No. 36.. of 50 copies of

A GAMBLE OF GODS

— THE ORDER OF THE DRAGON —
BOOK ONE

MITRIEL FAYWOOD

Mitriel Faywood

SIGNED BY THE AUTHOR

To Mum:

It's nothing like the books of Stephen King or Wilbur Smith,

but I know you would have been proud even so.

Chapter 1

Kristian

Life, ever so precious, is never without purpose. But it is our choice whether we open our eyes and face our destiny or close them tight, hiding behind curtains of self-pretence, until death creeps through the window one day and locks them for us forever.

All these years I'd spent at the university pretending I was making the most of it, so convincingly even I was blind to the truth. But deep down, I guess I always knew, as we all do, that in the end, I was just wasting time. Such disturbing notions are best kept buried under the distractions of the present, however. Or, as in my case, buried six feet under, anchoring the past.

A cool breeze rustled the leaves, a night-time ballad to match my mood, and I felt reluctant to lift my head, even when I heard his footsteps on the gravel. I knew it was him. With him, I was somehow always able to tell, and when I finally did look, the tall figure of Professor James Montgomery walking towards me between the graves proved me right.

He came to stand next to me, and together we watched the tiny, flickering light in silence for a while. It guarded the memory of my best friend, Raymond Emerson.

'May our souls always find their way back to the source of life,' the professor said finally, letting me complete the ancient orison.

'And never lose the light that unites us all,' I finished, and watched as hundreds of little stars rose from the gravestones to form the sign of Enderaste against the late autumn sky.

'I thought you had a class tonight in the laboratory,' he scolded me in a soft voice.

A guilty chuckle escaped me. 'And I thought you went to Ronar.'

'A change of plan,' he sighed. 'There was a technical problem at the port, and no ships are allowed to land until tomorrow. The committee meeting was postponed. But I spoke with the curator from the Messini Historical Society,' he added, almost as an afterthought. 'They are looking for someone knowledgeable enough on Satori symbols and artefacts to supervise a cave excavation on Thedos.'

I tore my gaze away from the spectacle above to find that he was watching me with an innocent expression. But I knew at once where this was leading and considered my response carefully, unsure whether my views on leaving the institution were best delivered cold right here in the cemetery, or in one of our heated debates later in the Grand Hall.

'I believe my current research keeps me—'

'Your current research does nothing to take your mind off the past and concentrate on your future. Kris, you need to take charge of your life!'

'But the university *is* my future!' I insisted. 'Spending my life here teaching is exactly what I want to do.' I turned back to stare at the grave in defiance.

'That's still your grief talking. What happened wasn't your fault,' he offered soothingly. A worn-out perception I was tired of hearing. Was there any point in telling people what had happened if they were only prepared to hear their own version of the truth?

'I know it's been seven years today,' he added.

'Yes.' Seven years that went by fast. They felt light and hollow. Like dry leaves scattered behind me.

He tapped the top of the gravestone and the flickering light re-appeared on the grave.

'The past is important,' he continued. 'It's part of who we are. But we can't let it dictate who we become.'

'But I don't, and it won't,' I stated firmly. 'I know who I am.'

'A shadow. A hermit, old before his time.'

'Is that what you think?' I laughed. 'Nice.'

'Harsh truths, Kristian. The ones we want to avoid the most. The ones that hurt. Facing those is what makes us all stronger. The truth is that you've been hiding behind that accident ever since it happened. It's time to let go and start living. To find out who you are and what you can achieve. To fulfil your potential. You'll never know how strong and capable you are unless you go and you challenge yourself!'

I said nothing. We'd had this discussion before. Undoubtedly, we'd have it again.

'Look, it's not that far. I think you should go. Just for a short break. Leave Alba for a while! Dr Miriam Rake is leading the excavation. I know you like her.'

The wind picked up, but the sudden chill I felt owed nothing to it. I gritted my teeth and let my eyes wander to the Shend. Out there in the darkness, Thedos made its slow orbits about the star.

'My place is here, James,' I said quietly but firmly. 'I'm not going anywhere.'

In the end, the bell saved me. Or that's what I thought at the time. Three huge tubular bells in the main tower played a short note. The bells rang, and we ran for the gates.

My name is Kristian del Rosso. I grew up within the walls of the University of Saint Mark, on Alba. An institution dedicated to preserving and expanding human knowledge, to making our world a better place through understanding and applying the laws of science, and by further exploring the universe. A white crystal citadel built from quartz. The pinnacle of millennia of research, standing proud among the peaks of the Ethrels. It was widely considered a symbol of progress and excellence. I always rather felt myself a part of its existence than it being part of mine, its history too vast, its significance too great to allow anything but admiration and obligation.

I was happy there, whatever James said to me on that ill-fated night. But it's easy to be happy when you choose to believe that your future has been decided for you. When you think you live where you belong. When you don't know any different. In hindsight, though, I hadn't the faintest clue what happiness really was. Or what it truly felt like to belong. That would have required me to drop the pretence, to go out and find what I really wanted. To fight for it, to love and suffer until I became someone who deserved it. Until I was forged into a sword sharp enough to cut my own destiny.

But no. I would have probably never left and looked for the life I should be living, had it not been that Death came looking for me first.

'What happened?' Professor Montgomery's first words to the Council of Masters as he stepped through the obsidian doors in the North Tower, the exquisitely carved panel sliding closed as soon as I entered behind him.

Eleven of the thirteen masters sat inside in a wide circle on ornamented chairs. Eleven of the thirteen masters looked at me as one as soon as I appeared, a ripple of disapproval overwriting the lines on their stern faces. As a lecturer, I had led various research projects, trying my hand at teaching classes, even had my own private quarters for these last four years, but despite my outstanding results, I would not be permitted to take my final tests for another three years. Even so. As an appreciation for my dedicated work, I was often allowed into council meetings. The unusual tension that I seemed to be the centre of puzzled me.

'An intrusion in the Armírion Wing,' Professor Rondoz announced. His aquiline nose and narrow, piercing eyes made him look like a particularly large bird of prey. His booming voice matched the authority he carried within these walls, his gaze a suggestion flickering between the two of us as though either of us should be able to continue the account of events from there.

'The laboratory?' I asked meekly, desperately hoping I was wrong for once.

'Precisely.' The head of the institution snapped his glare back to me.

'And the intruder?' asked Professor Montgomery.

'Escaped!'

My mind struggled to follow the words I was hearing. The university was like a fortress, with no reported intruders making it through its walls for centuries, let alone out. But this wasn't all.

'Your team have been terminated, son. Nobody survived. Their work should have been overseen by you tonight. Where were you?'

'It's my fault,' Professor Montgomery supplied quickly while I stood in confusion, oblivious to the discussion around me.

I thought of the students I'd been working with this past year. Lorand had been filling his cup when I left. That foul brew of his. Dead? He couldn't be. And Kendra? I've been meaning to talk to her about that research she was working on. She put so much work into it. She was just about to finish up. I thought about how I walked out of the door, telling the group that I needed a little time for myself. Out into safety, while those I cared about once again died.

My eyes regained focus, finding purchase on the glowing crimson circle on the seltenium floor. Its light grew stronger until panels moved around, and the circle opened upwards into a flower, letting Loreley, the university's main system, pour into shape from its middle. She printed herself into the form I admired the most. Beauty and intelligence combined in an exquisite metal body that looked both human and anything but. I walked up to her impatiently, as though cutting down the distance between us would result in the answers reaching me sooner, too.

She fixed me with those big golden eyes, her expression tinged with sorrow. 'Good evening, Kristian. Please accept my deepest sympathies.'

'How could this have happened?' I demanded, oblivious to my surroundings.

'The intruder entered the school disguised as one of the students and only revealed himself in the laboratory,' she stated.

I stared at her incredulously. 'That wouldn't have stopped you from identifying him as an outsider.'

'The disguise was perfect. There was nothing suspicious about him that would have alerted me,' she said apologetically.

'I don't understand. What do you mean *perfect*?' With any modern corporeal printer, you could change your whole body if you wanted to. So what? This was a ridiculous excuse. Even if it seemed a little excessive for anyone to completely alter themselves in order to look exactly like another human being, it was, I supposed, possible. But that changed nothing.

'She means that the intruder's complete DNA sequence matched the student's at the time of entering,' Professor Montgomery offered from behind me.

I span around, disbelieving as we locked eyes. 'That's impossible.'

His face remained serious under my incredulous stare. I turned around, expecting support from the council but found their expressions just as unfazed.

'We cannot explain how this was possible,' Professor Rondoz declared, 'but it is certainly the case. Professor Montgomery guessed it correctly.'

I looked back at my mentor's steady face. From him, it didn't feel like a guess.

'The impersonated student has been since found,' Professor Rondoz continued. 'He was on his way back from a visit to Ronar. I'm sorry to say, he's dead, too.'

'If we could perhaps watch the footage?' James requested.

There was a general murmur at this while Loreley silently transmitted a message to Professor Rondoz. Eyes narrowing into thin slits of concern, the head of the council considered her words. In the end, he pursed his lips and said, 'By all means, you may watch it with us, James, but I believe it would be best to do so without your apprentice here. I'm told the re-cording contains a certain amount of …' He paused, considering his next words carefully. 'Rather upsetting images.'

'No! Please!' The protest burst from my chest as I faced the council, but I could sense a growing concern behind me, leaving no doubt as to who would have the final say. 'I can watch it.' I turned towards Professor Montgomery. 'I need to watch it, please! I need to understand what's hap-pened.'

'Knowledge is as dangerous as any weapon if you don't know how to handle it,' he stated, unmoved by my outburst.

'It surely can't hurt me more than the person who did this would have,' I argued, my voice rising in desperation.

'Had you been in the laboratory, you would be dead. As simple as that. But seeing that you're alive, you are to do as you're told. Now—'

'So, teach me!' I cut across him, knowing it to be the only thing that might change his mind. 'Teach me how to handle it.'

He lifted a calculated eyebrow at that, and I knew I'd got my way. Well. Almost.

'On one condition.' He walked up to me until we stood barely inches apart.

'Anything.'

'You are to follow my instructions in this matter to the last word. Even if it requires leaving the institution for some time. No disputes, no hesita-tion, no questions. Are we clear?'

You find there's a strange calmness when you realise that you've willingly walked into a trap, locked the door behind you and thrown away the key. As though your brain were trying to persuade itself that this was the original idea all along rather than acknowledging such a massive embarrassment.

'Yes, Professor, absolutely.'

Such self-delusions seldom last long, though. Luckily, I had something more important to distract me.

The projectors jumped into life a few moments later, and the room around us turned into a recreation of the laboratory chamber. I walked between the ten students, who were working quietly in a group just as I had left them a few hours ago and positioned myself at the head of the long lab bench. Where I should have been.

'Now, that's interesting!' Meryl exclaimed suddenly on my left, running her fingers furiously through her hair the way she always did upon discovering something exciting.

'What's that?' This from Lorand, opposite her, adjusting his glasses so he could see in better detail what she was doing.

'Look!' Meryl again, clearly excited now, making the rest of the team look up, too, and start craning their necks towards our end of the table. 'Look at the reaction when it comes close to tetrium!' She lifted a small piece of the meteorite sample with a pair of remotely controlled elirion tongs and carefully moved it towards the clear substance in the dish inside the examination tank. As it neared the liquid, the meteorite piece changed colour, turning red. She lifted it back up, causing it to fade again to its original grey.

'Cool!' Lorand grinned at her in excitement, his green eyes glinting at the girl appreciatively behind the lenses. 'Isn't that like in the new Torello movie?'

'Do you mean the one with Shawn Hess?' Rin chipped in from his right, his eyes still on the meteorite sample.

'Meryl, what are you doing? Put that down!' Seneca was now next to her, his dark face taut with disapproval as he reached with his own remotely controlled robotic arm for the dish. 'Who said you were allowed to use tetrium in here?'

'It seemed like the right idea given the crystallography results so far,' she said defensively, placing the sample back on the main tray.

'Science-fiction movies are great fun but breaking the rules won't take you closer to finishing your assigned duties today,' Seneca scolded her.

'I doubt it's the furthering of modern science she had in mind in any event,' came Kendra's voice from behind him.

'Oh?' he turned to look at her.

'Please,' Kendra continued, placing her hands on her hips. 'It's quite obvious whose attention she's relentlessly after!'

'Because who isn't?' Lessa observed sarcastically, looking up from her notes at the other end of the table.

'Ladies.' Seneca chuckled at the brewing storm. 'As you all know, Kristian del Rosso doesn't date students.'

There was a general snigger at this.

'Kristian del Rosso doesn't date,' added Lorand with a smirk.

'No,' Lessa declared, bending back to her notepad. 'Kristian del Rosso never does anything that might be even remotely considered "fun".'

'Now, that's just sad,' an unfamiliar voice stated casually from behind her, making all of us look around. Its owner looked young, seventeen or eighteen perhaps. He had a shock of sandy hair and an innocent face sprinkled with freckles, but there was a certainty in his eyes that could have brought divine providence to its knees. 'But I heard he wasn't always like that,' he went on, seemingly enjoying their puzzled attention. 'I heard that he changed after that accident. Poor Kristian. I think we should help him. Play a little game with him. Don't you?'

'Sorry, who are you?' Seneca was first to find his voice as usual. 'It's Toman, isn't it?' he added uncertainly.

Toman favoured him with a wide smile. 'Now, why would we want to give him all the answers he should be looking for? Where is the fun in that?' As he spoke, he lifted two glass balls, breaking them against each other. The exploding shards slowed to a crawl around his hands, and it took me a few heartbeats to realise that Loreley had slowed the playback. Liquid metal poured from the broken balls, solidifying into two short, thin blades in mid-air, their ends broadening into elegant sword hilts.

Toman grabbed the short swords, and with a sudden flip in the air, he jumped onto the table. His landing smoothly became a spin, cutting Lessa's throat half-way through the circle. Completing the full turn, he straightened gracefully, assessed the exact position of the students around the table and, with a mocking smile, brought his right arm in front of his waist to make a humble bow. He turned the bow into another flip that moved him along the table. Another, then another. His features changed into someone else's in the process, someone taller, slightly older, with a different face pulled into the very same smile.

A deep sound started to reverberate across the room as death descended upon the living, effortlessly cutting them from this world with swift and precise strikes through each flip, until the last one brought him down to the left. From the slow motion of the falling bodies and spattering blood, I could tell he was moving at a speed no human should ever be capable of achieving. And in that moment, I wondered, in the midst of all that highly theatrical massacre, whether it was wrong to be grateful that they hadn't even had time to scream.

Meryl was the last to die, sinking to the floor gradually faster as Loreley turned the footage back to normal speed. The intruder let Meryl fall and turned his blood-splattered face to me, his dark eyes looking into mine with disturbing accuracy. He stabbed at my chest simultaneously with both blades, and despite myself, I jumped.

'Boo!' he yelled at me mockingly, and only then, between his laugh and reminding myself that I should breathe, did I realise that the deep reverberating noise I'd heard before was the distorted sound of the tower bells.

'Kristian,' he addressed me, looking apologetically in the general direction I was now standing, 'this really shouldn't have been necessary. After all, I only came to see you.' A menacing smile spread across his face. 'But never mind, I enjoyed it. How about you?'

A growing noise came from outside that made him look towards the door. He tensed slightly but then turned back and continued. 'You know, I heard you were meant for more than this.' He lifted his blades to indicate his surroundings. 'So, why are you hiding here? Why not come out and play? Or do I have to kill everyone in your soul circle, too? Preferably before they even get near the Bridge of Honour? Maybe that would get you moving.'

In that moment, the door opened, and a Hataroke entered the room. One of three the university boasted. One of the fifty our whole planet owned, in fact.

When you look at a Hataroke, it's not simply the huge humanoid robot you see. Nor is it the complex engineering miracle that could, in a split second, kill you with literally any tiny part of its intricately structured body. It is the eyes. The strange lights and the unsettling vibrations behind those crystal slits scratching against your senses. It's the way their intelligence has been cultivated around some of the most powerful processor chains ever built. The way your brain goes into panic mode in reaction to it. When you meet the eyes of a Hataroke, you find you can barely look away. You find that your mind becomes frozen into a prison of your worst nightmares. Except, on this occasion, of course, I was in such a nightmare already.

'You are under arrest under Federal Law. Identify yourself, outsider, and relinquish any weapons you may have in your possession,' it commanded, stopping not far from the entrance to assess the full scale of the situation.

The intruder eyed the android warily and slowly crouched down to place his blades on the floor. He let go of their hilts but remained squatting, palms flat on the floor, eyes cast down.

The Hataroke walked forward without hurry, its every move conveying its superiority and confidence. It only took three steps, however, before a sudden wave rippled across the black elbaite floor, cracking a hole into the metal and a smile across the intruder's blank expression. The area immediately beneath him broke from the rest of the floor and fell into the lower-level storage rooms.

The Hataroke slid into several pieces in an instant, sending a spectacular army of superdrones down after him through the hole in the floor. Yet it was the image of the silent laboratory, the bodies, and the blood, that crowded my vision and chased me from the room.

Chapter 2

Kristian

D-11, Alba, 7ᵗʰ Kostol 5102

A murderer had killed all ten of my students just to get my attention and make obscure threats. Who he was and how he knew me was all I could think about. I remembered that look in his eyes as he did it. His evident pleasure turned my anger into rage even now.

I sat down at my work desk with intent, the moonless night outside a pale imitation of the darkness my thoughts twisted around. Death loomed over me like a second shadow, cold and hungry. I invited it in. Somewhere out there, a killer was on the run. And I was going to hunt him down.

I stirred the holographic interface back into life and opened the system wardrobe. After selecting a set of regular items, I flicked down the menu options until I found the code, and as a privileged user of the university system, I began to overwrite the program. The fabric of my new outfit soon became interwoven with thyon, a metallic alloy that was both incredibly strong and light. Invisibility functions were not permitted inside the institution, but since I was leaving anyway, I grabbed my microelectronic cloak, too.

I left the tricky part till the end. No code was going to allow me to produce anything more dangerous than a kitchen knife. I had a bunch of practice weapons from martial arts classes, none of which would have given me an edge over what I was planning to face.

'Loreley, where's Professor Rondoz currently, please?' I called out. 'Still in the meeting room?'

'No, he's down in the Vectorium, overlooking the arrival of a new Hataroke,' came the answer. 'Would you like to talk to him?'

'Yes, but I'd better go and see him in person, thanks,' I said and left the room.

It was fairly late. The corridors were mostly empty, save for a cleaning droid here and there, with only the stars peering through the vast windows to watch my progress. On any other night like this, I would have called the place peaceful. Tonight, however, it all seemed eerily quiet. A cold numbness stretched across the halls, as though the massacre had wounded the building itself, leaking horror into its grand towers, leaving the institution abused and vulnerable.

The Vectorium was situated on the ground floor, the circular metal gate inside it presenting a second entrance to the world. Teleports were not a recent invention. They functioned in many places throughout the galaxy, transporting objects and materials. But it always irked me how we never quite managed to figure out how to teleport the living. Carcasses of endless test animals appeared at the target gates, the spark that had kept them alive quenched. No matter how hard we tried, we could never bring them back to life. Something somewhere along their journey sucked them dry of their essence, allowing through nothing but their hollow shells.

The gate was just closing following the Hataroke's arrival as I entered the large hall, the wide metal ring slowly narrowing as if finishing a tired yawn. Two masters and a handful of droids surrounded the new arrival. Professor Rondoz stood a little further away, talking to the hologram of a lanky, grey-haired man who looked familiar. Upon noticing me at the door, he beckoned me closer.

'Kristian, you remember Inspector Gorod?'

The inspector looked exactly as I recalled him. Seven years didn't seem to have changed him one bit. I had been only an impulsive adolescent at the time. I wondered if that was what he saw still when he looked at me. Given the anger that burned in me, who could have blamed him? I took a deep breath and tried to calm myself.

'Of course,' I said and joined them. 'Good evening, Inspector.'

'Good evening, Kristian. Not that we can really call it "good". But it's good that you're here as I will have to speak with you, too. Professor Rondoz assures me that neither you, nor anyone at the institution, has any information about the identity of this person. Or any knowledge on what might have motivated him when he attacked the students. So, you don't know why he might be looking for you?'

'That's correct,' I replied briskly. 'I have no idea who he is.'

The inspector nodded and continued. 'Did anything he mentioned sound familiar to you? That soul circle? Bridge of Honour?'

I shook my head. 'I don't know what any of that meant.'

'Well, we shall know more soon enough. He was detected less than half an hour ago in Dener. We have a considerable fraction of the federal land force combing through the area as we speak.'

'How can you identify him if he can change his DNA?' I frowned. The whole concept still sounded absurd.

'We suspect that he can't change it easily. He was spotted just as he was when he made his escape from the university. Perhaps he needs some sort of external aid to do it. Or more time and rest. Or maybe the whole thing was some sort of clever trick.

'Having said that, as an additional security measure, we'd like to relocate you until he's been caught. I hear the university has a small research base not far from here, with only a handful of staff presently resident. Having just a few people around you would prevent him from disguising himself as one of them so easily, and we can quickly secure the building due to its smaller size. Not that we'd allow things to progress that far, of course. But making your departure public with a false destination would hopefully deter even the thought of a possible repetition of tonight's events.'

'It all makes sense.' I nodded agreeably.

'Excellent. We'd like you to quietly leave early in the morning without a word to anyone. Professor Rondoz will make sure that you arrive at the base safely. Soon after your departure, we'll dispatch a small federal ship from the university to Ronar, with the official information being that you're on board. The crew with the ship will be arriving in about an hour, Professor Rondoz.'

'We'll look forward to welcoming them,' the professor responded.

'I'll be back with updates tomorrow. In the meantime, let's all stick to this plan,' the inspector told us, and without waiting for a response, he disconnected with a curt nod.

'Professor,' I called after Professor Rondoz, who was already on his way to join the others around the new droid.

He stopped and turned those sharp, narrow eyes on me. 'Yes, Kristian?'

'What happened to the Hataroke that chased after the killer? Has it returned yet?'

Professor Rondoz bit his lip and seemed to chew on the answer before spitting it out. 'No. He destroyed it.' He turned and walked on.

'Destroyed it? What? All of it?' How could he have destroyed a Hataroke? Not to mention alone.

'Yes.' He answered without stopping this time. 'All that was found of it were its eyepiece and a bucketful of dust.'

I made my way back to my suite after that. What the inspector said of course made complete sense. I had no idea what came over me before. Just what was I thinking? Let the professional soldiers catch the guy. Once they had him, there would be no more secrets. In the meantime, I could do some work at the base. Maybe I could finish Kendra's research and dedicate it to her memory. She worked on it so hard. Yes. That was something I could do and do well.

At the thought of her, the shock of the massacre washed over me again, filling my eyes with angry tears.

'Open the asclepeion, please,' I croaked and sat down at it, burying my face in my hands.

A small round table rolled into the room, stopping in front of me. On top of it, a clean cloth and a glass of altered water.

'Thanks, Loreley.' I reached for the drink.

'No problem,' Loreley responded through the speakers.

I wiped the tears from my face, drank the water and lay down.

'Apart from a little muscle tightness in your upper back area, there are only a few minor issues we should take care of. Would you like the full report?' Loreley asked.

'No, thanks.' The wonders of modern science. Asclepeions advanced and sped up our natural bodily functions while asleep, including memory functions, cell regeneration and other healing processes. As if I needed healing. Ten people had died, and I didn't even have a scratch on me.

'When would you like to be woken?'

'In four hours, please.'

'Would you like to choose a theme for your dreams tonight? Perhaps something nice and relaxing after today's events?'

I snorted.

'Have I said something wrong?' Loreley asked, reading in my expression that she had, yet not comprehending what. This was why AI, wonderful as they were, would never completely resemble human beings. For her, the suggestion was perfectly reasonable. Perhaps life would be easier if we, too, adopted their kind of thinking.

'No. Don't worry about it,' I said instead as I undressed. 'Actually, there is something on my mind that is bothering me. Aside from the murders, obviously. An odd sensation. Something I feel I should remember, but I don't. Do you know what I mean?'

'I'm afraid I don't. But in that case, perhaps it's best not to interfere tonight. Let your dreams develop naturally, on their own account. Ready?'

'Yes.' I stretched and lay down.

'Good night, Kristian.'

I closed my eyes and covered them with the electro mask as the top of the asclepeion slid into place. A light mist filled the air, with a faint smell of herbs, out of which I thought I recognised one or two. Loreley was clearly making sure I received the relaxation she felt was needed regardless.

I sighed, and two heartbeats later, I was asleep. Somewhere above my body, a light changed colour on a monitor. My heartbeat quickened, and dreams drifted across my world.

I ran up the outer stairway, taking two steps at a time. Entered the main building and took the north corridor, walking past empty classrooms and simulation units, my steps echoing from the cold white walls. Only a few doors stood closed along the way. I opened them all and looked in, searching for something. All empty. Even the corridor was completely deserted, not a single soul in sight. But somewhere ahead of me, fragments of a conversation filtered through into the silence and made me slow my steps. The unmistakable knowledge of who was in the room hit me at my core, as usual. I approached the open door and peered into the room.

It was semi-dark in there, the people inside hidden from me by a panel of screens, all turned off. I quietly crept in, rounding the internal wall. In the far corner of the room, Professor James Montgomery sat with his back to me. Opposite to him, a dark stranger. Between them, there was a small table with what looked like a candle on it. The candle was unusual enough, but it was the stranger that drew my attention. She was formidable. And not just in build. There was a dangerous energy to her, a presence that commanded obedience. I slowly crouched in the shadows, hoping to stay unseen. Fortunately, they seemed too focused on their argument to notice me.

'And just why do you think they would come all this way?' the woman asked James in a deep voice, sounding annoyed. 'What would they want? James, you've lived in retirement for over two decades since you deserted us. Ever since ...' She trailed off, thinking better of what she was about to say.

'Ever since Alessandra died,' James finished the sentence for her, and they both went quiet for a while.

I waited for them to say more. Alessandra was my mother's name. Surely, they weren't talking about her? I didn't remember her at all. She died when I was only five.

The woman sighed and closed her eyes for a moment. When she opened them again, her earlier frustration was all but gone. 'You loved her, James, I know that now,' she said quietly.

The candle sizzled between them in the momentary silence, as if wishing to add its own voice to the conversation. I very much wished to add my own, too, but hardly dared to breathe.

'And I understand why you wanted to look after Kristian. Even if I don't approve of you leaving our ranks because of it.' She leaned forward, arms resting on her knees, and looked down. A pose that would make another person look wary. She looked alert and sharp. Like a black panther, dangerous and ready to strike.

Another minute stretched in silence before I heard James's voice again.

'He is in my soul circle, Quede.'

'Well, well.' Quede straightened and cocked her head. The candlelight seemed to dance in her big brown eyes.

'Or I should really say, I'm in his soul circle. He's destined be a Tora. He's been able to sense my presence ever since he was a boy. Although we don't talk about it.'

'You would make him one of us?' There was an incredulity to her voice. Almost anger.

'Only if he decides to choose that life,' James said hurriedly.

'Oh, I think there's more to it than just him deciding in this matter. You know what his deranged father did to him! Sometimes it's still hard to believe that Tynan is your brother!' The accusation hung in the air. My mind was whirling. I had no memory of my father. In my records, it said both my parents died in a space shuttle accident, which also injured my head and caused amnesia. What did she mean he did to me and … brother? But wouldn't that make James … my uncle?

'He can control it,' came his dry response.

'Can he?'

Shreds of an old memory started to float back to me. A metallic taste in my mouth.

'Yes. I trained him myself.'

'You might have stolen him from under Tynan's nose, you might have changed his name, but you would have never been able to train *that* out of him! His father has broken his mind. He conditioned him. We both know this. We both saw the recordings.'

That metallic taste again. A large hall. Bodies on the floor. Somebody screaming. Somebody whimpering. Somebody laughing. Something red on my hands.

I gasped in horror, pushing the memory away as if it had burned me.

'We shall test … oh.' Quede looked at me. Her eyes found mine and bored into them. 'He's here,' she said.

'What do you mean here? How?' James asked, turning in my direction.

I jolted, tore the mask from my eyes and found myself sitting bolt upright, breathing hard, the asclepeion fully open around me. I pushed myself out and landed unsteadily on my bare feet. What kind of dream was that?

I dressed in no time, my head still heavy with sleep but bursting with questions.

'Loreley!' I shouted. 'Loreley!'

'Yes, Kristian?' came the answer immediately.

'That dream I just had …'

'What about it?' She walked into the room in her metal humanoid form.

'It was …' It was what? Strange? Shocking? Overly realistic? I lowered myself into a chair, unintentionally copying Quede's earlier position, if not her strength. I felt confused. 'It was … I don't know. It didn't feel like a dream. I'm not sure what just happened.'

'We can watch it back and analyse it together if you like?' she offered. 'Unless, of course, you'd rather watch it alone.'

'No.' I sighed. 'Stay. Sit.' I needed a second opinion on this. One that would tell me if I was going crazy.

Loreley took up a chair next to mine. She reached out with one hand, her fingers connecting to the output of the asclepeion. The other reached forward, an almost invisible projector in the edge of her palm painting me on the air in front of us. Dream-me ran up the stairs outside the main building.

'A wondrously vivid dream,' she commented. 'The details of your surroundings are remarkable.'

'I guess I've seen them enough times,' I muttered as I watched myself rush along the corridors. 'Now, this part.' I pointed as I saw my steps slow. 'There was this conversation I heard.'

'What conversation?' Loreley asked. 'I can't hear anything.'

'Turn the volume up. You'll see it in a minute.'

We watched me walk into the room, at which point the hologram disappeared.

'Hey, what are you doing?' I snapped. 'Why have you stopped?'

'I haven't.' Loreley stood up and walked closer to the asclepeion. She put both her hands on it, causing it to make a burring noise and flash all its lights. 'There's nothing after this.'

'But there must be!' I insisted. 'I remember it.'

'Well, somehow it either wasn't recorded or …'

'Or what?'

She looked at me coolly. 'Or it wasn't a dream.'

'What else could it have been?'

'I'm not sure. According to the data, you were asleep.'

'So … you think it was some kind of technical error?' I was grasping at anything now that made some sense.

'It must have been. Although, it is strange. There's no history of it at all.'

'Loreley?' I asked slowly. 'Where was Professor Montgomery while I slept?'

'In his quarters. Asleep.'

'Could I have somehow accidentally entered his dream?'

'Negative. Humans are incapable of entering each other's dreams.'

Of course, I knew that to be true. But it felt so real. Impossibly so. 'Say that I'd somehow done it. Would that have stopped the recording? In theory?'

'Only if you had stopped dreaming. But how else would you have been able to see his dream, even if such a thing was possible?'

That also made sense. Except … 'It didn't feel as if I was watching it. It felt as if I was there.'

'I think it's a lot more likely that the trauma you experienced is taking its toll.' She gave me a sympathetic look. 'Your brain is acting in unusual patterns.'

I guessed she was right. The more I thought about it, the less certain I felt. The whole thing was weird. Very dream-like. But still, there was one thing I needed to know.

'If me and Professor James Montgomery were somehow related, you would know. Wouldn't you?' I looked down nervously, avoiding her eyes.

'Of course. And no. You are not related.'

That, to my surprise, saddened me a little. I felt disappointed. As if I had failed an exam. But this whole thing must have been a dream. That was the only reasonable explanation. A strange dream, but nothing more than a dream.

'A little time away from here might be just the thing,' I said, more to myself than to her, as I stood.

'Yes, Professor Rondoz notified me about your departure this morning.' Loreley nodded. 'I'm sorry to see you go, but I hope it helps.'

'Don't worry.' I smiled at her reassuringly. 'I will be back in no time.'

'Do you need anything?' she asked, cocking her head to the side.

'No, thanks.' I picked up the stuff I prepared earlier and walked to the door.

'Breakfast?' she called after me.

I pulled a few energy bars from my pack between two steps and waved them over my head in answer.

Outside, the sun was already rising, the waking light breathing colour into the world all about. The quartz towers were the first to sparkle, gleaming among the surrounding mountain peaks, while the valleys stretched into the distance and slumbered on, thick blankets of morning mist hiding them from curious eyes. All was quiet, save for the occasional cry of a shale hunting for an early bite, writing majestic circles into the pale purple sky.

It felt surreal. It's hard to understand how such a beautiful morning can roll up as if nothing had happened, as if last night hadn't torn something out of life, leaving an ugly bloodstain on the fabric of the world.

I walked towards the Portus, where the university's vehicles were stored. A raw wind blew among the buildings, its cold fingers tugging at my cloak, hastening me along.

I entered the vast hangar through a side door, it being the closest to where the smaller land speeders were kept. Without hesitation, I pressed my fingers against the first one, throwing my bag onto the passenger seat before it was even fully open.

'You might want to retrieve that.'

I turned upon hearing the familiar voice. 'Storn?'

A dark shadow emerged from behind a nearby shuttle, a sharp contrast against the whiteness of the ship, heading towards me with an otherworldly grace. 'I was instructed to accompany you,' he said as he stopped in front of me and gave me a level look. I reached up to stroke his long, arched neck, running my fingers through his thick mane, temporarily forgetting all the anger and hurt I had to offer the world.

'Alright, then,' I said. 'Do you have the coordinates?'

'I do,' he said, then curled his upper lip, treating me to a close-up view of his perfect front teeth. 'But you should wait for the professor before we leave. He's on his way.'

I moved to get my stuff from the speeder, shaking my head. 'Well, I bet you're going to surprise the hell out of the exchange students at the base! I doubt they've ever seen anything like you.'

'I'm one of a kind,' he agreed. 'The professor built me to be exceptional.'

'Even if you didn't say a word and acted as if you were a real horse,' I added, 'I doubt they would know what that was.'

'Ha! I'm better than a real horse,' he snorted.

I kept my silence, trying to suppress a grin at his famous vanity. He called it pride. We both knew that neither of us had seen a living horse before, but I thought it best not to mention that now. Travelling with him when he was in a sulky mood could be considered an inconvenience. I called it a nightmare.

'Where was the professor living again when he had such animals in his keeping?' I asked.

'A very long way from here,' came the answer from the direction of the side door which I had left wide open, followed immediately by Professor James Montgomery himself. He closed it.

'How come I'm taking Storn?' I asked, my stomach unexpectedly tightening at the sight of him. I watched him carefully, but he gave no sign of anything being up.

'All the university vehicles are standard federal makes and therefore traceable,' he said. 'You'll be safer with something more difficult to follow. And while we're on safety: this is for your journey, too,' he said and handed me an A-type ionblaster with a leather shoulder holster.

I turned it around appreciatively. 'A K-317?'

'Works exactly like the K-20, you know, but it's even more collimated. Let's hope you won't need to use it.'

'Yes, let's hope,' I agreed. A tiny voice in the back of my mind begged to differ.

We walked out into the sunshine, leaving long shadows in our wake. I watched him from the corner of my eye. He seemed his usual self, yet somehow different. Or was it just that I saw him differently now? I tried to recall my earliest memory of him. My childhood memories were hazy.

I knew he adopted me. For a few years, we lived in a village called Dorsan, although I didn't remember much from that time and basically nothing from before. We moved to the university when I was eight. Seventeen years ago. Things were much clearer from that point onwards. But why wouldn't he have told me during all that time if he was my uncle? That made zero sense. Besides, Loreley confirmed that he wasn't. I was being silly. Of course, it was all just a dream. What else could it have been?

'It seems your wish is coming true, after all,' I said, a touch of bitterness lacing my words. 'I'm getting out of here for a while. I just wouldn't have expected my life to turn so grim in the process!'

A silence stretched between us until we came to a halt near the gates. 'It doesn't really matter what we expect from life,' he said eventually with a soft deliberation. 'But rather what life expects from us. It's our answers to its questions, our solutions to its problems, the actions we take to tackle the tasks it places in front of each of us that are important. Choose your answers, and you choose the person you will become. Choose your actions, and you choose your destiny.'

Big words for a short morning talk. 'I hope that wasn't by way of a goodbye forever!' I chuckled.

'Oh, no!' He laughed. 'I'll come after you soon. There's something I want to talk to you about.'

'Not another excavation job, is it?'

'Well, it's a bit like that, I suppose.' He hugged me even as I grimaced.

'Do you need to stay because of the investigation?'

'No. I have some other things to do,' he said. 'But it shouldn't take long. A couple of days, at most.'

'Alright, then. See you at the base!'

'Just be careful,' he said as I got into the saddle.

'You, too.'

I let Storn take me up to the gates. Once my mind was finally set on leaving, I didn't feel like lingering anymore. More importantly, I had hoped the university would be a safer place for the time being without me.

As I waited for the gates to open, a strange mood touched me. My skin prickled against a change in the wind, stirring a nameless feeling somewhere deep within my heart. A wonder. As if for a second, I had glimpsed something complex, something breath-taking, fading away in an instant, leaving nothing but an echo. A pause in the slow swirl of the stars around me. An impossible moment gone before it could be grasped. A feeling that something was changing. That a new beginning was leaking into the world. When all I was hoping to bring about was an end.

I chewed on my energy bar slowly, enjoying the view the vantage point yielded. The sun stood high in the sky, its light tumbling down the foothills onto the patchwork of the valley floor, painting it even brighter. Despite my sullen mood this morning, I'd enjoyed the journey so far. Riding gave me a sense of freedom and peace I'd found in no other means of travelling. I could well understand why James would miss these animals so much that he eventually created a replica. I turned from the view to look back at Storn. He stood on the road behind me, his head down, ears pricked up as he seemed to study something on the ground.

'Anything interesting there?' I asked. He had reflexive movements, originating from the body language of horses, but I didn't understand why he would lower his head. It wasn't like he couldn't see exceptionally well from a normal upright position.

'Ssshhhh.'

'What—?'

'You'll frighten it away,' he explained in a reluctant low murmur.

'Frighten what away?' But then I saw it. There was some kind of small forest bird hopping towards him on the road. It was always unpredictable how animals reacted to him. Some of them wouldn't look at him twice; others became uncharacteristically hostile; some others again, like this little one here, appeared downright curious. He, on the other hand, was fascinated with them all.

Storn stood still, letting the bird hesitantly approach him, its black bead eyes trying to take in the size of him. It was a brave one, it had to be said. The bird didn't stop until the distance between them was only an inch or two, and then, with a last defiant skip, it landed on Storn's muzzle. He looked at the bird in awe for a moment but then, just as quickly, something changed. I could tell from the way he pricked back his ears. His smitten expression became serious as he lifted his head and looked back, causing the bird to lift off in a golden swirl, chirping some offended complaint. But Storn didn't seem to care anymore. His attention was focused elsewhere.

'I'm receiving a weak signal,' he said and looked back at me. 'Sections of a coded message.'

'Who is it from?' I asked.

'I don't know, but the transmitter seems to be damaged or broken. The only thing I can get clearly is "University of Saint Mark".'

'Where is it coming from?'

'It's about twenty-five miles west-southwest, moving away from us with an average speed of 4.2 mph.'

'That's quite slow. Could it be some malfunctioning university droid?'

'It could be,' he agreed. 'But the code isn't familiar. It might be a little while before I can break it.'

I pushed myself up from the boulder I was sitting on. 'Let's go and collect it.'

'Shouldn't we be heading to the base?' he asked, surprised.

'The base is only a few hours away now,' I said. 'Even with a little detour, we should be there by nightfall at the latest.'

I flicked my lenses on as we neared the target, and Storn slowed our speed to a gentle trot. The university's welcome screen rolled across my vision, which I quickly waved away and opened my mailbox. There were no new messages.

'I can't believe you still use those,' Storn exclaimed.

'What? The touchgloves?' I looked down at my right hand, bare fingers sticking out of the black microleather glove. I never liked implants and used whatever I could to avoid them. 'They work perfectly fine,' I said and flipped the mailbox closed with my thumb.

He laughed at me. 'It's ancient technology.'

'Shouldn't you be watching the road or something? Stop scrutinising me!'

That earned me another snort, but he did go quiet for a while.

'I'm losing the signal,' he said eventually.

'How is that possible? I thought you said we were getting close.'

'I'm not sure. But I think it might be moving underground.'

'Send over what you have to my screen.' I sighed. I wasn't keen on wasting time playing hide and seek.

'What's this occasional background noise behind the message?' I asked after checking the content.

'It's the buzz of a flying insect. Judging by the wing-beat frequency, I would say it's a bluebee. Our droid has a constant companion, it seems.'

'But why would a bluebee follow around a droid so persistently? Unless…' I turned the picture around in my head, and realisation hit me.

'Storn, I don't think our droid has a bluebee companion.'

'What?'

'I think our droid *is* a bluebee, a Bluebee Z58 insectdrone. It must have come from the Hataroke that was destroyed last night.'

'That's a strange speed for a Bluebee,' he said sceptically.

'Not if it's sitting on something that's moving.' I double-checked the coordinates where the signal was last received from. We were only about a mile from it now, the road taking us downhill, winding around the mountain in a gentle curve.

Storn saw it first. 'Maybe we should just report this and turn back,' he suggested.

'You're right,' I said with mock concern, playing for his vanity. 'This could be a little difficult for you, and we wouldn't want you to get stuck in there somewhere. It's probably best if you just wait for me outside.'

'I didn't say it would be difficult.' He tutted. 'I can handle myself better than you'd think!'

The narrow opening of the cave loomed in front of us, yielding nothing but darkness. I dismounted and peeked inside. As my lenses adjusted, I could see that the tunnel leading into the belly of the mountain was a short one, opening into a large cavern further in. The next moment, something tickled my ear, and a large, dark nose pushed forward at the edge of my vision.

'Do you think we'll be able to find it in there?' the mouth beneath the nose whispered.

'I think we should give it a try.' I smiled and walked in.

The heavy silence that surrounded us was only broken by the clatter of Storn's hooves. We made our way through the cavern, entering a second tunnel at its end. The shaft wound on for a few hundred yards, its water-smoothed walls gradually widening as we progressed.

A little further along, my lenses highlighted several cave leeches sleeping in a group. Their dark grey, bat-like bodies could easily put anyone in mind of their friendly relatives. But these guys were nothing like them. They had venomous bites that would paralyse before they feasted on your blood with a ferocious appetite.

'Try not to wake them,' I whispered to Storn, hoping to avoid a noisy and potentially dangerous encounter with the little beasts.

Storn slowed, carefully placing one hoof after the other on the uneven ground. I followed, holding on to the saddle with one hand, my eyes on the leeches. There were seven of them, hanging upside down from the ceiling. My lenses made it possible for me to observe them carefully in the dark. Something they would have no trouble doing themselves with their night vision in return.

Unlike bats, leeches slept with their eyes closed—a habit I greatly appreciated just now as I looked at them one by one. A pointy ear twitched here and there, a nose, but otherwise, they all seemed unconscious. We quietly passed underneath them, and I was just about to turn my head to look ahead when the last one of them opened an eye and stared at us.

I froze, hoping that maybe it would just let us leave. Instead, it let out a high-pitched screech, waking its whole family, who quickly made descending on me their top morning priority.

'Don't kill them!' Storn lectured me as I tried to fend them off. 'Their population decreased significantly in recent years due to increased human activity in the area.'

'Not significantly enough!' I shouted back, but as it happened, my best defence against them offered no actual damage—at least, not permanent damage. Last year, when I had to spend a few weeks worming through the caves of the Ethrels, doing some research for the university, I made some manual adjustments to my lenses. The caves were full of flying serpents, and I preferred scaring them off to having to fight them. Fortunately, they didn't like strong light and my lenses—being able to emit a beam of light upon a command from my brain—proved useful when I couldn't use my hands. Cave leeches were similarly sensitive to bright light, especially when it hit them out of nowhere after their prolonged time in the dark. I expected three hundred lumens would do the job, but just to be on the safe side, I turned the setting up to five hundred. The temporarily blinded and disorientated creatures soon flew against the walls and crashed into each other in an attempt to escape.

'That's a clever trick,' Storn observed. His eyes lit up as he turned his head and looked after the departing leeches.

'Yes,' I said while checking my hands for bites. 'I'm pleased that it worked.'

'How long before they regain their sight?'

'I don't know. But now is not the time to find out. Let's go!' I walked ahead, my shadow stretching ahead of me. 'And switch those off. We don't need the light.'

'I found the signal again!' Storn announced behind me after a few minutes.

'Never mind that now.' I stopped so suddenly that he almost walked into my back.

In front of us, the tunnel opened into a void. A chasm divided the floor, the sound of rushing water rising from far below. At its narrowest point, it spanned around thirty feet. I cautiously leaned forward and looked down. Even without the exact figure indicated on the left of my vision, I could tell that stumbling into it would be the last slip I'd ever take.

'I might be able to make it,' said Storn from behind me.

I turned, knowing he could see the exasperation written on my face as clearly as if it was daylight. '"Might be"?'

'Well, I can't be one hundred percent sure because I've never jumped such a long distance before, but based on the parameters, if I also take into account the limited space I have to gain momentum, your weight and...' He trailed off under the look I gave him.

'Do you want to think about this a bit more carefully while you send me the new coordinates?' I suggested.

I pursed my lips as I considered our options. As crazy as this jump seemed to be, I had a gut feeling that what we were following could lead us to more information about last night. And whatever it was we were following, it was only about a mile ahead of us now. I wasn't keen on turning back when we were this close. I thought of the blood splattering across the laboratory as the killer cut through my students. The smile on his face as he'd done it.

'I'm eighty-three percent certain we can make the jump to the other side.' Storn's voice brought me back to the present.

I sighed, climbed into the saddle and positioned myself the best I could.

'Time to show-off!' I patted his neck.

Storn moved back further into the tunnel and took a moment to focus. For that moment, I briefly considered what I had to lose if we didn't make it. I couldn't think of much. But whether that was disappointing or liberating, I had no more time to establish. We shot from our position as if fired from a gun.

For the next few heartbeats, the whole world narrowed around us into the rhythm of Storn's charge, the sound of his hooves on the rock and the abyss rushing towards us at an alarming speed. We reached the edge, and Storn leaped off. Time seemed to pause, digging its claws into my nerves for purchase, keeping us over the void for an eternity.

Then we landed with a jolt, the edge of the cave floor crumbling into the deep under Storn's back hooves, but he pushed on and didn't stop until it was well behind us.

'We should probably find another way out,' I said as he turned and we looked back, my heart still pounding hard. I dismounted again, seeing that the limestone roof angled sharply downward ahead of us.

'Are you not forgetting something?' Storn looked at me expectantly.

'Forgetting what?' I did my best to sound innocent.

He brought his head close and bumped his muzzle against the side of my head.

'Okay, okay.' I laughed. 'It was a neat job. Well done!'

'It was an excellent job,' he corrected me, shaking his head.

'An excellent job,' I confirmed.

We set off once again and moved swiftly along the tunnel, with the echo of dripping water all around us, the walls growing so tight that we had to squeeze through in places. Eventually, it started to broaden again, and we found ourselves in a roundish cavern studded with glistening stalagmites.

We had walked around a long row of stalactites, descending like a curtain in front of us, when the distant sound of human voices reached us. Storn pricked up his ears excitedly, but I signalled him to keep quiet and fished out a small box from my bag. I pressed a button on its side to open it, letting a firefly lift into the air. It didn't have the same technological advances as a Bluebee Z58, but from this distance, it could still spy for us a bit. I set it to record and transmit back, and manually manoeuvred it ahead using my gloves.

I stood in the middle of the pitch-dark cavern, my arms held out in front of me as if conducting an invisible orchestra. The firefly flew through the space, my left hand controlling its flight, my right its view. The picture we received was surprisingly clear.

The source of the voices wasn't far ahead. We soon laid eyes upon five people, some standing, some sitting in a half-circle. I placed the drone up on a dry spot of the cave wall and zoomed in on them.

Just as I'd secretly hoped, our intruder stood among them. A dark smile spread across my face—a hunter's gratification.

'Are we all clear?' he said to the others. 'Lerkin, you and Seth go first.'

Lerkin, skeletal and pallid, looked up. On his left was another guy who looked just like him. His twin? Or could it be a clone, even? 'Should we not stay? To keep an eye on Kristian del Rosso in the meantime?'

'No. There will be too much attention on him for now.'

Lerkin shrugged himself from the wall. 'I can handle old Montgomery.'

The man sitting next to him on the floor laughed, a bald giant, thick muscles heaped along the length of him. 'Don't be an idiot!'

'Shut up, Aron. Nobody asked your opinion,' Lerkin retorted, pulling a long knife from his belt and twirling it.

Aron stood, easily dwarfing the whole group. 'Do you think Laro didn't challenge him at the university because he'd forgotten about him?' Aron growled, gesturing at the murderer. 'Just because James Montgomery has been in retirement for the last twenty years, doesn't mean he couldn't kick your tiny little arse all the way back to Coltron if he wanted to. None of us would be a match for him.'

There was this retirement again. What retirement? He'd been teaching at the University!

The knife in Lerkin's hand frosted over as if it had turned to ice and he smashed it against the wall, shattering it to pieces. 'You think?' My eyes widened in astonishment. How did he do that?

'Now, now,' Laro said. 'There's no need for concern. Just follow the plan.' He turned and set his palm against the wall, looking like he was pressing some buttons. There seemed to be something circular carved into it. I turned the zoom to its maximum to get a better view.

'Seth, Lerkin? Ready?' Laro asked, and in that moment, the whole circle lit up with a brilliance that temporarily blinded me. I could just make out Lerkin and Seth walking towards it as my lenses adjusted, stepping through its light-blue surface and disappearing into it completely. My jaw dropped.

For a second, I completely forgot about the remaining party standing in the cave and focused on the thing. The texture and the randomly swirling motion of its surface was reminiscent of the teleports I'd seen before. But could it be possible? Those guys stepped into it with practised ease, without the slightest hesitation.

As I watched, the intensity and the colour of the circle began to fade. I guessed that was how it closed, rather than the mechanical way I was familiar with. I tore my gaze away and turned the visuals back on the group. Laro was now talking to the only woman in the company. From how close they stood to each other, I suspected they were more than just passing acquaintances. Lovers, perhaps?

'Are you sure you won't need help with Conor Drew?' A seductive smile on an exquisite face.

Laro placed his hand under her chin and pulled her closer. 'I'm sure, Mara. You go to Earth with Aron, as we agreed. I'll take care of Conor Drew before he even hears of Kristian.' He kissed her and reset the gate.

I watched the woman and Aron go through it. I could still hardly believe it.

'Tell me about all this "attention" I have on me," I hissed to Storn, suddenly suspecting the horse had more duties than just to carry me where I was going. Storn turned to look at a nearby stalagmite and studied it with keen interest. 'When was the last time you reported to him?' I whispered.

'Just outside the cave.' He looked back at me sheepishly. 'The reception down here is terrible.'

'Give me the coordinates of his work desk,' I said as I watched Laro reset the gate a third time.

'What? What are you—?'

'Storn! The coordinates of Professor Montgomery's work desk in his study!' I cut him short. 'Quickly! There's no time!'

The coordinates appeared on my screen, and I set the firefly to its new destination. I drew the ionblaster from its holster and started running.

The gate had just started to fade, following Laro's departure, when I reached it, the swirling core of it inches away from my hot face. My heart hammered in my throat as I stared into the yawning oblivion, and for a second, I thought I wouldn't be able to step into it.

'Are you sure about this?' Storn was behind me.

I clenched my hand into a fist. 'I'll be damned if I let this Conor Drew die on my account, too,' I said through gritted teeth and entered the unknown.

Chapter 3

Conor

Kingdom of Coroden, Drelos,
18th The Month of Promise, 1575

Ancient belief has it that a traveller arriving at the hour of the owl is fated to bring a blessing and a curse. Yet people across the Nineteen Kingdoms are often blind when it comes to telling them apart. Word has it, my appearance is equally mistaken for both, regardless the hour, although I always prefer to fulfil my obligations after midnight.

Which explains why I'm not exactly a morning person. Dawn, in particular, never held any appeal for me.

I opened my eyes a tiny fraction. The amount of wine I'd consumed during the night, which was substantial even in my not entirely inexperienced assessment, told me to close them again.

I had ridden through the gates of Beren Castle at sunset, the clatter of horseshoes on cobblestone lost in the commotion surrounding the wedding of the duke's daughter. With fortunate timing, I missed the ceremony entirely, but was just in time for the feast. Weddings were never really my thing. Marriages are like hangings: best observed from a sensible distance before you turn away unsettled and ride to safety. Not saying that they aren't necessary for some. But I always held the view that no man should marry until there's an army outside his walls ready to raise hell if he doesn't.

Preparations for the festivities spilled out of the castle into the grounds, sprouting a dozen colourful tents emblazoned with the Beren family's coat of arms, a golden griffin on a black field. Around the tents, the wedding party gathered in groups, talking and laughing, hands variously clasped around goblets and tankards. Serving men hustled up and down, carrying trays, rolling barrels, turning joints of meat on spits above fire-pits. Kids ran around in numbers, chasing each other with wooden swords, ducal puppies racing along, yapping for their attention. I dismounted in the midst of it all, flipped a coin to the approaching stable boy, and made my way towards the keep.

I found the steward, Frederick Rolford, standing on the stairs. A solid, dark-haired fellow in his forties. He glanced at my pack before fixing me with an expectant look.

'Master Drew! How nice to see you return. A pleasant trip?'

The household staff always knew too much about their lords and ladies' business, if you asked me, but I had no reason to hold it against him on such a fine day. I gave him a confident smile.

'Wonderful, thank you.' If we didn't count the spiders, snakes, the rotting corpses and the legions of cockroaches. 'How is the celebration going? I should congratulate the happy couple.'

'The duke will be very pleased to see you! Let me escort you in,' he said and turned to show me the way.

After having been relieved of my sword, I followed Frederick into a large, crowded reception room. Guests in their best finery parted to port and starboard ahead of him, heads leaning together to babble in my wake. I kept my eyes to the fore, the ducal family coming into view at the heart of the assembly. The Duke of Beren, sporting a majestic grey beard, his face gleaming with pride; his wife, a chattering parakeet of a woman with a voice that drove me crazy half of the time; the groom, paunchy and dull, balding already … but in between them, a true beauty drew the eye.

The Lady Ameria Beren. A star descended from the heavens to shine upon our misery. Well, mainly on the misery of others. My only misery at this point lay in not being alone with her.

'My dear Conor!' The duke's rich baritone cut across the crowd. 'What excellent timing!'

'Your Grace.' I sketched a bow, then turned and bent to kiss the hand of the duchess.

'Conooor!' She made a singsong of my name with just a little too much enthusiasm. 'I hope you fared well on your journey. Let me introduce you to our son-in-law, The Duke of Sorpon, and of course, you have already met our daughter, Ameria?' This was followed by some elaborate description of the wedding ceremony I had missed and the marvel of the bridal dress, but to be fair, her words soon washed over me without registering.

After a quick bow to the groom, my attention moved over to the bride. Golden hair framed her pale angel face, a circlet of white flowers crowning her radiance.

'Lady Ameria.' She looked down at me as I bent and kissed her hand, a challenge kindling behind her green eyes. In response, I reached into my backpack, and with a flourish, I produced a small bundle of crimson satin cloth. The lady took it, raising a delicate eyebrow, and opened it to reveal an ornate hairpin. She let out a little gasp as she turned it around, allowing the rubies to glint proudly among the scrolling wire-work.

'It's breathtaking!' She looked back at me, her expression a mixture of joy and surprise. 'Is this from …?' She trailed off, a shadow of suspicion crossing her face.

'It is,' I interrupted hurriedly, before she had a chance to finish the question. Although I had little doubt that word of my recent travels had reached the ears of many of those present, it was best to keep a confidential manner. 'To suit a woman so dangerously beautiful.'

She favoured me with a dazzling smile, which, regrettably, I only had a moment to appreciate before the duke imposed himself upon me and gestured for me to accompany him out of the room. 'We have a bit of time before the feast starts in the hall,' he explained. From the corner of my eye, I noticed another man peeling off from the crowd to join us. An elderly, narrow-faced noble. 'Lord Simon Dranos, the king's closest advisor,' the duke introduced him to me later.

The three of us settled down around a table in the library with only the strains of music and conversation from the hall to disturb the silence. After a few courteous words, I opened my bag, removed a leather purse and placed its content onto a silver tray in the middle of the table. The duke and Lord Dranos leaned closer for a better view.

'Is this really it?' Lord Dranos asked, his voice carrying more astonishment than doubt.

'It clearly is,' the duke said, putting on a pair of dark gloves. 'Look at the craftsmanship! Not to mention it agrees with every description I have come across these last three years.' He carefully placed his hands around the precious metal and lifted it up. 'A red-gold crown, each of its points wrought to shape a rising phoenix with a pair of onyx beads for eyes. And in the middle …'

'The Lament of Andel,' Lord Dranos breathed. 'Said to be the largest blood ruby ever seen across the Nineteen Kingdoms.' He inclined his head and looked up at me. 'How did you do it?'

I shrugged. 'We all have our trade secrets, don't we?'

'They say nobody has ever returned from the Holt Catacombs before,' Lord Dranos pressed. He moved to refill my wine cup, perhaps familiar with the rumours claiming I was less shy about my achievements on nights out in my favourite taverns. 'Allegedly, the Earl of Twerbury sent down thirty mercenaries once. None of whom has ever emerged.'

'Forty,' I corrected after a mouthful. 'But yes, it's not for the faint-hearted.'

Not for the faint-hearted was a bit of an understatement. In truth, the place still gave me the shivers. Beyond its endless, dark tunnels, beyond the remains of the dead, beyond the disgusting, venomous creatures that made it their home, something else lurked there. It was in the foulness of the air. It dripped from the roof. It was woven into the spider webs criss-crossing the walls. A presence scratching against my mind with icy talons until my skull throbbed.

I shivered at the thought even now and tried to pull the blanket further over me. It appeared to be firmly stuck. I sighed and turned to wrestle my half away from the sleeping woman next to me. I heard that in some parts of the far east, it was a custom for men and women to sleep in separate beds. I really should look into how to introduce this clearly sensible tradition over here.

Once I made myself more comfortable, my thoughts turned back to the discussion last night. The duke had been so pleased at having acquired the crown that he couldn't help but tell me all about the reason he wanted it so badly.

'According to legend,' he'd said, 'the crown was cursed by the neglected mistress of Renold II, a Scarlet Witch, and was buried with her near four hundred years ago.'

'I'm familiar with the legend of the Cursed Crown, Duke Beren,' I said. 'Allegedly, the Lady Selia placed a malicious spell on it to take revenge on the king for abandoning her. They say the king, upon placing the crown on his head the next morning, went blind. And thus, the seed of the curse plaguing the royal line was planted.'

'Indeed!' the duke enthused. 'And having spent years researching the myths, I came to strongly believe that removing the curse from this crown would also remove the curse from the royal family.'

Curing the descendants of the Renol family tree by attempting to remove the curse from an ancient relic, when hundreds of healers, sorcerers and priests had failed to tackle the task, seemed more like chasing a miracle than carving a path to securing political advancement. But then again, who was I to judge? I'd done this job for a prize. A prize that would take me one step closer to my own goal. Chasing miracles seemed like a fitting description for that, too, after all. Not to mention that our current monarch was nearing his late twenties and the birthday when all his predecessors had gone blind. Who wouldn't do everything in their power, knowing that soon they would lose their eyesight for life?

'As much as I'd like to, I can't pretend to be an expert in lifting curses.' I emptied my cup and got up from the table. 'But I wish you all the best of luck and success with this enterprise, Your Grace.'

The other two men also stood. The duke rang a bell, and shortly, the door opened, half a dozen armed guards entering the room. One of them carried a small, elaborately wrought iron chest. The duke opened it, took out a small round object and replaced it with the crown I'd just given him. The guards left as swiftly as they'd arrived, presumably to carry it to the treasury. I didn't spare them a second glance. Since I'd first spotted the round object in the duke's hand, it had held all my attention. I furrowed my brow and swallowed, for once almost nervous.

The duke's smile widened upon noticing my interest. He held his hand out towards me, the golden disk glinting in his palm.

'As promised. Your payment, my good friend,' said he. 'Well earned!'

I took the medallion and studied its intricate design for a moment before slipping it around my neck on its fine chain.

'And now, let's get back to the festivities before my wife gives me a hard time for delaying dinner.' The duke laughed. 'Not to mention all our lady guests for hiding the famously good-looking Conor Drew!'

The feast that followed was one to remember. Even if the hosts seemingly made sure that the amount of wine consumed at the event was sufficient to wash it all into oblivion. I was seated near the high table, in between two exuberant noble families, who couldn't have looked at me with more excitement had I been a Temenesi street magician.

'You know, I travelled to the Lost Cities myself a few times when I was younger,' Lord Kenes announced to the lot of us while helping himself to more roast hog from the central plate. 'Had my sword crossed with a brigand or two.' Here he paused and lifted his fork into the air in doubtlessly faithful representation. 'Had a few fair maidens shed tears upon my departures.' He smiled to himself as he poured more apple sauce on his plate from a jug.

'Faaaather!' One of his younger sons on my left gave him a disapproving stare. 'Conor has been to the Lost Cities five times!' He put down his cutlery, straightened his back, lifted his chin and gave the overall impression of reciting his most recent lecture back to his tutor. 'He found the ancient scrolls of Serekesh, brought back seeds of the Meron fruit, defeated the Daloresi pirate captain in single combat, burned the Nemere Temple to the ground, and stole the map of the Death Islands from right under the nose of the Sint Overlord.'

I raised my eyebrows as I moved to let a serving man change my plate—damned if I remembered all that and in chronological order! Not to mention that the total demolition of the Nemere Temple wasn't strictly speaking part of the plan.

The serving man, a white-haired gentleman somewhere in his seventies, leaned close to my ear to communicate something quietly. Since it was the eighth occasion that evening, it didn't even take me by surprise anymore. In fact, I believe it was the first time I caught myself involuntarily leaning closer to him, too.

'I'm sorry, Master Drew, but the duchess once again would like to know how you liked the dish.'

I gave an almost invisible sigh and looked up towards the top table. The Duchess of Beren was looking straight at me, wearing a terrifyingly wide smile and an expectant look on her face. I re-arranged my expression into something that might resemble joy from a distance and gestured to express my appreciation. Thank the heavens she didn't know that I could play the guitar, too! I could just imagine her demanding a serenade.

In truth, though, it was all good. You could tell there was no expense spared when it came to marrying off their only daughter. Time after time, dancers appeared, jugglers, fools, comedians. The food was delicious, the musicians virtuoso, and every time I came near to emptying my glass, a pretty serving girl appeared and topped it up. Adjoining the hall was a larger room, where after dessert, guests who still felt confident enough to walk around were encouraged to socialise, and the fearless even to dance! Luckily for those fine specimens of womenfolk who caught my eye during the evening, I had solid experience when it came to socialising under such strenuous circumstances.

Back with my hangover, my stomach growled, presenting temporary competition to the peaceful snoring emanating from the other end of the room. I sighed. How could I be already hungry again? Sometimes, I really wondered if something was wrong with me.

I opened my eyes, and for the first time, I noticed a fruit basket on the bedside table, full of grapes. I reached out and seized a bunch. I stretched my legs and, stuffing the fruit into my mouth, I considered my surroundings. My clothes and boots lay on the floor, drawing a straight line from the door to the bed. On my right, the covers gently rose to follow the shape of an exceptionally beautiful woman. I watched her sleep for a minute or two, golden hair framing her pale angel face, a white rose petal here and there still visible among her locks. Given how the festivities concluded, I was fairly confident the whole castle was still deep in slumber.

I got out of bed and started to get dressed. In front of the dead fireplace, the Duke of Sorpon still slept noisily. Regardless, his presence served as a reminder that I should clear out of the newlyweds' bedroom before anyone took notice of me.

I was just pulling up my second boot with one hand, clutching a third bunch of grapes with the other, when to my astonishment, the door opened. It was the pretty serving girl from last night, the one topping up my glass so diligently. Despite having spent a few pleasant hours with her on one of my previous visits, I pretended not to recognise her.

'May I be of any assistance, madam?' I conjured up my most innocent smile. Although, the desired effect might have been somewhat spoiled by my voice being suspiciously close to a whisper. She gave a little shocked gasp upon seeing me, but it was too theatrical to be genuine. She knew I was in there.

'Master Drew! I hope you were not planning on leaving before fulfilling the promises you made to me.' She thankfully kept her voice low, but she had an iron resolution about her that I didn't like. I'd met religious fanatics with less conviction in their eyes.

'Promises? What promises?' I kept my smile in place as I tried to look past her into the corridor.

She grabbed the front of my shirt with both hands and shoved me against the wall. In my surprise, I let her. 'You know what promises!' she hissed so close that her lips tickled my cheek. Judging by the smell of her breath, she must have started the day down in the cellar.

'I didn't realise someone could get so athletic from lifting wine jugs all night! Looks like I'm in trouble, fair lady.' I grinned.

'Big trouble, too!' she said and firmly fastened her mouth onto mine.

'Mhmh …' I might have kissed back. Strictly in self-defence.

For a minute or two, it looked like I might get out of this. That was before she started unbuttoning my shirt.

'No, no, not here,' I mumbled and tried to push her off me.

'But *here* was good enough for the lady?' she spat bitterly and renewed her assault on my shirt. For the love of Torond the Great! Just what was it with women when it came to reason?

'Look, why don't we just—'

'No!' she retorted fiercely. 'Take me! Here! Take me now!'

I froze. She wasn't talking quietly anymore. The duke's snoring pattern became dangerously scattered, and I had no idea who might have heard her outside.

'Shhhhh! Listen!' I started again, but she clearly wasn't in a listening mood. In fact, it just seemed to agitate her further.

'What are you waiting for? Get on with it right now, or I scream to the world that you spent the night here!' she barked defiantly.

For a moment, I hesitated, wondering whether I should just knock her out. It turned out to be a mistake. Giving her a moment, that is. In the next, her shrill voice rang out so loud it could have woken the dead in the graveyard. On second thought, it could have woken the dead down in the bloody catacombs! Not that I had time for second thoughts.

I grabbed her and jerked her to the side before sprinting out of the room. Thankfully, no guards were stationed in sight, but I could already hear footsteps rushing up the stairs. I looked around for inspiration, and through the open windows, I spotted one of the large, well-pruned walnut trees standing fairly close to the building. With a swift jump, I gained the windowsill, and from there, I threw myself towards the nearest branch.

Judging by the shouts that went up by the time I reached the ground and sprinted off towards the stables, I had quite an audience following my progress from the windows. I ran across the gardens, dodging the seemingly random shrubs and ornaments. The open field beyond would have been quicker to cross had it not been for the tents erected for the wedding. And so it had happened that half-way through the tent-labyrinth, I was intercepted. It wasn't even the handful of guards yelling and running after me from the direction of the keep, although their reckless shouting probably contributed towards waking the bear of a man who emerged from a pavilion right in front of me. Normally the two large kitchen knives he was clutching would not have caused much concern on my part. Given, however, that my sword had been taken from me on arrival, I resorted to indignantly snatching up two pewter tankards lying on the ground. The man proceeded to show some competency with his choice of weapon—I guessed him to be a cook or a butcher. But no one could say I wasn't similarly accomplished with mine. Daily handling of any item will grant you some skills.

However, only one of them would train you to deal with a massive hangover, leaving me with the better stamina. I left the butcher unconscious after a few well-directed blows, but only got as far as the fire-pits before three guards caught up with me. Guards with swords. I threw the tankards away and snatched up one of the meat spits. A six-foot-long iron bar is an excellent way to extend your reach.

The first opponent to draw near was quick to learn the advantage of that reach when I smashed the spit's end against his sword hand, the blow strong enough to make him drop his weapon. It's also useful when it comes to preventing anyone getting close enough to do serious damage, as my second opponent realised when I forced him to back off with a series of strikes. And you know the handle at the other end? Oh, that's the best part! I turned the spit around, so it faced them, and thrust it towards the third guard, narrowly missing his head. He confidently advanced with a little smirk on his face, only to have the handle hit the back of his neck as I pulled it back and caught him in its angle. I twisted from my waist, changing his course and thrust him into the second guard.

The first guard stopped clutching his right hand with his left and decided to punch me in the face while I was occupied with his colleagues. I gave them a last shove with the iron spit, encouraging them into the closest tent, and sent the spit after them. It was all good fun, but I was running out of time. I blocked the next punch, and the third, delivered one myself, then skipped back three steps and snatched up a clay jar from a table left from yesterday's cooking. I lifted the lid and peered into it. To my disappointment, it was only salt. I threw it at the head of the approaching guard and missed. I snatched up a second jar, lifted its lid, too, but had no time left to check what was inside. Nonetheless, I shoved its powdery contents into the guard's face. The effect was immediate. Good old ground pepper.

I raced on towards the stable, picking up a sword on the way, shouting the name of my horse upon my approach, with an increasing number of men shouting mine not far behind. Not a moment too soon, I was in the saddle, prompting a hesitant stable boy to step aside, and rode out through the gates into the surrounding town. That was the second time that morning I thought I might just get out of this. And the second time that morning that I was wrong.

Chapter 4

Kristian

Kingdom of Coroden, Drelos,
19ᵗʰ The Month of Promise 1575

arly morning sunshine threaded the branches, teasing our eyes, trying to fool us into thinking we were back in the same woods, just outside the cave. I looked at the mostly unfamiliar trees we passed, the forest watching us curiously with a thousand eyes in return.

'Anything?' I asked again, for what felt like the hundredth time.

'There's still no signal. I have no idea where we are,' Storn summarised his earlier observations. 'All I can say is that the planet shares the standard parameters required for habitation. The percentage of oxygen in the air is very slightly lower than on Alba. The gravity is also a little weaker.'

'I still can't believe we lost him,' I grumbled. 'How did he disappear so quickly? We must have entered that teleport minutes after him, if that!'

Storn cocked his head to look at me. 'Um ... excuse me? Shouldn't you be still not believing how you've just survived teleport travel?'

I sighed. 'I suppose. Let's focus on finding this Conor Drew. And hope we can get to him before it's too late.'

Storn was right, of course. My thoughts had gathered around Laro like dark clouds at the expense of everything else. It was easier to focus on him than to allow other notions to complicate things. In fact, I needed something to fixate on. The loss, the shock of the massacre, still haunted me. A shadow of that strange, disturbing dream hung above it. At least my anger propelled me forward, while everything else only threatened to pull me down.

'Kris.' Storn's concerned voice jolted me from my pondering. Further ahead, the trees thinned, and a timber cottage stood near the road. Not far from it, something lay unmoving on a dark patch of the forest floor. Something large and furry. It looked like it might have been a dog. Without its head, it was hard to say for sure. I dismounted a good five yards from where the body lay rolled against a thorn bush. The forest, like a shocked witness, stood ominously quiet, the only sound the buzzing of flies around the carcass.

I walked on towards the cottage and pulled out my blaster. The door was ajar. I opened it fully. A figure sat on the floor, his back against the top of an overturned table. He was a burly man, well into his fifties, with dark eyes gazing unfocused below his short, ebony hair. He had thick arms laden with muscles. His fingers were clasped around the hilt of a blade driven all the way through his stomach, impaling him to the table.

The smell of blood woke something in me. A hot, vicious feeling broke free, like a dark poison spreading into my body and mind. A corruption both new and familiar, a memory of whispers that terrified me. I staggered back, shocked, wanting to run, wanting to free myself from that sickening sensation.

'Please …' The man's pleading reached me, his voice raspy and weak. 'Please help … please, don't leave me!'

I gritted my teeth and swallowed a few times, pressing the invading forces in me back into their place by strength of will. I opened my right hand, fingers shaking as I stretched them apart and pushed down. I pushed against an invisible shadow, both mesmerised and disgusted by the feel of it.

'Please …' The man spoke again, quieter this time.

My heart twisted at the sound of his cries, and the shadow suddenly dissolved beneath my fingers. I was myself again.

'I'm here.' I hurried into the room, crouching down next to him, recognising the language, although I'd never expected to use it outside the classroom. I looked behind the tabletop. The length of the blade visible on the other side made me nauseous. I assumed his body must have been in shock, immune, or at least dissociated from the pain enough to be able to talk. Nonetheless, I grabbed the biostick from my pack and switched it on. I selected morphine from the list of drugs available and gently inserted the emerging needle into his upper arm. He hardly seemed to notice.

'What's your name?'

'It's Declan.' He looked up at me with weary eyes.

'What happened here, Declan?' I asked, trying to control the anger rising in my voice in anticipation of the answer I suspected.

'A young man came by … asking questions … looking for Conor Drew.'

'You know Conor Drew?'

'Everybody knows Conor Drew,' he said, the corner of his lips curving into a bitter smile. His eyes defocused, as if remembering something, then he continued. 'Can't say I like the lad much … but my daughter is very taken with him …'

'Your daughter?' I glanced around uneasily, half-expecting to see a second body lying somewhere.

'Nera … She works down in Beren Castle.'

I looked down at the wicked object we'd been trying hard to ignore, wondering what the hell I could do about it. A quick glance at the interior, the obvious lack of electricity or even window glass, suggested we were likely on a pre-industrial planet somewhere. No help would come in the middle of a forest, and I had neither the equipment nor the experience to save him. The man seemed to guess what I was thinking, too, because he raised a weak hand to get my attention back and started talking with renewed intensity.

'Look, there's nothing much you can do here. But you need to go down to the castle and warn them, please! Conor Drew is expected there, at the duke's daughter's wedding. Please don't let this killer anywhere near my daughter. Please!'

'You told him Conor Drew would be at the castle?'

He didn't answer for a while, just stared at me in confusion, as if trying to remember who I was or what the answer to my question could be.

'No,' he said after a while, his voice growing steadier as the drug kicked in. 'I told him that I heard Conor went to the Holt Catacombs on some business on the duke's behalf. And that, as far as I knew, he was still there. No one ever returned from the Holt Catacombs. With some luck, he might be stupid enough to follow him there.'

'No one ever has returned from there? Why would this Conor Drew go to such a place?' What was the point of racing through half the galaxy to save him if he was stupid enough to walk into his own death without any assistance?

'It's a cursed place. But it's rumoured to hide some magical artefacts. The duke, like all the aristocracy, is a very keen collector.'

Magical artefacts? What? I frowned, but I kept my mouth shut as he continued: 'If anyone can get out of there alive, it's Conor, though and it might be only a matter of time before someone points this bastard towards Beren,' he continued. 'It's just down on the coast, not far. Go, please, and don't let this devil do any more harm there! Don't let him anywhere near my daughter! You've wasted enough time here. Just help me with this first…' His voice trailed off as we both looked down at the sword again.

'The blade went through your stomach. If I pull it out, you'll die,' I said tentatively, the reality of what might have to happen next only now hitting me.

'I'll die if we leave it in. Only slower,' he said. 'And I'd rather not have my Nera find me like this.'

'There must be a way,' I objected, desperately trying to think of one.

'There isn't,' he said simply, reaching out for my hands and placing them on the hilt, leaving his on top of them. I looked down at the blade, dreading what pain just moving it by an inch would cause. My hands shook as I looked into his eyes, unable to bring myself to take his life.

'There must be some other way,' I said again, angry tears filling my eyes now, blurring his face.

'Son, listen to me,' he said gently, one hand reaching up to my face. 'You're not doing anything wrong here. You're helping me.'

'I'm just so sorry that I can't do more,' I said, my voice cracking under the strain.

'You can't do any more than this for me now. But if you get a chance for justice later, I know you'll take it.'

'I will,' I said. 'I promise I won't let this killer anywhere near Nera. I'll catch him and make him pay!' My muscles tensed as more anger slipped into them with each word, giving me the strength I needed. A sudden yank and the sword came free, filling my world with hot blood, the man's howling, and the sharp, sickening stench of death.

It took some time before I stumbled out into the sunshine where Storn waited. Despite my earlier temper, a miserable exhaustion enfolded me as we set out towards Beren, and if I'd had to face Laro right there and then, it probably wouldn't have taken him long to add me to his growing casualty list. As it happened, however, the next section of the journey went uneventfully and fast as Storn flew through the forest with me in the saddle.

Eventually, the trees thinned around us, and a distant city came into view. Beren hugged the coast, walled off on its own peninsula. Behind the walls lay a carpet of single-story dwellings, their terracotta roofs gleaming red in the morning light, rising towards a rocky outcrop sporting larger structures—perhaps the homes and temples of a ruling elite. The castle stood on the very top, surrounded by another set of walls. I adjusted my lenses and zoomed my view in. Nothing within the city suggested heavy industry, just the thin smokes of individual smiths, tanneries and the like. Their narrow streets seemed unsuited to motorised transport. Out on the sea, no ships were at anchor other than those that depended on the wind.

'Look, look!' Storn said urgently. 'On the main road!'

Some commotion caught my eyes as I turned my gaze back towards the east walls where someone was galloping through the gates, followed by many others, their business seemingly urgent. I zoomed in again, something more than mere curiosity drawing me closer until I could finally see the first person's face.

'It's him. Conor,' I said. 'The first rider.'

'How can you tell?' Storn's voice sounded a little odd, but I was too busy trying to figure out why I was suddenly so certain.

'I don't know.' I had to admit it was peculiar. In fact, the more I tried to find some logic behind my assumption or just remember where I knew his face from, the less sure I felt.

'And he's leading an army?' Again, that odd slow voice.

I turned my attention to the riders behind him. They were all men, wearing various pieces of metal armour.

'It looks like it.'

'It's strange he's the only one not wearing any protection.'

I looked back at Conor. He seemed to be riding at full speed down the road, his head kept low. My lens' motion sensors highlighted a projectile passing close by him. It was an arrow, missing him by an inch.

'Now, wait a second …' A few more flew by before I spotted the archers and re-assessed my understanding of the situation. Chased by a whole army? Really? Seemed like the guy had a death wish one way or the other.

I pursed my lips, wondering what to do. After everything, would I now have to watch him die? At that moment, Conor looked at me, too. Given the distance between us, he couldn't have seen me. Yet somehow, we connected. In his surprise, he lost his balance and swayed in the saddle. He managed not to fall but slowed sufficiently for the others to catch up with him.

'Let's go!' I called out and gripped the reins. Storn didn't move. 'Storn!' I cried impatiently. 'Let's go, quickly!'

There was no response.

I leaned forward until my head was close to his. 'What's wrong?' Nothing seemed wrong with him. He just stood there.

'So many,' he said slowly.

'What?' I asked, tilting my head, trying my best to make him look at me.

'Horses,' he whispered, completely ignoring me.

I stroked the top of his head. 'Do you like them? What do you say we catch up and see if you can join them for a run?'

He looked at me then. Just for one moment. The next, I was holding on for dear life.

Despite our speedy approach, by the time we made our way down, the soldiers were long gone. I decided to move the ionblaster into my saddle-bag, hoping the city guard wouldn't want to go through its contents.

As we neared the gates, flags fluttered in the wind far above us on the battlements, and more and more people came into view. An elderly man passed by us on his way out of town, causally whistling as he led a heavily laden donkey. Ahead of us, two women entered, wearing long robes and carrying a large woven basket between them. I dismounted and pretended to lead my horse as I followed them through the gates. Within a few yards, three armed soldiers stopped me. A young, self-assured fellow stood in the middle of their half-circle and called out to me. 'What's your name, traveller?'

'Kristian del Rosso,' I said.

'Kristian de' Rosso!' His comrade standing on the left shouted back over his shoulder. Further in, near a large building, a woman sat on a bench behind a wooden table.

'I heard it myself, thank you, Rodrigo!' she called back, writing in a large book in front of her, presumably entering my name. I noticed she also had a tall, metal tankard next to her ink bottle, as well as what appeared to be a throwing knife embedded into the tabletop.

'And your purpose in the city?' the first soldier asked me again.

'I'm on business on behalf of the duke,' I told him with more confidence than I felt.

'He's on business on behalf of the duke!' Rodrigo called back again to the woman, who simply rolled her eyes. 'On your way, then,' he said to me, and they parted to let me go.

I only took a couple of steps, however, before a knife flew by, missing my nose by inches, and sank its tip into a log on a woodsman's cart. I turned to look at the woman who was holding a second knife already. 'And what business might that be, Kristian del Rosso?' she asked conversationally, twirling the knife between her fingers.

I looked into her big, dark eyes and confessed. 'Conor Drew.'

Her face split into a huge grin. 'Good luck with that!' she said and reached out with her arm, pointing her knife up towards the castle. She was pretty when she smiled. Mocking or not.

The vibrant streets soon swallowed us, drawing us deep into the heart of the town. A cavalcade of colours, sounds and scents invaded my senses, in stark contrast to the university's restrained atmosphere. My thoughts were drowned beneath the noise of carriage wheels, horseshoes on cobblestones, the chatter of citizens debating local news, the shouts of vendors, the laughter of kids chasing each other, the whistling of fisherfolk carrying their catch in heaped buckets, the frequent calls of seagulls from above.

We made our way up towards the castle. From many houses came the smell of fish frying over stoves, warm bread cooling on windowsills, variously mixing with the less pleasant odour of human sweat, the stink of pigs penned for market, stable doors yawning, their breath heavy with farm animals and hay, the sweet fragrance of acacia, rose and orange blossoms carried on a warm breeze from gardens.

Above all, my gaze was drawn to the faces of those who passed us by. On Alba, we were all shaped to perfection. Here, lacking modern technology, time and wear carved lines and imperfections with unforgiving hands, somehow still sculpting their owners to radiate deep internal strength and an innocent beauty.

Beren Castle, with its many towers and charming turrets, sat surrounded by a picturesque garden. It spoke of wealth and comfort, reflected in the girth of the men set to guard it, and in the obvious neglect of its defences in favour of ornamentation.

The same explanation I had offered at the town gate saw me through the gates and a boy appeared to lead Storn away. Storn, who pulled a rather concerned expression at this new development, soon cheered up upon realising their destination, and appeared to lead the surprised boy himself as they departed towards the stables. I stowed my blaster away, judging the saddlebag's biometric clasps to be sufficient impediment to anyone wanting to get hold of it.

I entered the castle in the company of a Frederick Rolford, who introduced himself as the steward. He quickly made it perfectly clear to me that, in his consideration, the chances of the duke granting me, or anyone for that matter, an audience to discuss any business regarding Conor Drew were very slim indeed. Nonetheless, ground down by my persistence, he left me waiting in a stunning, high-ceilinged library featuring magnificently carved bookcases, comfortable sofas and large, glass-paned windows providing views across the garden.

I walked along the shelves, inspecting the handmade volumes with interest. Many of them had wooden bindings, sometimes covered in leather with vellum title labels glued to their spines. A few were covered in textiles richly adorned with embroidery. Almost all of them were secured with small metal clasps. I examined several of them appreciatively, then turned to walk across the room and paused.

As my eyes moved past the contents of a shelf and its exquisitely detailed carvings depicting mythical beasts, they picked up on a familiar name on one of the book spines. I slowly turned back, half-convinced that I had only imagined it, but there it was. I reached for the volume curiously and opened it. Just like all the others, it was written in ink by hand. The only difference was that I knew this handwriting. I turned the pages slowly, scrutinising the elegant lines, but there was no mistake.

'I hope you find my library to your satisfaction,' an imperious voice addressed my back. It belonged to a tall man with sharp eyes and greying features. The presence of the steward and two armed guards behind him helped to convince me that this was the duke, who had entered the room while I stood there lost in surprise.

'I apologise, Your Grace,' I answered hesitantly, 'but this book here…'

'Is a rare and invaluable original, as I assume you must already know.'

I wavered under his steely gaze and reluctantly put *A History of Coroden by James Montgomery, G.M.* back in its place.

'Now, if you wouldn't mind telling me who you are and the reason for your visit, as it already happens to be an unexpectedly difficult morning for me,' the duke said, seating himself at a dark wooden table and indicating for me to join him.

'My name is Kristian del Rosso. I'm a scholar. I travelled here from Alba in search of a man called Conor Drew. I was told that I might find him here.'

'I've never heard of such place,' the duke said. 'As for Conor Drew, he's currently being held in the dungeons awaiting decision about his penalty, and as such is quite unable to attend to other matters, I'm afraid.'

'May I ask what he's done?'

The duke looked uncomfortable, his forehead creasing into complicated lines. 'A personal insult,' he said at last. 'One which has severe diplomatic inconveniences tied to it.'

I relaxed. That didn't sound too bad. 'Would there be any way to compensate you for these crimes and release him into my custody?' I asked.

The duke slowly shook his head, his lips curving into a sad smile. 'Not if you could offer your weight in gold. So, unless you have brought something even more valuable with you today, Scholar of Alba, I'm afraid this discussion has come to an end.' He looked at me expectantly.

I racked my brain. Even if the castle had been guarded better, it wouldn't take much for Laro to enter the prison and complete what he had set out to do. Hell, given what I'd seen here so far, he might even share a plate of delicacies and a game of cards with the soldiers while listening to a troubadour's performance beforehand.

'How about an invisibility cloak?' I offered suddenly, not seeing any other way out of the situation.

'A what?' The duke's eyebrows flew up in surprise.

'A magical cloak that can make its wearer fully invisible,' I explained with a confident smile spreading across my face. I used to teach classes. I could tell when my audience was hooked.

'Show me!' the duke ordered.

I opened my pack and pulled the microelectronic cloak out. It was of a greyish-blue colour, its material imitating cotton, with only the small monitor on its collar looking out of place. I stood and put it on, activating it with a few quick taps on the screen. I glanced up to take in the duke's astonished face, then pulled up the hood, too. I turned around to look at the other men standing at the back of the room, who, of course, could no longer see me. The steward stared, gaping, while the soldiers pulled their swords from their scabbards. I quietly walked back to the bookshelf and lifted *A History of Coroden* into the air, feeling like a magician as the people in the room simultaneously gasped. I put the book back into its place and pulled off my hood.

'Incredible!' The duke exclaimed in disbelief. Then he beckoned to the steward. 'Frederick, put it on!'

The steward's face turned horrified, and he glanced at the door for a second as if contemplating an emergency escape. Behind him, the soldiers exchanged excited looks, and one of them placed his hand on the steward's shoulder, who looked more and more like a scared rabbit under the butcher's knife.

'There's no need to be afraid; it's perfectly safe,' I tried to reassure him as I walked towards them, pulling off the cloak. I put it on the steward and activated the device. As Frederick disappeared from view, the two guards started curiously poking him, reassuring themselves that, despite it all, he was still there, laughing loudly, as if this was the best entertainment they had had in ages. The duke came over and joined them, slapping the top of the steward's head with a practised flip of his hand. His laughter boomed over the soldiers'.

'Take it off him,' he instructed me finally, his earlier distress replaced by enthusiasm. I did as I was told, and in turn, he sent his men to fetch Conor Drew while I explained to him how to use the cloak and how to adjust for size.

Once he had tried it on successfully himself, he turned to me and asked how I came to possess it.

'Cloaks like these are not that uncommon where I'm from,' I said carefully.

'Yes, this Alba is a very long way away, I'm sure.' He surprised me with a knowing smile.

'It is,' I admitted, unsure what he meant.

'You are not the first to come to our lands from a "far-away" place, Kristian del Rosso. Although, travellers like you are immensely rare. We call them Rachallans. There are stories about one or two in every generation, arriving from worlds beyond the stars, passing through our kingdoms, never staying for long.

'I love my books, and I read a lot. I came to respect the Rachallans for their unique skillset and knowledge. Unfortunately, few beyond these walls are similarly open-minded. Your fine manners, your strange accent and your unusual clothing give you away. Not to mention this cloak.' He glanced down at it, then back at me. 'You'll find this is a rough world, Kristian del Rosso. If I were you, I would try to blend in. What is your purpose with Conor Drew?'

'I need his help catching an assassin,' I said simply. Worried he might start asking questions I'd find more difficult to answer, I quickly added, 'This assassin has also killed the father of a serving girl working in your castle. Her name is Nera. I came across their cabin this morning, but I was too late.'

The duke's face darkened. 'I shall let her know.'

He rang a small bell on a side table and told the woman who appeared to get me a new set of clothing. I followed her up a staircase into a small guestroom and quickly changed before heading back down and out to the courtyard to find the duke with more of his soldiers standing around Conor Drew. It was the rider from the road.

Conor sported a few colourful bruises but seemed otherwise un-harmed, his hands still in shackles. He looked about my age with a scornful expression under his shock of messy, dark hair.

One of the guards presented me with an iron key, mumbling, 'All yours,' under his breath. I took it and walked up to the prisoner. Our eyes met as I released him, but neither of us spoke. Behind the soldiers, the stable boy appeared with Storn and another horse I presumed to be Conor's.

'Conor Drew, you are never to return here again,' the duke declared in a voice allowing no contradiction. 'You have two days to leave the city.' He turned to me, and his voice softened. 'Whereas, of course, you are welcome here at any time once your business with him is concluded.'

'I thank you for your kindness and your advice, Your Grace.' I bowed and turned to leave.

'Technically, nobody has proof that I've done anything wrong,' Conor said to the duke as I swung myself into the saddle. I was eager to get out of here and talk to him, to find the answers to my questions before Laro reappeared. This really wasn't the time to argue and further annoy the duke when he was free to go.

'Conor—' I started, but he cut me short with a raised hand and carried on.

'Your, Grace, just give me back what's mine! I don't even care about the rest. Give me back the medallion, at least. Nobody saw anything!'

'These extenuating circumstances are the reason you're still alive,' the duke answered coldly.

'You mean that killing me would confirm any rumours about what might have happened. It's in your interest, too, to let me go, as if it was all nothing.'

'Let me put it this way,' said the duke. 'One more word about this here or anywhere else, and the life of a cockroach will carry more enjoyment than yours!'

Conor raised his arm and pointed at the duke, presumably about to deliver his views on the finer details of legislative fairness, at which point Storn, sensing my impatience, let out a long, resounding neigh and pounded the ground with his front legs. Conor turned, wordless, his finger now pointing at Storn, quieting him with a murderous look on his face before walking to his own horse and getting into the saddle.

For my part, I was just relieved Storn had remembered to stay in character and hadn't reprimanded our new friend verbally. Then we would have never left.

Chapter 5

Conor

Beren, Drelos,
19th The Month of Promise 1575

Anger is like fire. Let it burn unwatched, and it will hurt you. Use it wisely, and it becomes what the gods intended it to be: fortitude. I've always found that one of the best ways to employ such a fire was by cooking up a plan.

I had two days to steal back the medallion from the duke. Two days I didn't actually need. All I needed was to make sure the act went unnoticed, and what better way was there to dispel even the shadow of suspicion than to have all eyes on me? To let people think, without the slightest doubt, that they knew where I was and what I was up to?

There was just the matter of ditching my new self-appointed guardian angel. To get rid of people, you have to politely listen to what they want as you take a good look at them and then give them what they need. For the best result, I decided we should focus on the two things he clearly needed the most.

'When was the last time you went out drinking with friends? Or spent the night with a woman?'

'What?'

'Oh, don't give me that look! It's bad enough when your horse does it.' The animal in question looked up at me as we unhurriedly crossed Merchant's Square. The streets quieted around us with the sun setting, heralding the arrival of the time of day I usually preferred.

'Conor, have you listened to anything I told you so far?'

Remember, as I said, you listen to them, or at the very least, you pretend.

'Every word of it.' I nodded sagely. 'We're both in mortal danger. This Laro could happen on us at any moment!'

'Does this not concern you the slightest?' He started to sound exasperated. Which was good. Tiring them can also help.

I looked at him, deeply troubled, and nodded a few more times. 'Now, let me recall when the last time was that someone tried to kill me.' I gazed at the crimsoning sky, as if trying to think hard but in fact remembering the wine-soaked table linen from last night. 'Aaaah, but only this morning!' I stopped my horse and dismounted. 'And I'll certainly perish from hunger before anyone else gets to try if we don't eat something soon.' I looked expectantly at the inn, and as if by magic, the innkeeper's son appeared to lead the horses into their stable.

'Be careful with this one, Ben.' I patted Kristian's horse as he dismounted. The animal seemed to have that annoyed disposition about it, as it had every time it looked at me. I grinned widely in response and rubbed its head behind the ear. 'Awww … who are we getting rid of now? Who? But who? This little opinionated horsie? It needs to go now and leave the grown-ups to talk privately! Oh, noooo!'

'It's best not to aggravate him,' Kristian stepped in, while the horse looked on as if he might complete the assassin's task the next minute.

'Pfffttt.' I turned and walked towards the door. 'Come on, Kristian,' I called back over my shoulder. 'I must introduce you to the local traditions.'

The Fisherman's Tale was packed to the gunnels with locals meeting up for a pint after the day's work, travellers from Savia or the Lost Islands looking to spend a night on land, others taking a short rest before sailing with the morning tide.

Heads turned as the creak of the door announced our arrival—some bored, some curious, all of them judging, making their own assumptions, each according to their nature and what best suited the next turn of their conversation. A quick glance around told me that there were no vacant tables, as was often the case on a fine, late spring eve.

There are several ways to get yourself a table in a crowded tavern. Usually, the less amicable, the more successful. But right then, for some unfathomable reason, I wanted to look good in front of my new friend. I wasn't even sure why. Maybe it was just that damn horse. In any case, I called out to Sarah, the innkeeper, loud and clear:

'Doreni High Ale for everyone!'

A resounding cheer went up at that, along with Kristian's eyebrows, while a group of regulars scrambled to their feet, and with the kind of unashamed affection that only the half-drunk can muster, patted my shoulders and persuaded us to sit down in their places.

The Doreni was so crisp and clear that nobody ever questioned the effort involved in carting the barrels over a hundred miles of bad roads from Orengwood. A sip would play a melody on your tongue, a tune of sweet, high notes underwritten by a sharply sour lament. A flagon would play a sonnet on your mind.

'Quite an entrance,' Kristian acknowledged, settling down at the table and looking around. 'I thought the duke kept your belongings.'

'He did,' I said.

'In which case, I'm not quite sure how you think we're going to pay for such an extravagant night out.' His questioning eyes settled back on me just as the serving girl placed a tankard in front of me.

'Ah, don't worry.' I shrugged and raised it in salute. 'We can always just sell your horse.' To his credit, Kristian returned my grin at the joke without missing a beat.

'I'm sure he'd find his way back before long. But I'd strongly advise against falling asleep in the meantime!'

I took a swig from my ale and started to enjoy myself. The noise of the inn washed over us in waves, conversations swelling, voices booming then softening until we could hear the repeated roll of dice on nearby tables. Someone hummed as they walked past our table carrying drinks. Occasional laughter cut across the air, the doors creaking as more guests arrived.

The windows stood open, letting the last of the daylight reach in. Outside, the sun drowned in the west, setting a field of night-flowers to bloom, first one, then another, another, then many. In sconces, upon the hearth, a faint and flickering glow blossomed in dark windows. Inside, the light pooled around candles on tables, around oil lamps on the walls, illuminating paintings nestled close, leaving others to the dark.

So, my rescuer wasn't rich, or he just hadn't much coin on him. I would have thought him rich. Even for a scholar, he had fine features. He had the hands of someone who never in his life had to handle anything more difficult than a teaspoon. Fingers manicured, hair freshly cut. He was bare-faced, like a woman. Not freshly shaved, but as if the hair had never started growing on his face. Nowhere a scar, or even a scratch, not a single strand of hair out of place. Even his blue eyes seemed to have an uncanny crystal clarity to them. He would be so easily manipulated, I almost felt sorry for him.

'I keep a strongbox here. The night's entertainment is on me,' I told him as a barmaid finally appeared with the stew I ordered.

'A strongbox?' Kristian asked, but he kept his eyes on his food, considering the contents of his bowl somewhat suspiciously.

'Yes. I keep my valuables in a handful of inns across the country,' I said and watched him closely as he watched the food equally closely. I noticed that, at times, his eyes went a little funny. As if he stopped seeing what he was looking at. Defocused. I'd seen similar on the faces of priests and spellcasters before, but that always lasted a lot longer than just a few moments.

'Oh, the food is fine. It's one of the cook's specialities, actually,' I said. 'It's—'

'Wild boar.' He finished the sentence for me as his eyes flicked back to normal.

'Yes, it is,' I said and wondered if I was just imagining things.

'So, strongboxes in inns?' he asked and started eating. 'You don't have a home somewhere? A family?'

'Heh, no,' I confessed as I tucked into my own. 'I'm not exactly a family guy. A home, a family are things you need to look after. I'm not keen on attachments. How about you? Is there a woman waiting once you hunt down this Laro guy? A place somewhere nice?'

'Not exactly.' He seemed to consider the answer before admitting. 'There hasn't been a woman in some years now. I had girlfriends while I was still a student, but once I started teaching, things changed.'

I nodded considerately as if I knew what he meant. I thought he'd said earlier they taught mixed groups of older pupils there. He was only a scholar, not a damned monk!

'I hear you are some kind of adventurer. You risked your life to help the duke retrieve a historical artefact?' he asked between mouthfuls.

'That's right,' I said, feeling suddenly more guarded.

'What was it? Was it worth all that risk?'

'It was an ancient crown, lost in the Holt Catacombs. An old graveyard buried 150 yards below ground.' I noticed with some satisfaction that for the first time, he looked impressed. I guessed he could know a little bit about me. 'There was good coin offered.'

I watched his eyes defocus and sharpen on me once again. 'Good coin?' He stared at me pointedly, as if he knew I wasn't exactly telling the truth. I didn't understand it. I was a good liar. And it wasn't even such a big lie. The medallion was, after all, a kind of coin, wasn't it? Maybe a little different, but not so terribly different. 'Well, it's a shame the duke took it all back,' he concluded as I failed to speak up in my turn, busy wondering how to distract him from the topic of my reward. 'What happened?'

'Conor Drew!' A female voice cut across as I struggled to come up with an honest-sounding answer. Oh, how I loved women calling out my name just at the right moment!

'Olivia Wade!' I turned around, my smile genuine. 'Where have you been? I haven't seen you in ages!'

'Around and about,' she replied as she reached our table, followed by two very attractive companions. I recognised them as dancers from last night's wedding festivities.

'Rubbish!' I claimed as I took in her pretty face, long brown hair and athletic body. Damn, she looked good. 'I would have known if you had been around.'

'Oh, shut up and let us sit down! This place is so packed. It's almost as if the beer was free.' Only after she planted herself on the bench next to me, drained my tankard and wiped her mouth with the back of her hand did she offer, 'Lady Merilla, the mistress of the Teshiri Pillow House, hired me to escort these ladies back to her distinguished establishment. She became unsatisfied with the services of the male mercenary who saw them here all the way from the south county.'

The ladies in question settled down around Kristian in the meantime, and I signalled to a barmaid for more ale. Despite my best efforts, Kristian had been very carefully keeping his alcohol consumption to a minimum, and I hoped that our new drinking buddies would assist me in encouraging him. Well, they'd better do if I was to ditch him somehow before I sneaked back to the castle.

To look at him, this promised to be a more challenging task than I had expected. He wasn't exactly immune to the charms of the two dancers snuggling up on either side of him. But it wasn't just his awkwardness that made him look closer to a statue wedged between the two women than to a flesh and blood man. His eyes were watchful, his attention on his surroundings never ceasing. It made me wonder just how dangerous this killer he talked about was. In all consideration, the whole situation didn't make sense as it was. If that guy was indeed as deadly as described, why would Kristian go after him all by himself? He didn't look like a fighter. He didn't even have a sword! Yet he wasn't a fool. And there was all this weird business going on. Like that moment before I was captured this morning. That was him, wasn't it? I recognised him! Somehow, even now, he looked familiar. Yet I was unable to tell from where. And all these oddly insightful looks of his. That must be a spell. A complex one I'd never heard of. Maybe there was more to this school of his than he let on. Anyhow. This puzzle had to wait till the morning. The medallion was more important.

I zoned in and out of the conversation, occasionally offering a 'Right!', 'A-ha!' or 'Noooooo!' like a ship captain keeping an eye on the general direction but leaving the labour to the others. Kristian mainly talked to Olivia, with the girls doing their bit and visibly becoming drunker and cuddlier by the minute but failing to influence the guy in the right direction. At the same time, Olivia started flashing him the kind of seductive smiles even I became jealous of. It was time I doubled my efforts and jerked that wheel back to ensure things were once again going my way.

I scanned the crowd until a temporary opening revealed an old, shady character between the shoulders of two guys hulking over him. I emptied my tankard and stood, intending to go and hulk over him myself. By the time I reached him, the others thankfully had cleared off.

'Evening, Rodmus, how's business?' I asked the short, bony man, wearing a cloak far too big for him.

'Not bad, not bad!' He looked up at me, his pupils way smaller than they should have been. I wondered how long he had before either the old witch or her potent brews were done with him.

'Boss is well?'

'She is. She's just got herself a new mansion in Goldwood Old Town.'

'Another one?' Business was good. 'Anyhow. Listen. Do you have any Pixies' Delight on you?'

'Pixies' Delight, eh?' He gave me a sickening smile that would have made me take a step back in the best of circumstances. But right now, I needed that bloody stuff too much, and so stayed in place like a good hound, eagerly watching as he reached into one of his many pockets. 'You're in luck.' He pulled out two small, cotton sachets, supposedly white, although that looked more than questionable in the candlelight.

'Half a sachet will make you feel like a god until at least sunrise. A whole sachet will bring you the most vivid, heavenly dreams you've ever had!'

'Give me them both.' I snatched them from his open hand and closed mine around them. I ushered him to the bar, got the innkeeper to pay him and add it to my tab. Next, I made sure my preferred room was still booked under my name for the night and managed to get the one next to it available for my new friend. I also ordered a bottle of sweet cherry wine, poured some into a small cup and started mixing the contents of the first sachet into it with a spoon. This Kristian was costing me quite a bit already, and I'd only just met him. The quicker we wrapped up his supposed business with me, the better. He somehow had the kind of influence on me I was usually immune to. And in my line of work, it never paid to have friends who cared about things like morals or responsibility. Or friends who could tell if I was lying. Or friends with overcritical pets.

'Conor, what are you doing?' The question came half-accusing, half-amused. I turned my head and looked at Olivia. All innocent.

'Helping out a friend. And it's not just me. You're helping, too,' I added hurriedly.

'I am? Why would I …? And wait! Isn't that far too much?' I ignored her and poured the contents of the second sachet into the cup, too. Women tended to worry way too much in my experience.

'Nah. He'll be fine,' I said, carefully stirring the drink. 'I brought him here to have a good time.' I put a finger to her lips to stop her from responding. Funny how that always worked. 'Now, we need to keep this quiet.' I moved my finger to my own lips in a conspiratorial manner and gave her a smile. 'He would never willingly agree to this. Do you know why?'

'Because people generally don't like being drugged without their consent?'

I shook my head. 'Heartbreak.'

'What?'

'He can't forget about her! It's been bloody months, and he's still hoping she'll come back. Just look at him!'

We both turned our heads and watched him. Kristian sat somewhat awkwardly, the head of one of his tablemates pressed against his upper arm, her arms wrapped around the rest of the limb. The other had a hand on his thigh and a coy gaze fixed on his face. He managed a lopsided grin every now and then, a small sip from his ale, but his eyes constantly wandered, carefully observing everyone around them, lingering on windows and doors.

'Despite my best efforts, he hardly eats anything,' I continued. 'He hardly drinks. He doesn't sleep.'

'That's terrible …'

I knew I had her then. But just to make sure, I leaned closer to her ear and confidentially added, 'I still hear him cry at nights.'

'Nooooooo.'

'So, you see, I've tried everything.' I took her hand in mine and squeezed it. 'I really need your help now.' I put the cup into her hand and closed her fingers around it. 'In fact, I've tried so many things, he doesn't trust me anymore. But I know you can make him drink it.' I poured wine into another cup for her and handed it over. 'It can only help. It's all herbal. Practically medication!'

She moved to go back, but I put my hand on her arm. 'Don't let him look at it for long,' I warned her. 'If he starts giving it much thought, he will hesitate and won't drink it, believe me!'

She nodded and left with considerable determination on her face. I leaned against the counter and smiled to myself. After a few hours with Kristian, it felt good to be able to sway people to my tune again.

I watched the proceedings from the safety of the bar, with just the tiniest degree of apprehension clenching my hand into a fist. I had faith in my infantrywoman. She cut across the crowd, claiming both its attention and admiration like a lioness going for the kill. Right ahead of target, she tipped the contents of the cup into her mouth. The wrong cup! But she didn't swallow it. A surprised Kristian did—right after his mouth was filled with the liquid as it opened beneath Olivia's sensual lips. The poor guy never had a chance!

The smile that spread across Kristian's face was so unlike him, he looked like a completely different person by the time I reached them. He was busy kissing one of the dancers while Olivia was busy rinsing her mouth—with my refilled tankard of Doreni High Ale! She ignored my feigned shock of disapproval, and I turned to look at this new person, who was now also watching me with joy sparkling in his eyes.

He stood suddenly, covering the distance between us with quick un-steady steps, and threw his arm around my shoulder, leaning on me as he affectionately announced: 'Conor, I'm so happy that I've found you!'

'Yes, isn't this nice?' I muttered. I patted his back and did my best to make him sit down on the bench. 'This was meant to be,' I tried to reassure him, sitting next to him, and he lowered his head on my shoulder, as if finding it too heavy to hold up.

'I know, right?' He turned his head to look at me, unable to lift it, which resulted in his face being now way too close to mine.

I raised my head instantly and looked around, trying to establish just how many people were being entertained by our little scene, but apart from Olivia, everyone seemed to be minding their own business.

'We'll get this Laro, don't you worry!' I raised my flask with my free hand. That jolted him up once more, and he stared at me wildly.

'We will?' He raised his own flask and touched it to mine. 'We will!' He lowered the drink uncertainly and followed it a second later, collapsing onto the table head first.

'Thanks for coming to save my life, by the way!' I commented.

'Any time,' he mumbled in a muffled voice.

'Right.' I stood, pulling him up with me. 'Bedtime!'

I escorted him up to his room with a little help from the innkeeper's son and closed the door on him. 'Done!' And with my guardian angel thus transported into his heavenly dreams, I paid the boy yet another quarter silver for his help.

I walked down the stairs, allowing myself a moment of self-appreciation before I reflected on my further plans for the night. I would sit downstairs with Olivia until the night grew darker around us and most of the customers cleared off. Then I would make my way up to my room, get what I needed from the strongbox, and leave through the window. My thoughts shifted back to the medallion. You don't lose something by others taking it from you. You lose it by not taking it back.

I found Olivia sitting at our table, smiling up at me innocently as I approached. The bench she sat on was otherwise empty. Too empty.

'Where's Kristian's pack?' I asked, not at all pleased with this new development.

'I just sent it after him with one of the barmaids. Is that a problem?' Sarah the innkeeper enquired from behind me.

'No, why would it be?' I dismissed the notion with a seemingly careless hand gesture. Damn. I had been rather looking forward to checking out that bag.

'So, what's the famous Conor Drew been up to lately? I hear you stole the Map of the Death Islands. Is that true?' Olivia brought her arms together on the table and playfully leaned forward, resting her chin on her hands.

I looked down into her big, green eyes. 'That's a veeery long story.'

'I could stay for a while ...' A suggestion of a slow smile was transforming into a promise.

'Well. It all started when a group of Sint deserters hired me to find the kidnapped daughter of their leader. They didn't have enough money to pay my usual fee, but they had something better to offer ...' I took a sip from my flask, thoroughly enjoying the relentless attention, and thought to myself how the allure of being a scholar was perhaps something I had utterly underestimated before.

It was late by the time I finally got up from that table and indicated we should go. And when I say 'late', I mean much, much later than I originally planned. We were well into the early hours, and if I delayed much longer, the crowing of the cocks would be the tune accompanying my little operation.

'I don't need to walk back all the way to our tavern tonight, do I?' Olivia asked me in a way that suggested she fully intended to stay.

'No, you can sleep in my room if you promise to be a good girl,' I conceded and turned to lead the way. Given the condition of my new pal, I didn't anticipate an early start in the morning, and I could nicely imagine Olivia both as an alibi and a treat for breakfast. We reached the first floor and walked past Kristian's door. It was all quiet in there, and I couldn't help but smirk as I pulled the key from my pocket to open the next room.

Inside, a single lantern burned, trimmed low, the pleasant late spring weather rendering the fireplace redundant. I lit a few candles, and while Olivia settled herself on the top of the bed, I went and pulled the old metal trunk out from under it.

With the key in my bag, still in the duke's castle, it took me a minute or two to open it. This was what happened when you had a lock made not just to keep thieves out but to intimidate them. Of course, you needed to be careful not to push this sort of thing too far. Unless you wanted to find the cream of the field queued up on your doorstep, drawn by the challenge.

'Has anyone told you before that when you invite a woman to your bed, there are usually other things to fiddle with?' Olivia looked down at me from the bed.

I feigned surprise. 'Never heard that one before!'

'Unless, of course, you have other plans for the night …?' she said as she watched me pocket a handful of items from the trunk.

'This won't take long. I'll be back before you know it and will happily undertake any required fiddling to the best of my skills.'

'Fine,' she said and suggestively stretched along the bed. 'But don't keep me waiting for long.'

Hmmm. That went easier than I expected. No objections. No questions asked. Just the way I liked it. In fact, things were going great tonight! I moved to close the lid of the trunk, then half-way down, I paused. Weren't things going a little too well though? Olivia hadn't even seemed that surprised by the fact that I was heading out. She'd expressed no further opinions on me getting rid of my friend for the night. I looked back up at her. If she somehow knew or at least suspected my plans …

In that very moment, a sweet smile spread across her face, a chasm that crossed the path of my thoughts, demanding I stop or fall. I stopped and smiled back. Nah. She just knew me too well. How long had we known each other? Sometimes it seemed like forever. All this stupid over-thinking, this suspiciousness, was Kristian's doing.

I looked back at the strongbox, intending to lower the lid and lock it, but a twinkle caught my eye through the gap. For a second, it reminded me of the light from a lighthouse out on a foggy sea. I briefly considered things again but drew a blank. If there was something wrong with my perfect picture, I couldn't see it. Nonetheless, I re-opened the trunk and took out the two short swords along with a double leather back scabbard. Initially, I only intended to take a dagger and a few emergency knives, not expecting to find the duke's night guard especially difficult to bypass, but perhaps carrying a few additional items on me would help to restore my composure.

By the time we had left the common room, it was so deserted there was no reason for me to climb through my bedroom window anymore, so I simply exited the room through the door instead. It was eerily quiet out in the corridor, the only sound the sputtering of candles here and there. I started down the staircase, the creaking of the old wooden steps forcing me into a slow, cautious descent. I was only about half-way down when I thought I heard a noise from upstairs. I turned and looked back towards Kristian's door. A pang of unexpected guilt spread through me. What if that alleged assassin of his found him while I was out?

So what? I said to myself. It didn't matter. I hardly even knew him! It wasn't exactly my job to protect him. And if he had got me out of the duke's prison, so what? It would only have been a matter of time before I got myself out of there without any of his help. Not to mention, that noise could have been anyone doing anything. The inn had a lot of guests staying overnight. But in any case, I wouldn't be away for long.

I resumed my descent and, for a moment, gained a clear view of the common room, lit by a sudden light, shortly followed by a slow, disapproving rumble of the skies. Somewhere, a window shutter swung against the wall, the strengthening wind eager to join in with the chorus of the heavens. Perfect! I might get soaking wet by the time I got back, but the storm would at least keep the streets clear.

In the temporary light, I spotted Rodmus in one corner, almost completely obscured by shadows. He seemed to have decided that the floorboards would do for the night. I was about to sigh and move on, but the sound of a door opening upstairs and someone fast approaching the top of the staircase stifled the urge.

'Conor?' It was Kristian standing up there and looking, to my biggest surprise, remarkably sober. He didn't seem especially happy, either. His expression was a mix of shock and anger, and I couldn't really have blamed him, except … he wasn't looking at me. He was looking towards the corner I had been looking at a minute ago. 'His neck is broken,' he said.

How the hell could he see that from up there? I walked to Rodmus's body and checked. Kristian was right. A blue glow lit up on the corpse, emitted by something that looked like a bumblebee, only bigger.

'He's here,' Kristian said in a grave voice. 'Laro is here.'

The blue bee rose into the air somewhat drunkenly and exploded into a bright light.

Chapter 6

Kristian

Beren, Drelos,
19th The Month of Promise 1575

We spend life chasing after an impossible moment. A mirage. Rushing around, trying to change our world until it's perfect. Then one day, the idiot whose life you're trying to save drugs you and two things happen: you turn into a god, stop time and carve your name into the flawlessness of eternity. Then you sigh, release your grip and let it flow again, just so you can go and kick his arse.

The flickering candlelight set shadows dancing on the walls. In contrast, I lay motionless, with the drug still pulsing through my veins. Deep down, under the artificial elation, an uneasiness lurked. The quiet of the night whispered its misgivings between the crackles of the dying candles. Horses whinnied outside in the stable, and a long, deep thunder purred along the edges of a brewing storm. I closed my eyes and let the narcotic drag me under, setting the shadows to dance on the veil of my imagination, keeping me entertained as my perception burned low.

The growling of an older storm rattled through my memories. Memories I'd long forgotten and were not meant to be remembered. The drug reached for them deep and ripped their seals free.

Over two decades ago, above the remote village of Dorsan, foreboding clouds mustered beneath a pale purple sky. A dark crusade marched to bring devastation down upon the land. The small houses huddled close together, an unnerving pressure building on their solar roofs.

The back door of one of the outer buildings slid open. Bright light escaped through the gap, quickly swallowed by the dusk. But something else also slid out with the light. A small, black shadow with amber eyes. It sprinted along the footpath, a touch crazy with the joy of unexpected freedom, and soon reached the edge of the surrounding forest, becoming lost from view among the trees.

The same door opened a few minutes later. This time, it was I who hurriedly exited. The silly cat must have noticed that I forgot to lock the door and ran off to explore the wilderness. This had happened once before, after he figured out how to flip the electromagnetic switch, and at the time, I was lucky enough to catch him before he got far. The land beyond the settlement wasn't a friendly place, to say the least. But now, he also managed to pick the worst possible time. Had I not been alone in the house, things might have turned out different. But since I was, it was my fault for being so careless. I knew he'd always been a daredevil by nature.

'Azraeeeel!' I shouted as I tried to wrap the coat around myself in the teeth of the gale. 'Azrael!' I checked the display of the device in my hand before setting off. Even at the age of six, I knew how to read a map.

The trees danced to the tune of the approaching storm, bending and bowing, torn leaves and twigs spiralling in the midst of them. I braced myself against the bitter tempest and trudged on, anxious now. How could I have been so stupid? I knew about the coming storm. Why didn't I pay more attention while I had the chance? I could have avoided this whole nightmare just by pressing a few buttons …

The first pieces of hail were small. One hit my shoulder early on; I scarcely noticed the pain. But soon, they grew as big as my thumb and tore through the foliage, striking the ground with enough force to shatter. I checked the screen again. The chip built into Azrael's collar was only about a hundred yards ahead of me now. No longer moving.

I sprinted on, and the world became a blur under the flashing lights, my shouts tiny among the rumbles of the storm, the moaning of dark trees and the howl of the wind.

Azrael lay unmoving near the foot of a large honeyberry bush, caught by a claw-trap, his fur glistening with blood. I crouched, trying to figure out how to release him. The hail temporarily ceased, as if to give me a break while I struggled to open the trap.

'Hey, boy!' I heard a deep voice. A large man stood in front of me with a girl who looked about my age huddled against him. Half of her face was covered in fresh scars. 'Who are you? Is this your cat?'

I nodded silently, squinting up at him in the wind.

'Why don't you come with us? This is no place for a sweet child like you in this weather!'

I took a step back.

'There is no reason to be afraid. Shalla here could use a friend.' He stroked her in strange places. She tensed under his touch. Her eyes reminded me of empty windows—wide, hard-glassed, inside the lights switched off.

A jagged light ripped through the sky, and the heavens roared in anger. Hail started to fall in earnest. Shards of ice scored burning lines across my face, a large piece hitting my hand as I raised it for protection. I snatched it to my mouth, tasting blood. He let her go and stepped closer to me, pulling a knife from his belt. I hesitated between running and wanting to release Azrael, the blood tasting strange on my tongue. Strange, but also familiar. Soon I could no longer feel the hail hitting my body. Nor the cold of the wind.

An unexpected joy filled me, pouring through me, and I took a step forward, eyeing his knife. Then another step. Each filled with strength. Easy and light. Every move precise. Bursting with power. A chasm opened in my mind, and what spilled out from there soaked me in an essence darker than the night.

I screamed in my head, pushing the dream away. Rain turned into sweat on my face as I fought to wake up, locked into place by the toxins, just as Azrael was trapped that night.

'James, James,' I muttered. I saw him in my mind's eye again, like I had back in that forest. Malice burned through my veins, demanding I hurt him. Then the world.

'You remember what we practised, don't you?' he asked, crouching down to me.

I remembered. I just didn't want to do it.

'Kris, please! It is not you. This anger, this violence is not you. Don't ever let it become you. Find yourself in the space around it. Concentrate on who you are.' He looked me in the eye, and I put the knife down. 'Can you feel the wrongness in you?'

I nodded.

'You know what to do. You can only reduce darkness by strengthening the light. Focus on your true self, and what isn't you will shrink away.'

I took a deep breath, closed my eyes, and did as I was told.

James did teach me to overcome this thing in me. That never should have been there in the first place. James, who was always there for me. Whom I was somehow always able to tell if he was close. As if the chime of a bell reverberated through my thoughts.

The same kind of sensation found me now, so many years later, under the thick layers of narcotics. Only the chime echoing in my head was slightly different. The steps outside the room were different. It was Conor. I was sure of it. He walked past the door outside and entered the next room. My uneasiness steadily grew, but I couldn't tell anymore what I felt uneasy about.

The drugs reached out once more and pulled me back into my delirium. I was back in the village. Back in that small house, wrapped in warm, soft towels. Azrael lay on pillows in a large basket, quietly complaining with an unconscious, weak whine. I'd never felt more horrible. Or more helpless.

'What did we say the first rule was when we adopted Azrael?' James asked as he took out a new syringe from the box in front of him.

'That I need to teach him to listen to me,' I said resentfully. It was so unfair. Azrael would never listen to anyone. He would always follow his nose.

'And the second rule, in case the first one failed?'

'That I needed to look after him. Keep an eye on him. Make sure he doesn't get into trouble.'

'Exactly,' he said and turned to look at me.

'He's going to live, right?' I asked even as I flinched, suddenly worried again, not at all sure what to make of his expression. 'He's not going to die, is he?'

James gave me a long look. 'If he makes it through the night, he'll live.' He gently put a hand over Azrael's back. 'Yes. He will live if he survives the night.'

My eyes flew open, dream and reality mixing in one quick swirl. I looked towards the door, the dark outline of my pack visible on the ground. I tried to rise, but my muscles wouldn't comply. My head felt like it weighed a ton. In the back of my mind, I could still sense Conor moving around next door. I couldn't believe just how much he suddenly reminded me of that crazy cat. He had no idea of the danger he was in and completely shrugged off all my warnings. 'He will live if he survives the night.' I heard James's voice again in my head.

I gritted my teeth and pushed myself up onto my feet. The floor seemed to sway under me, as if we were out on a stormy sea. Eventually, I reached for my pack and found the biostick. I clumsily fidgeted with the device until I finally managed to stick the needle into my arm. The cold wall felt soothing against my back, and I slowly slid down it as my legs gave way. I sighed and closed my eyes, waiting for the serum to work.

So, did this mean it was all true? This psychotic plague lurking somewhere deep within me … and James? James knew my parents, and he was my uncle? And Loreley? Loreley had lied to me! What else was there I didn't know?

I took out the thyon-reinforced clothes from my bag and hurriedly dressed, just as Conor came out of his room and walked past my door once again. A small, red light flickered on at the corner of my right lens, letting me know the battery was running low.

A quick flash outside was soon followed by menacing thunder. I couldn't believe this guy! He just completely ignored everything I had said. Did he worry about his life? Did he? Even now, he was heading out somewhere alone while a monster hunted him. In a bloody storm!

I grabbed the ionblaster from the bag. A few more days with him, and I swore, I might just kill him myself!

Looking down into the semi-dark common room, my lenses signalled the presence of two humans. One of them I already knew.

'Conor?' I called out, in case he didn't recognise me in the dark. The other one was lying in the corner, dead. Conor watched me, surprised, then turned towards the corpse.

'His neck is broken,' I informed him.

Did that mean Laro was here already? Was it he who killed that man? I studied the rest of the ground floor but couldn't see anyone else. Most of the tables and chairs had been moved and piled up along the walls, presumably to make cleaning the place easier before it opened in the morning.

The lenses flicked the image back to the body, on which the Bluebee Z58 switched on, making its presence known to us as it rose into the air.

'He's here!' I knew it! 'Laro is here!'

My hand tightened around the ionblaster's grip as I descended the staircase, my heart pounding hard as I pointed it at the droid. The bluebee amplified its glow in one quick burst, spreading white light across the room. It didn't show any intention of attacking us. Whether that was due to its instructions or damage, I wasn't sure. But it seemed to be recording what was going on.

I swiftly closed the gap between Conor and me, his eyes taking a few moments to adjust without the advantage my lenses afforded me.

'What the hell is that?' He squinted.

'It's … We're being recorded.'

'What?'

'What happens here can be watched back later. We might even have an audience right now.'

'You mean there are people looking through that, expecting some sort of performance?'

'I think that is exactly what they are expecting. A spectacle.' Massacre was probably closer to the truth.

As if on cue, the stone floor under our feet vibrated, and a good ten yards from where we stood, it began to crack. Moments later, a section collapsed, revealing a square hole. The floor tiles fell into what I assumed to be a cellar. Something was rising from the hole. A hooded head appeared first, the dark material covering the eyes of the person emerging at a steady pace and without any apparent effort but leaving visible a lopsided smile I'd seen before. Overall, the scene very much reminded me of the games Ray used to love playing when we were younger. A final opponent, arriving in some dramatic, visually impressive fashion that you needed to defeat before you could progress to the next level. I accompanied him on a campaign or two at the time but never really got into it as much as he did. The real world always held more appeal for me than virtual ones.

I heard Conor unsheathe his swords next to me while I raised the gun with two hands and pointed it at the figure in front of us, slowly landing on his feet. His shoes had magnetic levitation settings, just like mine. Too bad that in my hurry, I'd jumped into the ones Duke Beren gave me. Laro wore a sword on his hip, which surprised me, and that even my lenses couldn't detect any modern weapons or shields around him.

'Don't move!' I shouted, confident I could take Laro out within a second, but wanting answers to my questions while I still had a chance.

He raised his hands slowly, as if in answer to my warning, but then they moved to his hood and pulled it back. It was Laro as I knew him. As he had appeared on the video, murdering the students. As he had looked in the cave. As I'd pictured him in my head ever since I left Alba and sought this moment.

'Hello, Kristian.' He grinned at me as if we were old friends, and it wasn't the first time we had met face to face.

I didn't care for pleasantries. 'Why did you kill my students? Why are you after Conor? What do you want from us?'

'Just to have a little fun.' He grinned innocently.

'Fun? Really? Killing people is your idea of fun?'

'It's very satisfying, don't you think?' He drew his sword from its scabbard and stepped forward.

'Don't worry, I've got this,' Conor said beside me and moved forward to meet Laro, stepping right into the line of my weapon. 'I've had enough of this theatre.'

Exasperation had no time to hit me before Laro threw his own sword high above Conor and moved towards him by executing a few front handsprings at extraordinary speed. He propelled himself high into the air before he reached Conor, caught his sword nimbly and landed right in front of me. That was the moment the residual effects of Pixies' Delight finally died away in me completely, and my fast-evaporating bravado gave way to a sobering realisation of our situation.

Master Kam taught us that weapons were but an extension of our bodies. 'It's never the weapon that will kill someone; it is the killer's will,' he used to say. But of course, we learned martial arts at the university to keep ourselves fit and to study the philosophies behind them. We were never trained to actually kill.

In that split second, while Laro was up in the air above Conor, I had a clear shot at him. It should have been easy to pull the trigger. But I hesitated. Was it because I still wanted to know what was behind his actions and refused to dismiss him as simply disturbed? Was it conscience that stayed my hand, unwilling to take the life of another human being? Was I simply frozen with fear? I might never know for sure. The chance was gone. He landed in front of me, going to one knee while reaching for my ionblaster and melting it into something no longer functional. With his other hand he parried Conor's attack.

Conor showed no hesitation in making the most of his advantage, and I looked up from the mangled weapon just in time to see Laro rolling away from us in escape. His weapon skittered across the floor towards my feet. I scooped it up. He stood on a table now at the wall, holding one of those glass balls he stored liquid metal in. He broke it with one hand, sneering at us as he did so. There was something mesmerising about seeing the metal form into a long spear with a blade at each end, which he slowly twirled in his hand.

He jumped off the table and started to walk towards us at an even pace, making the weapon dance around him in complex patterns. It occurred to me then how easily he could have killed us by simply sprinting forward at full speed and thrusting his spear through us. But he didn't. He was a show-off, and he was enjoying this. Something that might yet be used to our advantage, I thought, just as Conor left my side and advanced towards Laro doing complicated things with double swords. A show-off Laro might have been, but he certainly wasn't the only one in the room.

'We have a policy here on starting fights for those who are not regular customers,' Conor informed him in a light tone.

'Don't worry about it!' Laro raised his spear with two hands to block the strike. 'We'll rewrite it. Together.' He leaned close to Conor's face and hissed, 'In your blood.'

I held back at first, trying to decide how best to proceed. The staccato chime of metal on metal rang in my ears, urging my whole being to rush in and help Conor. Even without my lenses analysing their moves, I could tell Laro wasn't playing for keeps. He favoured grand, spectacular strikes over effective ones, using speed to make up for the delay they caused him. It fitted right into what I anticipated from him. Unlike Conor, who took me by surprise. His techniques were precise and well-practised. It wasn't a fighting style he'd picked up on the road, as I expected. He had training. In fact, he was exceptionally good. He could have won under normal circumstances. But these were not normal circumstances. For now, Laro was just toying with him.

I looked down at his sword in my hand. It was a slender, elegant weapon. It felt much lighter than the practice blades we used in class. I cut through the air a few times, spun it around to get a feel for its balance as I approached, and I reminded myself how much I usually enjoyed sword-fights. I might as well make the most of it, given that this well might be my last.

'Look who's developed a taste for threesomes!' Conor remarked between slashes. 'Are you sure you know what to do with that, blondie?'

'I'm a teacher, remember?' I threw myself into the fight, giving it all I had. 'Watch and learn!'

Parrying Laro's attacks and trying to find a hole in his defences suddenly filled my existence to the brim. My lenses kept offering movements which were met by confident blocks every time. Yet I hesitated to abandon the scientific suggestions and trust my own instincts instead. At least with our simultaneous attacks, Laro had to keep up a continuously high, almost inhuman speed. I only hoped this would tire him quicker, too. Knowing just how fast he could move, I still thought he could have killed us if he really wanted to. What he was trying to accomplish instead was anybody's guess.

My thyon-reinforced clothing protected me up to a point. My hands, of course, were beyond this point. I managed to drop the sword as Laro's blade opened the back of my right hand, and I stared at it for a moment, trying to establish whether I still had all five fingers attached to it. That moment was all I had before Laro's right foot connected with my chest and sent me flying against the wall, my arrival rearranging a pile of wooden chairs.

Conor fought on while I tried to find something I could wrap around my bleeding hand. I wished my rucksack was nearby, and as I unconsciously glanced up towards my room, I noticed a figure standing upstairs in the shadows behind the balustrade, watching us. I was about to zoom in to see who it was when the noise of many things breaking at the same time demanded my attention.

Laro stood on top of the bar, looking down behind it. With Conor nowhere to be seen, I realised with a clench in my stomach that he had to be lying back there. Laro chuckled and jumped high to maximise the damage caused upon his landing. Suddenly, I found that I could stand up faster than I thought possible. I had no idea what he was doing to Conor, but the sounds I heard made me sick and kindled my anger.

'Laro!' I called out, racing towards them.

Laro raised his head from behind the bar and smiled at me apologetically. 'Kristian!' he said as he placed a hand on the polished wood and elegantly vaulted over. 'I almost forgot that you should probably watch this.'

He no longer had his spear, but as it turned out, he was just as efficient without it. I managed to avoid his initial kicks and even diverted a few punches, but soon he increased his speed again, outmatching me. He swept my legs from under me, and I found myself falling. I landed next to the sword I had previously dropped. I picked it up with my left hand, knowing I was near useless with it. Still, it seemed a better option than facing him without it. Once again, his kick came too fast, and before I could do anything, I found myself sliding back across the floor, slippery with my own blood. A kick to my face left me dazed.

'Now, it's important, when you're watching a presentation, that you sit still.' Laro gripped my injured hand hard and pulled me to the wall. Next, he grabbed my shirt, causing the thyon I had worked into it to move through the material and into his hand. He moulded the metal around my wrists, fixing them to the wall above my head, and for a moment, I wondered if he had done this to stop me losing too much blood and prolong my agony. But judging by the brutal kicks that followed, that wasn't the case.

The taste of blood reached into me like a living thing. Its fingers felt around, pushing their way into dark corners of my mind, lighting them up. A sinister sensation spread through me, numbing the pain and filling me with a craving that was both deliciously sweet and shockingly powerful. A smile spread across my face, causing Laro to pause and lean close to watch me. The next moment, a table swung in a horizontal arc and sent him flying headfirst into a pile of chairs.

Conor put the table down. He bent double, peering down at me. He didn't look good. I turned my head back towards Laro and zoomed in. He didn't seem badly hurt, but the impact had knocked out his own lenses. I saw them glinting in a puddle of beer beside him. He groaned, pushing himself up, opting to leave his lenses behind for now.

Conor grimaced and pulled something from a pocket. It was a large ring with a silver dragon curled around a bronze base. He slipped it on quickly, then turned and hurried towards the middle of the room where Laro's spear lay on the floor. He picked it up.

'I hope you enjoyed your little moment of victory.' Laro had gained his feet and was now carrying a sword. They circled each other slowly. 'Of course, it's only delayed the inevitable.'

'Inevitable …' Conor chuckled. 'If you only knew how many times I heard that word when I was young. Some fools believed I was fated to follow a path set out for me. That I would inevitably fulfil my destiny. Their version of it, anyway.' He aimed the spear towards Laro's heart. '"Inevitable" is a word for god-fearing folk. I myself am a big believer in breaking the rules and defying people's expectations.'

As he talked, he slowly slid his left hand along the spear until it was almost on top of his right, his fingertips pressing against the ring. A moment later, a small metal spike flew out of the ring, aimed straight towards Laro's neck. The whole thing happened so fast, I would have missed it if not for my lenses. Laro moved his sword to block its path lightning fast, his eyes round with surprise. Conor, in one swift move, stepped to the side in the meantime and thrust the blade of the spear through Laro's calf.

Laro's face distorted in pain, then he gave a sickening laugh. 'Is that it? I would have expected something a bit more …'

I'd never find out what he had expected. Conor swiftly turned, resting the length of the weapon against his hip, causing Laro's skewered leg to turn with him. He threw himself on top of Laro as he fell, twisting the spear. There was a loud crunch as they landed, breaking Laro's leg.

They struggled on the floor for a while before Laro managed to break free from Conor's grasp. I saw the glint of a medical spike which he stabbed into his thigh for pain relief and regeneration, followed by the metal weapons on the floor changing shape and flowing around his leg to provide support. It looked like he was better equipped to deal with injuries than I was. His leg might take a few days to heal, but for now, he was still able to carry on hammering Conor, his fast speed making the punches he delivered not just impossible to divert but also more powerful.

'Laro!' I roared. 'Come here, you coward!'

My whole being throbbed with a need for violence. Something I hadn't felt in decades, but now that I did, I embraced it with a long-lost lover's intimacy. I no longer felt the pain. I no longer feared death. I'd never felt more alive. I laughed. A dark, loud laugh that didn't sound like me at all. A laugh that didn't want to stop.

'What did you call me?' Another punch to my face as he was suddenly there. My mouth filled with fresh blood, and I chuckled, a euphoric storm building deep inside of me, making me feel invincible. The pressure kept on building in me, a power that felt too large to contain, looking to be released.

'It's over,' I slurred from a broken mouth. 'You lost.'

He leaned close, looking into my eyes, amused. 'And what is it exactly you think you can do?'

My sticky lips spread into a wide smile. I focused all that building energy on one single command in my mind, discharging all the power in me. 'Light.'

My lenses lit up with a force unlike they'd ever known. They would have caused damage to Laro's naked eyes even at their full capacity. Just like the cave leaches, he would have lost his sight for a while. But somehow, my brain managed to increase their intensity even beyond that. Judging from the inhuman screaming, way beyond that. Figures and graphs that flashed up a second ago on my right, showed values consistent with a laser.

Laro hobbled around on his broken leg, his palms pressed against his eyes, howling in pain. The bluebee flew down to him, clearly mind-controlled, too, and led him towards the exit.

The strength that had filled me left me rapidly. I could hear shouts from upstairs, swords being unsheathed, steps approaching. Suddenly, a group of people came down the stairs, led by Olivia. I blinked slowly. Someone else might have grumbled about all these people only showing up now, but I was glad they came when Laro was no longer in a fit state. I blinked again and saw he was no longer there, the door left open. The next moment, my lenses turned dark, and I blacked out, too.

Chapter 7

Conor

I wasn't usually one to spend two mornings in a row between the same four walls, except under exceptional circumstances. It usually required the right company and being sufficiently tired after the previous night's activities. Admittedly, the promise of a good breakfast also helped. Under very special circumstances, finding myself handcuffed and tied to a secure point might also be acceptable, presuming I'm soon compensated for the hardship with something delicious and rewarding.

All of me hurt. A fly buzzed around my face. There was no sign of breakfast. The décor, too, was distinctly lacking. Yesterday's dull prison cell was now decorated with Kristian and Olivia, neither looking their best or in any way interested in rewarding me. All in all, none of the morning's offerings came anywhere near meeting my requirements.

'Morning, sunshine!' Olivia spotted me squinting at my surroundings. For some reason, I struggled to open my right eye properly.

'Morning!' I lifted my head and tried to conjure a smile for her. It hurt.

'Hey.' Kristian's broken nose and colourful face made me grimace. Ouch. Well, he was definitely no longer competition when it came to Olivia. At least, not for a while. He wore far too many bandages. We both did.

'How are we here?' I asked, aiming the question at no one in particular.

'We rather hoped you'd know.' Kristian looked at me pointedly. He sounded pissed off.

'I honestly have no idea. But we're still better off here than dead. How are we not dead?'

'We got lucky,' he answered coolly. 'But it was a close thing. Because despite everything I told you, having fun was still more important to you than being cautious.'

'Says the novice tutor who left the safety of his school to go after a seasoned killer endowed with magical speed, alone and without even a bloody sword! I might be reckless, Kristian, but at least I'm having fun, while you're equally reckless, but just out of some weird sense of duty.'

'Weird sense of duty? That monster killed my students!'

'Better that than killing you!'

'Not everyone's only concerned with themselves!'

'Aren't they? Show me another schoolteacher dedicated enough to go after the killer of his students. You came because you were intrigued. You wanted to know why he did it. Who he was. Who I was. Why he was after us. Admit it: this is as much about you as it is about your students, if not more.'

'Conor, that's enough!' Olivia interrupted, using that voice she usually reserved as a last warning for men she was about to kick in the arse.

'Really?' I looked at her, hurt. 'You're siding with him over me?'

'Stop being a heartless prick! Besides, Kristian saved your life. You owe him.'

Did he? I looked back at him with surprise and even a hint of new-found respect. It was true; I had no idea what happened after I blacked out. But I did remember what happened beforehand. He must have done something.

'You killed him?' I asked. 'I'm impressed!' I was.

'No.' Kristian grimaced. 'He got away.'

'Well, thanks, anyway,' I muttered and cleared my throat, not sure what else to say. I usually worked alone and had learned to rely only on myself, apart from the occasional pub fight that got out of hand. Someone watching my back—and holy cat! Even saving my life—seemed both strange and unprecedented. I guessed I was grateful to be alive. I wasn't sure about the rest, though. I always liked going where I wanted, doing what I wanted, how I wanted. I picked jobs that interested me and went about completing them in ways that suited me. Outside my working life, I avoided commitments like the plague. I enjoyed the freedom. Owing someone your life sounded very much like a glorified relationship for an unspecified amount of time and with unknown commitments.

'So, we really don't know how we ended up in a prison cell in Castle Beren?' I asked instead.

'Sarah and I were tending to your injuries when the soldiers arrived.' Olivia shrugged. 'They wouldn't answer any of my questions.'

'Could it have something to do with your recent services to the duke?' Kristian asked.

'I wouldn't think so.' It was my turn to shrug. 'I delivered the crown he asked for.'

'And you've only taken in payment what you agreed on?'

'Of course!' I gave him a hurt look. 'Just what are you suggesting?'

'As if there was anything more important to him than that bloody key!' Olivia exclaimed sourly. 'Don't tell me he hasn't mentioned it yet,' she added, seeing Kristian's puzzled expression. 'I'm astonished!'

We both turned our heads towards her. I didn't understand where all this bitterness was suddenly coming from. Had I ever been anything but attentive to her?

'Or didn't he tell you why he risked his life getting an old, useless crown from one of the most dangerous places in existence for that pompous duke?' she continued.

'I understood it was just a job …' Kristian trailed off, suspicion turning his eyes back towards me. 'For *good coin*, wasn't it?'

'Well, technically, it was only one coin, but a very good one. A medallion, in truth.'

'So, let me get this straight,' he pressed on. 'You risked your life to fetch a crown for the duke, who in return gave you a medallion, but it is a key you're really after? Why did you want this medallion so badly, then? In fact, why are any of these items so important?'

I sighed. There was no point holding back now. I supposed sooner or later he'd find out about it, anyway. It wasn't exactly a secret. At least he should hear it from me.

'The duke wanted the crown because he thinks it might help with lifting the curse bestowed on the royal family. And I wanted the medallion because it's a tool that will help me find this key I've been looking for for a long time.' I looked at the barred window. I felt oddly self-conscious talking to Kristian about this, while in the back of my mind, little bells tolled in alarm. A suspicion that telling him of my obsession would somehow encourage him to seize it for himself when the time came. 'It's a lost key,' I explained. 'But not just any key. It's a very special magical artefact. Stuff of legends.'

'Let me guess. It opens any doors,' Kristian interrupted. I didn't appreciate his sarcastic tone.

'No. It's called a key because it interprets signs made by the Gods. One of its basic functions is to find anything you're after and to find a way to it by understanding and communicating these signs. Not necessarily just physical objects. People. Situations. Long forgotten secrets. It is generally known in the legends as the Supreme Key of the Dragon.'

'Strange, but I think I might have read about this only recently,' Kristian said slowly, frowning. 'My mentor, James, pointed me at it while I was preparing for a presentation on the history of cultural symbolism. A round, almost flat object. Dark, concentric, circular metal disks rotate upon each other, their surfaces engraved with runes, numbers, symbols. And I think it had a yellowish crystal in the middle. According to some of the earliest manuscripts, it was used as some kind of communication tool with higher beings in the Cathedral of Astalos.'

I looked at him, astonished. 'That's it!' It was the same description I had found. 'I can't believe this. You say it's in a church somewhere? Astalos?' I'd never heard of the place.

'Now hold on.' Kristian raised his uninjured hand to forestall me. 'Astalos is an imaginary place, and besides, we only know it was there a very long time ago.'

This note of caution left me somewhat deflated. But maybe Kristian knew more that could be useful. Maybe letting him stick around longer would actually turn out to be beneficial. He had already saved my life, apparently. We were best friends! He'd tell me everything.

'Why do you want this thing so much, anyhow?' he asked. 'I remember thinking at the time how it hardly sounded anything more than a fancy alternative for tarot cards or rune stones.'

'It was prophesied for me in the Temple of Mer as a child that I would be the one who finds it,' I said and did my best to ignore the look on his face. 'That it would open a way for me to the highest, mightiest place in the world and would bring great fortune. It's the key to my destiny.'

Here I was, talking earnestly about something very personal, something I had dreamed about all my life, while Kristian just sat there and laughed. And who was being a heartless prick now? Why wasn't he getting a reprimand? I took comfort in his scepticism, concluding that he had no obvious interest in trying to obtain the artefact for himself.

After that exchange, I fell into a brooding silence, which was only broken by the sound of footsteps and the rattle of keys. The heavy door of the cell opened, and the duke entered with a handful of guards—among them a dark, muscular fellow I hadn't seen before. The duke scanned the room with a murderous expression.

'Conor, where's the crown?' he demanded without preamble.

'How should I know? I left it with Your Grace yesterday,' I said, perplexed.

'Beorg.' The duke gestured to the new recruit, who promptly stepped forward, grabbed me by my shirt and shoved me against the wall.

'I don't have time to play games,' the duke said as he stepped close behind him. 'Do you have any idea what the king will do when he finds out that it's gone?'

I really had no idea. 'Be somewhat disappointed and cancel the midsummer celebrations next month?'

'Idiot!' the duke spat as Beorg's fist reminded my face where it already hurt the most. 'Lord Simon Dranos, the king's advisor, warned me just yesterday that Harag spies were looking for ways to steal it and smuggle it out of the country. Their overlord has no wish to see our royal family cured of its curse and restored to its former glory. Which you must already know if you're working for him? If the king finds out it was stolen from me, he might even accuse me of being an accomplice!'

Typical, I thought. Nobody even knows for sure whether that bloody crown would indeed lift the curse, but there was already a whole conspiracy woven around the damn thing in true Coroden fashion. I just wished I hadn't found myself caught in the middle of it.

'I'm not working for the Harags, okay?' I said with as much conviction as I could muster. 'And why should it be me? Anyone could have stolen it!'

To my surprise, the duke and his men broke out in incredulous laughter. 'Conor, half of my household saw you at dawn. Who are you trying to fool?'

'What?' What did he say? 'I wasn't here last night. I was at the Fisher-man's Tale.' I spoke slowly, frowning, almost as if talking to myself, as my mind shifted through my most recent memories. I mean yes, I had wanted to come and get the medallion back. But I never managed to actually set out on that little trip, now, did I?

'I saw you leave with the crown as clearly as I see you now!' one of the other guards grumbled as he wrestled with a tight bandage on his arm to reveal a nasty cut. 'See this?' He angrily shoved it into my face. 'You gave this to me when I tried to stop you. And I was lucky! Two of my comrades are dead.'

I had no idea what to say to that.

'Duke Beren,' Kristian's voice cut through the silence. 'I know that appearances suggest otherwise, but Conor was with us in the inn, just as he said.'

'And you can attest to this because you were together all night?' The duke turned to him in disbelief.

'Well …' Kristian swallowed while I stared, willing him to be a better liar. 'The truth is,' he said finally, 'that the assassin I told you about has the ability to temporarily make himself look like other people. I believe he's trying to implicate Conor.'

Hot rage spread its wings in my chest and across my face. 'And why have you not thought to mention this before?' I snapped. It's safe to say I wasn't exactly a big fan of this Laro as it was, but the thought of him parading around as me, committing idiotic crimes in my name, making me look like a fool, angered me in ways I couldn't even begin to articulate.

'Well, I don't know,' pondered the duke. He started pacing back and forth, pulling at his collar. 'Conor stealing the crown, as several of my guards saw it happen, and then getting beaten up by Harag spies in avoid-ance of payment is an easier tale to believe. You look like you even tried to help him.' He gestured at Kristian. 'A sorcerer assassin, who can change his appearance, steals a strongly guarded artefact just to implicate Conor. And to what end?'

'Let me go and find him!' I exploded, still furious. 'I'll bring back the crown for you, I swear!'

'Nice try, handsome,' said Beorg and he tightened his grip on me, pressing me harder against the wall.

'Oh, come on! Is this how you know me to be?' I asked. 'When was I ever caught stealing anything? If it was really me, there's no way any of you would have even seen me, let alone caught up with me. How do you think you managed to do that?' I asked the guard with the bandaged arm.

'You had a limp,' the guard said simply.

'A limp?' Clarity dawned on me. 'Of course, a limp! I broke his leg!' I paused and took in the puzzled expressions all around me. 'The assassin attacked us last night before he came here,' I explained. 'He got away. But I broke his left leg beforehand.' Their faces remained blank. 'Let me show you I don't have a limp!' I insisted, all enthusiastic now. 'Get me out of these chains.'

The duke gave a nod, and the guards released me. I stood, intending to stride across the room proudly. The first step turned into a stagger, and I almost fell on my face. I swore loudly and stumbled ahead with a slow, drunken gait. I knew that bastard had hurt me badly, but I hadn't realised it was this bad.

'You can hardly walk.' The duke stated the obvious. 'How do you think you'll catch him?'

'I'll go with him,' Kristian offered. I sighed. He was hardly in a much better state than me. 'I can help him recover,' he added quickly. 'I have some ...' He paused, looking for the right word. 'Some *potions* that will speed up his healing.'

'His eyes did look strange when we caught up with him at dawn.' One of the other soldiers admitted. 'Red inside, nothing I've even seen before. Certainly nothing like now. I'm no expert, My Lord, but some sorcery could have been involved.' The third man gave him a hard look for speaking up for us, but the soldier just shrugged.

'Who's to say Conor won't just disappear if we let him go?' argued the guard with the bandaged arm. He had a point.

'We'll keep his girlfriend here until he comes back,' Beorg suggested with his mouth twisting into a sly smile.

The duke considered this for what seemed like an age and then looked up at me. 'Fine,' he said. 'Let's try this. You have a fortnight to return with the crown, Conor. If you don't, I'll put the highest price on your head this country has ever seen.'

The guards helped me to a room—by which I mean they dragged me. In fact, I'm sure I would have been better off had I crawled up those stairs unaided and with my legs tied together. They clearly blamed me for the deaths of their friends, whatever my true involvement.

Lifting my head, I glimpsed my stuff on top of a large bed. I staggered towards it. I wanted nothing more than to check the medallion was there and then curl up under the covers. After a little rummaging, I found the velvet pouch with the medallion in it. I reached for it, and my fingers brushed against something else. I curiously pulled the object out. It was a small piece of parchment, carefully rolled up and tied with a black string. I opened it and read the writing on it, frowning.

Kristian entered the room behind me. I looked up at him. He had his pack over one shoulder. 'Storn brought it here from the inn,' he explained, misunderstanding my expression. Did he mean his horse brought his stuff up from the inn on its own account? I wondered for a moment. But then, what I held in my hand was more important. I passed it to him.

'"Bring me The Key. L.",' he read out loud. 'He doesn't even say where to bring it.'

'Well, of course not,' I explained as I gingerly stretched out on the bed. I felt exhausted. Everything hurt. 'Once we have the key, the key will lead us to him.' I closed my eyes, all my previous zeal leaving me.

'But even if we do find it, what if this key doesn't work?' Kristian puzzled. I let him. I honestly felt like I couldn't move a single muscle in my body. I needed to sleep.

'Anyhow. This will at least help,' he added, and I heard him put his pack down on the floor and walk towards me. I didn't care. But then I also heard a kind of short, strange, high-pitched noise I'd never heard before, which made me open an eye and look.

'What the hell?' I jerked my head up and stared at him wide-eyed. There was a weird-looking tube in his hand with colourful lights and symbols moving across its surface. But it was the long, thin needle at its end that held my eye. What did he want with that? He followed my gaze.

'What? The needle? Oh, come on! You'll hardly feel a thing.'

He stepped closer with clear intent. Suddenly I found I had the energy to move after all. He was upon me in a flash and pushed me down.

'What the fuck are you doing?' I shouted as I tried to sit up.

'It's very important that you just relax and don't fidget!' he said sternly. I did my best to wriggle away as far from him as possible.

'It will only take a moment. Conor! Stop!'

In the end, I learned that despite my initial judgement of him as a shy, hesitant guy who enjoyed theoretical musings, Kristian del Rosso was, in fact, both extremely practical and uncompromising when there was something he wanted to achieve. And just so you know, I will never, ever forgive him for how, despite my panicked whimpering as I struggled to squirm out of his reach, exhausted, in pain and barely alive, that cold-hearted bastard ruthlessly sat on me and jabbed that fucking large needle into my arse.

Chapter 8

Selena

I *still remember that old smell in the attic. The feel of the pages as they turned under my fingertips. That little beam of sunshine that found me through a crack in the roof. But I don't remember the title of the book. Or most of what was written in it. Only the last sentence. It said: 'And if they are not careful, they might lose themselves and never find a way back to who they truly are.' And in that moment, I knew that something inside me had snapped beyond repair, and there was no going back.*

'Miss Soto?' The nurse peered down at me in the corridor. I had no idea how long she had been standing there.

I stood hastily. 'I'm sorry. Yes?'

'I said your regular counsellor is away this week, but you can go into the room, and somebody will be with you shortly.'

'Somebody?' What I really wanted to ask was whether this somebody would know about the exercises I was supposed to have practised last week. I might get lucky and dodge a telling-off! The woman consulted her tablet while I pushed mine back into my rucksack. Best not to wave that around and remind anyone of any paperwork.

'Oh, it's Dr James Montgomery.' The expression on her face suggested I'd just hit the jackpot. 'He's extremely highly regarded,' she gushed. 'We're very lucky to have him help out in our facility for a few weeks!'

'Oh, is he? How fantastic!' I did my best trying to echo her enthusiasm. This Dr James Montgomery sounded way too important to have much time for me. He probably wouldn't go into much detail, especially if this was just a one-off. I beamed at the woman and strolled into the room.

The room at least appeared unchanged, although I'd never had a chance to properly look around it before. Usually, I just sat down in front of the desk, behind which Sarah Bektas, my Psychological Wellbeing Practitioner, would already be waiting for me. Today there was nobody there yet.

A screen covered the wall on my right, blazing out an advertisement for a fancy detox resort in the Grenadines. I stared at it wistfully. God! The vibrant colours were mesmerising! My eyes feasted on the sea and sky, drawn in infinite shades of blue, underlined by soft white sands. The state-of-the-art 4D visuals with the added smell of the sea made me feel almost as if I was there. Hummingbirds flew across my vision, their flights temporarily slowed for convenient observation. The camera moved around, featuring one good-looking resort guest after another in several "revitalizing activities", in truth mostly lying on various surfaces in different positions, all flashing expensive smiles and looking very pleased with themselves. I rolled my eyes and turned away from the screen. 'The Emerald Cove Detox Resort is rated seventh among the top ten private health resorts worldwide, tried and tested by travellers, just like you!' The soft female voice reached me, and I snorted. *Travellers just like me! As if I could ever afford it.*

Rain started splattering against the window again. I looked out into the gloomy world I lived in, scanning across grey buildings topped by a grey sky. My reflection stared back at me, the raindrops rolling down her cheeks, making her appear sadly disappointed with our life—blundering about in this darkness, waiting for someone to switch on the light.

'Miss Soto?' A gentle voice stirred me from my thoughts. I noticed a second reflection in the glass above mine. I turned to find a tall, lean man standing behind me. He looked as if he had just returned from that resort in the advertisement. He was well-dressed, clean-shaven, his skin lightly tanned. Despite his grey hair, there were hardly any wrinkles on his face. His angular jaw and pale blue eyes made him look attractive. No wonder the nurse became so excited when she saw his name. But it wasn't his good looks that arrested my tentative dislike towards him. He had a presence that was both friendly and reassuring. A quiet confidence that made the world around him pause and take notice. And above everything, he looked incredibly familiar. I was sure I knew him from somewhere.

'Miss Soto? I'm Dr James Montgomery.' He shook my hand. 'Why don't we sit down?'

I followed him numbly, still trying to figure out where I might have seen him before. Wherever it was, there was something about him that made me feel safe. Made me feel calm.

I yelled and jumped from my seat. Half-way through lowering myself into the chair, I caught a scuttling movement in the corner of my eye. A black shape on the arm of the seat. The familiar shock reached my stomach, half disgust, half dread. You'd think we'd turn away when something has such a negative impact on us. When we burn our finger, we snatch it back from the hot surface immediately. But we turn stupid when it's the mind being tormented. Not only don't we look away, our eyes widen, our pupils dilate, like an invitation for more. Of course, it's all designed to help you survive when you're in real danger. Fight or flight. Watching the creature lift one of its legs and then slowly crawl forward spurred me to do neither. Instead, I just stood rooted to the spot, feeling sick, my eyes widening even further.

Doctor Montgomery stood from his seat to see what I was gaping at. My eyes flicked at him for a second, then back to the spider. Somehow, it seemed bigger when it was only me looking at it.

'Sorry. Arachnophobia,' I managed before a thought occurred to me. My eyes slowly turned back to what I suddenly considered to be the bigger threat. My hands involuntarily moved in front of me in defence. Oh my God! He wasn't going to do some sort of flash-therapy inspired by the moment, was he? Like making me touch the thing or something? I stepped back a few steps as he approached, picking up the spider with his bare hands. Uggghh … I could see one of its legs sticking out between his fingers, twitching. I looked away, fighting nausea. Thankfully he walked towards the windows rather than towards me. I recovered with remarkable swiftness in order to rush ahead and open one for him. He put the thing outside on the windowsill and smiled. I shuddered.

This second time around, I wasn't in such a hurry to follow him back to my chair—to that ominous place of pure wickedness! Touched by those horrible legs everywhere, probably some disgusting web spit rubbed all over the surface. And what if it had a friend there, waiting for me?

But Dr Montgomery took my seat and encouraged me towards his behind the desk. His practical, perceptive response surprised me, impressed me even. My therapists were usually more theoretical practitioners. The ones who knew a lot about my conditions but had never experienced them. They were always aware of what advice to give, but never how I felt. Not that I could blame them. They were doing their best. But so often, I felt distanced from them. As if existing in two different worlds with a wall between us, through which we could talk, but they would never actually see me. Dr Montgomery seemed different. I couldn't help the feeling that he could see me just fine.

'So ...' He looked at me expectantly as he switched off the advertising monitor. 'Where shall we start? OCD?'

I puffed out my cheeks. Might as well.

'I saw in your file that Ms Bektas recommended the list approach a few weeks ago. How is that working out for you?'

'I saw in your file.' Oh, shit!

'It's fine,' I said. And it was. Ms Bektas suggested writing down a list of the things I repeatedly checked before leaving the flat in the mornings. Ticking them off on a piece of paper helped reduce the number of repetitions. Holding on to the ticked list once I left helped counter the compulsion to turn back, go home and do it again. 'Except when I'm running late.'

'It isn't as helpful with the added pressure, is it?' He smiled knowingly.

'No,' I admitted. 'It gets worse then.'

He nodded. 'Panic attacks. Have you experienced any in the last two weeks?'

'Not really.' The well-practised lie came easily. 'Apart from the occasional dizziness. But it doesn't last that long anymore.'

Dr Montgomery gave me a long look before he continued. 'Last week, you discussed Module 26/B, "Unhelpful Thinking Styles". Is that right?'

I shifted in my seat awkwardly. 'Yes.'

'Can you name a few of them?'

'Um ...' *Right. Here we go.* 'Um ...' I felt myself turn red under his intelligent gaze. God! Now he'd think I'm an idiot.

'How about assuming we know what someone else is thinking or predicting what's going to happen?' he asked.

'Um ... yes, that's jumping to conclusions.'

'Jumping to conclusions.' He nodded again. 'And blowing things out of proportion?'

'Catastrophising. Viewing situations as worse than they are.'

'Right. Yes. Well done! How about focusing on the negative part of a situation and forgetting the positive parts?'

'Mental filter.'

'Mental filter, indeed. Let's see. What are the positive parts of our current situation?'

I tried to feel around my mind for an answer, but it was empty. *The positive parts of this situation. The positive parts.* The room was quiet, apart from the rain tapping on the window. I looked down at my lap, seeing nothing. The positive parts of this situation. Come on! The positive parts! The sound of a mighty whip cracked the silence, followed by a deep, angry thunder and the sizzle of pouring rain outside. I couldn't help but grimace. Damn it! I didn't bring an umbrella.

'How about us meeting today?' Dr Montgomery suggested.

I looked up at him in surprise. What about us meeting today? Surely it was just a counselling appointment. Yet he was looking at me so attentively, smiling so kindly, I found myself easing up.

'Or do you find this so terrible?' He gestured around. 'Perhaps you think we are here to torture you!' he said with a pretend shock on his face that made me giggle. 'After all, we already tried to assassinate you with a house spider almost two inches long!'

'It's strange, but I feel like I've dreamed this moment before,' I admitted. 'Us talking here and laughing.'

'Ah, that's quite alright,' he said. 'Making your dreams come true is just part of the service!' He smiled that easy smile of his, then his face grew serious once again. 'I'm here to help you. The positive aspect of the current situation is that things will get better. That you will be well again.'

Me well again? Sounded like a foreign concept. Something we said out of politeness, but didn't really mean. Mental illnesses never fully disappeared. Even I knew that.

'You look sceptical,' he remarked. 'You don't believe it's possible, do you? Is this why you're not trying hard enough? Why you're not doing your exercises properly?'

I hung my head.

'But why is that?' he asked. I knew the answer to that. I just dreaded to say it. 'Because you think that with these exercises, we're only scratching the surface?'

It appeared he knew it, too. Anxiety returned and hit me in waves, ferociously clashing against my newfound safety barrier. Some things were best left unsaid. Undisturbed. Even just mentioning them might conjure the beasts. Dwell too much on them, and they'd take control of your mind!

'Miss Soto?' He leaned forward when I didn't respond. 'Selena?' he called gently again.

I looked up, my eyes welling. 'It's because I'm terrified!' I said hoarsely, fighting the sobs. 'I'm terrified that I'm losing my mind!'

He lifted his chair as if it hardly weighed more than a feather and brought it over next to mine. I reached up a hand to wipe at the tears, and as I lowered it, he took it in his. I looked at him, surprised. Again, there was something so familiar about him. As if I'd known him all my life. As if he'd been protecting me all my life.

I didn't want to say more. I'd never talked about these things to anyone before. What if he sent me to a mental hospital? What if I had to spend my remaining life locked away somewhere? But when he squeezed my hand and spoke to me again, I couldn't stop the words rushing out.

'The worst part of it comes at night,' I began. 'Not every night. Maybe once a week. Sometimes less often. I just stop feeling. It's like I lose the connection to my body. I try to reach out into my limbs, to take a breath, to move a muscle, and I can't! I just hang over what feels like the abyss of death, trying to cling on to life. And while there are other things, that's the single most terrifying experience I've ever had. Hanging helpless between life and death like that. And it doesn't get easier. There is no help, no cheat, no hiding when it comes. There's nothing I can do but silently beg for it to end. Beg to start feeling my body again. Beg for life.

'Then there are other times when I'm doing something, thinking about something, and suddenly it's like the train of my thoughts gets derailed. And I immediately have to stop whatever I'm doing and tear my thoughts back from wherever they went because if I don't, something terrible will happen.

'Those are the scariest ones. Followed by pure fear so strong some-times it feels as if it's actually doing physical damage to me. The rest is just annoying. Or perhaps I just cope with them better, I don't know. Like when my sight goes funny. I start seeing things differently. People change faces. I see objects that aren't really there. Shapes and shadows shift in and out. But I don't mind that so much because at least it's interesting. Then sometimes I go to bed, and I can't go to sleep, but I can hear all these voices as if I'm dreaming. Except there's no pictures, and I'm pretty sure I'm awake.'

Perhaps I should have stopped there, but I found myself quickly adding, 'And sometimes I have this strange sensation in my hands.' I looked down at the one he was holding, certain that on saying it, he'd let go. 'As if they're somehow leaching energy from others.' He didn't.

'I'd like to say that there's nothing to worry about,' he said finally, 'but I appreciate that these are some very powerful challenges you're facing. Nonetheless. It's going to be all fine with time, I promise. We shall treat the root of this.'

I looked at him in disbelief. Was that it? That didn't sound too bad! He didn't look too concerned or mentioned mental hospitals. But I needed to hear more, to confirm that there was no misunderstanding here.

'Isn't this all happening because my mind is a weak, broken thing?' I asked.

He laughed at that and let my hand go. 'No. It's the opposite, actually. Your mind is way too strong, and you don't know how to use it. It's like cutting yourself with a razor-sharp blade or burning yourself with fire. Except the mind is, of course, a lot more complex than either of those things, and the lessons that teach you how to use it are harder to learn and take longer. But nonetheless, these are lessons you will have to learn and learn with dedication. Otherwise, you'll just keep on hurting yourself with it.'

'So, you think that's really achievable? That I will be able to get rid of these things?'

'Oh, absolutely! But it won't be easy. And it won't be quick. It might take years.'

'I don't mind!' I would have done anything to not have to face those night terrors again. 'So, how do we start?'

'First of all, I'm going to give you a book to read.' He stood, walked over to the brown cabinet in the corner and pulled open one of its draws. 'A book that, in fact, I wrote myself.'

That sounded great! This man really knew his stuff. I was in safe hands! But my smile quickly faded into confusion. The book was a simple, black hardback without a dust jacket, the title and the author's name printed on it in silver.

'*The Order of the Dragon by James Montgomery, G.M.*,' I read aloud in surprise, thinking he must have given me the wrong book. When he didn't take it back from me, I opened it and flipped through the pages. 'So … is this Pantheon … a place?' I frowned, looking at a map inside the book, waiting for him to contradict me.

'It is.' He smiled. 'Don't over-analyse this. Just read it. You will agree with me afterwards that it helped.' He looked at me evenly, as if waiting for me to contradict him. Damn right, I would! Was this a test? Or a joke? I didn't get it.

'I'm sorry, but it just doesn't make much sense,' I declared.

He grinned at me. 'Says the woman who turns back from the street and goes home to check that she switched off the heating, after having previously checked it three times already?'

I opened my mouth in mock astonishment. 'Heeey!'

'Listen,' he quieted me before I had time to say more. 'Have you ever wondered why books have different effects on different people? Why some might love a book while others hate it? And then others again might be completely indifferent to it?'

'Yes.' This was easy. 'It's because all people are different. Their knowledge, experiences, tastes, moods colour their judgement. It's often more a reflection on them than on the book.'

'Very good. But that's only one set of variables in our equation. What's the other?'

'The contents of the book?' I ventured.

'The contents, yes. But there's more to books than what meets the eye. On a conscious level, people perceive descriptions, information, or characters, plot, themes as they read. Beneath all that, there is more. A complex rhythm of images and thoughts that direct your mind as you read it. A pattern of symbols that moves it along twisting paths. A vibe, an energy, that can be both powerful and intricate. In some cases, they can even mend a person. Or break them. Some rare books were written in a way that would only have a profound effect on a certain group or a certain type of people. On the rarest of occasions, on just a single one.'

'Are you trying to say that this book …?' I lifted the said item hesitantly between us.

'I'm saying that it will help you if you read it.' He lifted his eyebrows and added, 'I promise I will be here when you finish it, and if you find that wasn't the case, you can smash it over my head. Now, how is that for treatment quality guarantee?'

I really didn't know what to think anymore. Except, of course, I wanted to believe him. I wanted to believe that I could be cured. And I liked this man. He made me feel like we'd been friends for a long time. He was unlike any of the health professionals I'd met before, that was for sure. Yet he also appeared to be better than any of them. After all, wasn't he a highly regarded doctor according to that nurse in the corridor? But the really strange thing was that he genuinely seemed to care. Not just care. Care about me. He made sure I understood that he was there for me, and all he asked in return was that I respected his guidance, no matter how absurd it sounded. That I trusted him.

'Fine,' I said finally and put the book into my rucksack. Surely, I could give him a chance. It wasn't like I had a list of solutions to choose from. 'But this better work.' I grinned at him. 'For your sake!'

He offered his hand for a final handshake. 'Miss Soto, I expect to hear from you in a week's time.'

By the time I stepped out of the building, the rain had subsided. A brisk wind shepherded the clouds along the sky. It caught up with me on my short walk to the train station, pushing me in and blowing my hair into a mess full of cherry blossoms. I hurried to get out of its way, but it followed me down the stairs, and I only found shelter in the arriving train carriage. I sat down on an empty seat and started pulling the unwanted ornaments out of my hair.

The further the train took me from the hospital, the darker my thoughts grew. I thought of Dr Montgomery and how easily we had bonded, but even that cheeriness seemed to fade until I wondered whether the whole episode was nothing more than a mirage. Would he really be able to help me? Or was he just exceptionally good at talking to people? He'd certainly charmed me in no time!

The train stopped between two stations, the robot pilot informing us of signal problems or some such. I wasn't really paying attention. A sense of melancholy swept over me, a powerful longing for another place, another life. The sensation grew, gathering power, something in me reaching out to touch it, to pull away a curtain and show me more. A draft rose in the carriage, lifting my hair, a force of wonder intensifying, making my skin tingle in anticipation. My mind weaved itself into the motion, soaring to heights that frightened me, and I raced after my thoughts to bring them to a halt.

Suddenly, it all went dark. The screens and lights around us turned off, leaving the train stretched silently in the pitch-black tunnel. Passengers shifted uneasily in their seats, but no one said a word. After a few minutes, the power came back, and we continued our journey.

I reached into my rucksack and pulled out the book. I stared at it for a minute before opening the front cover and letting it steal me into another place and another time.

Chapter 9

Kristian

The stiff wind off the sea cracked the flags around me, straining through the teeth of the battlements and whipping my hair about my face. The promontory on which the castle stood jutted like a fist into the sea, weathered and defiant. The city of Beren spread beneath me, a confusion of colours and shapes moving around its streets in a random fashion—and yet, from up here, it all seemed to follow a rhythm, like a well-practised dance, vibrant and lively in the late morning sunshine.

I stretched my neck to see better and cringed as the pain shot through my back. The Arwenna Elixia I luckily stored in the biostick was highly efficient at speeding up the body's natural healing processes, but while I mixed Conor's dose with painkillers, I left them out from mine. I needed to think clearly. And besides, I was running out of supplies.

It was both strange and frightening to be in a world with no access to advanced health technology. In a land where people carried their pains without instant painkillers, endured broken bones for weeks or months, where they died of injuries, illnesses, childbirth or infections. Yet, despite death or maiming being an ever-present danger, the whole place seemed more alive than anywhere I'd ever known. Just a fall from this rampart would have seen me broken with precious little anyone could do about it, apart from watch me die. And yet there was an elemental beauty to this vulnerable existence. A thrill, an invitation to be a part of something more. An urge to take my place like a last piece of a puzzle completing the bigger picture.

Ignoring the pain and the fear, I climbed on top of the parapet and sat with my back against the tower wall. The threat of the fall yawned on my right, seeking to pull me down. I stayed where I was. As the wind filled my lungs with the salty tang of the sea, my ears rang with the cries of seabirds, the sun beamed down at me with all its glory, I tilted my head back and laughed. A long-forgotten joy of living spread through me, full of possibilities, yielding a profound peace and understanding. It wasn't me completing this new world. It was this new world completing me.

I pulled Conor's medallion out of my pocket and looked at it. It was a pretty thing that easily fit in my palm. On its face, a gold dragon swelled out from the round frame, curling around a key, with a silver tower in the background. All skilfully detailed and embellished with tiny, colourful gemstones. Had Conor been awake, I doubted I could have taken it from him unnoticed. But being drugged had relieved him of that responsibility. And since he had done the same to me, I had no qualms about taking advantage.

I lifted it higher, turning it slowly. The medallion's back was plain, and a simple line of thin ridges ran around its edge that lacked the precision of the image on the front. Nothing to distract the eye from the beautiful art that gleamed and sparkled in the sunshine. Yet there was something about that dull, milled edge that puzzled me. Wasn't it coins that people used to mill? To stop others clipping bits of precious metal off them? Who would want to shave bits off something so exquisite?

I slid from my perch and made my way down to the stables. I met several soldiers on the way, who curtly nodded to me; serving maids who giggled and bowed their heads together to gossip; young kids who rocketed down the corridor ahead of their nursemaids. Mouth-watering aromas filled the air as I passed the kitchens, the cooks preparing what seemed like a feast to my eyes, reminding me that the Arwenna Elixia needed more to work with than just fresh air in my stomach.

Outside, I walked down a stone-paved path and soon left the hustle and bustle of the castle behind, with only birdsong and the occasional cheerful neigh from the stables reaching my ears. I entered the wooden building, the smell of animals, hay, oats and leather still a new sensation but not unpleasant. I walked past the stalls of a dozen horses before I found Storn.

'All clear?' I asked.

'Yes,' he responded. 'No one's around.'

'Did you manage to charge my lenses?' I asked, hopeful.

'No. They are no longer functional, and repairing them or making something so intricate is beyond me. I'm sorry.'

'No worries,' I sighed. 'Thanks for trying, anyway.'

He lowered his head and pretended to study something on the ground. I knew that admitting he couldn't do something troubled him.

'Do you understand the local language, too? Wedan?' I asked to change the subject.

'Of course, I do. But I speak 752,392 languages, Kris. I was more surprised to hear you speak it! It's not exactly one of the most-known or most-used.'

'I know, right? What a coincidence! Believe it or not, James picked it for me. You know in third level, when your mentor selects a language and an old civilisation for you to study at the university?'

'So, you know where we are?' He lifted his head in surprise.

'Well, not exactly. When I learned it, it was allegedly the language of the old Peregen Empire on Tabu. But this is the Coroden Kingdom, and we're not on Tabu.'

'Given that Tabu orbits two stars, we're definitely not,' he confirmed what I knew.

'But I recognise other things from my studies, too. Biological things, like fruits, vegetables, animals and so on. Metals, obviously, and even some stones. Speaking of which, have a look at this.' I pulled out the medallion from my pocket. I held it up by its delicate chain for inspection.

'The object consists of forty-five percent pure gold. The rest is made of an alloy of ninety percent silver and ten percent copper. It is further ornamented by nine amethysts, seven prehnites, five apatites, three pieces of red lydium and a rhodochrosite. The art composition is dominated by a golden dragon, which strongly resembles the ones we often see in Therisi mythologies. Which is to say, it has large wings, a long tail, horns and whiskers. They are generally believed to be wise, friendly and fight the so-called evils of the world, rather than being the evils themselves.'

'Can you see the milling around its edges?' I asked.

'Yes,' he answered with noticeably less enthusiasm, seemingly unimpressed by my question.

'Can you see how unequal the gaps between the edges are? Several of them sit very close to each other, then there's a wider gap. A few close together again, then another wider gap.'

'So what?' Storn yawned. 'It was probably done by a person with lesser skills.'

'What if it's deliberate? What if it's a code?'

'In a primitive world like this?'

'Why not? People had used codes in more ancient civilisations than this.'

'True,' he agreed. 'Put it in my mouth, and I'll run a full scan.'

I carefully placed the medallion on his warm tongue and pulled my hand away before his massive jaws closed. A few moments later, they opened again, and I retrieved the object.

'This might take a little while,' he said. 'Even if we assume the corresponding language is the local native tongue.'

'Let's hope it is.' I nodded and turned to go.

'Of course, it's still going to be much faster than if you had one of those new S-type translators …' he continued undisturbed.

'I'll go and look for some food in the meantime.' I made a few tentative steps walking backwards towards the gate.

'… or even a federal ambassador droid …'

'I'm so hungry,' I continued stepping back and raised my hands in a futile attempt to quiet him.

'… not to mention …'

I turned towards the exit mid-step and added quietly, 'I feel like I could eat a horse.'

There was an abrupt silence then. I carried on without looking back at his expression. When you sense an impending explosion, sometimes the best thing to do is just keep on walking.

Early afternoon found me in the library the duke had graciously allowed me to use for research. It was a warm, peaceful day, my eyelids heavy as I slowly worked my way through several large, leather-bound volumes. I must have eaten more for lunch than I usually did during a whole week. Yet it was my head that now weighed a ton and needed propping up with an elbow.

It was apparently in the 1212th year of the local calendar that a fire destroyed the legendary tower of Ursul, the Wise. At least according to *A History of Coroden by James Montgomery, G.M.* The tower was alight for three days, and the flames could be seen as far as Tittere. Wherever Tittere was.

Once the fire was extinguished, priests of Meroth were called for to perform protective rituals against the evil spirits who might have entered the land where the destruction ripped into the fabric of the world. The priests carefully studied the charred ruins and collected all the ashes into one large pit, blessed by their elder. By the time they finished, the full moon lit up the night sky, and under its celestial gaze, the ashes started to swirl. A sparkle appeared in its cloud, then another and one more. Something born one twinkle at a time, brighter with every heartbeat of the kneeling priests. It rose from the ashes like a glowing star, bird-shaped, fast as the wind, delicate as a dawn mist.

The shimmering bird rose high above the land. It flew over forests and meadows, through locked gates and open windows, over todays and tomorrows, to forever and more, to the world's heart and soul, falling like starlight through the night, racing to reach its mark. When it finally stopped, it did a little twirl, then descended upon the forehead of a sleeping girl.

'Meditating over what you learned, wise scholar?'

'What …?' I hurriedly lifted my head from the table, heavy with sleep.

'Have you found anything interesting?' Conor asked. His voice from a bit further away now.

'Ummm …' I forced my eyes open and saw him standing in front of me, the amulet dangling from its chain in his hand. 'I thought I might figure out where we should take it and what to do next,' I said a little defensively. 'I thought the milling around its edges might hide some sort of secret clue.'

'No need for secret clues. You should have just asked me.' He lifted the book I had read earlier and closed it with a definite thump. 'The tower on the amulet is a miniature version of the Grand Tower in Iskahal, which is about three days' ride from here to the south. It's even called The Grand Tower of the Golden Dragon.' He turned to put the book back on the shelf.

'Well, that certainly makes a lot more sense than what I thought the clue around the edge was supposed to be,' I admitted.

He shook his head in mock dismay. 'Which was?' he prompted and raised his right palm as if I should place my answer there.

Feeling foolish, I buried my forehead in my hand.

'Oh, come on, I'm sure it's something good!'

He wasn't going to let this go, was he?

'Two storm crows flew past me in the cold night,' I muttered under my breath.

'What did you say?' He turned and looked at me.

I sighed, dropped my hand and repeated it more loudly. 'Two storm crows flew past me in the cold night.'

'Are you sure?'

I rolled my eyes and was about to say something I might regret later when I realised, he wasn't mocking me anymore. 'Why? Does it mean anything to you?'

'It's the first line of the Ballad of Borond. A well-known old song.' He raked his hand through his hair and looked away thoughtfully.

'Who is this Borond?' I asked.

'Not who, but what. Borond was a castle once, up in the north, built upon the shores of Lake Gelend. It's just a ruin now, though, nothing else.' He slowly walked to the windows and looked out over the gardens, his eyes seemingly lost in the distance. Then, in a low voice, almost to himself, he continued:

'Two storm crows flew past me in the cold night,
And I sighed as I glimpsed you by the moonlight,
My heart grew heavy upon seeing your grave,
Fallen hero of the north, noble and brave,
Under thick fog, gentle waves roll you to sleep,
Under the eyes of a thousand stars, you dream.'

'Sounds like a peaceful place,' I said.

'Well, it's not,' he announced and turned to face me. 'It's a nasty place no one ever goes to. Word has it originally King Gregor had it built for Duke Borond for his services in the Semerian Wars, hence the name. The duke died without an heir, however, twenty years later, and the castle eventually became the home of the notorious witchlord, Toleron, who resided there for the next two hundred years or so. They say neither the king nor his descendants dared to claim the place back from him. Toleron was feared all across the land. He was said to be a master of dark magic and thought to be immortal, until the Battle of the Four eventually claimed his life and destroyed his castle. Nobody lives there anymore, except this alleged monster that resides in the lake and feasts on the flesh of anyone who wanders too close. Toleron's curse, they call it.'

'Perfect. The Grand Tower of the Golden Dragon it is, then! You were right all along.' I shrugged and moved to get up.

'Now, hold on!' He gestured to me to stay where I was. 'This can't be an accident.'

'No, I can't see how it would be,' I said, which made him sigh and look at me as if it was all somehow my fault.

'The tower is three days' ride to the south,' he said. 'The ruins are four days' ride to the north. If we make the wrong decision here, we're going to waste a lot of time.'

'What can we expect from the tower?' I asked.

'The tower belongs to the Meroth priesthood. I was hoping to speak with their high priestess.' He looked at me expectantly.

I really didn't want to say it, but here it was: 'Who might still just send us up to Borond.'

'Yes.' He shook his head and flashed me a lopsided smile. 'You bring nothing but trouble.'

'I'm sorry.'

'No need.' He shrugged. 'Most people run from danger. But it was always my calling. Get yourself ready. We leave at sunrise.'

Chapter 10

Conor

*Kingdom of Coroden, Drelos,
21st The Month of Promise 1575*

At the break of dawn, we rode through the city gates faster than gold brings down a whore's drawers. The road to the north stretched ahead of us, empty at this hour, the fierce wind on my face cold yet still finding a way to light a fire in me. The rising sun tore through the clouds, bleeding colour across the hills of Emereth, in stark contrast to the grey dust we stirred up on the old King's Road.

Shooting towards your goal like a loosed arrow. Like an uncontrollable force. No rules. No fear. Just the knowing that with every heartbeat, you were closer to your dream. What was life worth living for, if not these moments?

I was finally on the right track. I knew it! After all those years of searching, looking, reasoning, all the clues finally aligned to show me the road to my destiny.

It had been almost two decades now since the Day of Revelations, yet I still remembered it as if it was only yesterday. Far to the north, in the misty mountains of Minar Desh, the Shield of Heaven Monastery had buzzed around us like a beehive. Everyone was busier than usual, preparing celebrations suited to the importance of our visitors. I'd watched the brothers get on with their tasks and training with some envy as I waited in the middle of it restlessly. Us novices were all lined up and made to stand outside the White Temple. I was almost last in the long queue. Only little Sam stood behind me, being six years old, whereas I was already seven.

On the Day of Revelations, all novices underwent a special ritual. Some kind of test, the details of which were kept secret from us. What we did know was that by the end of it, a high priest would take our measure and reveal what the future held for us. Show us what waited in the shadow of our tomorrows. Point us at the star we should follow.

The afternoon had dragged on, and by the time I got anywhere near the entrance, the sun had started to set. A chorus of songbirds and crickets

106   ❧   MITRIEL FAYWOOD

rose from the surrounding forest, trying to compete in vain with our own ensemble. Hauntingly beautiful music filled the air, stirring melodies swelling, cresting, receding and swelling again, a group of our most talented musicians playing on flutes, guitars, drums and pipes in the refectory. Fireflies swirled around us with the mid-summer breeze, while inside the buildings, legions of scented candles stood guard.

How excited I had been! Back then, all I wanted was to become a brother of the order and serve Meroth. I'd looked up to my teachers as if they were nothing less than Gods themselves. I was blown away by their martial skills, sometimes quite literally, and I trained all the time so that one day I could become one of them. There wasn't a more enthusiastic pupil, a more promising novice in the whole monastery. Except one.

The stars came out, and even the long-awaited fire moon had appeared in the sky by the time the boy in front of me was called in. Bjorn Whitehaven. Teacher's pet. Son of some famous warrior from Wolgland. They said his father took him to watch a battle when he was only five. Bjorn was a merciless opponent on the training ground. Nobody ever wanted to be paired up with him. Except me.

The door closed behind him, leaving me bursting with curiosity and impatience in equal measure. I looked around in the dim light. Two men walked into the scriptorium at the far end of the square, talking quietly between themselves. Light, laughter and delicious smells drifted from the kitchen nearby, where dinner was being prepared. But apart from little Sam behind me, I couldn't see anyone hanging around.

On impulse, I darted towards the old titan tree on the east side of the temple.

'Where are you going? Conor!' Sam called after me, his voice tinged with panic but too afraid to shout.

'Shhh! I'll be right back,' I hissed as I climbed, the knots and curves of the tree familiar under my fingers. Once I reached the branch I needed, I opened my arms for balance, ran along it, and noiselessly jumped over to the roof of the temple. There was a spot where a tile could be moved. I'd discovered this by accidentally tripping over it a few weeks back. I lay on my front and carefully lifted it.

Through the small hole, I had a limited but still a fairly good view into the hall inside. Bjorn was sitting on his heels in front of several priests. The priests, in turn, were comfortably seated in chairs and talking to him.

'According to our traditions, you will be tested tonight, and the purpose to your existence will be revealed,' the Dai-Osho, the head of our monastery, said from the middle of the assembly. He had his richly decorated ceremonial shawl wrapped around him that he only wore to New Year's Day celebrations. But his expression was just the same as usual. Stern, with a hint of that tension you feel before an approaching storm. From this angle, I was almost surprised to observe how wrinkled his face was. His sharp eyes tended to pierce your attention and hold it there. Getting released and allowed to look away was like coming up for fresh air. Whenever I could, I avoided risking the experience.

'We are all made of our past,' he continued, 'of our experiences. We are made of our blood and bone and spirit. But most of all, Bjorn, we are made of our choices. Despite how we might seem to the eye, we are in constant motion. We are always heading towards something that is the natural consequence of who we are and the choices we make. It is often obvious, yet people tend to be blind to it or too afraid to face it.

'Master Semaj is a high priest from the head temple who will conduct the ceremony and reveal this perception of your future. Veer from your path, and it will remain a dream. Stay on course, and it becomes destiny.'

Master Semaj, who wore a light blue robe and looked too young next to our Dai-Osho, but also somehow familiar, rose from his seat and walked to a desk on the left. He poured something red into an iron mug from a large jug and carried it to Bjorn along with a dark cotton bag.

'Drink this,' Master Semaj told him. He opened the bag and started taking out unusual-looking, small painted statues, which he placed around Bjorn in a circle. Once he was ready, he sat on the floor cross-legged, just outside the circle. He lifted his right hand. A moment later, the flame of the many candles lighting the room started to shrink until they looked nothing more than fireflies from above. The objects he placed around Bjorn flared up at the same time. It was only then I realized the statuettes were candles, too.

Only one other candle stayed properly alight, a massive pillar candle on the right, which stood nearly four feet tall. Behind the pillar candle was a man I didn't know. He held a simple, round iron shield. One of those the older students used for practise.

'Place the empty mug on your head and perform the Hundred Steps Kata,' Master Semaj instructed Bjorn. 'Make sure it doesn't fall off and that you remain within the circle.'

As Bjorn carried out each movement—each punch, each kick, each turn with painstaking care and precision—the candlelight around him kept changing colour. The candles illuminated him and his close surroundings in every shade of the rainbow until they seemed to settle on somewhere between blue and purple.

The last position of the kata was standing still with your hands in front of your chest, smiling politely and humbly, keeping your eyes closed.

'Hold it!' Master Semaj called out and once again raised his right arm. This time he pushed his hand forward, his palm facing towards Bjorn. The candles flared again, their flames dancing violently, sizzling in pain. The smile disappeared from Bjorn's face. His breathing became faster, and he started trembling himself. The mug fell off with a clatter.

'Hold the position!' Master Semaj called out again, this time louder. Bjorn shook badly now, his eyes shut tight, his mouth a thin line pressed against some complaint that threatened to escape.

After what felt like a long time, although probably wasn't longer than a few minutes, Master Semaj lowered his hand and told Bjorn to relax. He got up and walked to the man with the shield. The man held it higher now, as if he expected to defend himself against an attack. Master Semaj picked up a brush and a pot from the floor and started painting invisible lines on the surface of the shield.

'The Eight Star Kata! Fast!' he shouted without looking back. Bjorn obediently launched into a series of quick moves. The Eight Star Kata was an energetic one that contained a series of acrobatic kicks. Nonetheless, it failed to get my attention. I was too busy narrowing my eyes and trying to make out what the high priest was doing with the shield.

They finished about the same time. The candles, too, went out one by one, until only the large pillar candle was alight.

'Lanti Tierre,' Master Semaj said quietly now in the dark. Lanti Tierre was the name of an exercise where you were supposed to blow out a candle flame with a punch. Bjorn went closer and put his arm out to measure the right distance. He took up a fighting position, clenched his right hand into a fist and delivered a lightning-fast punch with a yell. The flame bounced around but carried on burning. He tried a few more times, each attempt faster and stronger but just as unsuccessful. I smiled a little smile. For once it was good to watch him struggle.

'Calm down and concentrate!' Master Semaj said, his voice both reassuring and powerful. 'It's not your speed that will make you succeed. It's your spirit.'

Bjorn stayed still for a minute. Then, rather annoyingly, he blew out the candle with his next punch.

For a moment, nothing happened. The darkness was absolute. But soon, the lines on the shield became visible. They glowed with a greenish light in the dark, forming a lotus flower in a circle above three straight lines. I couldn't help but gasp. A mix of disbelief, jealousy and outrage washed over me. A cold darkness settled on my shoulders, tight around me like a cape. Fortunately, voices were also raised down in the hall, some shocked, some supportive, but all excited, letting the involuntary sound I'd made go unnoticed.

I lay on the roof, unable to move, my eyes defocused, not taking in anymore what was going on below. That was the sign of our Dai-Osho. Bjorn was set to become the next leader of our monastery one day. I found it hard to imagine a higher honour or title. Not one that I wanted, anyway. And who would I be under his regime? I wouldn't want to be anyone. I looked at him, his delighted expression now visible in the once again well-lit room. He held his shield, proud and thrilled amid the congratulating masters. I hated him in that moment. I hated him more than I had ever hated anyone.

'Bjorn, you can leave through the side door,' the high priest said to him. 'Bring in the next one!' he called over to someone else I couldn't see. That took a moment to register, my mind still frozen with the discovery.

'Shit!' I cursed a heartbeat later. I clambered to my feet and started to run. *I will show them*, I thought to myself even as I practically slid down the tree. That's the only way. Bjorn surely won't be able to become the next Dai-Osho if there is somebody around who is clearly far better than him.

'Conor.' The current Dai-Osho indicated that I should sit down and pinned me with those sharp eyes of his. I defiantly held his gaze, but much of what he said afterwards escaped me. I stared at him, still trying to catch my breath, the beating of my heart like a war drum in my ears.

'According to our traditions, you will be tested tonight, and a purpose to your existence revealed …'

I knew what I wanted already. I didn't need a purpose. I just needed to be told that I would be the next Dai-Osho and not Bjorn.

'We are always heading towards something that is the natural consequence of who we are and the choices we make.'

I had made my choice already. It boiled in me with a determination that I could hardly contain. Yet somehow, through all that pressure, a cool sensation reached me. Like an icy touch on my face. A force that demanded my attention. Something more powerful than the weight of the Dai-Osho's commanding gaze. I had to turn my head and see what it was. But was that even possible? Not to mention highly inappropriate while the Dai-Osho was still talking to me. I shouldn't. I mustn't. I most likely couldn't anyhow. And yet the unthinkable happened. I stiffened and tore my eyes away in search of the source of that mysterious force. It took only a second.

The high priest stood and walked to me. In hindsight, it was probably the only thing that saved me from suffering punishment for my unprecedented rudeness. I wonder if he knew it at the time and did it on purpose. As for me, I was too startled to appreciate the gesture. His pale blue eyes bore into mine, making me feel like he could see right through me. As if he could tell everything about me just from that one look. All my secrets. All my dreams. All my lies.

'Breathe,' he said and put his hand on my head, his palm cool on my forehead. I closed my eyes, wondering what to do next. 'Just breathe,' he said again, as if answering my question.

I tried. I really tried. But in that stillness, a dreadful suspicion took hold of me. *What if he already knows my future?* I squeezed my eyes tighter and tried to imagine myself as the next head of the school.

A minute later, he let me go and went to fetch me the drink. The same red liquid in the iron mug Bjorn was given before me. It tasted strange. I drank it without the smallest hesitation. He put the candle figurines around me in the meantime, and I could now tell they depicted the twelve guardian animals of Meroth. I lowered the mug and waited for him to give me his instructions. Instead, he crossed his arms in front of his chest and looked at me.

'You know what to do.'

For a moment, I didn't move. I just sat there, frozen with guilt, pretending innocence. He waited. The priests shifted in their seats. Someone coughed. The high priest watched me, unconcerned. His eyes told me we would stand there until I did what I had to. That or failed the test.

I could feel myself turn red as I stood and put the mug on my head. He knew I had cheated and watched Bjorn from the roof. The rest of the room turned dark, hiding my audience in the shadows as I stood in the circle of burning candles and waited for the high priest to sit down. I took a deep breath and slowly exhaled. No matter what he knew about me, I would show him what I was capable of. He wouldn't be able to deny it.

He gave me an encouraging smile, then turned his back on me and walked to the man standing at the wall with the practice shield.

A little sound escaped me as I bit down on my tongue, half-way through calling after him to wait. He wasn't supposed to start painting yet! He was supposed to watch me! Whatever happened to following the rules?

'Begin!' he ordered before proceeding to pick up the brush and turning away from me. I swallowed and clenched my hands into fists, trying to contain my humiliated outrage. Despite it all, there was nothing left for me to do but my best.

I performed the kata perfectly. It was probably my favourite that I could have done well blindfolded on top of the roof. I practised it every day. But tonight, I made even myself proud. The candles around me flickered, their flames changing colours a couple of times before settling on a dark red. I took up the final position, closed my eyes, and since I had to, I smiled. It was a big smile. I had a lot to hide behind it.

'Open your eyes and put the mug down,' the high priest instructed me from the side. I did so. Ahead of me on the floor, Meroth's tiger watched me, the red flame above its head blown out by a mysterious gust a moment later.

'Lanti Tierre,' Master Semaj's voice reached me again, and I turned and slowly walked towards the only remaining light source in the room. The large pillar candle stood between me and the man I didn't know, holding my shield high. Master Semaj came and stood next to me, his eyes on me softer now. I looked at him almost incredulously. He wasn't going to feel sorry for me after everything now, was he? I pursed my lips and narrowed my eyes. Not once had I failed to blow out a candle with a single blow in my life. Not even the very first time.

I took up the fighting stance and positioned myself at the right distance. Deep down, anger still burned in me, mixed with a desire to distinguish myself. I raised my fist with determination. It was the determination of someone who'd just been slapped in the face by life but wanted to hit back.

I took a slow, deep breath, my whole being charged and ready to explode into that blow. I held it for a heartbeat. Two. Then released it.

Determination turned into horror as my fist connected with something solid, and for a moment, I was convinced I had lost my aim and hit the candle somehow. It didn't feel like hitting a candle, though. It felt like nothing I had ever touched. The flame of the candle, like an extension of my punch, flew on, shooting towards the shield and exploding against it. The man holding it jerked in surprise, but with no time to escape, he simply pushed the shield out a little more and turned his head away, eyes shut. Flames danced on the surface of the shield in organised patterns. The invisible paint the high priest had used burned in strange lines. Between the lines, I could make out two circles, two half-moons and a star. It looked nothing like the sign of my monastery. Yet it was familiar.

Gasps filled the room; someone even started murmuring the Prayer of the Magnificent. I bit my lip. I knew this sign from somewhere. But what was it? What? Then it came to me. My legs gave way, and I knelt, my eyes lost in the flames.

The Supreme Key. The Dragon's key. Meroth's favourite creation, given as his gift to humankind. The artefact that helped King Serhet defeat the weredevils. The same one that Darin the Great used to find a cure for the Black Plague. The key that opened a door to another world and helped the whole city of Gere escape from the shadow of the erupting volcano, releasing them back to a nearby island three days later. A wonder that human greed and jealousy lost for us a long time ago. A myth buried deep in the sands of our memories. Once our highest pride, now our deepest sorrow.

'Conor Drew.' Master Semaj put a hand on my shoulder. 'It befalls on you to find the lost key of Meroth, and after three hundred years, finally return it to us. The Supreme Key will heal the wounds of this world and once again bring glory to these lands. But it will also change you, Conor. It will open you up and release your full potential. It will open a new world for you. It will make you rich and powerful beyond your wildest dreams. It will fill your life with greatness, purpose and love.

'This is your destiny, should you accept and follow it.'

What can I say? I'd followed it ever since. From the next morning, I trained even harder than before. I no longer cared about becoming the next Dai-Osho. I no longer tried to compete with Bjorn to see who was better. He had his goal; I had mine. We often practised together until the sun went down. We changed in different ways over the years, though, and grew into very different men. He became obsessed with tradition, with rules. His mind was always focused on the classes, around the reputation or the future of the school. Whereas I … I don't know. It all started to feel too much after a while. Too dry. Too rigid. Like a cage. Then, of course, once I was old enough to be sent into town for supplies and started seeing girls … Let's just say, I realised that life in a monastery wasn't really what I wanted, after all.

The freedom, that delicious freedom I plunged into, was the best thing I'd ever experienced. I never regretted it. In fact, since then, I decided that staying in the monastery was never actually part of the prophecy. I was to find the key. And who said I couldn't keep it all to myself? Why should I hand it over to someone like Bjorn or a superior in the head temple? It would be mine and mine alone. I would decide what to do with it.

I never managed to punch fire like that ever again, though. It would have come in useful many times. Maybe the key would change that, too. I grinned as I reminded myself again how I was getting closer and closer to it, thanks to my new friend.

It was strange, but there was something in Kristian that reminded me of that high priest at the ceremony. The one who revealed my fate to me.

If I was honest with myself, it was part of the reason why I let him follow me around. I just couldn't put my finger on exactly what it was. Possibly the way he also seemed to know when I lied? That he took himself so seriously? That he was helping me find the key? They also both had blue eyes …

I glanced over at Kristian. He was riding with a silly grin on his face. He looked like the very manifestation of that joyous freedom I felt all those years ago. His horse looked just as enthusiastic. Like a stallion that had been kept in the stable for far too long. What was his name again? Ah, yes. Storn. In that moment, the horse looked at me, too. I almost lost my balance in the saddle in my surprise. He was a funny one. But at least there was no disapproval in his eyes this time. Instead, they glinted with something like joy as he tossed his head, watching me with expectation. Was I going crazy, or was a horse really trying to challenge me to a race now? I couldn't help but laugh. I winked at him and patted mine.

'Come on, Athos. Let's show these fools how to fly!'

Chapter 11

Selena

London, Earth, 21st May 2037

A nother week flew past, and not with the elegant sweep of a golden eagle. More like with the mad scurry of an over-ambitious chicken, flapping its wings feebly before meeting its inevitable fate: the garden fence.

My life was a puzzle in which none of the pieces fit together. The only certainty was time ticking away, as I rushed around in circles trying to arrange them, only to cut myself on their sharp edges. Constantly feeling the need to be better, stronger, faster, prettier, and failing on all accounts. The only comfort I could safely rely on rested with that masterfully crafted slice of Black Forest gâteau I was eyeing.

'Select Black Forest gâteau?' The question on the screen gleamed at me with the little box to tick jumping impatiently next to it. But I was still hesitating between that and the Dobos torte.

"If you'd like to chat with one of our staff members, review the ingredients or watch again how our famous Black Forest gâteau is made, just open the menu on your right!' a cheerful female voice announced in my ear.

Oh, for God's sake, all this pressure! Why couldn't they just give me more time to choose?

"Your current session started twelve minutes and forty-three seconds ago. Do you need more time to decide?'

That made me frown. I knew that even the most advanced VR glasses only read facial reactions and not your mind. It was still uncanny sometimes just how clear an insight the internet seemed to have into me. *Well, take this*, I thought and selected both cakes.

'Excellent,' the female voice said. 'Please choose your table.' I looked around the virtual representation of the Old Library Teahouse and was thrilled to find my favourite table free. I booked the table and added Keiko's and Rhia's profiles from my friends list.

'Invitations have been sent. Please allow us to track your journey here. This will ensure your tea is brewed to perfection and is ready to serve as soon as you arrive.' I clicked "yes". "Thank you for your booking. See you soon!'

I logged out and pulled off the headset. The Old Library Teahouse had over three hundred flavours of tea. Thank God I knew without question which one I wanted!

The 1012 bus I was sitting in came to a halt at the red light. I absent-mindedly looked out of the window. The miserable weather had held its grip over the city all week. Beneath the gloomy grey sky, the cold wind, laced with rain, chased pedestrians indoors. Crimson blossom petals swirled in the air, ripped before their time from the nearby trees, like the still-glowing embers of a dying love.

On the corner of the street, there was an old pub, its outside tables abandoned by its guests for the comfort of its cosy rooms, except for a beggar sitting on the ground with his back to the wall. He wore a long, dark cloak with a hood that completely hid his face. My eyes lingered on him. On that slice of darkness barely visible under his hood with his head tilted down. Had I been able to see his face, I would have ignored him without a second thought. As it was, I couldn't look away.

There is something intriguing about watching people when we think they can't see us. I kept my eyes on him, willing him to lift his head before the bus moved on. The hood he wore was slightly frayed around the edges, the material wet, heavy with rain. It somehow seemed so close. As if I could almost touch it. As if I could feel its cold surface. Smell it. If I could just will it back a little. Reach out. Pull it back. Just a little.

Something shifted, and I jolted. For a moment, I couldn't tell what had moved. It felt as if it had come from inside me. The man outside twitched and jerked his head up, looking straight at me. Except, I still couldn't see his face! Yet, I could swear he was staring at me. I felt his gaze penetrating me, reaching down into my core. It wasn't a pleasant sensation. I sat par-alysed, my heart in my throat as I watched him stand up and walk towards me. Yet, I still couldn't see his face! That scared me more than anything else.

Something told me I should run. But I just sat there, stupid in my shock, not daring to move, not daring to breathe, as if somehow that would solve the situation. The freak stopped beside the bus and put a hand on my window. His eyes held mine. Two gleaming yellow eyes that shone through the dark where his face was supposed to be. He slowly tilted his head to the side and then brought it closer to mine. An icy numbness washed through me. He spread his hand open on the glass, his fingers grotesquely long in a black leather glove. A weight settled on my chest, squeezing my heart. I tried to move. Tried to scream. But could do neither. I felt like an oyster sitting in an open shell, ready for the taking. The man slowly reached up to his head with his other hand. I was sure he was going to pull his hood off. Except now, I wished he wouldn't. I didn't want to know anymore! If he would just let me go. I thought I glimpsed something green and wrinkled, when suddenly the bus's engine sprang into life, and we drove on, leaving the horror behind.

By the time I stepped through the door of the teahouse half an hour later, only my hands still shook a little. The familiar smell of fruity teas and freshly baked cakes wrapped me in a reassuring hug like an old friend. I shut my eyes for a moment and let out a sigh.

'Your coat, madam?' The approaching waiter offered to help me out of it. He had a hard, narrow face, his long, brown hair tied back into a ponytail with a ribbon. He looked immaculate in his frilled, white shirt, dark waistcoat and trousers. I kept my face blank as I thanked him, although secretly I enjoyed being fussed over. With him looking like a 17th-century butler and our surroundings appearing even older, it was almost impossible not to be transported back in time and feel like a member of an old aristocratic family.

The teahouse had a warm, wooden decor. Shelves lined the walls from floor to ceiling, full of antique books and fascinating merchandise, further bookcases dividing the room into many small compartments. In the Old Library Teahouse, all books were re-printed to resemble antique tomes, whether they were classics or newly published titles. A wooden staircase in the middle led to the upper floors. Its steps creaked under my feet as I climbed them.

Keiko Nakamura was already sitting at our table, only the top of her head visible above a leather-bound volume. In front of her were two pots of tea and two cups on the table.

'Hi.' I sat down next to her.

'Just a minute,' Keiko declared without looking up from her book. 'This part is very exciting.'

I shrugged and lifted the crimson pot to pour myself some tea. The complex aroma steamed out of my cup in fast-moving, intricate little clouds. The Phoenix was a mixture of apricot, hibiscus, mango, papaya, rose petals, strawberry and about a dozen other things I kept forgetting. I blew at the hot liquid and sipped it carefully. It tasted even better than usual.

Two minutes later, Keiko was still deeply absorbed in the book. I leaned back and tried to see the page she was reading.

'How can it be already so exciting?' I bristled. 'You're only on the first chapter!'

'Shhh!' she retorted. 'Only three more pages.'

I watched her as her brown eyes widened in disbelief behind her glasses, disbelief shading into horror and finally astonishment within less than a minute.

'Seems intense,' I said as she finally lowered her book.

'It's very good. It's about broken children who get thrown into a big hole in an ice field by their own people. You should get your head out of virtual reality sometime and try some of this author's books instead.' She sipped from her tea and finally looked at me. 'What's wrong with you?' she asked. 'You look even paler than usual.'

'It's nothing.' I shrugged. In the familiarity of the teahouse, the whole episode on the bus seemed like a silly thing I half-imagined.

'Has something happened?' Keiko was one of my oldest friends. She could read me as if I was one of her books.

'Well, it wasn't anything major. There was just this homeless person sitting on the street. He sort of wandered up to the bus as it stopped at a red light. Right where I was sitting.'

'Did he say anything?'

'He didn't say or do anything. He was just weird. He put his hand on the window.'

'What did he look like?'

'I don't know. I couldn't see his face. He wore a long, hooded coat and a pair of weird yellow glasses or lenses. But somehow, he managed to really scare me, and I think I might have had a bit of a panic attack.'

'Oh, Selena.' Keiko set her cup down and put an arm around me. 'Is there anything I can do to help?'

'You're already helping.' I smiled at her weakly. 'Just keep distracting me. Talk to me about other things. What happened to those children you were reading about?'

She bit her lip. 'Why don't you tell me how your lunch with Jake went yesterday instead?' she asked with a triumphant smile, sure of having found a topic that would distract me even if the building was on fire.

'Um …' I hesitated as a young waiter arrived and placed a third pot of tea on the table.

'A Royal Affair for Miss Rhia Parker,' he announced, which meant that Rhia was just about to arrive. 'I'll bring your cakes in a moment.'

'I can't believe you didn't get promoted again!' Rhia pushed past the retreating waiter. She threw her bag on one of the empty chairs and flopped down into the other, her red, wavy hair flying as she spun around. She fixed me with a gaze that seemed to suggest it was all my fault. Typical Rhia. You could always trust her to make you refocus on the important stuff in life! 'Just how long are you planning to be a purchasing assistant for? Three more years?'

'Excuse me.' I attempted to halt her with a raised hand. This usually worked with the same success rate as stopping water spraying on you from a puddle by a speeding car. 'I'm a Sourcing Specialist.'

'Same thing!' she said. 'The point is that management only needs to snap their fingers, and you source them the only living Tibetan monk who makes some magic horse shit in his monastery's backyard—'

'Fertiliser,' I tried to interject. 'And it was a goat!'

'Magic goat shit,' Rhia declared, her raised voice like a hammer against a gong. The waiter reappeared at the table holding a tray laden with cakes and looking very much as if it wasn't just me under fire. 'The only thing out there that could miraculously cure the company's mascot bonsai tree from that Southeast Asian rot. They should have promoted you right then and there! But what happened instead? They threw some pocket money at you and gave you even more work, which you happily accepted!'

'It's just that she's really very good at her job.' Keiko sipped her tea next to me with zen-like tranquillity. 'I doubt they could ever find anyone like her.'

'Couldn't *you* do something about it?' Rhia turned on her. 'You work in HR, after all! I mean, even her surname sounds Japanese. Surely that must count for something? People don't need to know that it's down to her Spanish grandfather.'

'Nishida is the fifth largest company in the world,' Keiko said in a professional tone. 'Just because all three of us work at the London head office, that doesn't mean I have access to detailed information on you two. And even if I did, it's not like I could promote you myself.'

'I just get so frustrated every time this happens. She could do so much better. If only she wasn't such a scared little bunny sometimes!' Rhia, who looked like a film star, was fearless like a lion and worked in sales, got promoted practically every other week. 'She shouldn't let herself be used like that!'

'She was just going to tell me about her date with Jake when you arrived.' Keiko gave me an encouraging look. 'Who cares about work appraisals when Jake Black takes you out for lunch?'

Rhia's frustration instantly disappeared, and she looked at me in surprise. 'Jake Black took you out? Wow!'

'It wasn't such a big deal.' I hastily tried to manage their expectations.

'Of course, it's a big deal!' Rhia insisted, her perfect smile back in place. 'Selena, half the office has a crush on Jake.' Then, seeing my expression, she added, 'You didn't think it was just you, did you?'

'Well, no, but …'

'I'm honestly so impressed with you,' she went on, nursing her cup. 'I always knew how taken you were with him.' Her smile widened in excitement. 'So tell us! I want to hear everything!'

I slumped forward, buried my face in my hands and let out a groan. Jake Black was the hottest guy at work. He'd never taken notice of me before, and I only ever attempted to engage with him on a very few occasions.

Like last year, when I managed to seize the seat next to him at a work presentation. The way Sheila from marketing, who was two steps too late from securing the same position, had stared at me still haunted my dreams. A sixty-minute meeting, and despite me turning his way a few times, Jake didn't look at me once. And then there was that time in the office canteen when he waved in my direction. It took me a moment to realise that it was at another woman who was standing right behind me. That wasn't awkward at all! The memory kept coming back to me in unexpected moments, making me feel ashamed of myself. The happy eagerness with which I'd waved back. What a fool! Yet, I somehow doubted that he even remembered.

So, needless to say, when he appeared at my desk on Thursday afternoon and called me by my name, I might have forgotten how to speak for a minute. He asked if I would like to go to lunch with him on Friday, to the French bistro two streets down from our office building. When I agreed, he smiled sweetly and said he couldn't wait! I left work early that day, claiming I had a bad migraine, and spent the rest of the afternoon in our local beauty salon instead, feeling like I'd just won the lottery.

Jake had told me that his favourite table was upstairs, at the window, and that we should aim to meet there at noon. Which made sense, since the small place would be packed by one o'clock even on a Friday, and as the bistro didn't take table bookings for lunch, we would hardly find anywhere to sit, let alone get the table which was probably the most popular in the whole restaurant. So, just to be extra sure, I arrived half an hour early, triumphantly securing the table in question, and nervously waited. And waited. And waited. And waited.

By half-past-twelve, I was worried that something might have happened to him. He'd fallen ill. No. Surely, he would have texted then. He must have died! He was so excited to meet me that he ran down the stairs, fell and broke his neck! Or his ex-girlfriend heard that he was having lunch with me and killed him in a jealous rage! That was why I hadn't seen him all morning. Explained it all.

By quarter-to-one, I really thought I must have misunderstood. Had he meant next Friday? But just as I lost all hope, he finally appeared.

'I'm so sorry!' he said as he sheepishly took the seat opposite mine. 'My boss, Anthony, called me in for a meeting last minute. I hope you haven't been waiting long?'

'Oh, absolutely not,' I reassured him. 'What year is it? Still '37, right?'

'You're funny!' He laughed. 'Sorry, I should have messaged you.'

Damn right, I thought, *why didn't you?* But before I could say anything, he treated me to one of those heart-throbbing smiles and said, 'This is really nice. I'm so pleased that you were able to make it!'

'Me, too!' I beamed back at him, my annoyance evaporating like mist in the morning sun.

'Sooo, work is super busy at the moment, isn't it?' He frowned a little after he ordered a quiche.

'The same, please,' I decided on a whim. My stomach was back to the size of a pea. It didn't matter what I ordered.

'It's actually not too bad for me right now,' I confessed. 'Last month was crazy, but now I feel I can breathe again. What is it that's keeping you busy?'

'They decided to expand our antiquity division.' He sighed. 'We'll be selling Ancient Egyptian, Tibetan and Persian rugs, pottery, furniture and religious knick-knacks, too.'

'Interesting.' I sipped my lemonade.

'Because of all the hieroglyphics and pictographs, the company decided to offer a translation software, specialising in ancient languages and symbols, as an extra service to our customers. Anthony gave me the contract with this IT company we're getting it from to review.'

'That's so great,' I enthused. 'Actually, I have this old family heirloom at home with symbols on it. I don't think it's Egyptian, but it's really pretty.'

'Is it?' Jake picked up his fork as the waiter arrived with our order.

'Yes! It's richly decorated with interesting-looking runes, symbols and numbers that move around in circles.'

'Right. Sounds fascinating! So …'

'It really is! Maybe you should see it sometime.' I grinned.

'Um … yes … why don't you bring it in, and we can have a look?'

'In?' I frowned, taken aback.

'Look.' He leaned forward with a serious face. 'About this contract …'

'What contract?' I stared at him in confusion for a second before re-membering. 'Oh, the one you need to review?'

'Yes.' He wiped his mouth with the napkin. 'I'm not good at this stuff. Could you help me?'

'Me?' A sudden cold realisation hit me. So, this was why he asked me out?

'Yes. You're in purchasing. And everyone knows you have excellent attention to detail.'

'Really?' Was this really all he wanted from me? The obvious was star-ing me in the face, but I was desperately trying to ignore it, looking for any little sign that it wasn't true.

'Come on, Selena! I just need a second pair of eyes to highlight the important details, just to make sure I didn't miss anything crucial. All I need is a little summary separating the main points from anything that sounds odd or unusual. The whole thing is only sixty-nine pages long. You could do it in no time!'

For once, I was speechless.

He put his hand on top of mine on the table, stroking it. 'Look, you don't need to decide right now. Why don't you have a little think about it?'

I nodded, dazed. Jake Black was stroking my hand, smiling at me ador-ingly, yet inside I was numb with hurt. Here I thought I was going on a date with him, and this was all I was needed for. All I was good for.

'Now, tell me more about that family heirloom.' He laughed easily and squeezed my hand.

I found my voice again, but the words trickled out on autopilot. I let him pay for lunch and walk me back to the office. He was all charm, teas-ing me all the way.

I watched him with a polite smile on my face while my mind chewed on all the possibilities. I had to say no—he was clearly just using me. But if I said no, I would never get another chance with him. And wasn't this what I wanted? What I had yearned for for years? Him and me together? Him smiling at me like this? Holding my hand? Spending time together? But this was all wrong! This wasn't how I imagined it at all! If he'd truly wanted something, he wouldn't have waited until this bloody contract came up. And that thought hurt more than anything.

'Bastard!' Rhia blurted out, cross again.

'What did you say to him?' Keiko asked, her face stricken.

'I said no,' I informed them crestfallen, shame and embarrassment reddening my face. Keiko and Rhia had both been in loving relationships for years. I went out with a guy on this one date, and this is what happened.

'Well done!' Rhia put an arm around me. 'That shitface deserved nothing less!'

'Why did he have to be like that?' I bristled.

'He is clearly an idiot!' Keiko reached over and brushed a strand of hair out of my face. 'And you deserve someone better.'

'And where is this someone better? It's not like he's been banging on my door, is it?' I grumbled.

'I think you just need to get out and meet someone new.' Rhia pursued her lips. 'Leave it with me. I have an idea.'

Once I was back at home, I collapsed on my bed and thought of Jake. His face. His lips. His smile. I could surely forget all about that now. Maybe I should have helped him ... but, no! No, no, no! If he wanted to see me, he could call me. And if he didn't invite me out again, it would be completely, definitely clear that help with that contract was all he was after. Still. I wished I could know for sure. And could stop this silly, unrealistic hoping despite it all.

I reached under the bed, pulled out the redemeter and placed it on my lap. It was the old family heirloom I'd talked to Jake about. If you could believe a letter dated 1818 that used to be kept together with it in a box, this device was meant to determine divine intent. I'd never really been a religious person, but I always liked playing with it, consulting it on various matters and guessing what the answers it offered had meant.

It was a beautiful object. I loved the way the dark and golden circles complemented each other. The delicately painted symbols. The crystal—the colour of rich honey—sat in a metal frame, like the centrepiece of a small crown. I put my fingers around it and thought of my question. 'Will Jake ask me out for a date?' Then turned the centre part clockwise and let it go. The concentric circular metal disks rotated upon each other, the runes, numbers and symbols on their surfaces smoothly moving around. They soon slowed to a halt, three of them forming a line to give me the answer.

'Man. Meet. Woman.' WHAT? YES! YES! I couldn't believe it! What a clear sign. There was apparently hope, after all.

I jiggled around triumphantly before thinking of my next question.

'And what will happen on this date? Will he kiss me?' I grinned to myself even as I set the thing in motion again.

'Man. Fight. Woman.' What? No, that couldn't be right. No, no, no, no! Maybe I just asked the question wrong.

'What will we do on this date with Jake?' I said out loud and clearly.

'Man. Fight. Woman,' came the answer. Again? But that never happened. Okay. One more.

'So, what if I'm super nice to him? Will we fight even then?'

'Man. Fight. Woman.' Argggh! It didn't make sense! Had the thing broken? I lifted the round, flat object and shook it a few times. Maybe I used it too fast, too many times. *Let's just give it a little rest.* I put it back under the bed.

The main thing was that Jake was going to ask me out again. Wasn't he? Then I'd just make sure we had so much fun that he'd come back for more!

Chapter 12

James

Even the best intentions could lead to questionable outcomes. Often it was hard to tell whether one course of action would have resulted in something preferable or if you had done the right thing. Keeping Kristian safe at the University of St Mark seemed the most important thing for me twenty years ago. He was my nephew. And he was all I had left of Alessandra.

At first, he flourished there. He became strong, clever, honest, selfless. But with time, a tendency towards introspection deepened almost into depression. He became a passenger in his own life rather than its driver. I had hoped he would shake free of this passivity once his teenage years passed, but he just closed in on himself even more.

I thought I saw the same kind of resignation in Selena as I watched her wait for the bus. But whereas Kristian sealed himself off completely, her true self was still trying to break through the restraints. Like lava boiling under the surface.

She boarded a red double-decker, and I hailed a black cab. 'Follow that bus,' I said as I sat down.

'Please insert your bank card into the slot and say the name of your destination.' The car responded.

'Just follow that bus for now,' I repeated slowly, with more determination.

'Please insert your bank card into the slot and say the name of your destination.'

I sighed and pulled out a snooper from an inside pocket. I placed it on the card reader and watched as the black circle fastened itself onto the panel.

'Please insert your bank card into the slot and say … and say … and say … System override. System override.'

'Follow the bus ahead of us,' I said.

'Following the bus ahead of us,' the car responded as it took off.

Of course, a lot has changed here in twenty years. I would have enjoyed discovering the city again, but I didn't mean to stay for long. I just wanted to earn Selena's trust before taking her with me. Fortunately, time passed slower on Alba than it did on Earth. Kristian would still only be spending his first morning at the base back there.

I connected my lenses to the snooper and located Selena's phone on the bus. She was on a café's website, going over an impressive selection of cakes. The Old Library Teahouse. I transferred its location to the car's navigation system and flipped through the menu while I waited for her to make a decision. Rain splattered the windows, heavy clouds covering London's sky. It was just like the day we left her here. Some things didn't change.

I looked back at Selena's screen and saw that she still hadn't made up her mind. I wondered why she was taking so long. I took control of the Teahouse's system and prompted her to get on with it. She didn't seem to like that.

"Your current session started twelve minutes and forty-three seconds ago. Do you need more time to decide?' I asked, the snooper changing my voice to match the one used by the website. Immediately, she bought herself two cakes, making me smile and take note of her course of action under pressure. I wondered if her counsellor explained to her the impact of high sugar intake on anxiety symptoms or whether she was ignoring that rule as well. Either way, this would no longer be a problem if she came with me. I watched her choose a table and add the two friends she expected to join her.

I looked up as the car slowed, catching up to the bus at the red light. The pavements were mostly vacant, the street quiet. Nothing moved except the vehicles crossing our road ahead of the traffic lights. On the left, someone sat on the ground in front of a pub, wrapped in a dark cloak. I assumed it was a man because of his wide shoulders. His cloak was old and frayed at the edges, no bag or other belongings visible around him. The figure got up and unhurriedly walked towards the bus. My lenses finished analysing his features, and to my shock, it wasn't a human under that big cloak as I'd expected. *What the hell was a Preonian doing on Earth?*

'Wait here,' I instructed the car. I switched on the invisibility function on my coat, pulling up its hood to cover my head. I wouldn't have minded the creature seeing my face, but I didn't want Selena to glimpse me. I walked up to the Preonian, pulled out a laser stick from my belt and held it to his head. 'Let her go.' I said quietly. The creature lifted his arm slowly, his hand moving towards mine.

'Let her go,' I repeated and half-activated the weapon, making it hum with energy. The Preonian released his mental grip on the girl and turned to me. As if on cue, the bus took off.

'James Montgomery,' he hissed as he flipped out with his mental tentacles towards my brain. I blocked it.

'What is a Preonian doing on Earth?' I launched my own assault on the creature, my mind racing past his thoughts towards his memories.

'You are not a Champion of The Order anymore,' he protested in a strained voice.

'I only renounced my position, not my skills.' I pushed harder.

'You have no jurisdiction here!' He fought desperately. 'Why do you even care?'

'That's my business. Tell me yours, and I'll let you be.'

'I can't do that.' He tried to snatch the laser stick out of my hand, not realising that I already had him under my control. I lowered my arm, the stick no longer needed. The Preonian wasn't able to move on his own account anymore.

I looked through his most recent memories, not finding anything particularly helpful, but as I took a closer look, I noticed a chip in his cortex. The exact kind of chip The Order used to track someone, to record and transmit their observations. Were they using the Preonian as some kind of spy? Maybe he didn't even know. That would also explain how he got through a gate unnoticed, given that all skygates were monitored by the Order. Unusual, but if that was the case, I didn't want to interfere too much. Reluctant to simply let the creature go, I first deleted the memories that contained Selena and compelled him to hide somewhere. The compulsion wouldn't last longer than a few days, but that would give me enough time to check this out with one of my old colleagues.

I got back into the car and let it drive me to the teahouse. On the way, I cancelled the reservation of the table nearest to Selena's and booked it for myself. Of course, I could have just walked in and kept an eye on her hidden under my cloak. But damn, I wanted some of that cake now, too.

I arrived at the place shortly after her. The large, timber-framed building resembled a medieval inn from the outside. Inside, the décor shifted a few centuries, tastefully merging medieval with gothic. I was escorted to my table by a waitress dressed as a maid. Another poured a cup of tea and placed a slice of walnut cake in front of me as soon as I sat down.

The teahouse was packed, every table occupied, some by groups chatting loudly, others quietly reading books taken from the countless shelves that lined the walls and divided the floors into smaller areas. A large bookcase stood between me and Selena's table, too, its crammed shelves providing the perfect cover.

I fished out a small box from an inner pocket. Inside, I kept my latest creation: a droid disguised as a spider. It already knew Selena from our counselling session, so in no time, I had it climb over a large, leather-covered volume and watch her from the other side of it. In turn I watched her through my lenses, sipping my tea as I listened to their conversation.

Unexpectedly, my inbox beeped in my ear with an urgent message. Wondering who it might be, I switched my lenses over from the droid. The message came from an unspecified source. When I opened it, a video file started playing. It showed Kris secured to a wall, badly hurt. He was covered in blood, his face badly bruised, getting kicked senseless by the killer from the university. My hand tightened into a fist. The shock of seeing him so brutally beaten hurt with an almost unbearable pain. Anger and worry washed over me in waves—which was undoubtedly what the sender of the message wanted. I needed to calm down and pay attention. I needed to think. The footage ended abruptly, showing a different recording where his attacker addressed me, sitting lazily in an elegant chair in an expensive-looking room.

'He's still alive,' he said. 'Barely. If you want me to spare his life, come and see me immediately. Do not delay. Don't tell anyone. Don't bring anyone. I'm watching you. The smallest mistake, and he dies.'

I sat frozen for a moment. How did he find me? I checked all my system shields. Everything was in place. There was no way he could have followed me. Nobody could have, I was sure of that. I had been very careful. I looked around me. Could there be a hidden camera watching me? But how would he have known I was going to come here? Was he really watching me, or just bluffing? He sounded very confident on the footage.

The address he'd given was on Eris. I could be at the nearest skygate by midnight. Would I rush into a trap if I follow his instructions? Probably. Would I risk Kris's life if I didn't? Could it have been fake footage? According to my system, it was real. Who was this guy, and why did he bear such a passionate grudge against us? He called himself Laro Deathstorm on the video. Meant nothing to me.

I sent the spider into Selena's bag with a clear set of instructions and stood to leave. It was safer this way. Even within the Order, there were only two of us who knew of the location of the Key. And Ithorion would never betray it to anyone. At the same time, I knew that I couldn't desert her completely.

Outside, I took another cab back to the hotel. I quickly packed my stuff, checked a few things, then pulled out a candle from my suitcase. I had ways to contact people without using technology. Ways that were untraceable. A combination of my talents and ancient practices. The candle wasn't long enough anymore to reach out to Quede in the Pantheon, if indeed that was where she was. But if Ithorion, who had retired not long after I did, although for very different reasons, still resided on Drelos, I could just about reach him. Drelos was sister-planet to Earth, linked in many ways, and while a few galaxies apart, it was still closest by cosmic travel and range.

Once in the hotel room, I closed my eyes and tried to relax. I inhaled the familiar, complex scent of the candle, its chemicals preparing my brain for the task. I cleared my throat and slowly repeated the full name of the Order's most feared test master three times. Behind my closed eyelids, I saw his stern face. His prominent forehead, heavy brow ridge, and cold, green-grey eyes. His salt and pepper beard and hair. His thin lips that never smiled. His unyielding disposition. He had a family now. For their sake, I hoped that behind those unforgiving features we all knew so well, somewhere deep down, there was also a heart.

I made contact and waited ten minutes before he signalled back. Then I started slowly pulling him down into sleep.

'James.' He frowned at me once he sat opposite me in my dream. 'What an unexpected call.'

'Thanks for taking it.'

'I was half-way through reminding the butcher's son about the appropriate distance I required he keep around my daughter. It's thanks to you, he still has every part of his body attached to the rest. Anyway. What can I do for you?'

'I need your help,' I said simply.

'Is that so?' He cocked his head. 'It must be serious.'

'It is.'

He reached for the wooden pipe and tobacco I conjured up for him while I waited. 'Tell me all.'

'A week ago, a young man managed to sneak into St Mark's University and kill ten students before being chased off by a highly competent military droid. He was a trained killer. But he was also an identity-changer.'

'Are you sure? The last known identity-changer died centuries ago. It is not a natural trait to possess."

'I'm sure. Although there are some differences. There are signs to suggest that the transformations might be short-lived and might require longer breaks in between. It could be some sort of corrupted version of the original gift.'

'Chased off, you say? Does that mean he's still at large?'

'It does, I'm afraid. He seems to know Kris. Or at least, know of him. He wanted to meet him, potentially kill him, too, which he thankfully failed to do then.'

'But since we're here, I'm assuming he has him now?'

I nodded again. 'Potentially. I instructed Kris to get to a safe base nearby, and once he left, I came to Earth for Selena. As I've just found out, Kristian never arrived. He had one of my self-made droids with him, which has constant signal connection with the university. The signal was lost near the Andraida gate, which, of course, neither he nor Storn had any knowledge of. Allegedly, they were following a broken android transmission that they were investigating. Someone who knew about the gate must have led them there.'

'If the killer led Kristian through the gate, there would be a record of it. Your nephew isn't a member of the Order. Someone would have contacted you.'

'That's what I was thinking. But nobody contacted me. And a few hours ago, I received a video message from the killer to my private mailbox in which there's footage of him brutally assaulting my nephew and claiming him to be on Eris. He told me to go there alone. Said he's monitoring me and will kill Kris if I contact anyone.'

Ithorian leaned back in his chair as he processed all this. Then his steely eyes bore into me once more as he asked his next question. 'James, why did you go to fetch Selena?'

'Something the attacker had said in a video taken of him at the university. He claimed he intended to hunt down everyone in Kristian's soul-circle. Before they reach The Bridge of Honour and swear their oaths.'

The tobacco smouldered in the dark as he inhaled sharply. 'An identity-changer who knows about soul-circles, skygates and The Bridge of Honour. That can potentially mean only one thing. However unlikely that is.'

'A traitor.'

'But is he a traitor who left the Order with his memories intact or is he still part of it?'

'Or neither. He might be just getting help and information from the real traitor on the inside.'

'And you thought they might have found out about Selena?' he asked. 'But that would mean a traitor right in the inner circle. Surely, that's out of the question!'

'I couldn't be sure. And there were just too many questions following this attack. Something doesn't add up. I spoke to Quede but she wasn't being particularly helpful. In the end, I didn't want to take risks.'

'You sentimental old fool! You let your emotions cloud your sense of logic.' He exhaled, blowing out smoke in demonstration. 'Quede has never quite forgiven you for leaving her side. But she has a huge respect for you. She always counted on you. And she is still the highest-ranking leader in the Order, which she takes very seriously. If there's a corruption within, she is no part of it. I'm sure of that. You should have left Selena to be contacted by the Order. Not just rush ahead and take the matter into your own hands, like you always do … Thinking you know better than anyone else. And now here we are.' He leaned back and crossed his arms in front of his chest. 'With you inconveniencing me in the performing of my fatherly duties.'

I couldn't help but sheepishly smile at him.

'Oh, stop that, James Montgomery! Your charms don't work on me. Just finish your story and spit out what you want! I don't have all day.'

I nodded at him, my face once more serious, although deep down I knew I came to the right person and was glad to still count him as a friend.

'I doubt that the killer can really monitor me. At least, not the way he thinks. But I will have to go to Eris and investigate.'

'Sounds like he figured out how to get to at least one member of your nephew's soul-circle. Not that he seems to know who the others are.' He nodded. 'If he had really been watching you and knew all that he implies, he would have told you to take Selena with you, too. So, you're right about that. But what of Conor? Do you have any information on him?'

'Last I heard, he was still pursuing his sacred quest. The near-impossible treasure hunt we sent him on.'

'You mean *you* sent him on. Don't try to implicate me in this! I merely helped to make it happen.'

'I still believe it's the only way that might eventually win him over to the cause. His character makes it very difficult to rein him in. He is Kane's son. This was never going to be easy.'

'A near-impossible quest to accomplish a near-impossible feat. And they said I was the one who set bars too high!' He exhaled slowly. 'But yes, he was always a wild card. A dark horse that knows no limits when he wants something.'

'And this is exactly why, out of the three of them, I'm least worried about him. Nonetheless, I would ask you to check on him.'

'Consider it done. What else do you need?'

'Make sure he finds his way to the Key.'

'What?'

'Well, I can't stay here, and I can't take Selena with me. And whatever you say, I'm not going to leave her here alone in all this uncertainty. I will have to make my way to Eris. What if this Laro does have Kris? And if indeed there's a traitor in the Order, how can I know for certain who I can ask for help? A few hours ago, I found a Preonian with a Tereki chip in his head. On Earth! He had made contact with Selena. I deleted his memories of her, but the chip will have transmitted what happened. Chances are, that information may stay in safe hands. But I'm just simply not sure who I can trust anymore. So, let's have Conor protect Selena for the time being until I figure out more.'

'If there is indeed a traitor in the Order, we might need Selena more than ever before,' he agreed with a sigh.

The word 'we' pleasantly surprised me. What had happened to retirement? I drew my mental cloak tighter around me, hiding that particular thought from him. He was staring into the air with an expression on his face I had never seen there before. A sense of loss. I knew how he felt. We both dedicated most of our lives to the Order of the Dragon. It was always unquestionably secure and solid. Something we could rely on. The idea that all that safety was now potentially lost weighed heavily on us. Too much of our heart and soul went into building it.

'That is all,' I said when he stayed quiet. 'I need to get on.'

'Yes. Me, too,' he answered, his eyes still lost in the distance but filled with something new. Anger.

Despite it all, I woke with a smile on my face. Whatever wickedness was going on behind the scenes, it now had its days numbered with Ithorion back in the game.

Chapter 13

Laro

Y*ou never knew how often I watched you from the shadows as a child. Leo, the perfect. Leo, the strong. You were always our father's favourite, no matter how hard I tried. The glory was always yours. The punishment was mine. And believe me when I tell you, Father always knew how to hurt.*

Of course, you wouldn't remember. You left us when I was still in my mother's womb. But you left enough of yourself behind to make my life a misery. An uphill battle through hell that I had to fight naked and blind. While you lived in comfort and cared for by our uncle, who called you Kristian.

The waitress smiled at me sweetly again. I wondered if she'd looked up how much time she had left to try and seduce me. She acted like she knew. I pretended to check my phone instead of taking notice of her. I already had dessert on order. And I didn't mean cake.

The screen exploded with colours in my hand, drawing my eyes to it. I looked at it, but my mind was far away. I knew exactly what time it was. It was finally my time. And I had worked hard to get here.

Seven hard years of pain and suffering, but by the end of it, I had a power no one else had. I could become anyone. And I did what no one else could accomplish. I penetrated The Order of the Dragon. I learned about the skygates and how they worked. From there, it was only a matter of time before I could finally visit you.

I even found out how I could destroy the Order! All I needed was the Supreme Key. I just had to find it before the Order did. Ridiculous, but even there, nobody seemed to know where it was. Conor looked for it for years, but he was too stupid to find it. So, I thought you might help him. You're so clever, after all. Everyone seems to think so. I just needed to lure you out into the open somehow.

Dear Brother, you were so set on remaining in that little school of yours, clinging on with that ridiculous, rigid determination. I had to do something dramatic to unsettle you. To anger you. And it worked like a charm. Watching all those memories you left behind, learning about you eventually paid off. The curiosity and thirst for revenge I alone knew you would have, had you follow that little bluebee right into the cave. Right to the gate, where, for the first time, it was you who watched me from the dark. Watched me and took the bait. I pushed you further by leaving that dying peasant for you to finish off. And then again by hammering Conor in front of you. I saw the hate in your eyes. I saw the thirst for violence. You were no longer Uncle's little Kristian. You'd made your decision. The first step down the path which would lead you back to your true self again.

It would have made our uncle weep. You know, you truly are the most precious thing in his life. So, imagine my surprise, when following my attack, instead of watching over you, he suddenly left! Of course, that made my job a lot easier. I couldn't really complain. But I was curious. I was dead curious. What could be more important than you?

I sent Aron and Mara after him, but of course, I never hoped they could actually track him. That chance meeting with the Preonian changed everything, though. I watched later what the Preonian saw when it attacked her. Her most recent memories. Her meeting with our uncle. I watched James save her and delete the Preonian's memories of her. And I thought to myself again: who could be this important?

I'm here now, waiting for her while you're busy getting me that key, and I have to say, while I have some ideas, I'm still a little clueless. But I will get there, dear Brother. Oh, I will, trust me. I even got rid of Uncle, so it's only her and me now.

Learning about her was even easier than learning about you. These Earthlings know nothing of privacy. I now know her name. I know where she lives. I know where she works. I know who her friends are. But more importantly, I know who she is interested in. His face is reflected on the screen of my phone even now. And he is so looking forward to knowing Selena much better ...

Chapter 14

Kristian

Kingdom of Coroden, Drelos,
22ⁿᵈ The Month of Promise 1575

T he fire crackled merrily, as if it knew I'd built it simply for the joy of having one. It was a pleasant night. Not as warm as the ones we spent in Beren, but certainly warm enough to sleep out in the open countryside without having to worry about the cold. We sat among gently rolling hills and green forests, with small settlements and farmhouses dotting the lands in the distance. Conor was telling me about how he once saved the daughter of some famous court official, rather unsurprisingly, in return for a handsome reward, and I listened intently. I liked his stories. Even if half of them sounded rather far flung from reality. Magical items, ghouls, not to mention this key that he was prophesied to find. Yet, I increasingly found myself invested in the mechanics of his adventures, wondering what I would have done, had I been there.

As for the reward he received for the rescue mission, he pulled out a silver watch from an inside pocket, flipping its cover open with his thumb as he handed it to me.

'This unbinds all magic in a twenty-meter radius for exactly five minutes, up to three times a day. And since it was specially made for me, it only works in my hand.'

I took it and turned it over in my fingers curiously. Heavy steps behind me on the grass indicated someone else was approaching for a closer look, too.

'I can't believe your horse managed to untie the rope again!' Conor exclaimed as Storn's head appeared next to mine, pretending to nuzzle me in order to get a better view of the discussed item. 'How does he do it?'

'That's okay.' I patted Storn's muzzle. 'He's not going to run away.'

Conor and Storn stared at each other, one set of eyes frowning in suspicion, the other pretending innocence, while I raised the watch higher, trying to examine the delicate markings on it more carefully. It looked like a watch, nothing more. 'How can you tell it's magical?'

'Because I used it a number of times. Besides, if there's magic around to be undone, it flashes up briefly when you open the lid. But apart from that, yes, it often takes a spellcaster to actually see the magic bond to these things.'

'A what?' I couldn't help but smile.

'A sorcerer. An enchanter. A witch. A warlock. People who can wield magic.'

Well, that was pretty convenient.

'And where do these mysterious spellcasters abide? Can we just visit one on our way to the ruins?'

'Well, they are pretty rare.'

'I bet.'

'You know, for someone who tells me they arrived from a different world, following a killer who can change shape, you don't always seem very open-minded!' Conor observed, slightly annoyed with me now. He took the watch from me and snapped it closed.

I threw my hands up in surrender. 'I'm sorry. It's just where I'm from, we don't consider mysterious phenomena to be magic. We have scientific explanations. We understand how they work and can replicate them without the need for a bunch of enigmatic magicians, who are just likely to trick you.'

He gave me a level look. 'You've never seen magic before, have you?'

'There's no such thing as magic.'

He pressed his fingertips against his forehead and lay down, as if the weight of my ignorance was too much to bear. 'You've never seen magic before.' No longer a question.

'I don't believe in things I can't see, examine or test. One always learns something new, and I'm not against exploring things that are unknown to me. But if you want me to change my mind, you need to do better than this watch. Show me magic! Extraordinary claims require extraordinary evidence.'

He laughed at that. 'Oh, don't worry, we have that covered. What did you think I meant when I said Borond was a cursed place? That it was just a turn of phrase?'

An ominous thunderclap rolled across the sky, making us look up, but I didn't see any clouds.

'And anyhow,' Conor added as an afterthought, 'if you think everything can be explained by science, can you explain to me how our friend does his little shape-shifting trick? Or how one travels between worlds?' He widened his eyes at my hesitation. 'What? Surely if you came here, you know how to do it?'

'I heard all you had to do was click your heels together three times,' a sarcastic voice stated on our right. We both looked at the man standing at our fire, who in turn watched us with an unfriendly expression. 'I trust you two are having a nice evening?'

He raised his eyebrows, waiting for a response, but a dangerous light in his eyes told me there was no right answer. I stared at the man. Surely, we should have heard him approach. He was practically standing next to me! Not even Storn gave any warning signs about someone coming. If anything, he was now also eyeing him curiously.

'Not too bad.' Conor found his voice as he sat up. 'You're welcome at our fire and to what wine we have left, if you'd like.'

Why was he so trusting? We had no idea who this was! Could he have been some farmer whose land we trespassed on? He didn't look like a farmer. His grey hair and beard, the wrinkles across his face, should have marked him as an old man. Yet there was a fierce strength in the way he held himself, a sharpness to the gaze he held us with that hinted at no such thing. He wore a long coat despite the warmth, clean leather boots despite the mud and a sour expression on his face despite the invitation. Over his shoulder, he carried a long, dark bag.

'I will have some of that wine,' he said finally and sat down, facing us. 'You never know, it might help me endure all the foolishness I'm about to hear!'

Well, that wasn't very nice. What made him think we would tell him anything? 'It's not the best wine, but it helps me sleep,' I admitted.

'Oh, nooo!' he said in a mocking tone. 'You have trouble sleeping?' He pulled out a pipe from his coat and started stuffing it with herbs.

'I'm too used to the asclepeion,' I explained helpfully. Why did I say that? 'I've been struggling to sleep properly ever since I left Alba.' I closed my mouth tightly. I didn't mean to say any of that. What was in that wine? Did I now also have to explain what an asclepeion was? Conor was looking at me, confused, but the man didn't seem to care. He carried on fidgeting with his pipe and only glanced at me when I failed to volunteer more.

'I know what an asclepeion is, Kristian.'

A cold sensation washed through me. How did he know my name? Or what was on my mind?

'The more important question,' he carried on, 'is how come you're here? I'm sure you'll agree?'

'Yes, of course.' What? How did he make me say these things? I bit into my lower lip hard. There was no way I was sharing anything else with him!

'My name is Ithorion, and from what I've been told, you're not at all where I expected! So, I have to say, I'm a little intrigued now to hear what happened,' he said, looking untroubled by my defiance. 'Tell me all!'

And I did.

For what felt like hours, I talked, sparing no details, no matter how painful or embarrassing. I tried to stop a few times. To stand up and walk away. To stay and fight. It seemed I could do neither. As if talking had suddenly become the single most important act of my existence, and performing it required all of me. Conor initially looked like he might do something about my exploited situation, but upon hearing some of the details I'd previously kept from him, he seemed to decide he'd rather listen to me, too.

Once I could finally stop speaking, I hung my head, avoiding their eyes. I told them how I could sense whenever Conor was close. I told them all about how that vicious madness took over my mind sometimes. A condition I didn't yet fully understand but apparently could talk about in great detail. About how it made me feel, about my worries over what it all meant, how I thought it was slowly getting worse and what it might do to me in the future. I felt somehow dirty. Broken. But most of all, deeply ashamed.

Conor stood. I fully expected him to walk away. I wouldn't have blamed him. And he did start walking. But towards me. I looked up at him, but he wasn't looking at me. His eyes were fixed on something behind me. I had to half-turn to remember what was there.

He didn't stop until their heads were just an inch apart. For a minute, there was nothing but silence.

'Oh, come on!' Conor burst out finally, irritation colouring his voice. 'Say something!'

Storn looked at me instead, his nervous face so comical, it almost made me laugh. There was no use pretending anymore. I gestured to him to introduce himself.

'Hiiii,' he ventured, testing how this simple word might affect the progress of any conversation. 'I apologise for not being entirely honest with you about what I was.'

'You understood every word that I said to you? And to Kristian?' Conor asked incredulously.

'I did. I speak in 752,392 languages,' he added, his tone changing from careful to delighted.

'I bet it was difficult not to say something back at times,' Conor suggested.

'It really was.' Storn nodded. 'Especially when you told Kristian that I was stubborn. A characteristic not so far from your personality, if I might say so.'

'You.' Conor pointed at Storn. 'You were pretending to be asleep!'

'I was on stand-by mode. A little similar to human sleeping,' Storn argued.

'But you still heard everything?'

'Of course.'

Conor shook his head and sighed. 'I always knew something was off with you.'

'How so?'

'You don't smell like a horse,' Conor pointed out. 'You don't smell like anything! You need to change that if you want to fit in. People are bound to notice. If we stay somewhere longer, somewhere where they know me, they will start asking questions.'

If we stay somewhere longer. That didn't sound as if he was planning on walking out on us.

Conor went to his own horse and brought his waterskin over to me. I thanked him and drank deeply, only now realising how thirsty I was.

'You could have conjured up some water for him after making him talk for so long.' He looked at Ithorion.

'Conjured up?' Ithorion asked, appalled. 'My dear son, I'm not a magician!'

'So the way you made me talk … that wasn't magic?' I wasn't sure anymore which option I would have preferred. 'But if it wasn't magic, how did you do it? And how did you just appear at our fire without us noticing?'

'I suppose we could call it magic,' Ithorion agreed. 'Or we could call them special skills I practised and developed for a very long time. Part of a skillset specifically needed for a particular occupation.'

'Which is what? Head of the Royal Inquisition?' Conor offered.

'Nothing so primitive!' Ithorion bristled. 'I was Chief Test Master in the Order of the Dragon.'

'What is a test master, and what is the Order of the Dragon?' I asked.

'The Order of the Dragon is a secret organisation that assists the Gods, and above all, their highest and most powerful, the Dragon.'

'What do you mean by "Gods"?' I asked. 'Surely not immortal supernatural beings?'

'Well, they're not exactly immortal. Their lifespan is similar to the duration of stars. But otherwise, yes. They are the most advanced lifeform in the universe. Their very being is way too complex for our brains to fully comprehend.'

'If they are so advanced, why do they need a whole organisation to serve them?' I asked sceptically. I wasn't going to start believing in Gods now, too. What would be next?

'Not to serve *them*.' Ithorion rolled his eyes at me. 'The universe.'

'The universe? An organisation to serve the universe?'

'Exactly.' Ithorion exhaled slowly. 'The world order always needs protecting.'

'From whom?'

'From those who prefer chaos. Tyrants who prefer destruction to progress. The greedy who would see whole star systems drained of life before their power dwindles. Wars. Catastrophes. Madness. Idiocy. There is a never-ending list of problems that threatens life as we know it.'

'So members of this order …'

'Fix things.'

'Hmmm.' Gods aside, it sounded interesting. I looked at Conor, wondering what he thought of all this. He poked the fire with a long stick, his expression unreadable.

'And how does someone become a member of this order?' I asked, curious.

'All things are connected,' Ithorion started to explain. 'But some things more so than others. Everything has a soul, and souls form soul lines. These are like bloodlines, if you like, except soul lines don't require physical connection. If you've ever met anyone with whom you soon had a special bond, who felt like a soul mate, or visited places where you felt instantly at home, those were likely souls which belonged in your soul line. The members of the Order—we call them champions—usually come from a few specific soul lines.'

The idea of soul lines was completely new to me. But it reminded me of something Laro had said. 'Are there soul circles, too? What are those?'

'Along the soul lines, there can be individual souls that are even more tightly connected. These we call soul circles. Members of soul circles quickly form very tight bonds once they meet. Tighter than friends. Tighter than family.

'Champions sometimes work for the order alone. Sometimes they form groups with those who belong in their soul circle. Soul circles usually have a leader, called tora. A tora would have a few skills that help them form these groups and keep them together. They draw the others to themselves. They inspire them. They can sense them when they are close by.'

I opened my mouth to say something, but nothing came out. Once again, I looked at Conor, who rolled his eyes at the idea. I had to admit, it was absurd. There was no way I could lead him anywhere, let alone inspire him! Or anyone. And what if I suddenly lost my mind, turned blood-thirsty again and killed them? No, no way.

'Why are you so doubtful?' Ithorion asked me, reading my thoughts. 'This condition you described has arisen in you twice. Once in the forest hut and once when you fought with Laro. There was one crucial difference between how you behaved following the first signs. You say it.' He looked at me pointedly.

'First, I fought it, and then I embraced it,' I admitted.

'Exactly. You, Kristian, can control it. Indeed, you have to. It is and will always be your choice and your choice alone. Don't use it. It might make things seem easier in the short run, but as is the way with such things, later there's always a price to pay. As for Conor.' He shifted and looked him up and down. 'I admit that he might be hard work at times. But he's already following your lead.'

'We're following a clue,' Conor stated matter-of-factly. 'Besides, I serve only one person, and that's myself. Kristian can join your order if he wants to.' He looked at me. 'But the Gods can forget about me!'

'And what is a test master?' Storn asked the question I had quite forgot about, with a seemingly keen interest in the topic.

'Individuals who we know will potentially join the Order are repeatedly tested from an early age. They can only join if they pass them all.'

'Is this in some special school?' I asked.

'No. The Order doesn't have schools. Our classroom is the whole wide universe. The tests come in many forms and sizes, and they always remain concealed. The Order wants to see how potential candidates react to problems and how they solve them. They might lose something. Or someone. They might become seriously ill. They might meet someone who needs their help with something. A test master might appear only for a moment in their life, or they might become a challenging person, a neighbour, a boss, a new friend or lover, testing them for months or, in special cases, for years.'

'Does that mean we have been tested, too?' asked Conor, clearly taken aback.

'I wouldn't know. I retired decades ago,' Ithorion said. 'But it's likely.'

'But if you're retired, why are you here?' I asked, trying to make sense of it all. Or at least the parts that I could get my head around. 'And why are you telling us all this if it's a secret organisation?'

'Your uncle sent me to check on you,' Ithorion responded.

'My uncle?' The word was still strange on my tongue. 'Where is he? Is he well?'

'I don't exactly know where he is at the moment. But if anyone can look after themselves, then it's James Montgomery,' he added, seeing my expression.

'He's just a university professor.' I frowned at Ithirion, displeased by his dismissal. 'Anything could happen to him! Laro might want to kill him, too, if he found out that—'

'Your uncle isn't just a university professor, Kristian,' Ithorion cut me short.

'Professor James Montgomery was one of the highest-ranking officers in The Order of the Dragon for most of his life,' Storn supplied.

'What? And you knew of this?' I asked Storn, taken aback.

'Yes. He shared a lot of information about himself as part of my main programming.'

'Why didn't you tell me any of this before?'

'You never asked.'

'He never said anything to me about these things,' I grumbled, feeling slighted. James Montgomery working for Gods? Gods that exist? I still couldn't believe it. Maybe this was all just a strange dream. 'Did you also know that he was my uncle?' I asked Storn.

'Well, no, but I could see that the two of you were closely related.'

'And you never thought to ask about that or mention it?'

'It's a very personal question.' Storn tilted his head. 'Human reproduction is a subject I generally avoid in conversation if I can.'

'Great,' I said, burying my forehead in my hands as I tried to think. Had it been just this one man claiming the whole thing, I could have entertained the thought that he made it all up. But since Storn knew about it, too, it had to be true. Why else and how else would James have added it to Storn's memory such a long time ago? 'What am I to do now?'

'What are you talking about?' Conor asked hurriedly. 'We know what we're doing! This—' He gestured around us. '—changes nothing. We have the medallion that will help us locate the Supreme Key. We just need to get to Borond. Which we'll reach tomorrow.'

'And once we have this Key?'

'Once we have the Key, the Key will help us locate Laro.'

'Laro, who stole that ancient crown and will only give it back to us in return for the Key.'

'Exactly! We have eleven days to return the crown to the duke and get Olivia out of prison.'

'He'll also put the highest price on your head this country has ever seen,' Storn added helpfully.

'Nice.' Conor flashed him a sarcastic smile. 'Now that we're all once again up to speed on this, may I suggest that we try to get some sleep? Tomorrow is another long ride if we want to reach the ruins by sunrise.'

Ithorion put his pipe away and stood up. Was he just going to leave now? I wanted to hear more about this order and my uncle. 'If you're going to Borond, you might need these.' He opened his long bag and pulled out two swords in elegant leather scabbards.

'Thank you!' I stood, taking them from him. 'Do you know the place?'

'You could say that.' He sighed. 'Anyhow. Good luck!' He put his hands into his pockets and walked away from us.

'Do you have any advice?' I called after him.

'Try staying alive!' he shouted back without turning.

I looked at the swords and unsheathed one of them. The blade didn't seem like steel. Thin blue lines ran across the length of it like veins. They also felt surprisingly light.

'Is this why your uncle sent him? To give us these swords?' Conor wondered.

'Perhaps,' I mused. The James I knew would want to make sure I had with me what I needed. But then again, when the James I knew told me to get out more, I doubted that galloping off to a cursed place, allegedly filled with dark magic and monsters, to find an almighty key was quite what he had in mind. Or was it?

The next day we came to a halt at the sight that greeted us from the ridge. Lake Borond yawned between imposing hills. In the west, the sky still ached with echoes of the departed sun, an amber glow that lingered on the water, shading from distant gold to red around the dark ruins of the castle on the eastern shore. The shadowed remains of Castle Borond stood bitter and resentful, like the corpse of a once-merciless beast, broken by war, humbled by time, yet still seething, seeking revenge.

I threw my coat over my shoulders as the wind picked up, herding dark clouds together from the north, promising a storm in the wet hiss that already smelled of rain. The scattered walls looked to offer no protection against the weather. Or anything else that might find us down there to-night.

Conor seemed impervious to my concerns. His eyes twinkled with thrilled determination. His horse, Athos, tried to huddle against Storn, searching for shelter. Storn resolutely stared ahead, eyes wide and thoughtful. Above the ruins, a flock of crows circled, their screeches clawing into my already painfully throbbing mind.

'Doesn't it scare you?' I asked.

'What? This place?' Conor dismissed the thought with a wave of his hand. 'I've been to plenty of places like this.'

'I'm not talking about the ruins,' I said. 'I'm talking about me.'

'You?' He looked at me. 'Do you mean your violent tendencies?' He gave me a grin as if he found it difficult to think me dangerous.

'Yes.' There was something already stirring in me at the sight of the ruined castle. The way the setting sun painted the water around it red. The shadows that stretched behind the ancient walls.

'You can control it.' Conor shrugged. 'You said so yourself. The old man said it, too.'

'What if some places or circumstances make it worse?' I asked.

'You worry too much.' Conor patted my back. 'Let's go before it gets pitch dark. We don't have much time.'

We rode down a path that seemed scarcely used. The rain started spitting on us as we reached the outer wall, from where several crows watched us enter through what once must have been the main gate. The erstwhile fortress seemed completely deserted. Moss and ivy tried to cover it up under half-hearted greenery. The abandoned buildings were rotting and falling apart. With the sunlight gradually disappearing, the temperature dropped, and soon, I could see my breath smoking away from me in the damp air. There was something haunting, something twisted about the place, yet I kind of liked it. It called to me in ways I couldn't explain. Even my headache seemed to disappear, the pain numbed by the frosty air.

Suddenly, Conor's horse stumbled and screamed. We both dismounted, and I picked up the nasty, broken blade that previously stood buried in the undergrowth. Conor looked at the injured leg and quietly swore under his breath.

'Can I help?' I offered, standing behind him, trying to see how bad the cut was.

'I got this, thanks,' Conor said, and as he rummaged in his saddle bag, 'Just go and start looking around while I bandage him up. I'll join you soon.'

I nodded, thinking that the horse would almost certainly need some antibiotics, but that was something we could perhaps administer later. If I was honest, I was glad to leave them and be off to discover the place. It wasn't so much the key we were after—not that I even knew what exactly to look for. It was something else. Something that made me fidgety. Impatient.

'Stay here,' I said to Storn, and I left them there.

Dry leaves crunched under my feet as I walked up a series of stone steps littered with dead flora. They led to a building which once might have been a church. I placed my fingers on its grey, crumbling wall. It felt cold and wet to my touch. I absentmindedly stroked the old stones and looked down as something ruffled the leaves at my feet.

Behind me a second shadow stretched to my right, the realisation giving me a split second to turn before somebody threw themself at me with a loud cry. My upper back hit the wall, but I lost my balance under the sudden weight of my attacker. My legs gave way, and I fell, hitting my head on something in the process. I struggled to push the man away from me as blood seeped into my mouth. I must have bitten my tongue when I smashed my head.

The man on top of me was a big, burly guy, his face covered by a muddy beard, smelling of worse. His eyes were full of madness. That, more than anything, made me aware of the change that started taking place in me. A velvety, sweet sensation, promising strength in place of tiredness, pleasure to wash away my pains. It filled me with a powerful desire to hurt the man. To cut his eyes out. His tongue. To burn him alive. I struggled to remember how to stop it while trying to keep the madman's hands from choking me. What did James say again? Concentrate on the part that was me. Find a space around the sensation. Find myself.

The man's hands tightened around my throat, making me waver in trying to control the dark menace inside me. What if I just used it a little? Could I come back to myself afterwards? Or was there a point of no return? Did it really matter if I died otherwise? But what if I lost my mind and hurt Conor afterwards? My body longed for the relief which filled my limbs with that intense energy. Anything to be able to push this man off me and get air into my lungs again. Maybe if I just let it flow through me very briefly, then fought to stop it …

Something crashed against the man's head from behind, and he collapsed on top of me. Conor helped to roll him off.

'Are you alright?' he asked me.

'I think so,' I croaked, massaging my neck.

Conor turned to look at the man.

'Is he dead?' I asked.

'I didn't think he would be … he might be.' Conor said, checking him over. 'It's probably better this way. Come on. We'll give him a burial once we've found the Key. There's no time to waste!'

He pulled me up, and after a last look at my attacker, we started off towards the next part of the building. A terrible, ear-shattering sound behind us made me stop in my tracks. Someone screamed, howling in pain, the sound turning into a low, deep growl as I turned.

The supposedly dead body of the man stood where we had left him, his head flopped to one side. In its place, there was a new one that looked like a bad animal experiment gone horribly wrong. From its side, four more arms sprouted, all absurdly thin and long, the skin on them very red and glistening with something wet. I unsheathed my new sword without taking my eyes off the creature, which in turn gave out another loud shriek and started running towards us. On my left, Conor held out his watch in front of us and flipped its cover open. The man collapsed mid-run, one of his new limbs hitting my right boot as he fell and slid.

Part of me was trying to work out what the hell just happened, while another seethed against Conor stopping the upcoming fight. I wanted to yell at him in anger. I wanted to hit him in the face. *Concentrate on who you are! Find the space around the darkness. Find the space around your rage.*

'Don't just stand there doing breathing exercises!' Conor scolded me. 'We have five minutes to chop up the body before the watch stops blocking the magic.'

I let out my frustration on the twisted corpse, our blue-veined swords working with an efficiency that went beyond my expectations. We dug out a reasonable hole in the wet earth with broken roof tiles found in a nearby heap, and buried the corrupted parts. By the time we finished it, the storm was upon us. Lightning flashed nearby as thunder gave voice to the tension around us. I felt it spoke for me, too.

Conor walked ahead to examine something around a window, and I turned away from him. From the corner of my eye, I noticed something glinting on a nearby wall. It was a large bug with a golden back, emitting a faint light. Now that I looked around more carefully, I discovered two more where the wind cleared the ground. And another further up. They were all headed in the same direction. I decided to find out where they were going.

I walked around the church and discovered a cemetery on the other side. The bugs seemed to be congregating on the graves, especially around one in the far back under a big oak tree. I had a feeling I knew what was there. I didn't know how. I just did. I walked along the rows, pausing here or there to read the headstones or to admire some of the broken stone sculptures. But deep down, I knew I was delaying the inevitable.

I tried to ignore how I felt. It came at me in waves, each stronger than the one before. Making me feel strong and certain. That I could do anything. That I should be afraid of nothing. Least of all, death.

By the time I reached the grave in the last row, the rain had started falling like it meant it. Lightning flickered through the dark sky, and the thunder in response was so loud it sounded as if the heavens threatened to collapse on the place, too.

Conor appeared next to me, shouting his questions through the storm. 'Have you found anything?'

I nodded towards the gravestone, illuminated by the phosphorescence of the strange bugs. Conor frowned and moved to clear away the ivy that partly covered it. I didn't think it was necessary. I could clearly tell what name was carved into it without his assistance, but his concern made me smile. He stared at it for a minute, shocked, then looked back at me.

'Are you alright?' he asked, for once clearly concerned.

'I'm absolutely fine. Don't worry,' I reassured him and put an arm around his shoulder. 'I've never felt better.'

The gravestone stood clear and proud now. Like the name inscribed on it. It was my name.

Chapter 15

Conor

Borond, Drelos,
23ʳᵈ The Month of Promise 1575

Are you alright?' I asked him. He didn't look alright to me. There was a dangerous look to him that made me take a step back.

'I'm absolutely fine.' He gave me a frosty smile the king's executioner would have been proud of. 'Don't worry,' he said and put an arm around my shoulder. 'I've never felt better.'

The hair on the back of my neck prickled as we turned back towards the grave. I stared at it, still not getting it. Just how the hell was there a grave here with "Kristian del Rosso" written on it? I briefly wondered if it was seeing that that made him crack. Somehow, I doubted it.

I took the watch out of my coat and snapped it open. It flashed up as I did so, and I looked back at Kristian, eager to see if it helped.

In response, he narrowed his eyes at me in a way that suggested it definitely hadn't. His grip tightened on my shoulder with a strength I hadn't realised he had. Then came that cold, sinister smile again. Slow and mesmerising. Like a snake creeping up on you in the dark.

'Shit,' I muttered and turned my head away, staring blankly ahead, wondering what to do. 'Wait!' My eyes caught on the gravestone.

'What is it?' He followed my gaze.

'The gravestone.' I nodded. It looked darker now and a little shapeless. But most importantly, the writing on it was gone. I closed the watch. The gravestone changed back to how we'd seen it before.

'What the …?' Kristian walked towards the stone, seemingly gripped by curiosity. For a moment, he was back as he'd been at our first meeting. Someone who wanted to understand everything. Sparked to life when faced with a puzzle. It was like a challenge he couldn't resist.

He reached out to touch the gravestone carefully, as if it might jump if startled. As his fingertips connected with the engraving, a tremor ran through the ground. For a moment, a silence fell, heavy with foreboding. The next moment, the grave shook, and amid complaints of hidden chains and the rattle of invisible cogwheels, it slowly sank into a void below. A staircase revealed itself, leading down into a pool of darkness. Around us, the strange bugs opened their wings and flew through the opening, descending with a golden light like shooting stars on the night of the Silent Prophet.

'Wait, it could be a trap!' I called, but Kristian ignored my warning and walked into his grave without the slightest hesitation. Above us, another clap of thunder split the clouds and let torrential rain give me a good washing. I swore and started off after him.

The straight descent soon became a spiral stairwell, leading us deeper and deeper, round and round. I counted 277 steps before reaching the bottom, where a level tunnel led away into darkness. The walls were wet and mossy, poorly lit by the golden light of the bugs pulsing ahead of us. There was an old torch fixed to the wall near the bottom of the stairs, at first glance, it seemed held there only by thick strands of spider web. After treating it with a little lamp oil, I lit it with a flint and steel I'd snatched from Castle Beren.

Oh, Castle Beren. With all its comforts and its sweet lady. Typical that I was in a bitterly cold, wet underground tunnel instead, with at least one wild creature who looked like he might decide to kill me at any moment. A heartbeat later, I reminded myself why I was there in the first place and hurried after him.

Our footsteps echoed in the tunnel, but they weren't the only sounds. Water dripped at places into pools. A small rock fell in the distance ahead, rolling across the hard ground. A heavy door creaked nearby. The scurrying of quick, light feet echoed occasionally from side tunnels, which we noted but didn't stop to investigate.

I tried to catch sideways glimpses of Kristian without being obvious. He still had that creepy smile on. A dark determination glinted in his eyes, his expression edged with an arrogant self-confidence I hadn't seen on him before. I would have thought it a mask had he not worn it so naturally. He looked like a stronger, taller and bolder version of himself in the torchlight. Just not one I recognised. The way he stared at me at times made me wonder whether he had trouble recognising me, too.

The main tunnel turned left after a while, and we found ourselves at a large wooden door. A scratching noise came from its other side. I looked at Kristian, who nodded, and we both unsheathed our swords. The blue lines on the blades now emitted a soft light. I sighed and rolled my eyes. So much for using this sword if I ever wanted to surprise anyone in the dark.

Kristian put his hand on the ancient iron door handle and carefully pressed it down. The scratching noise stopped. The door didn't open. I handed him my sword and the torch, and crouched to examine the lock. It was a simple enough design, one that I had dealt with on countless occasions. It took me less than a minute to unlock it. I took my sword and torch back from him with a smug smile and nodded for him to open the door.

He pressed the handle again, pushed the door, pulled it, but apart from the scratching noise re-starting, this time louder and with more urgency, nothing else happened. He raised an eyebrow at me in a way that made me shove the sword and torch back at him and look at the lock again. It appeared unlocked, and I couldn't see anything that might be blocking the door, at least not from our side.

I sighed, pulled my watch out again and opened it. The watch flashed up and the scratching noise stopped. I pushed down the door handle, and with a loud creak, the door opened.

'And this is how you deal with long-dead, dark witchlords like Toleron and their lingering spells,' I supplied as I spread my arms and victoriously walked into the hall, turning back towards Kristian mid-step for effect.

There are those moments in life when death, swift like a viper, closes its fingers around you. Much later, when telling my stories to the folks in the inn, of course, I much prefer implying that it was my quick reflexes that saved me on these occasions. My training. It's good for business. But the truth is, I couldn't tell you if it was the sudden breeze or a sixth sense that made me look left and jump. Or simply luck.

A large iron ball hanging from a chain whooshed past me, one of the sharp blades sticking out of its middle narrowly missing my chest. The next moment I landed on my back with all the air escaping my lungs, just in time to glimpse the glimmer of torchlight on a falling cleaver aimed straight at my head. I rolled to my right. The first cleaver only just struck the ground when a second, and a third, and a fourth chased me across the rough stone floor, impacting with a series of clanks. I rolled out of the way

of the last one and sighed with relief. And that was when the ground underneath me collapsed into a pit. I found myself barely hanging on to the
edge of the cavity, dangling above a multitude of snakes, sounding rather
unhappy to be woken. I could barely make out the squirming heap of reptiles in the dark; trying to see where my watch had fallen was pointless.
Not that I didn't try.

All the angry hissing under me almost made me miss the sound of approaching footsteps, unhurried and even. Kristian stopped near the edge
of the hole and looked down at me.

'Help!' I called out to him, a sudden cold sensation running through
my spine. He stood there, eyes hard and calculating, filled with a malicious
intent that shocked me to my core. 'What's wrong with you?' I yelled at
him, more out of desperation than because I thought he would actually
tell me. In any case, I thought I had a pretty good idea.

I tried to find a ledge with my feet, or anything that I could step up on,
but the wall of the cavity was flat and slimy. All that my wriggling earned
me was that my grip on the edge loosened, my fingertips desperately trying
to dig into the hard-stone floor to keep me sliding further in. The hissing
under me intensified at the excitement of the approaching feast.

I looked back at Kristian. He didn't move. But either I imagined it
because I wished it to be true, or his expression softened a little. He looked
down past me into the pit with an idle curiosity, as if my current situation
was merely one of the experiments for his precious university studies.

'Kristian.' I tried to speak calmly, as if we were having a normal every-
day conversation. His eyes found mine and once again hardened, but I
didn't flinch this time. Whatever this madness was, the guy who I had
travelled with, who had saved my life only recently, was underneath it.
My… friend? Was he? Friend? Fuck friend! Didn't Ithorion say I was in
his soul circle or whatever? What happened to special bonds? To being
closer than friends, closer than family? I bit my lip, half in anger, half in
frustration. 'Kristian!' My fingers slipped some more, but I still didn't look
away. 'Kristian, for heaven's sake!' I shouted at him, before lowering my
voice again, remembering what he told us last night. What his uncle had
said to him a long time ago. "Kris, please! It is not you! Find yourself in
the space around it. Concentrate on who you are!'

He blinked. Then again. The next moment the sinister expression was gone. He put the swords and torch down, lowered himself next to the edge and gripped my arms.

Within a minute, I was out of the pit, still panting from the effort, torn between wanting to hug the guy and hit him. In the end, I jumped on him, threw one arm around him and pounded his head with the other. In his surprise, he laughed, and I laughed with him at the relief, at the craziness of it all. At the joy of being alive instead of being eaten alive.

'Lucky I remembered those words!' I told him.

'It wasn't the words,' he said.

'What? Sure it was. I saw it on your face.'

He shook his head dismissively.

'What was it then?'

'I don't want to talk about it,' he said, sounding upset. Then his voice softened again as he added, 'Maybe ask me again later. It isn't fully over just yet.'

I shrugged and looked around. There had to be something I could use to eliminate all those snakes and get my watch back. I lifted the torch, grabbed my sword and carefully walked towards the wall, along which a series of long boxes were lined up. As I neared them, Kristian caught up with me and made me stop.

'I think those are coffins,' he said.

I had suspected as much. 'Don't worry,' I said. 'Coffins are my speciality.'

I walked to the one that was the most richly decorated. It was positioned higher than all the rest, with a few stone steps leading up to a base. It was a painted, cast-iron coffin with three clasps on the side, which was a little unusual. I put the sword down and opened the clasps, one after the other. The third one was followed by a noise, like a panel shifting from its place somewhere. I waited a little, then slowly opened the lid. Rather unsurprisingly, a skeleton lay in the coffin. Rather surprisingly, though, its bones looked like polished marble and glowed with a pale light. There were two light blue topazes where its eyes should be. There was also a sword next to the bones, which by contrast, seemed rather boring and unremarkable.

I was just about to reach for the gemstones when something at the feet of the skeleton caught my eye. There was a painting on the inside of the coffin. I shifted position and leaned closer to examine it, lifting the torch higher to see it better. The skeleton's toes twitched, as if a slight ripple had run across the bones. I turned my head to see if there was something causing the movement or if it was just my eyes deceiving me in the torchlight. To my horror, I found the skeleton sitting with a straight spine, its topaz eyes moving in their sockets as they examined me.

It reached out and grabbed the torch from my hand. That finally spurred me into motion as I jumped and almost lost my balance on the steps. The skeleton lifted the torch, as if saluting us, and then pushed it against a small nook in the wall. The nook, which turned out to be a stone basin, lit up, and from it, the fire spread across the walls along gutters filled with a strange-smelling oil. The old door through which we had entered the chamber slammed shut with a mighty thunder. For a moment, the silence was absolute. Then dozens of coffins opened with one creak all around the walls of the vast hall, and shining skeletons started climbing out of them.

I turned towards Kristian, who, to my utter dismay, looked to have changed back into his dark maniac self again. I took a step back, uncertain upon seeing his wicked smile, but when his eyes found me, he simply nodded. 'I've got this,' he said. 'I need this!' He raised his sword, turned, and with a roar that sounded strange from his lips, he ran towards the emerging army. The skeletons crowded around him, completely ignoring me.

Kristian fought the armed skeletons with a speed and skill that left me staring speechlessly—and that's saying something coming from a guy raised among martial monks. He didn't look like he needed much help, either, which was just as well. I stood there frozen in awe, watching the performance as if it had been the best show I'd seen in my life. In fact, I was so distracted that for a long minute, I didn't notice that I wasn't the only fan staring. Next to me, sword in one hand, the torch still in the other, stood the skeleton I'd woken. I hit its skull hard with the back of my elbow, leaped for my sword and turned to send it back to sleep.

I had only fought such creatures once before, but ever since, I'd wondered what kept the bones together when dark magic rose them from their graves. At the time, I used a war hammer and cared little about where it hit them. Now, though, just where was I supposed to aim with a sword? For some time, I didn't much need to concern myself with the question as the skeleton turned out to be a rather accomplished swordsman and parrying his strikes took most of my attention. Then, when the opportunity finally presented itself, I took aim at his neck. The blue veins of the sword flared as the blade slid between the small bones of the creature, separating its skull, which fell. The rest followed a heartbeat later. I bid farewell to my opponent, triumphantly getting the torch back and raising it high with a victory cry. Sadly, my theatrics drew the attention of some of its friends and soon, I found myself back to back with Kristian, at the heart of the battle.

By the time the last of the skeletons fell, I felt so exhausted I briefly considered sitting down among them. Kristian, behind me, fell to his knees, his hands around his head as if trying to keep it together. He let out a pained cry and collapsed.

'Kris!' I rushed to him and tried to lift him into a sitting position. 'Don't you die on me now! You hear me?' I yelled at him. That didn't seem to bother him. I frantically tried to find his pulse, his skin icy cold under my touch. But he was still alive. I slapped his face a few times. 'Wake up! Wake up!' He slowly opened his eyes, looking weak and tired. 'Here, take a few sips of this.' I pushed my old metal flask to his mouth. He drank briefly before a violent cough stopped him.

'What the hell is that?' he asked when he finally could.

'It's a powerful herb spirit that I only use when everything else fails. It's very good at restarting your system. I know it burns like fire, but trust me, your colour is already much better.'

I changed the flask in his hand for the waterskin. 'Take your time,' I said to him as I stood and looked around, feasting my eyes on all the gemstones that would find their way into my pockets.

'We need to find a way out of here,' Kris said as he pushed himself up from the floor.

'I just need to get my watch back first,' I told him. 'Then I can open the door again.'

I casually picked up a topaz from the floor and raised it to my eye. The pale blue gemstone was beautiful. It was so clear that I found I could see right through it. And when I did, the world around me seemed a different place.

'Hey, pick one up and try this!' I cut across whatever Kris was about to say and motioned him to follow my example.

'There are markings on the walls,' he said as he looked around.

'I know. Any idea what they might mean?'

'There's some on your hand, too.'

'What?' I turned my hand to look at it. There were black markings on it, like a drawing with coal.

'And some on mine.'

'Yours looks like a part of a lizard.' It actually didn't look bad and was somehow familiar.

'It connects to yours.' He moved his hand next to mine.

'It looks like the dragon from the medallion. Except that part of it is missing.'

'The wings.'

'Right,' I said. 'That still doesn't explain the markings on the wall.'

'No, it doesn't.' He lowered his hand and turned to examine the wall. 'Most of the symbols repeat themselves. There's only one half-circle. But there are many triangles, suns, moons and stars. Lots of snakes.' He turned to give me a look, then carried on. 'There are only two hand symbols, though.'

'Are you thinking what I'm thinking?'

He shrugged. 'We can try.'

'Seems a bit easy,' I said but plastered my palm against the symbol anyway, just as Kris did the same a few steps away from me.

The sound of gushing water echoed around the chamber, loud and coming from multiple locations. I swore and rushed back towards the pit, hastily picking up a few more gemstones on the way. I knew it was too easy. The pit was filling up with water and fast, giving me even less of a chance to find my watch, which would most likely stay at the bottom while the snakes would swim up. Water poured out of newly revealed holes in the walls as I hurried to the door and tried to open it. It stubbornly refused my efforts. I pushed, I pulled, I yanked, I banged. I even scratched it a few times, just in case. Nothing. The water kept on surging into the hall.

Kristian stood where I'd left him, with his back to me, still looking at the symbols and trying to figure out their meanings. Suddenly remembering the cleavers that tried to end my life earlier, I hurried to pick one up and fell on the door as if it were a living enemy. But whatever magic shrouded it, it repulsed my efforts and showed no sign of damage.

'Conor!' Kris shouted over the noise I was making. 'Come here!'

I reluctantly left the door and ran back to his side, sloshing through the water as I approached.

'What is it? Have you found something?'

'Look at just the star symbols. Disregard everything else. What do you see?'

'Um … star symbols?'

'It looks like a constellation I saw in the sky as we travelled. What is it called?'

I raised the topaz back to my eye and looked again. He was right. 'It's called the Reaper.'

'Nice.' He grimaced. 'If that rotated half-circle is supposed to mean a gate, the scythe goes right through it.'

'There was that painting in the coffin I opened,' I remembered suddenly. 'I think they might be connected.'

'We should probably have another look.'

The water was now knee-high and rising fast. Snakes slithered around the base of the coffin. Some were headed our way.

The torch and the sword helped with approaching the coffin, but with the water level rising, I knew they wouldn't be much use for long.

I hurried up the steps and jumped into the empty coffin. As if that had been a signal, the snakes across the hall raised their heads as one and started swimming towards me.

'Kris, here! Run!'

He sprinted up the steps and jumped in next to me. I threw the torch into the water, aiming at the nearest snake, then pushed him down and closed the lid on us.

At first, it was just strange and dark. I could hear angry hisses coming from outside, water sloshing against the steps and Kris's breathing next to mine.

'What now?' he asked.

'I have an idea. If this works, we'll be out of here soon,' I told him.

If this worked, it would also be the weirdest and creepiest shit I'd ever done, and I had a rather admirable collection of those already. I didn't tell him that, though. In truth, I couldn't help but wonder if this whole episode was one of those tests Ithorion talked about. His old friends messing with us. If so, this was a touch too crazy.

The painting I saw earlier on the inside of the coffin depicted Darq, the black angel. According to myth, the creature had the power to transport souls between bodies. Whether the destination had to be still alive or not was, to my knowledge, never specified. I still remembered hearing that noise when I opened the clasps on the side of the coffin. Like a panel moving aside. I just had to lock them again somehow, and hopefully, an exit would reveal itself.

'*Reme et reon se beron. Wero et beron se reon,*' the inscription read around the painting of Darq in the old tongue. 'Reach for the blessing, and you shall receive the curse. Cast aside the curse, and you shall receive the blessing.'

I guess the main point was not to have my soul transferred into Kris's body. That wouldn't be much help right now. Could that be avoided if he joined me?

'So, what's the plan, exactly?' he asked. 'Can I help?'

I briefly thought about how to explain it and decided against it. If I was wrong, I would sound very stupid, and then we'd die. This way, we just died. Besides, we had no time to argue.

'Just give me your hand for a moment. We need to lock those three clasps I opened earlier.'

I placed my palm against his, our fingers pointing towards our heads, my thumb reaching around his hand to keep them together, while he quietly contemplated what I'd just said.

'Those clasps? But aren't those ...?'

I took a deep breath, and before I had time to change my mind or Kris could finish his inquiry, I pushed our hands out above our heads, where I remembered the painting to be. For a moment, nothing happened. Then my fingertips went numb, as if I had put them on ice. The feeling was painful and very unsettling, so much so that I would have snatched my hand back straight away had I been able to. The freezing numbness progressed across my arm with alarming speed and poured into my torso. Whatever poison the painting contained, it worked fast. I squeezed my eyes shut in a vague attempt at defence against what was coming. A moment later, all my feeling was snuffed out.

There was quiet. There was peace. There was an ungodly heaviness on me, like the mother of all hangovers from hell. I awkwardly pushed myself up, swaying as I stood. I reached out with my hands to steady myself and slowly opened my eyes. I would have thrown up, had I still had a stomach. The bones of my arms and hands glistened with a pale light, naked in the water. Something tugged at my leg, and I looked down to see a snake coiling around it. On my left stood another skeleton, staring at me.

I pointed towards the coffin and shuffled towards it as more and more snakes wrapped themselves around the skeleton that was now the new me. I tried to fend them off, but my movements were slow and drunken in the water, and I didn't think even a sword or one of those cleavers would have improved my chances much. In any case, I didn't need much time. Not if it was all as I had guessed and all I had to do was lock the three clasps on the side of the coffin. And if I was wrong … then it was too late for us anyway.

I managed to locate the clasps before a snake coiled itself around my skull and covered my gemstone eyes. I blindly reached out, another of the reptiles pulling my arm down, and with great difficulty, I managed to lock the first clasp. My arm was harder and harder to keep upright under the increasing weight, my hand shaking with the effort that made my job even more challenging. But finally, the second clasp was in place, too.

Then there was a terrible cracking noise. My upper body remained floating, one hand holding on to the second clasp, while the rest of me was pulled away, broken off from my spine. I let my right hand drop, heavy under the weight of the reptiles, the momentum turning me around in the water as I blindly struck out with my left hand—and missed my target! I could feel the snake on my skull move lower, wrapping its body around my neck bones and squeezing them harder and harder. The next moment there was another crack.

I opened my eyes to pitch darkness, gasped and threw myself upright into a sitting position. The now locked lid of the coffin reminded me why this wasn't such a good idea. I fell back, rubbing my forehead with my hand, the hair on my head reassuringly normal, reassuringly me. Kris next to me was also moving, careful not to follow my example.

'You locked the third clasp?' I asked, hoping for a yes.

'I did,' he said slowly. 'A moment before I died as a skeleton which I died into a few minutes ago?' He sounded like he was asking me.

'Didn't you say you wanted to examine and test magic for yourself?' I tutted. 'That extraordinary claims required extraordinary evidence?'

'I think some sort of hatch opened through the base,' he said coldly by way of a response, ignoring my point.

I felt around. It was just big enough for us to squeeze through, and some sort of ladder led down underneath it. 'So it worked. I'm a genius!' I informed him and slipped down through the hatch.

Chapter 16

Selena

London, Earth, 28ᵗʰ May 2037

T he first rule of waiting for a guy to call is not to expect it. Because to have your heart jump every time your phone rings, to stub your toes on the bed as you rush towards your various devices, or to drown your disappointment at the end of each day in wine is really not that all good for you. But surely, everyone knows this. In theory.

'Selena here … oh, hi, Jake!' I said to my phone while lying on the bed, using the most nonchalant voice I could produce. I grimaced into the camera, cleared my throat, and in a slightly lower tone, I started again. 'Hallo? Who? Oh, Jake, right, sorry! Of course!'

I frowned at my own reflection, reached for the hairbrush on the side table and combed a rebellious lock back into place. 'Yes, it's Selena …' I singsonged, even as I put the brush back and reached for the wineglass.

The phone in my hand burst into a shrill ringtone, and I dropped it, knocking over the glass in the process.

'Selena, it's me.' Rhia's voice blasted over the device even as I tried to reach after it, fishing blindly in the small crevice between the bed and the wall with one hand, doing my best to clean up the mess with the other. 'Shit,' I muttered, stretching my arm until it hurt, wondering if I should move the bed, just as the doorbell rang. I rolled my eyes, but in that moment, my fingers finally connected with the thing, and I yanked it out with a triumphant smile. 'Hi!'

'What are you doing?' Rhia's face was full of excitement. 'Go to the door. I've got you something!'

I signed for the package, transferring the call to the house screen system on the way to the front door, and finally flung myself down onto the sofa in the living room.

'What are you waiting for? Open it!' Rhia beamed at me from the large screen as if she were getting a present and not me.

'What is it?' I lifted the delicate fabric out of the box. 'A costume?'

'Mother is away in the States, so I decided to have a little fancy-dress party in our Hampstead mansion on Saturday!' Rhia grinned mischievously. 'So, what do you think? Do you like it?'

'Do I like it? Rhia, it's beautiful!'

It was a stunning red dress with a phoenix under its low-cut back and long-flared sleeves resembling wings. It came with a half-face mask, featuring flames and additional feathers attached to its side. A long, thin coat completed the look.

'This must have cost a fortune.' Just the phoenix on the back was a work of art. A combination of silk and cotton transformed exquisitely with sparkling crystals and beads. 'Let me pay you back.'

'Don't worry about it!' Rhia waved the idea away. 'Just relax. We all deserve a little fun. And you might meet someone—I invited a lot of people!'

Rhia's mother was a very successful actress, and currently on her second energy tycoon husband, so I knew I shouldn't really feel bad, but I still did. Despite my rushed words, I probably couldn't have afforded a costume like this. Still, when I tried it on a little later, it fitted me so perfectly I could have cried.

As I stood in front of the mirror, a longing crept into my heart. A longing to find that Mr Someone Better. For him to see me in this dress and appreciate me. To wrap me in his arms and kiss me. Keiko and Rhia had been in relationships like that for years. Why was it taking me forever to meet the right guy? I always thought love like that would just find me. But maybe they were right, and I needed to do more than just sit around and wait.

The next day I was back to being disappointed and let down, now by Dr James Montgomery. Unexpected personal business or something along those lines had him urgently called away, and I had to do my session with yet another replacement, which by comparison, felt like a waste of time. But at least I enjoyed Dr Montgomery's book, which was a rare accomplishment. I wasn't a big reader. Never really understood what Keiko saw in books. I got bored of them after a few pages. Gosh, sometimes even after a few lines! But there was something about this one. A simple need to keep returning to it. Like coming home in the evening.

By Friday, I had given up on Jake, too. He had no interest in me. How silly I was. Playing around with that stupid ancient thing and making myself believe that there might be a date and what exactly? True love? True love only existed in fairy tales and other people's lives. I was cursed to only ever attract egocentrics, bad guys or a combination of the two. I was much better off concentrating on my work and getting that long overdue promotion. Maybe I could even look around for a new job. Or pick up a new hobby—learn something new!

The phone rang, and I stared at it. It was Jake. *Get a grip, girl. What if it's just another contract?* I told myself and greeted him coolly. He was all charm and sweet talk. He said he'd very much like to see me again! He asked if I fancied meeting him tomorrow afternoon in the teahouse for a little treat.

'It's not about that contract again, is it?' I laughed nervously.

'What contract?' He sounded genuinely puzzled.

'Ha-ha, yes, let's not worry about it!' I agreed, relieved. 'There's just this fancy-dress party Rhia organised for tomorrow ...'

'So, why don't we meet in the teahouse and then go to the party afterwards?' he asked causally, as if nothing was more obvious.

'Yes, sure,' I replied, astonished. Jake Black was taking me out for a date and then coming to a party with me! Was this real? It seemed like I had completely misjudged him. Maybe I was just really bad at reading men. Maybe I just needed some kind of user manual.

'Great,' he enthused and told me he couldn't wait to see me.

So, here I was, sitting in a cab, my heart in my throat. Remembering our lunch from a week ago, I'd decided to bring the redeemer with me. When I'd talked about it to him, he'd said, 'Bring it in sometime and we can have a look.'

Looking at it with him at work wasn't really what I'd had in mind. But if nothing else, I thought the teahouse might be a better place for it. I looked at the large jute bag on the seat next to me. But on second thought, did I really want to carry it in and then out? I wanted him to see me in this outfit, looking exquisite. With that large jute bag, I looked like I was headed out to the market to do a week's shopping. No. Just no!

When the cab stopped, I paid for it to be taken to Rhia's.

'I'm sending you something with a cab,' I messaged her. 'I need it later. Could you please put it somewhere safe for me? xxx' Then I took a deep breath and stepped out into the late afternoon sunshine, which after weeks of grey gloominess, felt just as unreal. As if even the universe had been trying to tell me that finally good things were headed my way!

I entered the teahouse and let the approaching waiter take my coat while another led me to the table. Heads turned in my wake. Admittedly, I was a little overdressed for a cup of tea and a slice of cake. Jake was already at the table, waiting for me—another welcome change, I noted. Even more surprisingly, he had taken the effort to dress up himself. He always struck me as a little too lazy to make the effort for these kinds of things, at least as far as company events were concerned, but he had clearly decided to impress today. And boy, did he pull it off!

He stood as I approached, giving me the chance to fully appreciate his dark costume. I would have guessed him an assassin at first sight, but then I spotted the unmistakable laser sword on his belt. A Sith, then.

'Don't you just look gorgeous?' he greeted me, which prompted me to do a little twirl for him. Partly to show him the beautiful design on my back, partly to try and hide how red I felt my face was turning.

'A phoenix?' he asked.

'The Red Phoenix.' I took the mask out of my bag and raised it to my face. 'It's from a video game,' I added when his face remained blank. I was surprised he didn't seem to know it. It was pretty famous. 'It's called *Dark Rising*. I used to be a huge fan a few years back.' As Rhia knew only too well. I smiled as I remembered how relentlessly she used to tease me about it.

'Shall we?' He gestured at the table.

'Can I see your lightsabre?' I asked, impressed. 'That is so cool!'

His smile vanished, and for a second, I didn't think he would actually show it to me, but then he detached it from his belt.

'Sure,' he said as he placed it in my hand. 'Just be careful with it.'

'Right.' It must have been expensive. I gingerly took the gadget from him and admired it with a huge grin. I turned it around but couldn't see a brand name or logo on it. 'Can you actually switch it on?' I asked.

In response, he took hold of my other hand and gently placed it on the sabre, too. He stepped behind me, moving the toy weapon a little away from me and pushing a red circular button with my forefinger under his.

I expected some holographic image to spring out of the handle. What appeared instead took my breath away.

'Oh my gosh, this looks so real!' The light that pulsed in front of me had an edge to it. A red aura that shimmered. At the core of it, the glow was so bright I had to look away. 'What a beautiful red!' A shade so vibrant it made my dress seem pale by comparison.

'Do you know why it's red?' He switched it off as I lifted my hand, my finger curiously questing towards the light.

'No, I don't,' I admitted. He pulled out my chair, waiting for me to sit down. He pushed it in as I did, and bent down, his head inches away from mine, his voice suddenly cold, distant in my ear.

'At the heart of every lightsabre, there is a kyber crystal.' He switched the sabre on again, its blade very close to me this time. I could feel the heat radiating from it on my face. 'kyber crystals,' he repeated, 'also called living crystals. A rare wonder of the universe that the Jedi had a very special, very strong personal connection with. But the Sith never had the same kind of connection with them. They had to kill the Jedi, take the crystals from them and bend them to their will. The crystals resisted them at first, but the Sith were stronger. They pressed on until the crystals bled and turned red.'

He eyed me expectantly, as if I should admit some guilt and apologise. I was more puzzled than ever.

A user manual. Seriously. Maybe there were classes for lost case women like me. I should look that up!

'Well, it's very beautiful!' I managed eventually, hoping for the best. 'It suits you well.'

He cracked a smile at that. It wasn't one I'd seen before.

I studied his face more carefully as he took his seat on the other side of the table. There was something out of place with him, something I couldn't put my finger on. Yet, as I reminded myself, it wasn't like I actually knew him that well. We'd hardly ever had a proper conversation in the past.

It took a few minutes, but once we started eating, I managed to relax again. I don't know if it was the familiarity of my favourite cake, which definitely helped, or just the new topic of our conversation: gaming. I never took Jake for a gamer, but here I was wrong again. He was just as passionate about the features that worked for him in the virtual world as I was. Passion looked good on him.

'People often praise the best games for their good stories, for their realistic designs. But the person who stands behind the most compelling games and is rarely mentioned—is most often a good psychologist,' he said. 'Understanding and manipulating the gamer is the real game.'

'You seem to know a lot about it. You don't have a secret second job, do you?' I teased him with a smile. He returned it with one of his own. I put my cup down and let my arm rest causally in the middle of the table, hoping that he might put his hand on mine like last time. He didn't.

'I studied psychology for years,' he said instead.

'I thought your degree was in business studies,' I ventured, remembering his CV which I had looked up earlier.

'Well, that's what I say at work,' he admitted. 'It fits my profile better. Psychology can really come in handy when negotiating with clients, though.'

'I bet.'

I was wondering if I could ask him for some tips on how to get myself a pay rise as he went on talking about some of the best-known experts in the field, until a familiar name snapped my attention back to the conversation.

'Did you say "James Montgomery"?' I asked.

'I did. Have you heard of him?' he asked, sipping his tea as if not really interested in my answer at all.

'Absolutely!' I enthused, before giving a second thought to what turn the conversation might take if I blurted out more and quickly dialled back. 'One of my friends has counselling sessions with him.'

'Counselling sessions? Are you sure?' he raised an eyebrow, doubting me. 'Montgomery's work is mostly in research. He isn't known to do regular counselling sessions.'

'I'm sure,' I said defiantly. 'Unless, of course, there might be two James Montgomerys …' I trailed off as he pushed his phone towards me.

'Do you think this might be him?' he asked.

I looked at the photo on his screen. Yep, that was Dr Montgomery alright.

'I think it is,' I answered, feeling his eyes on me. 'At least, from the description my friend gave me.'

'Your friend must be either very important or very interesting to have sessions with him,' he concluded.

'Oh, she just got lucky,' I said hurriedly. 'He's just covering for her regular counsellor.' As soon as I said it, I realised how that sounded even less believable.

'You know who else is very good in this field?' he asked, moving his phone back to switch the picture.

'Who?' I asked, relieved to change the subject.

'Kristian del Rosso. Do you know him?' The phone screen was suddenly in front of my eyes again.

A powerful recognition shot through me like fireworks, blossoming into a million explosions of sparkling joy. My heart filled with something profound, something sweet, washing away the whole world around me. The whole world, except him. I stared at the face on the photo, blue eyes holding me with such intensity, I felt like he was actually looking back at me, too. I was vaguely aware of Jake talking to me, but I didn't take in any of it. I couldn't look away from the screen. 'Yes, he is …' He is … who? Suddenly, I realised I couldn't actually tell who this man was or how I knew him—which was a very strange, almost scary sensation. Honestly, what was wrong with me? Or more like, what wasn't?

'Selena?' I heard Jake's voice again, muffled and far off. His grip on my hand tightened, making me aware that he was holding it.

'Aaaaah!' I cried out at the sharp pain, trying to snatch my hand back, but he wouldn't let go. If anything, he pulled it closer to him, although the grip eased as my eyes once again focused on him. He looked a little bleak, a little off-colour. As if a big, dark cloud had hidden the sun away.

'I'm sorry, I think I was mistaken. I don't know him, after all.'

He raised an eyebrow at me. 'Are you sure? You seemed quite captivated there for a second.'

That made me feel ashamed. What was I doing leering at another man's photo on a date? On a date with Jake Black! He just told me how he was into psychology. Shit. If this was some kind of test, I'd definitely failed. 'I'm sorry,' I repeated, more sincerely this time. 'I've no idea what came over me.'

'Let's not worry about it.' He smiled and slowly raised my hand to his mouth. He watched me with a new hunger in his eyes as he softly kissed it, making my heart beat faster. My phone buzzed in my bag. I didn't want to reach for it and break the moment. I had a pretty good idea who it was in any event.

'Probably Rhia,' Jake supplied the answer with a little smile.

'It must be. She's probably wondering if we're on our way yet.' I rolled my eyes.

'Well, let's not keep her waiting then.' Jake stood, not letting my hand go.

I smiled at him and reached for my bag with my other hand. As I put it on my shoulder, through the thin material of my dress, it almost felt as if something had moved in it. But I was sure it was just a nerve.

'I have something to show you later,' I said as we waited for a cab outside.

'I'm sure you do.' He grinned wolfishly.

'Do you remember that family heirloom I mentioned to you last week?' I asked, meekly trying to wave away the idea that I was thinking of anything else. 'The one with the interesting symbols on it?'

'Oh, yes.' His smile disappeared. In its place was that intense, searching look again. 'It's not a round, flat object of dark circular metal disks with a crystal in the middle, is it?' he asked. 'Because if it is, I would do anything to see it!' He caressed my face as he leaned closer. 'Why don't we go to your place, and you can show me?'

I felt very confused for a second. I was sure I hadn't told him how it looked. But I clearly must have. Another thing I should probably mention to Dr Montgomery next week, provided he turned up this time. But even more importantly, now he wanted to come back to my place to see it? How stupid of me to send it to Rhia's! I never expected him to be this ...

willing. Not after how he'd been before. Today he was so different. I would have to somehow send it back to my place when he wasn't looking.

'It's okay if it's not that,' he said, misunderstanding my fallen face. 'I'm sure it's something worth seeing anyway.' He stroked my hair and turned to flag the finally approaching cab.

'Let's just go to Rhia's party first,' I suggested as we got in.

I sat down next to him and looked into his eyes. He smiled at me. It was a smile to light up the world. I still couldn't believe it! Here I was, sitting in a cab with him, holding hands. I was going to a party with Jake Black! After all those years, I should have been crazy happy. And I was. Except ...

I looked out of the window, pretending I was suddenly interested to see where we were. Yes, he was different to what I expected, but there was nothing wrong with him. If anything, he was even more interesting than I had thought him to be. More exciting. There was a lot more to him than I'd realised before. I felt like I was discovering a completely new person. And yet something had happened that was messing with my mind. As if the train had unexpectedly run onto a new track and there was no going back. I thought back to the photo he showed me. My imagination painted it across the moving landscape, the world washing into a swirl of colours in the background, that face the only constant. What was it about him that had such an impact on me? His eyes told me he knew. Maybe if I just looked at them a little longer ...

'Selena?' Jake turned my head back towards him, holding my chin gently as he leaned closer. 'Is everything okay?' He was barely an inch away, a fire to him that melted me completely.

'Yes,' I whispered, my voice lost in the numbness of attraction. 'I think we're getting close.'

'I think so, too,' he murmured as his lips found mine.

Those last miles flew past while I was lost in that kiss. By the time the car stopped in the private street where the Aldridge mansion stood, and the loud music coming from the party wrapped us into an uplifting piece of melody, I was pretty high already. He got out of the car and reached for my hand, pulling me up to him once more for a kiss. Whistles and high-pitched cheers on our right signalled that we were no longer alone. We walked through the front gate with his hand on my waist and a smile on my face, big enough to hurt.

The whole garden was completely transformed with tables, trendy decorations, flickering flame-like lights, leaving a large area in the middle for guests to dance in front of a DJ booth.

'Look who's finally here!' Rhia called out as we approached her.

'It's good to see you, Selena.' Estelle wrapped me in a friendly hug. Estelle, who was a very popular piano teacher, and looked like a perfect Barbie doll even on her worst days, captivated half of our company ever since she first turned up at the Christmas party two years ago. The fact that she came along as Rhia's girlfriend and was holding hands with her all night did nothing to stop our male colleagues wistfully discussing her in small groups on their cigarette breaks. She was dressed as an angel now, which suited her personality perfectly, while Rhia sported a devil's outfit. Next to Estelle stood Rin Soroko, a popular Japanese anime character, and her samurai bodyguard: Keiko and her architect fiancé, Rob.

'How many people did you invite?' I asked Rhia once greetings were over, trying to speak loud enough to be heard over the music. The place was heaving with guests, many of them I didn't know or recognise in their costumes.

'Enough to fill the house.' Rhia shrugged and smiled in a way that told me she'd had quite a few drinks already. I turned around once more and caught Jake from the corner of my eye looking at a dark-haired woman in a long, black dress, standing on the upstairs balcony. The woman narrowed her eyes at me when she saw me looking, then turned her back on us, making her waist-length hair fly luxuriously around her in the process. She marched back into the house, closely followed by a large, half-naked guy dressed as a gladiator.

'Excuse me for a second,' Jake said. 'I just need to talk to someone.' I watched him walk away into the house with a sinking heart.

I turned back towards the others, their faces full of sympathy.

'I know what you're thinking, but I swear, he has been very attentive all afternoon,' I protested loudly, my voice sounding desperate even for me.

'I don't think you have too much to worry about.' Rob tried to smile at me reassuringly. 'Did you see that guy she was with? We saw them arrive at the party together arm in arm. He seemed very protective of her. Whatever this is about, Jake will be back very soon, I bet.'

Keiko nodded a few times in agreement. 'Rob will get you a drink in the meantime,' she said. 'What do you want?'

I shrugged and said I didn't mind.

'I really thought this might be going somewhere,' I admitted when he was gone. Despite our first date and how indifferent he'd been all week, I was ready to forgive him everything based on how he'd been this afternoon.

Keiko put an arm around me. 'Sometimes, I just feel that you're a little too desperate to belong somewhere. Belong with someone,' she said. 'But it's perfectly understandable, given what you went through with your parents.'

Estelle looked at Keiko with concerned eyes, clearly not knowing what she was talking about.

'It's okay,' I hurried to reassure her. 'It's not as bad as Keiko makes it sound. My mother left us when I was young and moved abroad. She wanted to take me with her, but I wanted to stay, and my father wanted me to stay, too. My father remarried, but I never really got on well with my stepmother. And so, when I was eighteen, and they moved to the States, I decided to stay again, this time alone. So, both my parents have now spouses and children with them, their own happy families, where I'm always invited to stay, and I do visit them almost every year. I just don't really feel that I truly belong in either place. Hence Keiko's psychoanalysis.' I hated to admit that she might have been right.

'Selena, you're so gorgeous, sweetie.' Estelle squeezed my hand warmly. 'And this dress is stunning on you! Any guy here would be lucky to be with you, and you could easily find someone much better than Jake!'

I managed a weak smile, wanting to show her that I appreciated her efforts. Even if her words felt like something any friend would say in a situation like this.

'I just felt so good with him,' I mumbled. 'Like I matter ...'

'Of course, you matter! You are important!' Rhia stated loudly.

'To whom?' I protested, letting self-pity take over.

'To us!' Keiko joined in. 'And a lot of other people. You are bright, lovely, kind, practical. A loyal friend and a fantastic colleague. Good at so many things!'

'Like what? Finding stuff on the internet?' I took the cocktail from the returning Rob and sipped it. 'So cool. I'm sure many guys would be into that!'

'Not just on the internet,' Keiko insisted. 'Remember when we were in Nice on holiday? You found that amazing restaurant just by walking into it. And you found my sister's lost cat!'

'And my phone,' Rhia chipped in.

'Maybe I should start hooking up with guys through lost property message boards,' I mused. 'Any of you boys are looking for something?' I called around. 'Just come to me!'

'Silly!' Keiko chided me. 'Here, try this. You'll love this one.' She exchanged my glass with hers. I sipped the yellowish drink and grinned approvingly.

'It was too sweet for me, but I knew you'd like it.' She smiled. Always right.

The crowd in front of the DJ desk started making a lot of noise, and more people joined in from the sides as a new track started playing.

'Not this again,' I grumbled. 'Aren't people sick of it yet?'

'We should go dance!' Rhia said. 'Why don't you go and ask the DJ for a song? Give me your coat and your bag, I'll take them inside.'

I gave her the coat but kept my bag. Jake was still nowhere in sight. What if he tried to call me?

'Nobody's going to call you,' Rhia said, reading my thoughts.

'Look who's talking,' I said defiantly, holding my bag closer.

'What do you mean?' Rhia asked.

'How many times did you call me today?' My phone kept buzzing, even as I was kissing Jake in the car. Lucky that I usually kept it on silent.

'I didn't call you,' Rhia said, shaking her head. 'Go ask for a song. I'll be with you in a minute.'

'Strange.' I pulled the phone out of my bag and saw that I had no missed calls. No notifications. Why was it buzzing, then? I'm sure it had been!

'Oh, I put your thing in the library,' Rhia said. 'I'll leave your coat next to it. It's locked. Nobody will touch them there. You are still authorised to instruct Amariella.' And she went inside.

I made my way to the DJ. She seemed to be in her early twenties and looked very cool with her glittery purple hair and tattoos on her face. She was focusing on a set of monitors in front of her, tapping along instructions on them with both hands.

'Sorry, can I ask for a song?' I shouted at her, trying to make myself heard over the music.

'Just a minute!' she shouted back and continued with whatever she was doing.

I put my bag down next to the stand and looked around while waiting, checking out what costumes others wore on the dance floor and looking around once more, just in case I could spot Jake. I couldn't. I looked up at the balcony. It was full of people. Nobody I recognised.

I looked back at the DJ, who seemingly tried to ignore me, probably hoping I might go away, and when I didn't, she sighed and asked me which song I wanted.

'Could you play "Summer Fire" by Noemi Taylor?' I asked.

'Sorry,' she shook her head. 'I just played another song by Noemi not long ago. Maybe later.'

'How about "Fatal Love" by Drem?'

She gave me a disapproving look. 'I don't play songs by Drem!'

'What about "Wait for Me" by Troubled Times?'

'That's a slow song,' she explained as if talking to an idiot. 'Maybe towards the end.'

'Right,' I said, suddenly out of ideas and completely disheartened.

'Wait!' she shouted, just as I was turning away.

I turned back, thinking she might have changed her mind. 'What?' I asked when instead of looking at me, she again looked at her monitors, frantically tapping on them.

'How are you doing this?' she asked, her face angry.

'Doing what?' I asked, puzzled, as the rhythm playing gradually changed and the first chords of "Summer Fire" were mixed into them.

'This!' She gestured around, as if that should help me get her meaning.

'I'm not doing anything,' I told her, just as Rhia jumped on me.

'There you are!' she shouted in my ear. 'What's taking so long? Have you given her a whole list? Come on!' She dragged me to the middle of the dance floor where the others were, just as the energetic track of "Summer Fire" erupted from the speakers on full blast, and the crowd went wild.

After it, "Fatal Love" started playing, and I wondered what changed the DJ's mind. Probably seeing Rhia with me. But I had quickly forgiven her for her dismissiveness for playing all my favourite songs, as if she had somehow acquired a set of my playlists.

I was on my third cocktail when Jake reappeared, gaining my forgiveness even faster by passionately pulling me close and kissing me in front of everyone. A few songs later, I stumbled, and he caught me, closing his arms around me.

'Are you alright?' he asked. 'Why don't we go and sit down?' He signalled to the others reassuringly and escorted me off the dance floor. 'Let's go and find some cold water for you.'

I only just remembered then to pick up my bag that was luckily still at the foot of the DJ stand. Jake led me to the kitchen, got a glass of water and asked someone to give his seat up for me. I sipped my drink quietly, its freshness clearing my mind as I rested, wishing very much that there weren't so many people around us. Then it came to me. Rhia said the library was locked and empty!

'Are you feeling better?' Jake asked as he leaned down to me.

'A little,' I said and stood. 'Come on. I'll show you something,' I said and led him upstairs.

I found the library easily. Rhia's mother invited us for a posh afternoon tea there last year. Just as Rhia said, the door was locked. I looked at Jake with faked distress. He tilted his head with a smile, waiting to see what I was up to, not concerned in the slightest.

'Watch this.' I grinned. 'Hey, Amariella!' I said loudly. 'Open the library door.'

'I'm sorry,' the home system responded through a small speaker just below the doorknob. 'I cannot do this right now. Please try again later.'

'Hmmm. Let me try again,' I said. 'Hey, Amariella! Unlock the door to the library.'

'I'm sorry,' the home system repeated. 'I cannot do this right now. Please try again later.'

Damn! Did I need to go all the way down to find Rhia? Or should I try calling them? Would any of them have their phones on them even? I was sure Rhia didn't.

While I mulled around my options, Jake put his hand on the doorknob and gently tried to twist it left and right. Not that he would be able to open it like that, I thought, but to my surprise, the door opened.

'How did you do that?' I looked at him, astonished.

'Magic.' He smiled and opened the door for me.

The lights switched on as we entered, Jake closing, and what even sounded like locking the door behind us. The library was surprisingly quiet, not even the music from the garden audible in here, and it made me remember how Rhia mentioned once that her mother, another book lover, just like Keiko, had it soundproofed.

'Alright,' I muttered as I looked around for my bag. 'It's going to be here somewhere.'

'What are we looking for?' Jake asked.

'Surprise!' I said as I turned the corner and walked towards a small table against the wall. I was half-way there when my phone started buzzing again.

'This again!' I exclaimed as I got the phone out of my bag.

'Who is it?' Jake came after me, curious.

'It's no one,' I said. 'Look.' I handed him the phone. 'It keeps buzzing for no reason!'

'Interesting,' he said, turning the now still phone around with one hand, his other slipping around my waist.

'Just a minute,' I giggled. 'Let me just show you this thing.'

'If it's so important …' He sighed dramatically and let go of me.

I hardly took a step when a song started playing through hidden speakers around us. It was "Wait For Me" by Troubled Times. The only remaining song I requested from the DJ which she had yet to play. I stopped and stared. Something strange was going on. Jake also looked around, then shrugged and turned back to me. 'Would you like me to try and switch it off somehow?' he asked.

I considered the question for a moment, the slow, sweet melody reminding me why it was one of my favourite songs. 'No. I love it, actually.' I smiled at him.

'Come on, then.' He reached his hand out to me. 'One more dance.' A heartbeat later, I was back in his arms.

Chapter 17

Kristian

Borond, Drelos,
24th The Month of Promise 1575

O r was this not the kind of magic you wanted me to show you, sweetheart?' Conor grinned at me, his overfriendly teasing hiding a touch of guilt. He had been in this ecstatic mood ever since we had found our way out of that deadly chamber, clearly enjoying himself, while I was still stunned by what had happened. *'Most people run from danger. But it was always my calling,'* he told me once. I clearly didn't fully appreciate before what that actually meant!

'You killed us both,' I pointed out.

'Only temporarily,' he protested. 'And it had to be done. I had to make sure we touched the painting at exactly the same time, otherwise our souls might have just swapped places.'

'You still should have asked me first.'

'It would have taken too long to explain, and we were running out of time!'

'Did you know exactly what would happen, or was it just a guess?'

'It was a guess,' he admitted.

'A hell of a guess!'

'It worked!'

'Have you done anything like this before?'

'No.'

The tunnel we walked through was dimly lit by the torch Conor had taken from a bracket, close to where we emerged from the coffin chute. Its light didn't reach far into the darkness ahead of us. It perfectly resembled how I felt.

'You'll be fine,' he insisted. 'You'll get used to it all soon.'

'Why, are you planning to kill me a few more times?' I turned my head and gave him a hard stare.

'Only if you're foolish enough to walk into your own grave.' He smiled back innocently.

'The weather was terrible outside.' I shrugged.

'Only because you took too long getting acquainted with the locals,' he pointed out.

'They were persuasive!' I could still feel that man's fingers around my neck.

'Lucky I was there.'

'Indeed.' I sighed. 'Fine. Tell me about magic, then. How does this all work?'

'Well, I'm no expert. All I can tell you is that only a very few people can do it. Some are born with it, others develop the traits later, but it's rare in both cases. It's not something you can just learn. You either have it or you don't. The more powerful spellcasters can attach magic to objects or to places in a way that lingers. They say spells cast on people or animals are more short-lived.'

'That's reassuring,' I mused.

'Don't worry. Spellcasters don't just walk around, casting spells on people. I only ever met two in my life. Three, if we count Ithorion.'

'Do you think he's watching us somehow?' I asked.

'I was thinking that earlier. If not him, maybe someone from his order. It all feels somehow a little structured in here. A little organised.'

'But didn't he say those tests were more simple things, like illnesses, losses, specific problems you had to solve?'

'Maybe they've been saving the good stuff for us!'

'Why would we be so special?'

'Wasn't your uncle some high-ranking officer? Also, they might want to see how you cope under pressure with your … condition.'

'Hmmm. I'm not sure I passed that test.' I frowned.

'What happened? You said you could control it. Ithorion said you'd always have the choice.'

'I did have the choice. At the start. When that man attacked me outside.' I thought back, running through it all again in my head. 'I think it's blood that triggers it. It never used to. Only since the night of the massacre. The sight of it affects me a little. The smell of it more. But it's the taste that really gets it going. When I fell out there, I bit my tongue, and that started it. I had my chance to stop it, but I hesitated. I thought I was going to die. So, I let it flow through me for a moment, which was a mistake. It became very hard to control afterwards.'

'And at the snake pit? You said it wasn't what I said that helped you snap out of it. What then?'

I sighed. 'You know how I can sense it when you're close to me?'

'Yes.'

'Well, it turns out that I can sense when you're close to death, too. And it's really, really not a good feeling, to say the least.'

'This is why I was no longer in danger afterwards?' he asked after a pause. 'From you, I mean? When you fought the skeletons, you didn't want to hurt me.'

'Yes,' I admitted. 'Whatever happened at the snake pit, it left a lasting impression.'

'And what about in the coffin? Could you not tell what I was up to?'

'Hard to say,' I said. 'It happened so quickly. I still felt sick, and we were in a situation where death seemed inevitable one way or the other.'

'You didn't look too good back then. The old man was right when he told you not to use it. Are you feeling better now?'

'Strangely enough, I feel absolutely fine.'

A low, menacing growl rose ahead of us in the dark that made us stop.

'Well, don't get too cocky about it,' Conor suggested. 'It might not last.'

I unsheathed my sword and warmed up my wrist by cutting figure eights into the air. 'I'm starting to learn that with you around. I could even say you'll be the death of me one day! Except, oh wait …'

'Better me than that vicious thing ahead of us,' he offered with a grin, effortlessly making his sword dance in his hand in a complex yet beautiful pattern that made me jealous.

'Or you could just stand aside and hold that torch for me while I sort out the situation,' I suggested.

'Just try not to fall and bite your tongue, champion!'

'I won't if you don't get too close to death.'

'Oh, don't worry, Mother, I'll be fine.'

I stared ahead into the dark, trying to make out the contours of the creature. I could see nothing. 'Why is it not coming towards us? What is it waiting for?'

'You intimidated it with your fancy swordplay.'

'So modest!' I looked at him and added, 'Will you teach me that flourish you just did once we're out of here?'

'What? This?' He smiled and made the sword dance even faster than before.

'Yes,' I said, half-expecting him to mock me in return.

'Well, I tell you what. Help me find the key, and I'll teach you everything I know.'

'Splendid. In that case, let's get going,' I said, trying to ignore that old obsession I detected in his voice. Somehow, I doubted he would be willing to concede to Laro's blackmail and give him this key once we found it, whatever might be at stake. Still, that was a problem for another day. Right now, staying alive, preferably without dying in the process, was much higher on my priority list. That and not letting all the killing turn me into a monster, too.

The creature growled again, much closer this time, yet I still couldn't see what we were facing. Our quiet, careful footsteps sounded unnervingly loud to my ears, my imagination conjuring up all sorts of horrors that might jump on us at any moment from the dark. Whatever this monster was, its hostility was almost palpable, pressing on us like an invisible weight. My heart quickened with each step, demanding that I stop, turn, and run, or at the very least, consider biting my own tongue and gain some reassuring advantage for the fight. I pushed back against that desire and carried on walking.

Something came to me then that I'd learned from James. Exploration, doing new things in life, always came with risk. The greater the reward, the greater the risk. The only question remained: was it still worth doing? I thought about that for a second. Was it really worth catching this Laro? Laro, who kept trying to kill me and those close to me? Laro, who seemed to know more about the world, more about me, even, than myself? A world where things went against everything that I knew. Where human teleportation was possible—which James must have known all along. James, who never once mentioned that he was my uncle or that my father still lived. Or that in some parts of the world, animated corpses, Gods, shapeshifters, telekinetic powers existed. And ancient spells could make me spiritwalk through death.

I looked at the sword in my hand. The blue veins in its blade that had pulsed in the fight before, now stayed dull. I wasn't sure if that annoyed me more or that I was already in a mindset where, despite all sense, I expected my magical sword to light up and help. I felt toyed with and angry. Angry with my uncle. Angry with the world. Angry with myself.

I fastened my grip on the hilt and yelled into the darkness, 'Come on, then!'

Two red eyes lit up in response, framed by the black mass of a large hound. I raised my sword and ran at it. A throaty growl shook the air as the hound took off too and raced towards me. Like a rocket burning up fuel, I poured all my anger, frustration and confusion into that charge. The distance between us narrowed within seconds, bringing into sight the dog's mangled fur, powerful muscles and slobbery jaws. The beast leaped, and I jumped to meet it, the razor-sharp blade angled to take its head off, its stink hitting me mid-air. And nothing else. My sword cut through space just before I landed, clumsy from disorientation and spraining my ankle. I crouched around the pain for a moment before looking back, not seeing anything apart from Conor running to me.

'Are you crazy?' he yelled at me.

'Where did it go?' I asked, confused.

'It wasn't real,' he said.

'What?'

'It was a ghost.'

'A ghost? Are you sure? I couldn't see through it. It looked real.'

'See through it?' He tilted his head curiously. 'Can you see through ghosts where you're from? They can't be too scary.'

'Well, they don't exist. That's just how people imagine them.'

'Did you bite your tongue?'

'What? No!'

'You *are* crazy!' No longer a question.

'What? It was only a rabid dog ... with weird bioluminescent eyes.' Now that my anger was spent and my mind calmer, that did seem a bit strange.

'That wasn't a dog. It was a hellhound. Massively stronger than any dogs. Had it been real,' he added.

'So concerned about my life all of a sudden!' I mused and turned my attention back to my leg, rolling my foot around and trying to put weight on it. 'Ouch.'

'Why wouldn't I be?' He shook his head. 'Can you walk?'

'I can,' I said. 'Might be a bit slow for a while.'

'Come on, lean on me,' he offered, clearly eager to make up for his previous recklessness.

'It's not that bad,' I protested, feeling foolish.

'We can walk faster that way,' he stated, watching me hobble around.

'Okay, fine.' I relented and put my arm around his shoulders, shifting my weight. 'Just for a bit.'

'If all goes well, we won't need to go far now anyhow.'

'What makes you say that?'

'Ghosts normally guard things. Most often treasure. The key might be near.'

'About time!' I grumbled.

'I've been looking for it all my life,' he said. 'You can last a few more miles.'

'I still don't really understand what it can do and how. Isn't it just a flat, round thing with symbols on it and some crystal in the middle?'

'The symbols move around, giving you directions and answers to your questions.'

I detected a strain in his voice I recognised. He sounded like I did when I had to explain something to the students over and over again. I couldn't help but grin as I pushed him. 'What else?'

'It can open doors into other worlds.'

'Sounds more interesting. Anything else?'

'It will make me rich and powerful beyond my wildest dreams. Release my full potential. It will fill my life with …'

'Hold on.'

'No, seriously. It was prophesied …'

'Shhhh. Just be quiet for a second,' I urged him. 'Listen. Can you hear it, too?

'Hear what?'

We looked at each other. From his eyes, I could tell he heard it, too. From his expression, that he had no idea what it was, either. We looked behind us. The torch lit our immediate surroundings, its light soon swallowed by the blackness of the tunnel. Somewhere in the distance, the sound of pattering. Like rain, but harder. It steadily grew louder as we listened. The torchlight shook violently under a sudden breeze, as if it panicked in our place.

'I have a feeling we should get going,' Conor said and fastened his grip on me.

'Me, too,' I agreed, ignoring the pain in my left ankle as I tried to match his steps.

The source of the sound kept gaining on us, like a thousand metal sticks knocking on the stone floor.

The tunnel abruptly ended, opening into a huge cavern. Conor pushed the torch out into the open space, trying to see how far away its walls were. The light didn't reach any of them. Beyond our feet, a void, its depth similarly hidden.

'Do we have any rope?' I asked as I turned back, trying to look for a stone I could throw down to see how far it would fall before hitting the ground. Looking back down the corridor, I saw a swarm of fist-sized brown insects on the wall, marching towards us on many needle-like legs.

'What are those?' Conor asked.

'I was hoping you'd know.' There were a lot of them. 'How can there be so many? What do they even eat down here?'

'Based on the speed they are coming our way with, I'm not sure I want to know!'

'So, rope?' I demanded, hopeful. My eyes remained on the fast-approaching wave.

'Just a … wait a sec,' he said and took a step back towards the abyss. 'Hey, lady!' he shouted. 'A little faster, please!'

I tore my eyes off the danger and turned, perplexed. The sight that greeted me made me shiver. In the middle of the dark, empty space, an old wooden boat moved towards us through the air, its side mostly covered with barnacles and algae that emitted a greenish-yellow light. In the boat, a woman sat, sculling with a single oar. She had long, blonde hair that partly hid her naked body. Half of her face was a decayed, skinless mess, with an empty hole for an eye.

A sharp pain in my foot made me look down and see one of those insects on my boot, punching through the leather. I shook it off, only to be surrounded by dozens more, a vanguard of the advancing army. They soon had me jumping around, brushing my hair and arms as they fell from the ceiling, too.

'Kris, come on!' I heard Conor's voice. He stood in the creepy boat, reaching out towards me.

I got in, and in that moment, an invisible force pushed the unnatural vehicle away from the tunnel, making it move in the opposite direction. It swayed under my feet as I turned, just as if we had been on open water.

Had we just escaped the frying pan by jumping into the fire? I sat down at the end of the boat, as far away from the woman as possible. Conor naturally moved closer to her with a smile on his face. Why did he always have to be like this? He wasn't just enjoying danger; he was literally courting it!

The woman said nothing. The left side of her face was innocently beautiful. The right side was terrifying. Her naked body was similarly divided. Her left breast big, round and full. Her right, nothing more than a shrivelled, desiccated, shapeless piece of flesh, the skin peeling off it in pieces.

I looked down into the dark but could see nothing. There was no machinery built into the floating vessel that could have kept us up. How was this possible? Could it be that either the fluorescent algae or the ship itself had some unique component? Something that would defy gravity or perhaps create a strong magnetic field?

A steady breeze blew my face, and a few creatures flew past us that looked like bats. Conor had given up trying to talk to the woman and was looking at me now, grinning, as if all this were just a bit of fun, a harmless, exciting ride in a simulation game. Was he crazy, or was it me who was taking things too seriously? I knew he was right. I did worry about him too much. And why? He was a grown man I hardly knew. Yet, Ithorion's explanation rang true to me. I could feel the connection he described. Conor might not have looked up to me, but I certainly felt protective towards him. Even just admitting that to myself sounded pathetic. Maybe this was all just an aftereffect of the massacre and nothing more. Maybe I should just let things go. In an ironic twist, Conor was the worst possible person in the world to be worried about. I took a deep breath and tried to relax.

The boat glided peacefully through the emptiness, and I started to see in the distance where we were headed. An entrance to another tunnel yawned in the middle of the cavern wall, larger than the one we had left behind. In the tunnel there was a blue light. As we got closer, I saw fungi covering the walls in patches that emitted the light. As the other end of the boat gently hit the wall just in front of the entrance of the tunnel, I actually smiled. We had made it through. I really did worry too much.

We both stood and stopped. The woman's hand reached out in front of Conor, palm up as if asking for payment. I was stopped by an invisible wall that seemed to stretch vertically, separating me from them. A chill ran through me as I pushed against it and could do nothing to make it move. Conor reached into his pocket and dropped a topaz into the woman's hand. That didn't seem to satisfy her, so he grudgingly took out a few more and gave them to her, too. Her hand remained as it was.

'I don't think I have anything more valuable than that.' Conor laughed nervously as he spread out his arms.

'Wrong,' the woman spoke for the first time, her voice ringing clear and loud. She slowly rose, letting the gemstones fall without any notice, and stepped closer to Conor until their bodies touched. She put her arms around his neck, one of them almost entirely skeletal. The next moment, a black substance broke out from her fingers, pouring down around Conor's body, forming a web, solidifying into thick wires full of spikes fastening him to the boat.

'No!' I shouted, hitting the wall in front of me with my fist, making no impact.

The woman opened her mouth impossibly wide, revealing a set of sharp teeth, and sunk them into Conor's neck. Conor roared in pain, which in turn made me hit the wall harder, shifting my weight left and right, causing the boat to sway wildly. Neither of which seemed to make much difference, but I thought I saw her lose her balance just for a moment. So I rocked the boat even harder. So hard, even the gemstones fell out. The woman narrowed her eyes at me over Conor's shoulder. The next moment, only my half of the vessel turned, rotating violently. In my surprise, I stopped shouting. It was only Conor's howls that still rang in my ears, or so I thought, as I fell into the abyss.

Chapter 18

Conor

Borond, Drelos,
24th The Month of Promise 1575

I n my line of work, you learn how to deal with some of the most dangerous creatures in life. Women, especially. This was nothing. I made myself take another step forward into the tunnel, my leg comically shaking. I'd been searching for the Supreme Key for so long! It had to be close now. It had to be! I couldn't die now. It would be simply very bad timing. Just one more step. One more!

My legs gave way, unable to support my weight anymore. I lowered myself to the ground, half-sitting, half-lying, my head against the wall, all of me trembling. Maybe I'd just rest a bit first. Just a few minutes, nothing more.

It was strange to be alone again. So quiet. So free to do anything I wanted. No more worries over what Kris might think. Like it ever mattered! I groaned. Typical of him to go like that. He worried too much about me. I didn't need anyone to worry about me! I had strong survival instincts. And when those failed, I always had luck. Most men disliked me for it. For that, and for how their women looked at me. Conor Drew, that lucky bastard, they all thought jealously behind my back. And this was why I hardly had any friends. Let alone anyone who cared. Or worried. I chuckled. What a fool! My eyes misted, and I swallowed hard.

I was disoriented at first when the undead witch let me go. It took me a moment to remember where I was and why, as I grabbed my stuff and struggled out of the boat onto the stone floor of the tunnel. I looked around, my vision blurry, yet clear enough to realise that the witch and I were alone, and Kris was nowhere in sight.

'Where is he?' I asked the witch, who had been sitting quietly, smiling, as if waiting for me to ask the question. Her face and body were whole now, looking beautiful and healthy. Easily mistaken for a vulnerable young woman. I gripped the edge of the boat with one hand, and with the other, I pointed my sword at her, and all but roared, 'Where is he?'

It was a weak, clumsy move, leaving myself open to her cruel counter-strike.

'He fell,' she answered, still smiling. Two words, one blow. So obvious, yet somehow it still hurt more than all the rest she'd done to me. I hadn't the strength to wield the sword, and we both knew it. Instead, I slumped to my knees and stared into the pitch-black emptiness below.

'Kris! Kriiiiis!' I shouted, my voice echoing back to me, empty of response, full of meaning.

The witch had just left me there then. Weak and stupid with grief, I was no longer worthy of her attention. I stayed on that edge for a long time, hoping against hope that he'd somehow mysteriously reappear. But of course, he didn't.

Even now, lying here in this godforsaken tunnel, I still couldn't believe he was dead. Hadn't his uncle allegedly worked for Gods all his life? You'd think they would look after their own. This couldn't have been a test, surely! What, exactly, did they expect to happen? The only thing that did happen was that I finally got rid of him. And now that I had, I missed him more than was reasonable.

'I hope you're happy now!' I called out in case anyone was listening. 'But let me tell you that you made a huge mistake letting him die like that!' I closed my shaking hand into a fist. 'He was great! You hear me? He would have made an outstanding member of your Order! The best champion you could have ever had!' There was nothing but silence in return. The best friend I could have ever had.

I closed my eyes, utterly exhausted now. Would I die, too, if I fell asleep here? I wondered. Nobody would know. Nobody would care. Not anymore. A peace enfolded me, pulling me into its calming depths. Dreams drifted across my consciousness, and I left the world behind me.

I slept for what could have been hours or days for all I knew. When I finally woke, I was still weak and viciously hungry. Whatever food I'd had on me, we had already eaten. It was only Kris who still had some of our provisions in his pack. I'm not sure if it was the loss of him or of our remaining food that I regretted more in that moment. I was too hungry to even think. I eyed the glowing blue fungi from the corner of my eye. Would it kill me if I tried one? It was either that or hunger. I reached out to grab some.

'I wouldn't if I were you!' a voice called out to me from further down the tunnel.

I turned, half-disbelieving, half-amazed. Kristian del Rosso was walking towards me with a huge smile on his face. I couldn't understand how, but right then, I didn't care. I grinned back.

'It's good to have you back,' is what I should have said. 'It's good to have the food back,' is what I did say.

'Um … about that.' He hesitated. 'I'm afraid it all got completely soaked in the water I fell into.'

'Where is it?' I demanded. Soaked or not, I didn't mind!

'Don't worry. I have something else.' He presented me with a smallish, colourful slab.

'What is that?' I asked suspiciously, looking at the strange thing in his hand.

'It's my uneaten breakfast from a week ago. Which actually feels more like a lifetime ago. An energy bar,' he added. 'Here, let me open it for you.'

I shoved the thing into my mouth, bit off some and started chewing. 'It's good,' I said. In truth, I could hardly taste it at the speed I wolfed it down.

'You're lucky I still had it.' He watched me bemused. 'I knew you were hungry, but I didn't realise it was that bad!'

'Did you only have the one? How can someone have just a small thing like that for breakfast?'

'Don't worry.' He smiled. 'It's more than it looks. Just give it a few minutes, and you'll see it's quite filling.'

My stomach rumbled, disagreeing with him.

'How's your neck?' He leaned closer. I turned my head, letting him have a better look.

'It's not as bad as I expected,' he said in a voice that made me wonder if he wasn't quite telling the truth. 'Let's see what we can do about it.' I watched him get that funny-looking tube out of his pack with the moving symbols on it.

'Not that thing,' I warned him, quite serious.

'Don't worry,' he laughed. 'No needle this time.'

'So, if it works without one, why did you have to skewer me last time?' I asked.

'It depends on the problem, on the medication, and on how urgently it needs to enter your circulation,' he explained as he started to clean the wound. 'In some cases, it's sufficient to apply the remedy to your skin and let it penetrate your body that way. Other times, it's better to inject it into a part where you have a lot of muscle.'

'I have a lot of muscle in many places. Why did you have to—?'

'A lot of muscle and no injury.'

'Ah.' That made sense now, thinking back.

'And in some cases,' he continued, smearing something on the inside of my arm now, which was strange as I didn't remember it being cut. 'Keep looking left until I finish it!' he snapped at me when I tried to turn my head and look.

'Sorry,' I mumbled and let him fuss some more.

'So, in some more serious cases, it helps if the medication gets delivered straight into the vein.'

'Are you saying you would pierce that long needle right into someone's vein?' I shuddered at the thought.

'Yup! Close your hand into a fist.'

'Lucky mine's not so serious.' I relaxed and did as I was told.

'Yes. Now hold still,' he instructed.

'Fine!'

The pain shut me up. Not the honest, quick cut of a blade. A wicked, unnatural pain of something solid and cold creeping up in the middle of my arm. An unfamiliar threat that stopped me moving, not knowing what might happen if I did. By the time I did turn my head and managed to look, he was already pulling that blasted needle out of my arm.

'It needed to be done,' he stated matter-of-factly. 'Now, let me bandage your neck, and we're done.'

I was too stunned to even respond. How come he always knew when I was lying but not the other way around? This whole soul-circle nonsense was completely unfair. But I guessed at least my hunger had disappeared, so he was right about that energy bar thing. Even so, he should have been more considerate. A little nicer. Wasn't he a little too chilled and collected? A little indifferent? Not that I expected him to jump for joy upon seeing me alive, but still. I was thrilled that he lived, just usually much better at pretending nonchalance.

He fell into water. I guessed that was lucky. But wasn't he going to ask me how I got away? Didn't he care?

'How did you know I was hungry?' I asked.

'What?' He sat opposite me now, putting his things away.

'You said you knew that I was hungry. How did you know?'

'Um … you don't remember?' he asked, looking a little awkward.

'Remember? Remember what?' I asked, puzzled.

'I'm not sure how to explain this …' He hesitated.

'Why not start at the beginning?' I offered, damned curious now.

'The night after the murders, I had a strange dream,' he started.

'When I said "at the beginning", I didn't mean way back when—'

He silenced me with a raised hand. 'Do you want to know or not?'

'Fine, fine,' I relented and stretched out, trying to make myself more comfortable. It sounded like this might take a while.

He sighed. 'In short, we spoke in your dream.'

'We did what?' I sat straight back up, a vague memory returning to me now. 'How did we do that?'

'So, the night after the murders, I had a strange dream,' he started again, and this time around, I listened intently. 'I think I somehow wandered into my uncle's dream. I don't know how. But suddenly, there he was, having a conversation with a tall, black woman. They seemed very surprised when they saw me there. It was as if they had used that dream to discuss something. Like you'd use a room. But I woke up and didn't have a chance to ask him about it. At first, I thought it was all just a dream. My dream. And with everything going on, I quite forgot about the whole thing until now.

'When I swam to the surface of that lake today, it was completely dark. I couldn't see the flying boat above me or anything at all. I shouted, but there was no response. It took me a while, but eventually, I found a shore and climbed out. As I wandered around, I came upon a small cave where the air was surprisingly warm. It was blowing out from a crevice in the ground. I sat down there to dry my clothes. I thought about you, wondering if you were still alive and whether I could sense it if you weren't. And as I sat there in the warm, feeling exhausted, I dozed off.

'I was looking for you in my dream until I came upon a lake that was upside down. Through its surface, I could see you sitting here, your eyes half-closed but not quite asleep. I called out, but you couldn't hear me. Then I reached out to you through what looked like water but wasn't, and sort of … pulled you down. You stood next to me, but you were also still above us, sleeping.'

'Some of it is coming back to me now.' I frowned. 'Us looking up at me. You said I looked very pale.' I couldn't recall more, no matter how I tried. And I tried. I wanted to remember the part where he was overjoyed to see me alive. 'I don't remember any more of it,' I confessed, defeated.

'Your body was still in trauma after all that blood loss,' he said. 'You should be just happy to be alive.'

I should be happy?

'What about you?' I blurted out, not quite able to control myself.

'Oh, I remember everything.' He shrugged, then sensing my sulkiness, he added, 'How are you feeling now?'

'Much better, thanks,' I said and stood quickly, trying to get a grip on myself. 'I feel like I could run for miles.'

'That's the energy bar,' he said. 'I told you it was more than it seemed.'

'So, what else did we talk about?' I asked, and he stood to join me. I still couldn't believe he just made me fall asleep from a distance. I hoped he hadn't heard my lament about him to the Gods. There already seemed a little cockiness to him that was new.

'Not much,' he said. 'Mainly just how I fell into the water and how the vampire-witch let you go once she was done with you.'

'That's women for you.' I grinned.

He looked like he was going to say something to that, but then he closed his mouth.

'What?'

'Nothing,' he said, but with a very strange smile, and he started walking.

'Hey! What were you going to say? You need to tell me now!' I hurried after him.

He slowed his steps and reluctantly looked at me. 'After we talked …'

'In my dream?'

'In your dream,' he agreed. 'I wanted to see if I could talk with my uncle, too. I have so many questions. Unfortunately, I couldn't find him like I could find you. But as I was just about to give up, I found someone else. A woman.'

'You were flirting with a woman while I lay between life and death?' I knew there was something odd about him since he came back. He was so calm and … happy?

'You were on the mend. And we didn't flirt. We didn't even talk.'

'You didn't talk? What did you do?' I turned to him, put an imaginary pipe in my mouth and in a deep voice added: 'Tell me all.'

'Nothing like what you're thinking.' He laughed. 'We just looked at each other. I think she's like you.'

'Like me? In what way?' I asked, confused.

'Part of our soul circle. Remember how we connected from a distance on the first day we met? It was a bit like that with her, too. Only … a little more emotional.'

'Interesting. I wonder how many of us are out there …'

'Oh no,' Kris groaned. 'That thought never even occurred to me. But honestly, I'm not sure I could cope with many more of you!'

'Oh, rubbish.' I chided. 'By the time we've explored this place, you'll be a lot more resilient. Let me just throw myself into a few more snake pits or take another turn or two with that lovely boatwoman!'

'That's not funny,' he declared in his warning voice.

I liked him better when he was more fun. But now, maybe I knew a way to make that happen.

'So did this woman you saw have a name?'

'She probably did. We didn't talk.'

'But she was pretty?'

He smiled then. There it was. I knew it!

'She was pretty,' I concluded.

'I liked her.'

'What did she look like? Dark or fair?'

'Is that a torch on the wall?'

'What?' I looked. He was right. Ahead of us on the wall in an iron holder, there stood a torch.

'Feels a bit convenient with the fungi gradually disappearing around us,' he mused.

'True.' I took it down and lit it with practised moves. 'So, dark or fair?

He was eyeing the road now, which forked three ways ahead of us. 'We still have no idea how to find this key. What if we just circle around for weeks?'

My eyes caught on something red that glinted on the ground of the rightmost tunnel. It was a perfectly round ruby with unusual circles around it. I stooped to pick it up. Whoever cut and polished the stone clearly knew what they were doing. I'd hardly even pocketed it before I spotted a moonstone a little further up. Then a stunning yellow sapphire not far, also completely round.

'This is the point where we can stop pretending that this isn't a test. And whoever prepared it clearly knows you well!' Kris stated behind me.

I hesitated, just for a moment, before protectively closing my hand around the sapphire. 'Even so, I'm not going to just leave these here.' I turned back, my eyes following the line of colourful stones waiting for me. 'I already lost most of my topazes in that flying boat.'

And so, we went. Me stopping every few steps, raising gemstones high and admiring the beauty of them in the torchlight, Kris with his hand on his sword hilt, exploring the tunnel ahead of us or looking behind, preparing for some unknown enemy. Not that any came. It was only us and the gemstones until the tunnel once more broadened into a vast cave. The ceiling vaulted away from us into darkness, the floor shelved into a lake unstirred by any breath of air. Far out across the black expanse of the lake, the cave roof gradually descended once more, narrowing the gap between water and stone until, at last, they met. How far and how deep the waters might run, I couldn't say, but nor did I care. The ground in front of us was covered with black sand and scattered with scores, if not hundreds, of gems and precious stones. All were round, shaped and polished to perfection. Further ahead, a thick circle of bricks made of gold.

'I think I'm going to need a bag,' I said and stepped forward to lay my hands on the nearest gem.

'Wait!' Kris stopped me mid-step.

'Why?'

'There's just something about how this is all laid out. See those spots?'

I held the torch higher. There were a few small, round patches where the sand was white amidst all the black. Now that I looked closer, there was a white spot like that under each of the gems, too.

'Some stones have already been taken,' I acknowledged defiantly, seeing no reason why I shouldn't gather the rest.

He pointedly looked at my pack, bulging with my growing collection. I didn't like where this was going.

'Could you light those other torches on the wall for more light?' I knew he just wanted to keep me away a little longer, but I did as I was told. A bit more light couldn't hurt.

He walked around the edge of the gemstone field, his hand raking his hair as he looked at the stones from different angles.

'Can I just take some of these near the wall?' I tried my luck.

'No. I think we need to put some back,' he said.

'Put them back?'

'I don't think these are random patterns.'

I tried to see what he was getting at. There were no clear circles or squares. I couldn't even make out constellations.

I walked over to where he was, skirting the area around as he did, rather than walking through it. But even from there, it all seemed unstructured to me.

Something made me turn and look behind us. The edge of the water was only a few meters from us, crystal-clear and unmoving. Maybe we could fill our waterskins once we were finished here.

'I think it might be a map,' Kris said suddenly. That snapped my attention back straight away.

'A map? How?'

'A space map. Depicting part of a galaxy.'

'You lost me.'

'Your planet, your world circles, orbits around a star. Your sun. And you also have a moon that orbits around your planet. Where I'm from, we also have a moon, a bit similar to yours if I'm not mistaken. But our planet orbits around two suns. Along with sixteen other planets. See that yellow sapphire there?' He pointed at a stone nearby. 'That could be a sun like yours. And all those round stones nearby planets circling it. Of course, it's not an accurate depiction. It's what we call an Ethorinian map. The planets are shown far closer to each other and bigger than they are in reality, so we can see better what we're looking at. The distances are so vast that otherwise, the planets would be too small to see.'

'And your point is …? '

'Let's put some stones back in the empty places and see if anything happens.'

I sighed and pulled out a handful from my pack. 'Here,' I said and moved to place a pale blue aquamarine onto the white patch next to the sapphire.

'No, wait!' Kris said. 'That colour suggests an icy planet. Anything that close to a sun would have lost all water from its surface thanks to the heat. We need something brownish, red-brown or dark yellow. No, nothing that big so close!' he said, dismissing my next suggestion.

I sighed and poured all of the stones out onto the ground.

'This one.' He picked out a striped, dark agate. 'This might do.'

I watched him measure distances with his fingers and place a few more gems around the area.

'Can I put the aquamarine here further away?' I asked. 'There's another blue planet nearby already.'

'Yes, go for it,' he confirmed after a quick look.

I put the stone in its place like I knew what I was doing.

A metallic sound came from somewhere, like two swords clanking together. Next to the golden circle, a long gold pole rose into the air from the ground.

Ten minutes later we were both on our knees, lost in the puzzle, our stuff in a heap outside the gemstone field. Around the circle three more poles were standing. It looked like there was space for four more.

I lifted a blue-green opal next with a lot of white swirls in it. It looked different from the other stones. It felt different, too, a little warm against my palm. The other stones were more beautiful. More perfect. I would get a lot more for those ones anywhere. But this blue gem was more interesting. Its green shades shifted into yellow and brown here and there. But it was those white swirls against the deep blue that covered most of its surface that really stood out. I felt almost a connection to it. I couldn't say why.

As I looked at it, another sound hit my ear. Not from Kris's direction, crouching in front of me, a little to the left. The sound came from behind me. Like water splashing. I slowly turned. The surface of the lake rippled gently, but I couldn't see anything in the water. I slipped the stone into my pocket and went to fetch a torch.

'What is it?' Kris called behind me as I eyed the water, holding the torch high.

'I'm not sure,' I said. 'I thought I heard something.'

'Do you need me?'

'Oh, no. You just carry on. I'll let you know if I see anything.'

I stood there, watching the lake that once more lay still. Its water was remarkably clear near the shore, but what creatures it might hide further in, it was hard to say. Hopefully, only fish. Speaking of which, I didn't like how I couldn't see any. I walked back to where Kris was sitting on the ground.

'How are you getting on?' I asked him.

'Only a few more stones to go, and one pole,' he answered. 'It's starting to look like a tower in a way.'

I looked towards the construction we were building. He was right. Could this be the tower the medallion referred to?

'See this system here?' He pointed as I crouched down next to him. I saw another large golden topaz, surrounded by seven stones, reddish-or-angey ones closest, blueish ones out at the end. 'I can't find what comes here.' Kris placed his finger above a white patch where the third stone should have been.

I reluctantly pulled the blue opal from my pocket. 'This can't be it, can it?' I asked uncertainly. 'I mean, those are all reddish-brownish colours around the hole. The blue ones are all over there.'

Kris smiled as he took it from me for a closer look. 'See, this is different from those! The white swirls and all that blue are clouds and oceans. And those green-yellow-brown patches are land. For these conditions to form, a planet can't be too far away from a sun, and neither can it be too close. Still. These guys seem to be particularly lucky! We have less than a third of their water on our planet.'

'And that's important?' I asked, trying to follow.

'Water is very important,' Kris said, giving the stone back, indicating that I should put it into its place. He turned to watch it as I did so. 'It's … hey!'

He jerked his head back to look at his legs. A snake-like creature coiled itself around his right ankle, greenish grey and slimy, its long body stretching all the way back into the water. I swore, and with our swords out of reach, I jumped to my feet to get a small dagger out of my belt. Kris cried out. Despite his best efforts, he was already being dragged towards the water, one violent tug at a time, scattering gems as he went.

'Catch!' I threw the dagger to him, then rushed to grab a sword. As I leaned down for it, a shadow fell on me. Next, I was seized by three long tentacles and pulled into the lake in one swift motion. It happened so fast I didn't have time to empty my lungs by screaming. But neither did I manage to fill them much with air before finding myself underwater. I turned the sword in my hand and thrust its point down with all my strength. Scraping the bottom of the lake slowed me sufficiently to get a second dagger out of my right boot, much smaller than the first but sharper. I slashed at the nearest tentacle around my torso. They all tightened around me as the creature jerked in pain. I tried not to panic, not that it was easy, and attacked the same tentacle. It slipped from me after what felt like minutes but was surely less than that. Either way, I still had one around my hip and one coiled around my left leg, and my lungs were already begging me for air. I looked down and hacked at the next limb, but rushing, while struggling against being pulled further in, caused me to cut my hip, too, mixing my own blood with the creature's around me. The beast chose that moment to yank on me once more, making me lose my grip on the sword hilt, and it pulled me further into the belly of the lake—and undoubtedly towards its own, too.

At that moment, something else caught my arm from above, and I almost stabbed it before realising it was Kris. He somehow managed to pin his foot into a crevice on the roof of the cave, which this far in, was much lower. He finished removing the tentacle I already half-severed while I got rid of the one on my leg. Then he shoved me towards the shore while he swam for the sword.

My first thought upon breathing air again was that strangulation underwater was becoming a theme here that I would do anything in my power to avoid for the rest of my life. My second, turning back, was to wonder what all that blood swirling in the water was possibly doing to my friend, who had yet to re-surface. Would he let those dark powers in him take over once more? Had he gone after the monster and was cutting it into pieces even now? My question was soon answered by him bursting out of the lake, followed by five more tentacles. I rushed back with the other sword to help him.

I looked at him quickly as I joined his side. He seemed himself. 'You resisted it?' I shouted, impressed.

'I did,' he yelled back, stepping out of the way of a jabbing tentacle and slitting it apart with an elegant move.

'Well done!' I stabbed at another limb reaching for me. 'Keep it up!'

Fighting off the tentacles as yet more emerged was one thing. The wall of the cave above the lake starting to tremble and pieces of it falling into the water was quite another. A high-pitched, furious shriek filled the air, followed by another thump and more rocks falling into the water from the cave wall.

'Kris, go! Finish the map!' I shouted at him. 'I'll keep it busy in the meantime!'

He looked at me, clearly reluctant.

'That tower might be exactly what we need. This might be our only chance to finish what we started here. Go! I'll be fine, just hurry up!'

He ran off, and in no time, I heard another click behind me, signalling that the seventh pole was about to rise around the golden circle. I wanted to see what we had accomplished but was still too busy to look. The tentacles kept coming, no matter how many I cut.

'Conor, come on!' Kris shouted. 'I think we need the medallion here!'

I turned on my heel and started running towards the tower. The gold poles were joined by three gold rings higher up, but past it all, I could see Kris standing in the middle.

Half-way there, a few tentacles seized me again and lifted me into the air. The monster had clearly decided to change tactics and smash me against the ground from high up. I cut its tentacles in the air, having gained considerable practice in the last few minutes, and carried on falling towards the tower.

I caught one of the poles and jumped down from the lower gold ring next to Kris. I tried to ignore the lake creature's swarm of tentacles hunting around the base of the poles and the thumps against the cave wall becoming more frequent, causing more destruction.

I ripped the medallion off its chain around my neck and thrust it into a small, round recess at our feet. A bright light filled the inside of the tower. Outside, the gemstones rose into the air, all moving, some faster, some slower, circling around the large yellow topazes or some other, darker crystals. Further out still, the cave wall started to tumble down, water cascading through the breaks, and something huge moved in the background, pushing itself closer.

'Welcome to the North Sentry Gate, Conor Drew,' a female voice said in my head. 'Where to?'

'Can you hear this, too?' I turned to Kris, nervous all of a sudden. He knew how these things worked more than I did. Surely, he should take over now?

'I can. But she's asking you. Answer the question!' he urged me. 'Quick!'

The sea monster's tentacles were now trying to pull the poles apart, its huge body pressed into the narrow space that had opened in the cave wall. Water washed the ground outside the tower, and doubtless more was to follow once it finished pushing itself through the gap.

'Where to?' the female voice asked again. I looked at the swirling stones. Did I have to pick one?

'To the Supreme Key of the Dragon!' I said instead. There was nothing in this world I wanted more. A second thought occurred to me then, which was that we had left the horses outside and had to come back for them somehow later, but I didn't say anything. It was best not to over-complicate things.

The light within the tower intensified. Under our feet, the ground became so bright I couldn't look at it anymore. Small golden specks travelled from it up into the air above us, where a white disk formed. I couldn't tell if it was liquid, solid or gas. It didn't look like anything I'd ever seen before. A hot wind blew, drying my clothes almost instantly, and a noise unlike anything I'd ever heard before filled my ears. I was vaguely aware of the monster outside making its way into the cavern. I heard my heart beating in my ears like crazy, until suddenly a force flew us up, and I stopped hearing altogether.

I travelled through space in a dream-like state. It felt as if my body had fallen apart into a million tiny pieces, while my soul remained whole and was now flying through darkness faster than thought. I lost all sense of time. When a light blue circle suddenly appeared in front of me, I couldn't have said if it was a heartbeat or a lifetime later.

I stepped through the circle, answering its pull more by thinking of doing it, rather than actually moving my legs which I still couldn't feel. Not until my feet reached the ground on the other side. All the feelings rushed back into me in one swift motion then. Light, sounds, smells, colours, warmth, having something solid under my feet, the thrilling memory of what had just occurred. It was staggering. Suddenly, I also remembered that it might be here that I finally got to see the Supreme Key and steadied myself.

Kris stood next to me. We were in a library, not unlike the one in Castle Beren. In front of us, a couple stood in an embrace. My eyes naturally moved to the woman's face, and I stopped breathing. She looked at Kris, then looked at me. A mad joy filled me as our eyes met, pushing everything else in me aside. Nothing else mattered but this moment. I opened my mouth, wanting to call out her name, but no words came.

Her smile faded, and she tore her eyes from me, shifting her gaze to Kris once more. She almost looked guilty, or was it scared? I couldn't tell. I looked at my friend. His face was unreadable, as if too many different emotions were trying to take over his expression all at once upon the sight that greeted us, and the jury was still out on which one he might settle on.

I looked back at the woman and answered my earlier question. 'So, she's fair.'

Chapter 19

Selena

That evening, I really felt as if a dream had finally come true. As if in a story, where despite all odds, the female lead finally gets her fairy-tale ending with her prince charming. In that magical moment, when everything feels just right, the change in the soundtrack tells you that this is the last scene of the movie. THE END. But no! Instead, I had two other guys arrive out of nowhere. Two other princes, who I felt like I knew, but not really, although they certainly watched me as if they knew me and left the million-dollar question hanging in the air, unspoken: "Girl, what the hell are you doing?"

What the hell *was* I doing? I was staring into a pair of sharp blue eyes like nothing else in this life mattered. Or even existed. He was here! The guy from the photo was here! My heart almost jumped out of my chest, and I thought I could fly away with happiness. If only I hadn't been kept firmly on the ground by two strong arms, belonging to the man I'd been snogging all night.

Kristian del Rosso looked confused, yet knowing; happy, yet somehow disappointed. But why did that make me feel so guilty? I was a grown woman, completely entitled to be in the arms of a man who I actually knew. Who wasn't a … what? Time-traveller? Alien? That library door was locked for a reason! It wasn't me who—forget knocking—practically ripped the world open and stepped through!

I stared wide-eyed at the circular blue swirl behind him. What was that? A stargate? Only I could be woken from a dream by another one.

The dark-haired guy smiled sweetly. It filled me with joy. My heart told me he was here for me. That I could rely on him. "Everything is fine!" a warm look in his eyes told me. "You're with us now." Like that was all that mattered. And I wanted to believe him. Except, I could still feel those questing blue eyes on me, making me feel as if I should explain myself. Not that I had to. Yet, for some reason, I wanted to.

'Kristian?' I called his name out hesitantly, and he blinked, as if that single word had broken a spell. His expression softened, and for a moment, he looked like he wanted to say something, but his eyes shifted to Jake instead and widened in shock. Jake was still holding me protectively, and I moved to step forward, pushing his arm down.

'Back!' Jake practically growled the word, and for a second, I wasn't sure if he meant it for me or for them. The lightsabre hummed in his hand, its red laser blade against my throat. The two newcomers drew swords as one in answer, their weapons sizzling with a blue light.

'Jake!' I tried to turn my head to look at him.

An unfamiliar face looked back at me. 'Hello, Selena!' He smiled.

I stared, unbreathing. It was the same look in his eyes. The same smile. But a different face. Younger. A different voice. Deeper. And wasn't he a little taller, too?

'Who ...? Who ...?' I started, unable to articulate the question.

'My name is Laro,' he said. 'And there are two things you need to know right now. This laser sword is not a toy. And I will kill you in a heartbeat if you try anything,'

'Let her go!' Kristian said. 'It's me you want dead, isn't it? Why don't we swap?' He lowered his sword. 'Take me and let her go!'

'If I had wanted you dead, you'd be dead by now,' Laro responded in a frosty voice.

'I heard you stumbled away from him blind last time,' the third guy interrupted with an expression of strong dislike on his face.

'*You* I should have killed back then! And trust me, Conor, you're not getting away this time.'

'Try me!' Conor snapped back, anger flashing in his eyes.

'Enough!' Kristian ordered, stepping between them. 'Just tell me what you want. You said you don't want me dead. So, what *do* you want?'

'I want you on my side,' Laro said, giving Conor a despising look. 'Instead of his.'

'What?'

'You heard me. I know you're capable of a lot more than this. You're too good to be wasted as a Champion. The two of us would be unbeatable together. We could do anything.'

I felt something crawling on me in rapid motion and I looked down. A large, black spider was running up my stomach. Something flashed, causing Laro to wrench his hand away and drop his weapon, while I instinctively screamed and, without thinking, jerked myself out of his reach, trying to get the spider off me. It nimbly jumped away from me, landing on Laro, who already had his sword in his left hand and reached after me with his right. An apparently painful spider bite, followed by two blue blades, stopped him from catching me.

'You have a little trick up in your sleeve every time we meet, don't you?' Laro asked Kristian between sword strikes. 'Very clever!'

'Why me?' Kristian asked back. 'How do you even know me?'

Laro didn't respond. It seemed to me that he was focusing more on what he was doing instead. He was fighting against two, yet he had an unnatural speed to him that evened out the odds. An unnatural speed that was being eroded by the spider's venom. He had bursts of fast movement every now and then, but less and less often. My eyes found the spider again. It had jumped off Laro as soon as he tried to catch it and ran away into a corner. It was almost as if, just like me, it was watching the proceedings from a safe distance.

Kristian, who kept inserting himself between the other two, was forcing Laro further and further back, until he eventually knocked the lightsabre out of Laro's hand and had his sword pointing at his neck.

'Why me?' he shouted at Laro. 'How do you know me?'

'You are my brother,' Laro said, his face stern.

'That's impossible.' Kristian wavered, shocked by this revelation. 'We don't even look alike.'

'Different mother. Same father.'

'I don't believe you,' Kristian said, but he lowered his sword, looking at Laro more carefully.

'You can do better than this. You are more than this,' Laro told him. 'You know what I'm talking about. Remember who you truly are. Let it reclaim you!'

'No,' Kristian flatly refused.

Laro moved like a cobra. He jumped and kicked and punched and turned, too fast for my eyes to follow, until Kristian lay on the floor, his head against the bookcase wall.

'Stop right there!' Laro pointed a narrow black tube at Conor. He flicked something, turning on a little red light on its side, and it let out a short, high-pitched beep, repeating it every few seconds. 'You might have slowed me down with your poison, but I have my own tricks, too.'

'Conor, stop!' Kristian shouted when Conor ignored the threat. 'He can kill you with that in a second.'

'Drop the sword!' Laro ordered Conor.

Conor looked at Kristian, who nodded.

'Now move!' Laro walked Conor off towards the light blue stargate that still swirled in the background.

'You stay there!' he called out to Kristian. 'And cut your hand!' He tossed his head towards Conor's dropped sword.

Kristian grudgingly took up the sword and cut the back of his hand.

Laro stopped Conor not far from the gate, training the beeping tube on him.

'Taste it!'

Kristian licked the back of his hand, then angrily threw the sword away from him.

Then there was a pause. We waited for something to happen. I didn't know what it would be, but I had a bad feeling about it. I desperately tried to think of anything I could do. I hadn't dared to move a single muscle for a while, and I wasn't entirely sure that I still could. And what could I say or do to save the situation? Whoever this Laro or Jake was, he had clearly just used me. He wasn't interested in me or in my feelings. I wasn't a martial artist of any sort. I hadn't even been to the gym lately!

'Let it flow through you.' Laro was still talking to Kristian. 'Stop resisting it.'

Conor stood motionless, his face concerned. The way he was looking at Kristian made me think that he wasn't worried about himself; he was worried about his friend.

'Stop resisting it, I said!' Laro shouted at him, his face flushed with anger now. 'Otherwise, I will have to do something that will break you into submission. Starting with your friend here.' He looked back at Conor. 'I will enjoy killing you!' he said to him. 'You useless piece of shit! You had one job to do. One! To find that fucking Supreme Key. And you couldn't even do that. Conor Drew, famous thief and adventurer, couldn't even find his own treasure—his call of destiny!'

All that talk about finding something important made me remember something else. I quietly slipped towards that small table I wanted to go to right at the start. My bag was on it. I reached into it and pulled out the redemeter. I turned with it, terrified, but the others were paying no attention to me. Laro had seemingly decided upon executing Conor no matter what, and Kristian was begging him not to.

'Any last words, Conor?' Laro asked, a wicked smile on his face.

I stepped forward a few steps and lifted the redemeter high, showing its circular symbol-ridden rings to them. As I did so, the crystal in the middle lit up of its own accord, its golden light slicing through the room like a ray of sunshine.

'Hey!' I yelled at Laro. 'Isn't this what you want?' I really hoped it was. Or that it was something that would at least momentarily distract him. In the afternoon, he had looked very eager when I mentioned it.

Both he and Conor stared at me open-mouthed, with no words to articulate their surprise. Then Laro closed his mouth, and his eyes narrowed. My focus shifted as something pulsing drew my eye to their right, giving me an idea. I turned the round object, holding it as if it were a frisbee, and threw it.

'Catch!' I yelled and watched it sail towards the middle of the stargate.

'Noooooooooooooooo!'

Laro threw himself after it. His hands closed around it as he caught it, and at first, I thought my plan hadn't worked. But as he touched the stargate, it sucked him in, and the whole portal vanished as he disappeared through it.

For a second, I thought he wasn't truly gone as I could still hear his cry that ran out like an alarm as I took my throw. I needed a moment to realise that it was Conor making that noise. He was on the floor, his hand on his forehead, Kristian leaning over him to see what was wrong.

'He's okay.' He turned and smiled at me. 'It's just the shock.'

'No, he is not okay!' Conor insisted, lifting his head from the floor and looking at me, clearly upset. 'What have you done? How could you have done that?'

I looked back at Kristian, confused.

'What Conor is trying to say here—' He gave him a friendly pat. '—is: Thank you for saving his life!'

'Are you sure?' Conor was looking at me as if I had just killed his mother.

'Absolutely! That was a brilliant move. Thank you, Selena.' Kristian smiled again, a truly warm and happy smile this time, and I relaxed.

Conor mumbled something unintelligible, but I was too busy returning Kristian's smile and enjoying it. After a moment or two, it occurred to me that I should probably say something or ask questions, but I had no idea where to start. He might have been coming to the same conclusion himself, and his face grew more serious as he said, 'I'm sorry about your boyfriend. Jake, is it? But he might be alright, you know. Laro can make himself look like other people. That wasn't Jake.'

'Oh, that makes complete sense,' I said. It was strange enough how Jake acted today. Completely out of character, if I was being honest. How could I have believed that, after all that time, he was suddenly really into me?

'As I said, he might be fine,' Kristian repeated, seeing my expression.

'Oh, it's not that.' I waved the notion away. 'He's not really my boy-friend.'

'He's not?' he asked.

'Well, it's …' I trailed off. What could I say? It's complicated? After all that had gone down here tonight, my relationship with Jake was complicated? It really wasn't that complicated, at all. But do I tell him that Jake wasn't actually interested in me and let him think me a loser? Or should I just shrug, signalling that I didn't need to be in a relationship with someone to be privately intimate with them? And what exactly would that make me?

Conor chose that moment to step into our little circle, and I looked to him for help.

'We need to get that thing back.' He pointed at where the stargate had stood. I looked back at him, lost.

'Well, can't you just … you know?' I waved a circle in that direction, meaning to re-open the gate.

'No, we can't re-open that gate from here,' he said. 'It's very possible that it can never be opened again from anywhere. And I don't know where we are or how we can find our way back.'

'I'm sure I can help you with that,' I said reassuringly. 'I'm really good at finding things, you know.'

He rolled his eyes at that, as if I had made a joke.

'No, really. It's true,' I insisted.

'She already had the Key once,' Kristian added for my benefit.

'How did you find it?' Conor asked me.

'It was always ours,' I said. 'My family's. It's an old family heirloom,' I explained. 'But honestly, it's nothing special. Sure, it looks pretty, but it doesn't even always work.'

'Or maybe you just don't know how to use it properly,' Conor retorted defiantly.

'Maybe not,' I conceded. 'Actually, there's some old writing about it in its box, too. It never meant much to me, but it sounded interesting. I'm happy to give that to you, if it's so important,' I said, and I meant it. He seemed so nice earlier. I wanted to be back in his good books.

'Well, that could be a start,' he relented. 'Is it in this room?' He turned and looked around the library.

'Oh, no,' I said. 'I don't live here. This is my friend's mother's house. I'm here at a party.' I gestured towards the window, suddenly aware of how quiet the house sounded under the soundproofing of the library. But at least lights were still flashing outside, backing up my story. 'But you're welcome to come over with me right now. Or even spend the night. I live on my own, nobody will be asking any questions.'

"Shouldn't you be asking questions before you invite two strangers into your home?" Keiko would have asked me at this point. I looked at these two strangers. They didn't feel like strangers. Kristian walked away to investigate something in the corner while I looked at Conor and asked, 'Have we met before?'

'No.' He grinned at me. 'But I know how you feel.'

As he moved, I could see a few cuts on him. Some of them were still bleeding.

'Hold on, there's a first aid box here somewhere.' I remembered it from last year when I cut my finger at afternoon tea. A papercut! Seemed hilarious in comparison. I found it and tried to make him deal with his injuries. If anything, Conor just looked embarrassed and told me they were nothing to be concerned about.

'Listen to the lady,' Kristian said, walking back to us, picking up and pocketing Laro's lightsabre hilt on the way. 'Actually, can I please have a plaster for my hand, too?' he asked, turning it my way. In his other hand sat the black spider. I took a few involuntary steps back.

'I'm sorry.' I grimaced. 'I'm a little nervous of spiders.'

'Lucky it's not a spider then.' Kristian smiled.

I looked back at the spider, puzzled.

'It's like Storn,' Conor guessed.

'Yes,' Kristian agreed. 'He means a robot,' he told me.

'A robot?' Despite myself, I moved closer. 'It looks so real. Can it talk?'

'I can talk,' a vibrant voice responded. 'But I was instructed not to unless there were specific circumstances. Such as Kristian or Conor being around and nobody else.'

'Instructed by whom?' Kristian asked.

'By my creator, James Montgomery,' the spider responded.

'You *were* there!' I exclaimed, the memory returning to me. 'At my counselling session. That was you, wasn't it?'

'It was.'

'And when you were on me before you were there …'

'To protect you. One of my core programming modules.'

'Why? I mean, why am I so important? How do I fit into all of this?' I gestured widely around.

'I don't understand the question.'

'Artificial intelligences don't think like humans do.' Kristian turned to me. 'Core programming modules don't require reasons or explanations. It's just something they are meant to do without question.'

'Do you know,' I asked him, struggling to get my head around it all, 'how I fit in?'

'Sorry.' He smiled ruefully. 'I don't know. But if you want to find out, I'll help you.'

I nodded. Then I took an antiseptic wound spay out of the first aid box along with some wipes and turned to sort out Conor first.

'Are you happy to travel in my pocket, spider?' Kristian asked the droid once I concluded my nursing activities. 'We can talk more once we're at Selena's place.'

'I'd rather go back into Selena's bag, if that's okay with you.'

'It's okay with me,' Kristian laughed. 'Is it okay with you?' He looked at me.

'My bag? Were you in my bag all day?'

'I was.'

The day's events quickly rushed through my head. The interrupting buzzing. The angry DJ outside, accusing me of messing with her music. Even the house system that didn't want to let me in here. I looked at the spider suspiciously. Just what else was there in its core programming? 'What kind of things can you actually do?' I asked.

'All sorts,' the spider said, its response rather pointed and smug. Had I been able to see its eyes, I wouldn't have been surprised to see it wink at me.

I gathered my coat and bag, opening it for the droid. 'Come on, then,' I said and bravely watched it climb in, my stomach still turning a little as it happened. 'Dr James Montgomery would be proud of me,' I informed no one in particular.

'I'm sure he would.' Kristian gave me a warm smile and presented me with his arm. 'Shall we?'

I took it and looked at Conor. He stood on my other side, offering his arm, too. 'Did you say there was a party out there?' he asked with a lop-sided smile. 'I think I could use a drink.'

'I'm not sure we're dressed for the occasion, Conor,' Kristian stated as we headed out of the room.

'Oh, no, actually, you're perfect,' I reassured them. 'It's a dress-up party. Everyone looks weird.'

'Heh, weird! Thanks!' Conor mocked my choice of word, feigning hurt.

'You'll see what I mean soon,' I laughed.

'Bring it on,' he mused and pushed the doors open.

The noise hit us from outside, and it was strange to realise that the party had just continued as normal, while we could have died in that library. As we passed guests in corridors and rooms, I felt as if everyone was watching us. By the time we reached the garden, I realised two things, though. One was that it was a predominantly female interest we were generating—although I flattered myself into thinking that occasionally one or two men turned after me, too. Second was that apart from me, no one else understood what the two guys were saying. Nor did they understand what everyone else was saying, either. Had we been talking in a different language all along, and I didn't even realise it? What language was it? I tried to separate the two in my head as I translated short conversations. Both came to me naturally.

I thought it might be easier if I asked them what drinks they wanted and then went to fetch them myself, but somehow, just a few steps into the garden, we all had glasses in our hands and a circle of women standing around us.

As I looked around, hoping for a way out of the situation, I spotted Rhia and Estelle heading towards us. Rhia seemed to have lost her devil horns somewhere, leaving her luxurious red hair in disarray. She was practically being dragged by her perfect angel girlfriend. As they reached us, Rhia pushed a way through to me and all but fell on me, wrapping me in a drunken hug.

'Estelle says we need to call it a day and go to bed now,' she complained loudly in my ear. 'At my own party!'

'I'm sure Estelle is right.' I smiled, trying to make her stand on her own two feet.

'Well, as long as you're having fun, darling. After all, I organised it for you!' She cupped my face in her palms, then looked at my male companions approvingly. 'You're having fun, aren't you?'

I reassured her that I was, then helped her back to Estelle.

Estelle squeezed my hands before they left. 'I told you that you could easily find yourself much better guys than that Jake. Well done!' She looked happy for me. Then she gave a quick smile to them and led Rhia into the house.

'Good night!' I called after them, watching Conor turn next to me, as if helping to tuck the girls in was on his mind.

Kristian reached out and put a hand on his shoulder. 'Drink up!' he said without looking at him.

'Why can't we spend the night here?' Conor argued. 'I'm sure Selena's place is lovely, but this is such a big house! We could get that letter in the morning.'

'No,' Kristian said, still not looking at him but politely smiling at the ladies in front of us.

'Are you a model?' one of them, dressed as a princess, asked Conor.

Conor tilted his head towards me, waiting for me to translate.

'She asked if you're a model,' I said.

Conor turned to the woman, smiling, wanting to say something, then tilted his head back to me. 'A model of what?' he asked, puzzled.

'Modesty and saintly behaviour,' Kristian stated. 'Come on, let's go!'

He politely parted the circle and dragged us after him. Conor still managed to fetch a beer from a tray as we made it to the front gate.

'Hi!' Keiko greeted us outside. 'We wondered where you disappeared to.'

'We called a cab, and it's almost here,' Rob said. 'You could come with us if you wanted to … but I'm not sure it will be big enough for five.' He frowned.

'Oh, that's okay,' I said. 'I think we're just going to take the tube.'

'Are you sure?' Keiko asked. 'Where is Jake? And who are these guys?'

'Um. Jake left already,' I said. 'And these guys …' I turned and looked at them, playing for time. '… are my cousins from my mother's side of the family. As it turns out, they travelled up to London to surprise me with a visit.'

'From Eastern Europe?' Rob asked, surprised.

'Cousins?' Keiko stared at me. *You never mentioned them*, she was clearly thinking.

'Second cousins. Twice removed,' I responded, having no idea what I'd just said. 'We very rarely see each other.'

'Best to go,' Kristian turned to me. 'We don't want to bring trouble on anyone.'

I gave Keiko a reassuring hug and wished them good night. I hated lying to her, but I didn't want her to worry, either. In any case, we had already got into trouble tonight and escaped it. It was all behind us for now. Or so I thought.

A little later, we took the Northern Line from Hampstead, their swords bundled into my long, red coat and carried by Kristian. I was holding on to Conor, or tried to, who couldn't stop staring at the many wonders surrounding him.

'He comes from a pre-industrial planet,' Kristian told me quietly when Conor stopped to watch a red double-decker pass us by.

'And you?' I asked. It seemed to me that he enjoyed looking around just as much as Conor did, if not in such an obvious way.

'Oh, we're way ahead of you, I'm afraid.' He smirked.

'Oh, is that so?' I grinned. 'Please forgive us for our rusty farm-wagons that await us under the ground!'

Inside the station, the same ad was playing on a giant screen that I had seen in the hospital a few weeks ago. The Emerald Cove Detox Resort in the Grenadines. It was only 2D, but even so, Conor stood in front of it mesmerised. To be fair to him, that was how I felt, too, as I joined him. An upbeat remix played in the background as we watched the painfully beautiful bird's eye view footage of the white sand beaches, slowly stroked by the warm Caribbean Sea that gradually shaded from turquoise to the darkest deep blue. We gazed at the elegant resort, the tropical gardens, the hummingbirds, women receiving beauty treatments and drinking cocktails. People wearing very little, partying on a boat. Quick views of the surrounding islands. The twin Pitons of St Lucia. The Dunns River Falls in Jamaica. Then suddenly, it was all over, and the screen jumped to show the station departures.

'Come on, you two, this is not the time,' Kristian said softly behind us. We obediently turned, but Conor still shot me a grin with such an excited happiness on his face, as if he had somehow soaked up all the magic the real place had to offer.

'Nice, isn't it?' I grinned back, the bitterness I felt last time I saw the ad forgotten.

I paid for tickets, and we took the escalators down. It was two o'clock in the morning, and the platform was almost empty. Now that we had left most of the excitement behind us and were just standing quietly, waiting for the train, I could see how tired they both were. By the time we exchanged trains at Camden Town and sat in the last carriage towards Mill

Hill East, Conor on my right seemed to have decided that it was safe to doze off. With his head on my shoulder and his right arm half-protectively, half-lazily around my front, I wondered if he might have actually forgiven me for throwing the redemeter through the stargate. I wanted to ask him why it was so important to him but didn't want to ruffle his feelings and have him upset again. I might just find out eventually anyway.

I closed my eyes for a moment, too. I shouldn't have. The events of the past few hours chose that moment to catch up with me in one powerful adrenalin rush. The otherworldly beauty and mystery of the stargate, the violence, the anxiety, the strangeness of speaking an unfamiliar language, the powerful connection I felt to these two people. A sickening feeling of unreality spread through me, the terrifying fear of losing my grip on the world and becoming disconnected from my body. My head span, but my eyes flew open, and I turned my head to look at Kristian. I tried to focus on his narrow face. The dimples in his cheeks appearing as a slow smile pulled his lips slightly apart. His eyes found mine, anchoring me to the world, to the now.

'All good?' he asked me. His eyes flashed to Conor, then returned to me, checking if I was okay with his overfamiliar position.

'Ah, yes, don't worry,' I hurried to reassure him and turned my head towards Conor with a smile. 'I really don't mind.'

Kristian's smile faded into a sarcastic one. 'Women usually don't. Just be careful. He has a big appetite!'

He turned away from me and looked at the advertisements on the walls. I closed my eyes again, cursing myself for being such a fool. How was I supposed to tell him that while I liked the guy straight away, it wasn't Conor who took my breath away? That instead, it was him who lit me up with joy every time he smiled at me? How could I have said anything that might have sounded half-believable after spending the night canoodling with his half-brother—and now I was sitting there, letting his best friend cuddle me in his sleep? No, it was hopeless. Only God knew what he thought of me! And anyway, just how did you even impress a guy like him? A guy who could have clearly walked off with any one of those women at the party. I wasn't anything special. I racked my brain as to what I could tell him that might sound remotely interesting. My eyes caught on the colourful pharmaceutical ad playing on the wall. 'Pantheon.'

'There's a Pantheon in the book I'm currently reading, too,' I informed him. Kristian del Rosso seemed like one of those people who might be impressed if I sounded like I read on a regular basis.

'Oh, yes?' he asked, waiting for me to volunteer more.

'Um, yes. In the book, it's a sacred, celestial city where members of a secret order live. They work for Gods.'

'What book is that?' He frowned at me.

'It's called The Order of the Dragon. Dr Montgomery gave it to me to read it. I think he wrote it himself.'

'How do you know Dr Montgomery?' he asked.

'We only met once,' I admitted, unsure what else to say. Here I was, trying to look good in front of him, only to bring this up. 'He covered for my regular counsellor last week at my therapy session.'

'What kind of therapy are you doing?' he asked with a serious face, and I felt myself turn red with embarrassment.

'My brain does funny things sometimes. Nothing serious! Just anxiety attacks and that sort of thing,' I said.

'And was Dr Montgomery able to help you?'

'Oh, yes, he was really good, actually!' I enthused. 'I mean, he obviously wasn't able to fix things completely with just one session, but he made a very good start at it. And this book seems to be helping, too. I don't understand how, but it does!'

'But you might need more than that,' Kristian said, with some concern in his voice.

'Oh, no, I'm fine. Really! I've been like this for a long time; I'm used to it. It's nothing.'

'It's not something to be embarrassed about,' he said. 'Actually, I, too, had some mental challenges lately. But eventually, I was able to cope. And it's because meditation and mental self-control has always been part of my education. A lot of it I learned from Dr Montgomery himself.' He smiled. 'Maybe I could help you. If you wanted me to.'

'That would be nice.' I smiled back, enjoying that spark of affection that returned between us. It disappeared as quickly as it started. The next moment, he looked up, and his face hardened.

'Conor? Conor, wake up!' He shook Conor's arm. 'We have company!'

I turned and looked to see what he meant. A tall, dark-haired woman entered the carriage. The same one I saw at the party, looking down at us from the balcony. The huge, muscly guy was behind her once again. Kristian seemed to recognise them from somewhere, too, because he stood, stepping protectively in front of me.

'Where's Laro?' the woman hissed at Kristian.

'He decided to take a bath,' Conor responded, standing up with a long knife flashing in his hand. 'Don't worry, the water is lovely. We tested it for him already.'

'Enough of the silly jokes! You're going to tell me now, or you all die here.'

I stood awkwardly behind them, looking at the handful of travellers who moved to the other end of the carriage, one pulling the passenger alarm.

'Ladies and gentlemen, this is your driver speaking. I'd like to inform you that one of our passengers has pulled the passenger alarm,' the robot driver announced through the tannoy rather cheerfully. 'We'll be pausing our journey at our next stop while we investigate the nature of the problem. Our next stop is Highgate.'

'This is our stop,' Kristian said. 'Why don't we just all get off and discuss things peacefully?'

The woman started laughing, as if this was somehow hilarious. She lifted her hands in the air and rolled her eyes back until only the whites showed. My anxiety attack returned at that, as if a pair of invisible hands had started ripping the fabric along its seam, unravelling something unknown, something terrifying inside me. My mind rushed like lightning into a far-away place. I tried to stop it, far more scared about what that might do to me than about anything else that crazy woman might attempt.

A powerful force tangled itself around my neck, choking me and forcing me to kneel. I saw Conor and Kristian in front of me dropping similarly. A breeze rose, lifting my hair. Glass broke around us, shards flying. I saw Kristian slowly push himself up against the woman's power, while Conor struggled, whereas I simply ignored her attack altogether. Behind the pain and breathlessness she was somehow causing, there was something much more horrifying going on in me. I wanted to scream for help. To point out what was happening to me. But I had no name for it.

No air to scream. No strength to do anything. With a final effort, I reached out and grabbed the back of their shirts, my fingers pushing against them for help or to just feel close to them as I died. A moment later, something in me exploded, and everything went dark.

Chapter 20

Kristian

Pantheon, Styx, BD19S2 11-77Δ

he's going to be fine,' Terek repeated for about the tenth time. It wasn't enough. Was he even medically qualified to make such a judgement? 'She just needs some sleep.'

I looked at Selena, the way she lay there on the bed, like a pale, lifeless doll. I say "bed", but it was a low, soft platform with pillows that covered half of the room.

'All rooms around here are submerged in Ethiria, a sacred lifeforce which will heal all your internal and external injuries. It also relaxes the mind and clears your energy paths,' he continued. That didn't impress me much. I wanted a full-body scan and an asclepeion for her. Figures and results that I understood displayed on a monitor where I could keep an eye on them. But I guessed the others had left Terek in charge for a reason, and they all seemed like intelligent and highly competent beings.

'Really, Kristian, this is the Pantheon. Just relax. You are safe here!' Terek tried to reassure me once more. He was a reptilian humanoid with blue-white skin and ears that shared something with horns. They pointed down to either side, making his skull take on the appearance of a crescent moon or a strange axehead. 'Nobody will disturb you here, I promise,' he added.

Conor decided then that the moment when he simply couldn't stay awake anymore had come and he started to take off his boots. I couldn't blame him.

'We have the neighbouring rooms free and waiting for you,' Terek offered politely, which Conor promptly ignored. He took two folded blankets from a nearby pile and crawled onto the platform next to Selena. He gently put one of them over her. The other he pulled over himself and laid down, facing her. A heartbeat later, a quiet snoring indicated he was asleep, too.

'We'll be fine here, thank you, Terek.' The V-shaped lines on his blue forehead disappeared at the change in my tone. 'I'm sorry if I was difficult. It's been a long day.'

'Not at all,' he said. 'I know this place might be a lot to take in, and you must have several questions, but I promise you that can all wait until you're rested first.'

I had more questions than he could count, but deep down, I knew he was right, so I left it at that.

'There's a room through that door where you can wash yourselves. You'll find clean clothing there, too. And someone will be around with food when you wake up. If there's anything missing or anything you need, just tell them to call me. But I'll be back later, anyway.'

'That's very kind, thank you,' I said, wishing he would just go now. Exhaustion overwhelmed me, and I couldn't believe that the last time we had a proper sleep had been when we were still a good day's ride away from Borond. How many hours ago that was I had no idea. It must have been a lot. I thought of Storn and hoped he was alright. I hoped he freed Conor's horse, too, and the two of them were far away from that dark place.

'I'm sorry?' I said, realising Terek had said something as I sat down on the bed.

'I only said that you were welcome. James is an old friend, and it's a pleasure to have finally met you, too.'

'Same here.' I smiled. 'Oh, and Terek? Sorry, just one question. The way Selena brought us here …'

'You mean how she teleported you?' Terek's dark blue mouth widened into a smile, and for a moment, he looked excited.

'Yes. Is that common around here? Are there many others here who can teleport people the way she did?'

'Oh, no.' He laughed. 'Never. Nobody has ever done anything like that. This gift is unique to her.'

'Thanks,' I said and watched him finally leave the room, closing the door behind him.

I kicked off my boots and, following Conor's example, took a blanket from the pile. I climbed up to Selena's other side and leaned close to her. Her face had several thin cuts across it where flying shards of glass had hit her. Conor's was the same, and I knew I must have had them, too. She was otherwise deadly white in the dim light of the room, her breathing so shallow, my face had to be almost touching hers to be able to detect it. Not a single muscle twitched anywhere, as if that faint breathing took up all her remaining strength. Despite the blanket Conor put over her, her skin still felt cold to my touch. I looked at the blanket I had for myself. I wasn't even sure why I had one. I wasn't cold. If anything, I felt a little hot.

I laid down behind her, put my arm around her and pulled her close. I'd thrown the blanket over both of us, and before I knew it, I was fast asleep.

I woke, feeling a peace in me that was unlike anything I'd experienced before. A delicious, complex aroma reached me, and my stomach rumbled in response. I sat up and checked on the others. They were both still fast asleep. Conor was smiling in his sleep, and as I looked at his face, I realised that the cuts had indeed disappeared. Selena's skin appeared similarly healed. Her breathing was now much deeper. Her expression somehow more natural. There was a little colour to her cheeks. My gaze moved over to her lips, to the delicate curve of her neck. Then I closed my eyes and pushed myself away from her before my mind could wander further.

Several tables now stood at the end of our bed, heaped with food. There were bowls of what looked like both raw and cooked fruits and vegetables, stews, fried fish, soup, various types of bread, cheese, butter, boiled eggs, yoghurt, pasta with piping hot sauces and more grilled vegetables and colourful fungi. Even cakes! It took me a minute to understand what our hosts were trying to achieve. I believed they were assembling food from both Conor's and Selena's worlds. I had to laugh when I couldn't find anything on the tables from our regular fare at the university. Just where was my exciting vitamin jelly and altered water?

As I buttered some freshly baked bread that was still slightly warm, shreds of my dream started coming back to me. We were sitting around a table, eating—Selena, Conor and me. Laughing and talking and stealing each other's food. But not here. We sat outside, somewhere in a garden behind a big house, with sunshine on our faces and bird song around us.

It felt like a place I knew. That felt special. More special than a sacred city full of celestial warriors and healing energy-infused sleeping rooms.

I heard movement and watched Conor carefully climb through the bed and wordlessly join me. With his sole focus clearly on the plates, I waited until I thought he was more or less full before I told him what was on my mind.

'She's pretty special, isn't she?' I asked quietly, without looking at him.

'I only wanted to be close to her so I could protect her if something happened again,' he bristled.

I grinned into my bowl upon realising where he thought this conversation was heading. 'No, that's not what I mean,' I said as our eyes met. 'Don't you think it's curious how she brought us here? How, just like you said the Key would, she opened a door for us into a different world?'

Conor didn't say anything but chewed his food slower as he thought about it.

'You said the Supreme Key communicates with the Gods. It interprets their signs,' I whispered. 'Selena saw a sign which had this place's name on it just before we were attacked.'

'No,' Conor said, frowning at me.

'What no?' I pushed on. 'Just think about it! "The Supreme Key has its own mind. It's like a living thing." Those were your words, not mine. And when you asked at the gate to be taken to the Supreme Key. Once it opened, it wasn't facing some small table in the corner of the library. It was facing her!'

'Just what are you trying to say?' Conor asked, his voice raised. He knew what. But I told him anyway.

'That I think whatever Laro said to you in the library, he was wrong. You *did* find the Supreme Key.' I looked back at Selena and added, 'And most importantly, you didn't just find it. You still have it!'

'What about those descriptions of the Key being a round object?' he protested.

'What were you told originally?' I asked. 'When you heard the prophecy. Did they tell you what the Key looked like?'

'No,' he admitted. 'I only found those descriptions much later.'

'Maybe those were meant to mislead you. And everyone else.'

'But she said she'd used it herself. She said it didn't always work.'

'Conor, I don't think it was that thing that didn't always work,' I said. 'I think it was her mind.'

He wiped his hands on a wet towel and climbed back onto the bed. He settled down in his previous spot, crossed his legs in front of him and just watched her.

'I'm gonna go wash off the dirt,' I said. 'According to Terek, there are some clean clothes waiting for us in the other room.'

He nodded. I went in and closed the door behind me. I knew he needed some time alone with what I'd just made him see.

By the time I emerged, Terek was back and discussing something quietly around the table with Conor.

Selena was still asleep. I thought she would be awake by now.

'She will wake when she's ready,' Terek tried to reassure me when he saw me checking on her. 'Kristian, why don't we go for a little walk while Conor gets changed?' He added, 'We'll be back soon.'

I sighed and let myself be steered outside to the elegant terrace through which we had previously entered. There was a stunning view of the surroundings that I failed to appreciate amidst the chaos of our arrival.

Had I stood here, thousands of years earlier, I would have looked at the rugged charm of the place and never thought that anyone could, or should, attempt to build here. Plunging ravines, waterfalls tumbling into spray, greenery clinging defiantly among the bare rock. To construct anything here, let alone grand golden buildings that soared cathedral-like to threaten the sky, would have seemed madness. First and foremost, because of the engineering challenge, and secondly, because of the affront to the wild beauty that the place was blessed with already. But amazingly, the architects had managed to build a series of towering wonders that somehow both preserved and enhanced the original. A lazy, dark honey-coloured sunshine cut across light pink clouds, painting everything more vibrant, making the city sparkle with a spellbinding charm.

'Beautiful, isn't it?' Terek asked. 'Why don't we take a little turn just across the main square there, and then back through those bridges?' He pointed. 'I'll show you all around more after the initiation.'

'Initiation?' I asked, caught by surprise.

'Of course. I'm afraid you won't be allowed to leave here, at least not without your memories adjusted, unless you become initiates,' he said.

'Well, why don't you tell me more about the Order and this place first?' I smiled and gestured for him to lead the way.

'I'm so sorry! Silly me!' Terek shook his head. 'It's just that usually, by the time we welcome newcomers here, they know all about these things already. They would have passed all their tests. They would be ready to start their probation period. But of course, they don't normally just teleport here by themselves, either!' He gave me a pointed look before turning and slowly making his way down the steps. 'I'm not even sure where to start.'

'Why not start at the beginning?' I suggested and followed him down.

'The Order exists to protect the world,' he told me once I joined him at the bottom of the staircase, stepping onto a flagstone path that was bordered by narrow lakes on either side, blanketed by water lilies. 'Its purpose is to secure peace, to safeguard freedom and the spiritual and technical progression of species. And all this, of course, without ever being noticed. Without claiming credit. Without making ourselves known. It is simply our duty. Our duty to the Order and to the Gods themselves. *We are the fire that keeps away the dark.*'

'I'm not someone with a strong sense of faith,' I admitted. 'What if I find it difficult to believe in Gods?' It was still strange to think that James had served in this order. He wasn't a religious person, either.

'It's not a question of belief,' Terek said. 'You will meet them. Or, more accurately speaking, experience them.'

'How? Will they be at this initiation?'

'No. Not at the initiation. At the initiation, they usually send a sign, indicating which of them you will belong to. They will appear at the ceremony where you are made Champions, full members of the Order.'

'All of them? Are there many?'

'There are eleven altogether, and no, not all of them at the same time. Even we, who are more experienced, would find it difficult to meet more than a few at once. Their presence can be overpowering. Especially the presence of the Dragon, who is their leader and the most powerful.'

'Do you think we would belong under the Dragon?' I asked.

'It's difficult to imagine that Selena wouldn't. She is the Dragon's Key, after all. And, of course, your Uncle James was a Champion of the Dragon, too.'

'When you say Selena is the Dragon's Key, what does that mean exactly?'

'Our bodies are not generally built in a way that makes interaction with the Gods easy. Dictos and Test Masters receive visions from them, identifying possible candidates and tasks, but most of us are simply not equipped—are not born in a way that makes communicating with them straightforward. Imagine being an ant and a human such as yourself trying to talk to you. Make you understand what they wished you to do and why. Selena's spirit has an unusual combination of elements which enabled the Dragon to make an adjustment in her case. To add a divine particle which will help their communication, and also give her unique powers, such as teleporting between worlds.'

'I don't think she has an understanding of these things yet.'

'No. But she will gradually learn them once you become champions.'

The way he spoke about it sounded so definite. Like there were no alternatives. Yet, when I looked into my heart, I knew he was right. It didn't feel like a choice that had been made for me. It felt like a path I wanted to travel. A life with higher purpose that I wanted to live. A realm where James had excelled himself already, and by the sound of it, I had some big shoes to fill.

'I'm in,' I said, 'but Selena should still be given a choice. It's just not right otherwise.'

'Of course. You will be all given that choice,' Terek confirmed. 'Which brings me to Conor. He said something to me earlier which sounded like he didn't want to join. He made it sound like a joke, so I wasn't sure what to make of his comment.'

I sighed and turned to watch a group practising unarmed martial arts in a green area nearby. 'Leave him to me,' I said. 'I think he'll change his mind.'

My words sounded more confident than I felt. On one hand, I really couldn't imagine what he would do after all this. Would he go back to his old life and leave me here alone? Were there any treasures left on Drelos he hadn't already found? On the other, was I just being selfish? Didn't

Conor deserve a choice, too? Just because I didn't want to lose him, shouldn't he be left alone to walk away, if that was what he wanted? I thought of the bond that had formed between us in the last couple of weeks. Was it strong enough to keep us together? I guessed a time was coming when we would find out.

The group of practitioners sat on the grass and watched an instructor in a black uniform show them a few complicated moves with a longsword. That took my thoughts far away from Conor to other, more painful questions. Was Laro really my half-brother? Why was he pursuing me with such determination? He must have found Selena through his search for the Supreme Key, although why he wanted it, too, I couldn't fathom. Just the thought of them being together the way we found them turned my stomach and filled me with a jealous rage I hadn't even known I had in me.

'Terek, was there anyone else in my family who had previously been a member of this order?' I asked.

'No,' he responded straight away—a little too fast, I thought. His large, green eyes were fixed on me, as if trying to see into my thoughts, his face suddenly more serious than before, his gaze colder. I decided then that those questions could probably wait until I met James again.

'And what is it like to be a Champion?' I asked, conjuring up an easy smile for him, trying to move the conversation back to friendlier waters.

'Oh, I'm not a Champion.' He smiled back, seemingly pleased by my mistake. 'I mostly deal with what you'd call the running of this place. But of course, I do know a bit about Champions. I've been working with them all my life, after all.'

'Ithorion said some of them work alone while others work with their soul circles,' I said.

'You met Ithorion?' he asked, looking both surprised and impressed. 'And of course, he's right. We have some Champions working alone, but mostly they work with their circles. They often give themselves names. Like the Golden Circle or the Deadly Fangs. These are not official names. But we use them, nonetheless. It's better to work within your circle than alone.'

'Sometimes I worry about them too much,' I admitted, not comfortable with the thought of Conor or Selena risking their lives, whatever the cause.

'That's partly unconscious self-defence,' Terek said.

'Self-defence? How so?'

'Well, you are a tora. Have you started sensing their minds yet?'

I smiled with embarrassment and nodded. 'I often find it's easier when I'm not looking directly at them. But even then, I don't get exact thoughts or feelings, just a kind of vague blur of both. With an occasional object thrown into it all. I feel a little guilty about doing it, but I can see how it could be useful with an occupation such as this.'

'It usually starts with sensing feelings.' Terek nodded. 'You can't stop it from happening. And I imagine it must be nice, as long as they are happy. But as soon as you three get into trouble, this will change. On top of your own fear, you will feel their fear, too. On top of your own pain, you'll have theirs. So, in a way, it is in your interest for them not to suffer. It is not uncommon for toras who've lost members of their circle to retire. They say the sense of loss is so unbearable they feel too broken to carry on.'

We stopped in the middle of a long, graceful bridge, moving aside to let others pass. I looked across the city, or the Pantheon, as they called it. With my eyes firmly on the breath-taking white-gold buildings, my mind travelled back to a much darker place. To that awful skeleton hall of Borond, where Conor nearly fell into a pit full of snakes. I remembered that overpowering sense of dread, so strong it cut across even my own psychopathic madness. And again, when that bloodsucker had him in her grips. And again, when Laro had threatened to kill him in the library. Would I be able to face that again? And again? That something like that could happen to Selena, too, didn't even bear thinking about. Maybe I should do this alone. But then again, Conor was apt to get into danger, regardless. Maybe it was better if I was around and had at least a chance to protect him?

As if on cue, a little signal in my head that was unique to him, had me turn and look to the right. He was stepping onto the bridge in the company of a tall, young man, who wore his long, dark hair in a ponytail. I guessed he was in his late teens.

'Selena is awake and well,' Conor announced once they reached us, making it look like it was him who was able to read my mind. 'And this is Ramin, by the way.'

'You didn't leave her there alone, did you?' I demanded.

'She's not alone,' Ramin said. 'And Aiki was just on her way to meet her, too.'

'Aiki? That is good,' Terek stated. 'Aiki is Quede's daughter, who is the leader of the Order,' he explained. 'You'll like her. Everyone likes Aiki.'

'Quede? Quede is the leader?' I remembered her dark face. Her sharp eyes. Her fierce spirit.

'You've already met Quede?' Terek turned to me.

'Only in my dreams,' I said. Then realising how funny that sounded, I added, 'Actually, in my uncle's dream, to be precise.'

Terek gave me a long, thoughtful look which Conor interrupted with his own questions.

'Is Aiki also a Champion?' he wanted to know.

'No,' Terek said. 'Aiki is training to become a Test Master.'

'Like Ithorion?' Conor frowned, the answer taking him by surprise and not in a good way.

'They are not all as curmudgeonly as him.' Terek laughed. 'They are often quite friendly and supportive. Besides, Ithorion was the chief of all Test Masters, second only to Quede in command. But he's long retired. You don't need to worry about him testing you anymore.'

'So, are you going ahead with this?' Conor asked me.

'I am,' I said. 'And you should become an initiate, too. There's a probation period. You can still decide whether you want to become a Champion by the end of that.' I looked at Terek for confirmation, who nodded. 'Otherwise, they will erase your memories of this place very soon and we'll need to say goodbye to each other. And you won't even get to know Selena. Your special treasure you spent half your life searching for!'

'You think Selena will want to join this Order, too?' he asked, taken aback.

'I honestly think there's a very good chance that she will,' I told him.

'Fine. Sign me up,' he agreed with a newfound eagerness that might have fooled Terek. But I suspected this was just so he could spend more time with Selena and have a chance at talking her out of it, too.

'What else can we expect at this initiation?' I asked.

'Most importantly you will be allocated to a Dicto. It is basically some-one experienced in the Order who will supervise you and to whom you will report.'

'We'll be given a boss?' Conor turned on Terek. 'I thought Kris was our leader.'

'Yes,' Torek explained patiently. 'Kristian is your tora. The leader of your soul circle. But you, meaning mainly him, actually, will still report to an esteemed member of the Order we call a Dicto. Dictos report to Dicto Supremes, who form the Council of the Order and report to Quede. Dic-tos won't accompany you on your assignments. They are simply there to give you tasks, to aid your learning and progression within the Order, and to support you. Test Masters similarly have their own hierarchy, just as we, who work on the operation of the Pantheon do. But in the end, Quede is in charge of us all.'

As we talked, we carried on walking over the bridge, and soon, we were on a walkway leading back to where we started off. On the other side of the terrace from our allocated room, in front of a graceful waterfall, there was a bench. Two women sat on it, and although I could only partially see one of them, due to the several men standing around them, I knew the other one to be Selena.

'The Golden Circle.' Terek indicated with his head.

'Champions?' Conor asked.

'The best. They are the only circle who directly report to Quede, her-self,' Terek said. 'Their tora, Clive Walker, is the one in the middle. He can be a little cocky sometimes, but he's a really good guy otherwise.'

'He has four members in his circle?' I could only see his back. His dark blond hair, light blue shirt, black trousers, black boots. With his left foot up on the bench between the two women, he leaned forward as he spoke. He was leaning close, a little too close, to Selena.

'Yes, four men,' Terek confirmed. 'But they are all very chilled and tactically minded by nature, so I think he's rather lucky with them.' He gave Conor a sideway glance, who in turn looked at me quizzically.

I dismissed his unvoiced question with a shake of my head. This was not the time. Clive Walker turned his head and looked us up and down as we approached.

'And here they are!' he announced in an over-friendly manner as we reached them, pushing himself away from the bench and lowering his foot to the ground. 'Welcome to the Order, guys! We're just back from Earth, where we tidied up a few things after your little accident.' He laughed. 'Don't worry! I'm sure you'll get the hang of things soon,' he added in a slightly condescending tone.

'Thanks for the help,' I said hurriedly, placing a seemingly casual hand on Conor's shoulder that I would have preferred to plaster over his mouth, had that not been too obvious. 'We'll aim to do much better next time.'

'No worries. That Mara was quite something! But nothing that me and my guys couldn't handle. Here, let me introduce you. This is Matt.' He pointed at a short, skinny man with olive skin and a dark beard, who shook my hand with a friendly smile.

'Kris,' I introduced myself and moved to greet the next member. They all offered a few kind words, and I did my best to give them all my attention, but it was hard with Selena on the bench. I avoided looking at her, delaying it for as long as I could, not keen to display any weakness of affection in front of this crowd. I knew it was coming, though, and I was both longing for it and dreading it. Her attention on me, like a sweet little hook in my chest, pulled me closer, yearning for me to finally look at her and meet her eyes.

After that dream I had in the cave, where I somehow found her and we connected, I wondered if my feelings for her had something to do with the soul circle. Ithorion said relationships between members formed quicker and became stronger than usual. And I had never believed in love at first sight. But surely, that couldn't be normal! I doubted soul circles could function well in the Order if toras just fell for their team members.

But whatever it was, I could hardly stop thinking about her ever since. As if, even while I was still in those dark tunnels, she was pulling me ever closer to her.

'And this is the wonderful Aiki,' Clive was now gesturing at the young black woman, who stood to introduce herself. On Alba, I'd seen many perfect beauties. But Aiki was more than that. There was something mesmerising about her. A playful but fiercely intelligent look in her big, dark eyes. A natural sensuality to the way she pushed her skilfully braided hair back. I could tell Conor next to me was captivated with her straight away, just as I would have been, were my heart not thoroughly occupied by someone else. 'I'm Clive Walker, tora of the Golden Circle,' Clive continued. 'And this lady I don't need to introduce to you.' He smiled at her.

I still didn't look at her. 'I'm Kristian del Rosso,' I said instead, 'and there's really nothing interesting about me I could tell you. Conor Drew, here, on the other hand, has been a legendary adventurer all his life. His latest achievement was locating the long-lost Supreme Key for the Order!'

There was a little general applause at that as the focus of the group shifted to Conor, and as he started talking, I slowly turned my head and looked into the soft brown eyes of Selena Soto.

'It's good to see you're feeling better,' I told her quietly, doing my best to keep my face straight, despite the warm, crazy joy that rushed through me like a wild horse. I didn't know how much of it was my happiness and how much was hers. All I knew was that I desperately wanted her in my arms and my lips on hers. But even if that was a good idea for us, and there was ever a place and a time to do so, this was not it.

'… But really, I usually work on my own,' I heard Conor saying now, 'which suits me fine, and I'm honestly still considering returning to it once we're done here.'

'Well, in that case,' Clive said with another award-winning smile as he reached out to Selena to help her up from the bench, 'maybe we could borrow the Supreme Key every now and then. I'm sure you wouldn't mind.'

Conor made a face that suggested that he would actually mind that very much, and putting an arm around Selena, he pulled her close to him and away from Clive. 'In your dreams, pal!' He grinned at Clive.

'Aaand we actually have a long overdue circle meeting to attend,' I said and put my hands on their backs to steer them away. 'It's been great to meet you all, but we should really be on our way.'

'See you around,' Clive responded with an amused look and turned away to talk to the others.

Soon, I was marching Conor and Selena down the road towards a large garden, which in true Pantheon fashion, seemed to have been crafted with an ambition to leave you in awe. We walked under a mighty tree full of huge, dark purple flowers. It had a few large low branches that stretched out close to the ground, one of which we settled on.

'You've been very quiet,' I told Selena. 'Is everything alright?'

'Yes,' she said. 'I think I'm just a little overwhelmed. I feel as if I lost my footing on reality at some point last night, and I've just been drifting along ever since.'

'I know perfectly well what you mean.' I laughed, watching her. Her lips curling into a smile, transforming her face. The way her wavy, soft blonde hair fell on top of the light green dress she now wore.

'Everything that Dr James Montgomery wrote in that book is true!' she exclaimed. 'I read it thinking it was fiction. I mean, who would have thought that a place like this—' She gestured around. '—could exist? It's incredible!'

'They do serve a rather good breakfast,' Conor acknowledged with a nod behind her.

'You probably know way more about it than us,' I told Selena. 'We've never read the book!'

'Did it mention any fun activities?' Conor asked.

'Fun activities?' Selena wrinkled her forehead as she tried to remember.

'All he means is social gatherings with a lot of alcohol where he can freely engage with the opposite sex,' I explained with a grin.

'Hey!' Conor reached around Selena and punched me in the shoulder. 'That's not all I mean,' he said, but he was grinning, too.

'Is it not?' I quickly reached around Selena, too, grabbed his tunic and gave it a good yank so he would lose his balance on the branch, laughing when I succeeded. 'What else?'

He adjusted his position and moved to do the same to me, but I was ready for him—or so I thought. A heartbeat later, I was on the ground and he on top of me, laughing.

'Other stuff! Okay, Kris? Other stuff!'

'What other stuff?' I twisted and had him change places with me in two moves, blocking his arms with a lock. 'What other fun activities are there for Conor Drew? Treasure hunt?'

To be fair, I thought he could have easily escaped my lock, had he moved fast enough, but he was still too busy laughing. By that point, we both were.

'Ahem!' Someone cleared their throat near us. Someone with a deep voice that definitely did not sound like Selena. I looked up to see a tall, robust man with a considerable moustache and raised eyebrows observing us.

'Yes?' I said, releasing Conor.

'My name is Hans. The Council of the Order requests your presence for an audience. If you would please follow me when you're ready.'

I got up and brushed off my clothes, then half-turned and smiled at Selena as I reached my hand out towards her. She caught up with me and took it.

'So, what's the plan?' Conor joined us on her other side as we followed Hans.

'Well, my suggestion is that we say we want to join the Order and become initiates. That way, they won't erase our memories of this place just yet, and we'll gain some insight into what it would be like to be proper members, Champions here. I've already made up my mind that this is something that I would like to do, but if the two of you decide after this probation period that it's not for you, you are free to walk away.' I looked at them. 'Unless, of course, you'd like to do so now.'

'And have my memories erased?' Selena asked with her voice raised. 'My memories of …' She didn't finish the sentence. But I knew what she meant.

'Yes, I suppose that would include your memories of us, too.' I looked over at Conor, then back at her. 'But you could probably just go back home then. Wouldn't that be something you'd like? To go back to your friends and family? Back to …' What was his name again? 'Jake?'

She gave me an incredulous look, let my arm go and quickened her steps to catch up with the man walking ahead of us.

'Nice one,' Conor said, patting my back.

'I just needed to know.' I smiled after her.

'And no better way to find out?'

'No time.'

'You can be such a cold-hearted little bastard sometimes.' He shook his head at me.

We entered one of the Pantheon's majestic buildings, the one they called the Claw, climbing stair upon stair, passing elaborately carved golden pillars in narrow corridors as we hurried after Hans and Selena. Ahead of us, a large double door loomed, and in front of it, a man and woman stood guard, wearing the gold, red and black uniform of the Order.

They opened the doors for us, letting us into a round hall. From up there, stairs led down to the middle of the room, where a solitary figure stood looking up at us. Quede. Around her were benches in tiered concentric circles, where around fifty Council members sat, who also turned their heads our way.

'If you could please join me down here,' Quede called out to us.

A soft murmur ran across the hall as the doors closed behind us, and the three of us made our way down the steps, Hans remaining outside.

'Welcome to the Order of the Dragon,' Quede addressed us in a formal voice. 'I trust you're finding your stay in our home pleasant?' Her hair was cropped close to her skull, as if not to let it distract anyone from her beautiful, hard face, sharp eyes and no-nonsense expression. Her mostly black uniform complemented her dark skin and made the gold amulet at her neck stand out even more. She had the same fierce, energetic disposition I remembered from my dream.

'We've been having a very enjoyable time,' I said. 'Thank you for your hospitality.'

'Good,' Quede turned on her heel, her black cloak flying after her as she took a few steps, then turned back to us. 'I would hate to hear that the nephew of James Montgomery suffered any inconveniences while he stayed at the Pantheon. Your arrival has been somewhat unusual and took us a little by surprise, but this is not something that will ever happen again.'

I frowned at the turn of her words, not exactly sure what she meant by them, but I had something more pressing on my mind I wanted to ask.

'Honourable Quede Ocana Idashi,' I said, remembering how Terek advised we address her. 'You mention my uncle. May I ask if you know his whereabouts? I haven't been able to contact him ever since I left Alba. I'm starting to worry.'

'James Montgomery abandoned this Order a long time ago,' Quede announced in a frosty voice. 'His whereabouts are neither my business nor my concern. I suggest you do your own research.'

Her unfriendliness took me by surprise. Had I done something wrong? 'But Terek told me that—'

'It doesn't matter what Terek told you,' she cut across my reasoning. 'You and Conor will have your memories of this place erased and will be sent back to your individual planets this afternoon.'

'But … the three of us were hoping to join the Order …' I trailed off under her hostile gaze.

'Were you now?' She walked slowly back to us, giving me a hard stare.

I was very confused. Was this some kind of test? What was her problem with me? Memories of that dream I saw her in started to come back to me. Hadn't she been arguing about something with James even then? Weren't they arguing about me?

'Are we not allowed?' I asked.

'Of course, you are allowed,' she responded in a mocking tone. 'As long as we can find a Dicto for you. Without a Dicto, unfortunately, nobody can be a Champion of the Order.'

I nodded uncertainly, not sure where the catch was. But I was sure there was one.

She looked away from me and turned slowly in a circle to address the Council around us.

'Respected Members of the Council of the Dragon! I hereby formally request that you volunteer, or volunteer someone under your supervision, as Dicto for the three people standing in front of you. To be in charge of and to be responsible for the actions of the attending Kristian del Rosso, son of Alessandra del Rosso and Tynan Dorion. The man we long suspected of involvement in the running of the Darkstar Alliance. The man who has for decades been blasphemously making his own poor copies of the divine gifts only the Gods can bless us with!' She turned and pointed a finger at me. 'Who even broke his own son's mind and spirit, and tainted him with demonic powers!

'And Conor Drew. Renowned thief and adventurer of Drelos. Who, in fact, doesn't even want to join this Order at all! Who has no interest in serving the Gods, serving the Order, or anyone else apart from himself. Who, even now, is more concerned about lining his own pockets than what happens here next. The two of whom would join this woman, who has never even been tested in a consecrated bond.' She pointed at Selena. 'The Supreme Key of the Dragon, who has the potential to become the greatest blessing and asset of this Order, or its most dangerous curse and downfall. Who among you, dear members, is willing to take responsibility for their joining? Who would guide and conduct them? Who is willing to accept this challenge?'

There was a deep silence around us. I turned and looked across the faces of humans and other races. Nobody was prepared to meet my eyes. Quede's words had them all cowering in their seats.

'I'm going to count to five.' Quede looked at me. 'If by the end of that count nobody comes forward, you won't be joining the Order. After the meeting, you will be taken to have your memories erased. Of this Order and of each other. One ...'

I looked at Selena, half-expecting tears in her eyes. But instead of sorrow, there was a fierceness in them I hadn't seen there before. Was she planning on something? Would she be able to teleport us from here before it was too late?

'Two ...'

But what then? Would we be hunted for the rest of our lives by a secret order whose fanatical members possessed supernatural powers?

'Three ...'

I moved my eyes over to Conor.

'I'm sorry.' His voice was barely a whisper. 'I'm sorry I let you down.' There was a profound sadness to him that was so unlike him, I thought it would break me then and there.

'Four ...'

I looked around once more. In the front row, a white-haired woman looked at me with concern, as if she wanted to say something. Quede walked up to her and stared at her until she looked down.

'Five!' Quede turned, and for the first time, there was a smile on her face. 'Well, I'm sorry, Kristian, but—'

'I will be their Dicto!' A loud, clear, deep voice cut across whatever Quede was about to say. She frowned and looked towards the doors. We all did.

'As previous Chief Test Master of this Order, I officially request my reinstatement as Dicto for the three recruits present.' Ithorion stood at the top of the stairs, wearing his long, dark coat. With his head held high, he slowly descended the staircase. There was a graceful strength behind each step. Steel in his eyes, sharp enough to cut diamonds.

'Ithorion.' Quede's voice wavered slightly, clearly taken aback. 'You would come back to the Order into a position so beneath your skills and experience?'

'I would,' Ithorion said, reaching the ground level and making Quede take a step back. 'Unless, of course, you have any objections to me re-joining the order?'

If the silence around us was deep before, now it pressed down on us so heavily, I thought I could hear Selena's quiet breathing next to me.

'Of course not,' Quede responded after a moment's pause. 'How could I? Few of us accomplished, or indeed can dare hope to accomplish as much as you've done for this Order.'

'I was hoping you'd say that.' Ithorion put his hands behind his back and shot an assessing look our way, as if estimating the price of three sheep he was about to buy at market. He nodded a few times, then looked back at Quede. 'Are we done, then? They're all mine?'

'Of course.' Quede reached a hand out towards us. 'All yours.'

'Excellent! I already have a task for them in mind, so if we could have the initiation at sunrise, please.'

'No problem.'

'Alright,' Ithorion said, then looked at us. 'Follow me!'

A babble of voices rose around us as everyone started talking at the same time. I numbly scurried after Ithorion, closely followed by Conor and Selena. We were almost at the doors when Quede's voice reached us again.

'Oh, and Ithorion?'

'Yes?' he turned.

'Welcome back.' There was a smile on Quede's face that didn't quite reach her eyes.

'Thank you.' The doors in front of us opened. 'Out!' he told us. 'Quickly now!' A heartbeat later, we were all in the corridor again, and the two guards closed the doors behind us.

'In there.' He pointed to our right. We piled into a small room with a large mahogany table in its middle, surrounded by a set of carved wooden chairs.

'Sit.' Ithorion gestured as he took a seat himself. Conor and Selena did as they were told, but I stopped and looked at him.

'Thank you.' I wanted him to know how much I appreciated what he had done.

'Don't,' he said in his cold voice. 'I didn't do it for you. I did it for James.'

'Do you know where he is?' I asked, hoping again that someone could finally tell me.

'No, not yet,' Ithorion said. 'But I'm investigating.'

'Terek said all human teleports were monitored by the Order,' I pointed out.

'And what Terek didn't tell you was that some information went missing here. There's no record of you or anyone leaving Alba on the day you did. Nor would I advise you to start making inquiries about this matter while you're here. Leave it to me. Just concentrate on the task I'm going to give you and trust me to deal with this one. Alright?'

I nodded and sat down opposite him, between Selena and Conor.

Ithorion pressed his fingertips together in front of him, and without any preamble, he cut to the chase. 'Back on Drelos, the Kingdom of Coroden has been ruled by the Renol family for half a millennium. According to records, about four hundred years ago, King Renold II was cursed by his sorceress mistress, Lady Selia, and went blind at the ripe old age of twenty-eight. But the curse didn't just affect him. His son, Renold III, who followed him on the throne, also went blind when he reached the same age. So did his son and his son and his son thereafter, right down to the father of the current ruler, Sirion I.

'The current king, Sirion II, is nearing his twenty-eighth birthday, and understandably has been working rather hard on trying to avoid the same fate. For years, the court has been requesting the expertise of mages, priests, healers, who have all failed to suggest a convincing solution to the problem. Especially given that many of their suggestions and practices had already been employed and failed when they were trying to break the curse and cure his father, who has since passed away due to white fever.

'Most recently, the Duke of Beren, an important member of the nobility, who has done considerable research into the legends, came up with the idea that the curse might be linked to an old crown. It is generally believed that King Renold II went blind upon placing his crown on his head on the morning of his twenty-eighth birthday. The Duke of Beren believes it is this crown the curse should be removed from, which in turn would break the curse on the royal family, too.

'For this reason, he employed the services of the famed adventurer of his kingdom, a certain Conor Drew, who recovered the lost relic from the treacherous Holt Catacombs. Unfortunately, before anything further could be done, the crown was stolen from the duke's castle the following night. The word on the street is that it was stolen by the very same adventurer for a handsome reward from the Harag Khagan, the ruler of the neighbouring Harag Empire. Reason being, it is not in the empire's interests to see Coroden get stronger again upon breaking this curse. The Kingdom of Coroden has been a politically weak sovereignty ever since the curse was placed. The only reason it's managed to maintain peace and ensure a relatively good life for its subjects during these centuries was clever governing. Tactical trade deals, well-arranged political marriages, sacrificing disputed border territories to its neighbours.

'Now, however.' Ithorion shifted in his seat. 'The king has unfortunately made a mistake. With his birthday only ten days away, tensions in the court are running high. Due to what we might call a miscommunication with the Harag delegates around the issue of the missing crown, the Harag Empire is now preparing for war against The Kingdom of Coroden. Coroden hasn't been involved in any serious military action for centuries. Its defences are few and neglected. When the Harag army makes its move on the king's birthday, there will be no war. It's going to be a massacre.

'Your task is to stop the upcoming conflict and to cure the royal family of this curse.' Ithorion tilted his head. 'Any questions?'

'I didn't steal the crown, and we don't have it,' Conor stated.

'That's not a question,' Ithorion pointed out. 'Any *questions*?'

'You talk about this curse as if it was a real thing,' I said, watching him raise his eyebrows at that. 'Had anyone talked to me about curses and magic a few weeks ago, I would have laughed. But on Drelos, I saw animated corpses, headstone engravings that disappeared, boats that flew without any apparent power to do so, and I could go on. Even you said your skills could be considered magic. Does magic really exist?'

'Does magic exist? That rather depends on your definition of magic. You can sense when Conor, Selena or even James are nearby. Would you call that magic? You can communicate with them in their dreams. Is that magic? Selena can teleport you into another world. Is that magic? And with that said, why is it so difficult to believe that others can animate corpses or make things fly? We all have the capacity within our skulls to do more. In a lot of people, these kinds of abilities never manifest. But you, by finding each other and stepping onto a path that leads to forming a sacred bond with the gods, have woken a special part of your brains. Have woken it, and by serving in the Order, you will strengthen it further and possibly have new powers manifest. We call these gifts. You would call them supernatural powers.'

'I have not experienced anything of the sort,' Conor bristled. 'No gifts.'

'And I wonder why that is?' Ithorion retorted.

'I was already told by the priests once that upon finding the Key, it would take me to the mightiest place in the world, where I would become rich and powerful. I found the key, and where is all that, then?'

'You are in the Pantheon, Conor. The place where Gods and lesser creatures form sacred bonds. A place which exists to protect all that is precious. A place filled with wonder and extraordinary warriors who possess divine powers. This is the mightiest place in the world! As for riches, Champions are extremely highly rewarded. They are given substantial breaks between assignments in which to spend those rewards in any way they like, on whichever planet they wish. And as for becoming powerful, if you join the Order, you will learn. You will get stronger. And eventually, you might even start using your brain more, too. In every sense. Well, one can only hope! But yes, in return, I will boss you about. Your dear friend, Kristian, here will boss you about. You will swear an oath to the Dragon and pledge allegiance to the Order. You will serve and follow the rules. This Order, this place you seem to think so little of, will matter to you!'

'And the task you've given us would be our first assignment?' Conor asked.

'First assignment? No. In my books, this is called "sorting out your own mess". Which reminds me, Kristian. Champions of the Order are not supposed to carry objects made with modern technology to less advanced worlds in case they are seen by the occupants. Leaving them lying around, or Gods forbid, giving them away is strictly forbidden. So, if you could please collect that invisibility cloak from Alba while you're at it. Next question?'

'Is this the type of task the Order usually gets involved in? I mean, obviously, this is important to us since it's Conor's home, but what scale of problems do you normally tackle? And how do you decide which conflicts are the most important?' I asked.

'Dictos usually receive visions from the Gods about situations that might start a chain of events escalating into serious worldwide or even galactic problems. But when not prompted in such a way, Dictos may choose assignments they consider important and fitting for the skills and level of the circle they are in charge of. Initially, these would be small-scale events. As Champions gradually progress and become stronger, more experienced, more gifted, the scale and the difficulty of the tasks increases.'

'And everyone who can do magic in the world, everyone who is gifted in this way, are basically in the Order?'

'Well, no. Sometimes gifts manifest in beings outside of the Order. Depending on what these are and who they are, the Order might get in touch with them. There's a lower tier of membership, if you like. They've never been here, they don't know too much about us, but they know we exist. We have a secret alliance with them.'

'And those corrupted gifts Quede mentioned?' I forced the words out, feeling ashamed. 'And all those things she said about my father. What he did … I don't remember.'

'All true, I'm afraid,' Ithorion said, and for the first time, I thought I saw something in his eyes which could have been mistaken for compassion. 'James saved you by stealing you away from your father's citadel after your mother died. You were barely five years old. Then he spent the next three years training you, healing your body, your soul and spirit. Fixing your mind. He couldn't make the corruption completely disappear, but he taught you to overcome it. Then he did something we call in the field of mindwork, "covering your past". He didn't erase your memories. He simply hid them away in your brain, so the trauma wouldn't hurt you any longer. The truth is that erasing years from someone's memory takes a big toll on the subject. When it's their first five years of life, it could destroy their mind completely. This is why I told you not to use those powers.

Every time you do, you're straining that mental cover until it will eventually rip open, and what's behind it could poison you once more.'

'Why didn't James tell me that he was my uncle?' I wished I had known.

'You will have to ask him yourself. But my guess is to protect you. The fewer people knew who you were, the less danger you were in. With time, your father seemed to lose interest in you. If I were you, I would be glad for it and keep it that way. Next question?' He looked around.

'How can I speak two … languages?' Selena asked. 'Or three? What language are we even talking right now?'

'It is Elesean. You are using it through your connection with Kristian. Soul circles are one of the strongest bonds in the universe, and their strengths can manifest in many ways. In your case, it seems you're tapping into your tora's communications skills. Which is not unusual. It mostly means that both Conor and you are able to understand and communicate in any language Kristian can, to the level he can. As long as you're near him.'

'That's handy! He seems to be quite fluent in this one.' She smiled at me.

'And so he should be,' Ithorion responded. 'It's his mother tongue.'

'How far can we go from him before we stop understanding the people here around us?' Conor asked.

'That you will have to test for yourselves, I'm afraid. And, of course, your brains will gradually pick up any languages you learn this way, if you use it often enough.'

'Speaking of learning,' Selena ventured, 'are there truly no courses, no training of any sort, before we head out to save the world? I might be the Supreme Key, but so far, I'm only aware of one gift I might have, and I'm not even sure how to use it. As for anything else, I'm not exactly fit, and there are so many things I don't know … It's not that I don't want to go. I do! But how can I be of any use like this?'

'You think yourself useless, and yet you've already saved the arses of these two twice in less than a day. Don't worry about the things you don't know. You will learn. Focus on the things that you *do* know. In here.' Ithorion pointed at his head, then to his chest. 'And in there.'

'But what about martial training?' I asked, remembering the group practising outside.

'Your circle's physical preparation is not my responsibility.'

'But then whose …?' I trailed off under his gaze.

'What? Did you think I was going to do push-ups with them?"

'Right. Sorry.'

'But I still don't understand how I can learn to use my gifts if no one will teach me?' Selena objected.

Ithorion abruptly stood and, with decisive steps, walked over to us. He stopped in front of Selena. Out of nowhere, there was a dagger in his hand. 'I'm going to move the point of the dagger towards you,' he said. 'Try to stop me.'

Selena tensed, but nothing changed. Ithorion's hand moved ever so slowly towards her.

'Concentrate!' Ithorion ordered in his cold voice. 'There's no resistance coming from you at all. Let's try again. Concentrate! Concentrate! Nothing!'

He grabbed Selena's arm and yanked the sleeve of her dress up, pinning her wrist to the table. He raised his blade over her slender arm, this time with speed. 'Last chance!' he hissed. 'Do it!'

It wasn't just Selena who strained now. A tension from Conor gripped me from my right, mixing with my own. Ithorion looked like he would actually stab Selena's arm if she didn't stop him.

'Finally! Now I can feel something,' Ithorion said with his hand shaking ever so slightly. I let out a breath I didn't realise I was holding and relaxed. 'But it's practically nothing.' He moved the dagger down lightning fast, and I watched in disbelief as he carved a bloody line into Selena's forearm. We both stood then, Conor and I, making the chair legs screech on the stone floor in protest. Ithorion snapped his head around to give us a warning look. 'Now, now …' Then he looked back at Selena and added, 'Heal it!'

'How?' Selena asked after a moment of pause.

'I don't know,' Ithorion stated. 'I don't have this gift. But my guess would be to move energy into that area from here.' He poked a finger into her stomach. 'Maybe it helps if you combine it with your breathing. Feel free to practise these two things in any free time you might have in the upcoming days.'

'Do you know what other gifts I have?' Selena asked, sucking her arm.

'No.'

'But you knew about this one,' she insisted.

'No,' Ithorion repeated.

'What? You didn't know? So, I might not even have it? Then how could I—?'

'Just keep practising.' Ithorion shrugged off the question. 'That way, we'll find out either way.'

His attitude somehow didn't seem that bad when I was the target of his ire, but watching him be like this with Selena infuriated me.

'Any more questions?' he asked. 'Only if they are clever and not a waste of my time!'

'What if Laro catches up with us again?' I asked. 'He has supernatural speed and can work metals with his mind. Last time we met, he even had a proton gun. How can we protect ourselves if we have no useful gifts and can't carry modern weapons with us?'

'You already met him twice, and yet you're sitting here perfectly fine. You are more capable than you think. Stop whinging!'

'And how are we supposed to break a four-hundred-year-old curse if we don't understand how magic works? If we don't understand how these gifts work?' I asked, angry now.

Ithorion looked me in the eye with a gaze that could have frozen the sun in the sky. 'Figure. It. Out.'

I held his eyes a moment longer before feeling a calming hand on my shoulder. The way I usually stopped Conor when he was about to say or do something foolish. At first, I thought it was him doing the same to me. But then I looked and saw that it was Selena who seemed to have picked up my technique.

'Right. We're done here,' Ithorion concluded. 'Tell Terek what you need for your trip, and he'll have it ready for you in the morning. You'll leave shortly after the initiation. I'll see you all on the Bridge of Honour at sunrise. Don't be late!'

Chapter 21

Kristian

Pantheon, Styx, BD19S2 11-77Δ

hat a lovely place!' Conor stated bitterly as we left the building, casually waving away a golden butterfly that tried to land on his hand.

I put one arm around him and the other around Selena. 'At least we're still together.'

'Oh, is that suddenly so important to you now?' Selena gave me a hurt look, then turned away. Her pain throbbed in my chest, and I was grateful for Ithorion not mentioning to them this ability that had slowly grown in me. Sensing their minds. I'd rather tell them myself—I just wasn't sure how. I hated to think that they might be uncomfortable around me once they knew.

After everything we just went through in the Claw, I needed a minute to work out why she had said that. It had to be what I asked her before we entered the building. I couldn't believe she was still upset with me because of that! I needed to fix this and soon. I had to talk to her alone.

A warm feeling reached me, and I thought that she might have perhaps already forgiven me, only to realise it was coming from Conor. His bad mood lifted like mist disappearing into sunshine, and I had to look up to see what was causing this profound change.

Aiki was coming our way, smiling at us warmly. She clearly didn't share, or possibly wasn't even aware of, her mother's disposition towards us. As I looked at that stunning woman, there was only one way I could think of describing her: Godsent.

'Aiki!' I called out to her in a friendly manner. 'Perfect timing! Conor here thinks he might still need some testing before the initiation takes place tomorrow.' I pulled him in front of me by his arm.

Aiki's smile faded into a slight frown of confusion upon my words, only for her eyes to light up with meaning as I wildly gesticulated behind Conor, asking her to occupy him for five minutes and that I owed her one. She narrowed her eyes, and with one look, she managed to convey that she would definitely be back to collect that debt. Then she softened her gaze again and shot Conor a playful grin.

I took Selena by the hand and led her under a big magnolia tree that stood in the middle of a nearby garden. I turned to face her, and reluctant to let her hand go, I found myself reaching for the other one, too. I looked down at them as if I could read the lines on her palms and, from them, know what to say and how.

'I'm sorry for what I said before,' I started, raising my eyes slowly to meet hers. 'But was it really such a stupid question? Whatever gifts you might or might not have, however noble they make all this look, I have no doubt that these assignments will be dangerous. You could die out there. And even if you don't, between jobs we will have to train. You will have to learn how to defend yourself. How to control your mind better. We might need to study other things, too, to research places. It would be a completely different life for you, away from everything you know. And we want you with us. *I* want you with us. But would you really not miss what you have on Earth? Would you really not mind leaving all of that behind?'

'Not if I'm with you,' she said, melting my heart. 'I've never in my life felt like I truly belonged anywhere. Not until I met you and Conor. This place, this way of living, feels right to me. But yes, I'm scared, too. Not scared of being hurt or dying. I'm scared that this might all just be a big misunderstanding. That I'm not good enough for this. Not strong enough. And you, dismissing me the way you did back there, like you don't care whether I stay or not, doesn't help!'

'I'm sorry.' I pulled her into my arms. 'I didn't mean it that way. Of course, I care. And we all have our doubts and insecurities about whether we are good enough.'

'Conor doesn't,' she countered.

'Maybe not,' I agreed.

'And I bet he isn't afraid of anything.'

I couldn't help but laugh. 'You'd be surprised.'

That finally made her smile.

'For what it's worth,' I said, 'if this is really what you want to do—and I hope it is—I promise I will always be here for you. Always.'

I could tell that meant a lot to her. She relaxed and moved closer, resting her head against my shoulder. 'I will be with you all the way,' I murmured into her ear. 'Wherever this road takes us. Are you with me?'

'I am,' she sighed. A few of those golden butterflies circled around us as we stood in each other's arms, reluctant to let go.

'Should we head back?' she asked eventually. 'Our time is probably up, and I wouldn't want Aiki to be annoyed with us, too.'

'Don't worry,' I said, stroking her back. 'I'm sure those two can handle each other just fine.' I kissed her hair softly. I wouldn't have wanted to be anywhere else in the world in that moment.

Sometime later, the three of us were sitting in a circle on the bed of our allocated room, debating what to do. Outside, the last rays of sunshine were bleeding into night, and a lazy breeze blew the sweet smell of acacia trees through the open window.

'So, we have ten days to break a four-hundred-years-old curse and stop an impending war, and we have no idea how,' Conor helpfully recapped the situation.

'That sums it up,' I agreed.

'And this is a probationary task? What will we have to do later?' he mused. 'Unless Ithorion just handed this to us to fail and get rid of us.'

'Why would he do that? Why save us in the council meeting only to see us flunk? That wouldn't make any sense. Think about it. He was Chief Test Master of the Order. He wouldn't send us to do something if he thought we had no chance of succeeding. But given his reputation, I don't expect it to be easy, either. No, he's throwing us into deep water and expects us to learn to swim in the middle of the lake. I imagine now that he's become a Dicto and for the first time has a team, he will want to show off with us. "See, my circle solved that on their first assignment!"'

'Do you think we should look for that crown?' Selena shifted uneasily. 'Could it really help?'

'No,' I declared a little too quickly. Laro had wanted the Supreme Key in exchange for the crown. The very idea of Selena getting anywhere near him again filled me with foreboding. 'We have no idea if the crown will definitely work, and searching for it might see us run out of time. There has to be another way.'

'I'm not so sure the crown is the answer, either,' Conor said. 'I didn't want to dishearten the duke at the time, but my watch didn't detect any magic from it. If there had been such a powerful curse tied to it, I'm sure it would have flashed up. On the other hand, the royal family has been keeping meticulous records on the onset of the curse and every attempt to raise it,' Conor said. 'Maybe they missed something. The answer could lie waiting to be discovered in the library of the Royal Palace in Caledon. And the palace would also be the best place to find out just how far this conflict with the Harags has escalated.'

'So, we should go there,' I said. 'We have no time to waste.'

'Easier said than done.' Conor grimaced. 'How do we get in? And surely, they wouldn't consider us important enough to talk to about any of this. Without the crown, they are likely to just arrest me on sight.'

'Couldn't we give them something else useful instead of the crown?' Selena suggested.

We both looked at her, the same idea forming in our minds.

'We could say we brought a powerful sorceress who can break the curse.' I looked at Conor for confirmation.

'A Scarlet Witch from the Isle of Yres!' He nodded. 'Like the Lady Selia was. They very rarely visit Coroden.'

'Have they not already tried to break the curse?' I asked.

'They are refusing to accept the Coroden court invitations. In their books, Lady Selia cursed the king, her lover, because he was awful to her. And once the king was blind, she was captured and executed. Having the king think we managed to convince one of them to help would instantly give me a royal pardon. And while the Scarlet Witches have been incredibly stubborn on the issue, I have a bit of a reputation when it comes to making impossible things happen—and, of course, to charming women.' He scratched his chin and grinned.

'But how can I pretend to be a powerful sorceress when I can't even do any spells?' Selena protested.

'You don't need to do any spells,' I told her. 'Just get us in and buy us some time. Say you need to spend a few days with the king to assess his condition. Or that you need to put together a talisman during the upcoming week. Gather herbs for a potion. Whatever you like. Just give us a reason to hang around and look at those records. Besides, your gifts might start manifesting while we're there, too. You might sort out the situation with a wave of your hand while we have a beer with Conor and relax!' I grinned at her.

'And what if anyone asks for some proof that I'm actually a Scarlet Witch?' She frowned.

'I'll come up with something.' I promised her.

'We will have to dye your hair red,' Conor said. 'The Scarlet Witches all have red hair.'

'I'm sure Terek will have something for that,' she said. 'I'll ask him later.'

'Good,' I said. 'So, that's settled, then. Is there anything else?'

'What you said earlier regarding my family and friends.' Selena looked at me. 'Don't worry,' she added hurriedly. 'I haven't changed my mind. But I'm not sure what to do about my sudden disappearance. I don't want them to wonder for the rest of their lives what happened to me. And I'm not sure I have the heart to make them think I'm dead, either. Maybe I could say that I'm moving to another country for a new job? Both my parents live abroad already. But I can't make up my mind on what exactly to say to them and how.'

'I can cover for you for the time being, if you like.' A fourth voice reached us from the nearby table that stood empty, except for Selena's bag. The spider droid climbed out from it.

'I quite forgot about you,' I admitted as it scurried onto the bed with us.

'But what could you do, exactly?' Selena asked, wrinkling her forehead.

'Take your voice or video calls and make calls on your behalf, to start with,' the droid said in Selena's voice.' I can create a video image of you in real time and broadcast it to any device.'

'Wow, that's really good!' Selena fished her mobile out of her bag. 'Do you even need this?' she asked, putting it down next to the droid.

'Not really.' The spider spoke in its regular voice again.

'And what about the passwords on my laptop and other home and work stuff? Won't you need those?'

The spider didn't say anything for a while, just bobbed up and down on its long legs. I wondered if it was laughing. 'No,' it said eventually.

'Great. You should probably call my boss first thing and say that I'm ill.'

'I was thinking of negotiating a sabbatical,' the spider said.

'That would also be good,' Selena agreed. 'But be careful. He's really hard to negotiate with!'

'Just leave it with me,' the spider said confidently.

'Fine,' Selena said. 'I'll double-check with Ithorion tomorrow. But maybe he wouldn't mind. We already have robots in my world. Probably not as sophisticated as you are, but who knows, really? Some could already exist somewhere in a secret military base!'

'What's your signal range?' I asked the droid.

'I have ionospheric bounce technology built in, so practically planet-wide,' it responded.

'Impressive,' I complimented James's skills with a sudden urge to take the thing apart under a microscope and see how he'd managed to do it. Sadly, I didn't have the time. But I did have an idea how to take advantage of it.

A knock on the door announced Terek's arrival.

'We have a rather long list of items that we'll need for tomorrow, I'm afraid,' I told him.

'No problem,' he said. 'In fact, Ithorion sent me word earlier that you're going to Drelos, and I already have some things prepared for you. But we can add more.'

'I will also need to dye my hair red,' Selena chipped in, 'to look like a Scarlet Witch from the Isle of Yres.'

'Hmmm.' Terek tilted his head. 'I will send someone around to help you with that about two hours before sunrise tomorrow.'

'Can't we do it now?'

'Everyone's at the feast tonight in the Hummingbird Park. In fact, I just came to tell you that you should come, too. The tables are already filling up.'

'Perfect!' I announced and ushered Selena and Conor out of the door—not that the latter needed much encouragement.

Once we were on our way, I gradually slowed my pace until Terek and I were out of earshot of the other two.

'Terek, how long do teleport journeys take? Are they instantaneous?'

'No, they are not—although it might feel that way for those who travel,' he said. 'It really depends on the distance to the destination and on what time speed zone it is in.'

'Say from here to Drelos—how long would that take?'

'Almost two hours at this end,' he answered, 'using the metric time system of the Pantheon. It would be more for those waiting for you on Drelos. Time moves a little quicker there. During the day, there's usually a clerk at the Pantheon's gate. They can always give you the exact numbers and calculations.'

'And how do the gates work? Do you only need to think of where you'd like to go?'

'Well, there are two possible options,' Terek said. 'The first is much safer and so more generally used. It is travelling between existing skygates. There are over a million of them, all well hidden on planets across the universe. If you've already been to the destination gate before and can visualise it very clearly, that should be sufficient to get you there. But again, it's much safer to use the symbols carved on the inside of the skygate. Every gate has a unique symbol code. You just need to know them.'

'And the other option?' I asked.

'The other option is to think of and visualise any existing location. The mental image has to be a lot sharper with this method. The gate that opens on the other side is only temporary. If you think to travel one way only, it will disappear shortly after your arrival. If you think about travelling back, too, it will stay open longer, but even then only for a few hours at best, depending on the strength of your mental skills. And immediately disappears after your departure.'

'The one we used on Drelos wasn't like either of those.' I frowned.

'Which one was that?' Terek asked.

'I think it was called the North Sentry Gate?' I said. 'We practically had to build it up by solving a puzzle.'

'Oh, that one.' Terek smiled. 'That gate is different from the rest. It was created by your uncle and Ithorion.'

'By my uncle?' I could see that. James always liked handing me things to solve, whether they were complex equations, playful riddles or short detective stories to improve my logic. Building it with the Chief Test Master himself could have only meant one thing. They built it to test those they thought might become Champions. But who from Drelos could have solved it? Was it for others who had come from different, more advanced worlds? Like me? A strange thought occurred to me then. Surely, they wouldn't have built it explicitly for us? Was that why my name was on the grave? I puzzled over it briefly, but then decided I had better questions on my mind.

'But the gate that opened was a temporary one,' I thought out aloud. 'To a place where neither of us had been to before. Conor just said he wanted to go to the Supreme Key. And we appeared in the library of a grand house we hadn't even known of.'

'That is because Conor used a much stronger connection than anyone can conjure up in their minds by simply thinking of a place. He used the bond of your soul circle. His bond with Selena.'

'It worked even though they'd never met before?'

'That doesn't matter. Being together physically or not, knowing each other physically or not, doesn't matter. Your souls are still connected.'

'But he didn't even know the Supreme Key was a person. He thought it was an object.'

'A carefully selected group of us within the Order always knew that the Supreme Key was a being. We just didn't know who or where. But someone must have known. That knowledge must have been there somewhere when you opened the gate, hidden inside you or Conor, or the gate itself.'

I thought about that for a second. The key being that fancy wheel-like object had always seemed somehow wrong to me. But had I really known the truth? I doubted it.

'So, we can just think of each other if we want to travel to them? Instead of a place?' I asked.

'Technically, you can. It's just not recommended. What if Selena had been waiting to cross a busy road and the gate opened right in the way of the vehicles speeding by? What if she had been in a small room, where there wasn't enough space for the gate to open? Maybe it would have demolished a wall, or worse, materialised inside it. I think you just got lucky.'

'And when you say an option is safer, what do you mean exactly?'

'For one thing, already existing skygates are hidden, and so the chance of inhabitants of a given planet seeing you arrive is practically zero. Whereas if you just teleport anywhere, that could always happen. But also, if your mental image of the destination is not clear enough, you might end up somewhere else, or even lost in between, trapped, until you slowly die.'

'Thanks,' I said. 'That's certainly useful to know.'

We talked some more before catching up with the others, just as they were about to enter the park. Young Ramin joined them on the road, almost dancing around them with excitement. I wondered if Conor was telling them about some of his adventures.

The park itself looked lovely and inviting, enchanted by soft, glowing lights woven around the limbs of ancient trees. Tiny, colourful birds flitted around artful flowerbeds and little ponds that sparkled in the moonlight. A gentle music played from somewhere, staying politely in the background while members of the Order sat around long, wooden tables cheering, talking and laughing. Selena stood enchanted in front of a bush full of ruby-red flowers, pointing out a hummingbird to Conor. As I watched them share a smile, I felt a sudden pang of sadness for having to miss it all.

I walked with them to a table where there were still some empty seats left but remained standing as the two of them sat down. Terek walked over to speak to someone serving food, while Ramin stood next to me uncertainly, as if not sure whether he could sit with us without a clear invitation. I gestured for him to step away with me and quietly asked, 'Do you think I could borrow you for a few minutes?'

'Of course,' he said, looking pleased at having been asked. 'Whatever I can aid you with.'

'Let me just talk to these two first.' I nodded towards the others. 'Then I'll meet you at the entrance. Thanks!'

I walked back to the table, where Selena politely waited for me to join them before eating. Conor was already busy wolfing something down.

'Kris!' He turned when he noticed me. 'Hey, try this! This is delicious!' he said and pushed some kind of pastry roll into my mouth.

'Mmmm.' I nodded, chewing. It was good.

'Come on, sit down.'

I finished swallowing the food, then told them, 'I'm not going to stay here with you tonight.'

'What?' Conor asked, taken aback. 'Why not?'

'There is just something else I need to do.'

'But what?' They both looked quizzically at me now, the "With whom?" clearly the next question on their minds. But while Conor just seemed intrigued, there was a tiny shard of jealous suspicion in Selena's eyes that concerned me more.

'Well, if the two of you will be good tonight, I might tell you later.' I winked at her, hoping that it would dispel any doubt she had.

'But if you leave, how will we even communicate with the others?' Conor protested. 'We won't even understand each other.'

'I don't know.' I threw up my hands into the air. 'Maybe use sign language?'

'Sign language? Well, that won't lead to long conversations!' He pulled a face.

'Good,' I said. 'Eat your food, have a little fun, then go to bed. We have an early start and a busy day tomorrow.' I reached over his shoulder and took a few more of those pastry rolls. 'And don't wait up for me!'

With that, I turned and walked back to the entrance, suppressing an urge to tell Conor to look after Selena. I knew he would. I saw the way he looked at her. Not the way he looked at other women, with that mischievous challenge in his eyes. There was an attentive care in Conor's every move when it came to Selena. Putting a blanket on her when he thought she might be cold. Protecting her when he thought she was in danger. He'd shown more affection towards her during the short time since we'd met her than he did to any other woman I saw him with, including Olivia. Poor Olivia, who was probably still in prison, yet whenever I brought up the subject, he dismissed it with a wave of his hand, claiming that the Duke of Beren was too soft-hearted to keep the girl in prison for long, and convinced that she'd be treated more like a princess than some common criminal. Having seen the place for myself, I guessed there might have been some truth to that. But still, his unconcerned attitude towards Olivia stood in sharp contrast with how he barely let Selena out of his sight. But then again, she was his Supreme Key, his most precious treasure!

I looked up to see Ramin waiting for me on a bench under a big walnut tree. He stood when he saw me, excitement in his eyes. I really wasn't sure what he expected we would do. Nothing anywhere as spectacular as the feast I was keeping him from.

'Do you know where the Pantheon's skygate is and how it works?' I asked him.

'Of course,' he said. 'Would you like me to take you there?'

'If you don't mind,' I said. 'I just need to stop by our room first.'

'Are you planning on going somewhere?' he asked, baffled. 'Now?'

'Tomorrow morning, we will have our initiation ceremony where I become a leader of my circle, and soon after, we'll depart for Drelos,' I explained. 'In front of Conor and Selena, I need to look like I know what I'm doing, or they will never respect my lead.'

'So, you want me to show you how to open the gate to Drelos? You don't actually want to go there now, do you?'

'I thought I might, if we can keep this between us.' I gave him a conspiratorial smile. 'But you don't need to come. You can go straight back to the feast. I just ... need to see for myself what it's going to be like. I will come back straight away.'

I watched him absentmindedly chew his tongue as he thought it over. Then he seemed to decide that the whole thing was probably innocent, re-tied his long ponytail and nodded.

'Thanks!' I gave him my best smile. 'I owe you one!' That seemed to please him.

I guessed what I was about to do wasn't strictly speaking against the rules. At least, not based on what Ithorion had told us. But I suspected it was a bit of a grey area, and for that reason, I didn't want to involve the others. It was best if only I knew about this, in case I got caught.

I made Ramin wait at the bottom of our staircase as I ran up to our room and got the spider droid out of Selena's bag. It seemed a little concerned when I asked how to switch it completely off and back on, but luckily, James had the foresight to give me the highest level of clearance in the droid's base programming.

Once the spider was safely in my pocket, dead to the world, so to speak, I raced down the steps and re-joined the boy.

'So, are these initiation ceremonies a big deal around here?' I asked him as we walked.

'Not really. They are fairly boring,' he admitted. 'You just say "yes" to everything Quede asks, and then at the end comes the only interesting bit: one of the Gods sends a sign of approval. It's often like a specifically shaped cloud or a shadow covering you. Sometimes an animal might appear, like a hawk that sits on your arm or a cat that rubs itself against your legs. Some of the best ones I saw were meteor showers, swords materialising at the feet of the initiates, and in one case, a flame ran across the side of the bridge.'

'And are they well attended?' I asked.

'Not many would go to watch an initiation ceremony here. It's different when you become Champions. On those occasions, there are plenty of people and a large celebration. But few would go to an initiation ceremony. Even fewer as early as sunrise. But I'll be there!'

'I hope the sign will be interesting enough to make it worth you getting up so early.' I smiled.

'It's not just the sign,' he said. 'It's the three of you. I mean, Conor is so great! He's so brave! I really want to be more like him. And you are James Montgomery's nephew. *The* James Montgomery! And the two of you have the Supreme Key. You even have Ithorion as a Dicto now. I think that's awesome!'

His enthusiasm touched me, even if I knew he was only young and the way he saw us leaned closer to fantasy than reality. I just hoped it was a fantasy we, with time, would grow enough to measure up to.

Five hours later, I was hurrying back down the road, the journey feeling a lot shorter. As I made my way up the stairs again, I could see that the light was still on in our room. It was quiet, and I stopped on the terrace before entering, suddenly unsure what I might walk into. Through the open shutters, I saw them sitting on the bed. Selena was drawing something on a board, Conor behind her, watching. In front of them, half a bottle of red wine and two glasses on the table. Part of me felt like joining them, getting a third glass out and making them tell me what I'd missed. But deep down, I knew I had to start acting more responsibly than that.

Suddenly, Conor burst out laughing. 'I mean, I can't … I can't even … tell if it's supposed to be a dog or a horse, Selena. How could I teach you the right word?'

Selena laughed with him, until realisation hit her and she said, 'Wait … wait, Conor, I can understand you again!'

'And I you,' he responded as they looked at each other, then towards the door.

I knew they couldn't see me out here in the dark, but I also knew that my time was up. I wiped the smile off my face, and as I walked through the door, I put on a more serious expression.

'Right, you two,' I said. 'Bedtime!'

Selena giggled as she pulled a blanket over herself and laid down, already wearing a set of comfortable-looking, light blue pyjamas. Conor, who I now noticed sported a similar set of dark grey clothing, uncertainly shuffled towards his spot on the big platform.

I still felt the buzz of the teleport travel in me, keeping me tense and alert, and so I picked up one of their glasses and poured myself some wine.

'What are you doing?' Selena inquired, watching Conor hesitate mid-crawl.

'I just thought I would sleep where I did last night.' He grinned. 'Unless, of course, you want us to piss off.'

'What? You slept here last night, with me?' she asked incredulously. 'Both of you?'

'Yes,' Conor said. 'We all slept here together, like a big, happy family. Although, you were pretty much out of it the whole time.'

'Out of it?' Selena's hand unconsciously moved to her neck, her cheeks flashing red.

'Oh, completely.' Conor unsuccessfully tried to suppress a laugh. 'Just ask Kris. We were playing noughts and crosses on your forehead all night.'

He made a fake hurt noise when a well-directed pillow landed in his face two seconds later.

'Enough,' I said softly. 'We can go next door.' I gestured for Conor to get up.

'No, it's fine,' Selena insisted. 'Stay. I would feel safer that way,' she added with a smile, and she knew she had me.

I finished my drink in one move and put the glass down. 'Alright,' I said, 'but I want you both asleep in five minutes.' Then, without another look at them, I marched into the bathroom to wash off the dust I collected in the dark caves of Drelos.

'Nervous?' I asked him.

'A bit,' he admitted. It didn't look like a "bit" to me.

It was still dark, dawn nothing but a hesitant suggestion in the eastern sky. A soft breeze ruffled the surface of the water at our feet, blurring the reflection of the city's twinkling lights. I looked up at the elegantly curved stone bridge upon which the ceremony would take place soon. As far as I could see, it was still empty.

'Is it Quede that worries you?' I asked quietly.

'No,' Conor shrugged off my suggestion.

'Ithorion?' I asked, surprised.

'No,' he said more firmly.

'Then what …?' But then I looked again at his taut face, and suddenly I knew. 'It's the commitment, isn't it?'

He let out a sigh in response.

'This isn't final.' I tried to make him look at me. 'You know that. You can leave at any time, I promise.'

He turned away, not meeting my eye, suddenly finding the pebbles alongside the road more interesting than my face. He picked one up and skipped it along the surface of the lake. I sighed, too, and followed his example.

'From what I heard, it's not even supposed to be a big deal,' I said and threw a stone, watching it kiss the water again and again. Without meaning to, my thoughts were filled with Selena again. How I longed to pull her to myself last night and kiss her hair again and again. Instead, I kept a good distance as I was supposed to and made myself fall asleep the way James had taught me many years ago. And for that, I was especially grateful to him now. I very much doubted I would have got any sleep otherwise.

Even then, when someone knocked on our door four hours later, it barely felt like five minutes had passed. Selena had been faster than either of us getting up, and before we knew what was happening, she had already reassured us that it was just a woman Terek had sent to help with her hair.

'Are you going to be alright alone?' I had asked her, sitting up and rubbing my eyes.

'Don't worry. I've got this.' She patted my head and disappeared a few minutes later, telling us that she'd meet us there. We hadn't heard from her since.

I re-focused my eyes on Conor, wondering what to do about him. Maybe if I managed to distract him somehow. 'So, how was last night, anyway?' I asked.

'Fine.' He shrugged. 'It turns out Test Masters speak a lot of languages, so eventually, we had someone translate for us.'

'Find out anything interesting?'

'The Order has some prison facilities on a planet called Uruth. That's where that woman and the man who attacked us on the train were taken to.'

It was reassuring to know that they were safely behind bars. But that still left two guys in Laro's crew who I remembered from the cave the day I left Alba. The twins. One of them with the power to freeze metal. And probably anything else he wanted.

'Hm. Clive was at the feast, too, I guess?'

He pulled a face at that, signalling to just drop the subject.

I heard some noise and as I looked around, I started seeing small groups slowly walking towards the bridge from all directions. Selena wasn't among them. I saw Terek coming with Ramin and a few more members of his team; I saw faces I recognised from the council meeting, the white-haired woman who nearly spoke up for us, being one of them. Aiki walked up behind Ramin, and with a smile, made him flash so red, I could see it all the way from where I was. I saw Quede and Ithorion discussing something as they slowly approached the west side of the bridge.

'Just how long does it take for a woman to dye her hair?' Conor asked next to me.

'Where I'm from, probably like five minutes,' I said. 'Here? I have no idea.'

I shifted my balance from one foot to the other and continued watching the small gathering crowd. Conor shuffled and slowly turned around.

The next moment, he put his hand on my shoulder and tapped it. I turned to see what he wanted, and I'm pretty sure my heart skipped a beat.

On the east road behind us, framed by the rays of the rising sun, Selena walked towards us.

'Hope I'm not late,' she said. 'I was getting a little concerned, but Saya said something that sounded like not to worry. I'm the Supreme Key of the Dragon, they will wait for me!' She laughed. 'So, what do you think?' she asked when neither of us responded.

I tried to move my jaw, only to realise that my mouth was already open. 'You ... look ... good,' I managed finally. Understatement of the year. Her previously shoulder-length blonde hair was now a cascade of red wonder, reaching down to below her hips. She wore make-up that made her eyes not only larger but somehow more seductive, too. The colour of her lips made me think of the kind of dark cherries that were always the sweetest. Her intricate dress tightly followed every curve of her slender body, emphasising the round shape of her breasts and providing a view of her cleavage that would have had a monk reach for himself.

'If I understand correctly, this is the kind of clothing Scarlet Witches wear on Drelos?' She was talking to Conor now. 'It's not too much, is it?'

'Yes.' Conor was shaking his head next to me. 'No, I mean, yes. You look perfect!' He smiled at her, and suddenly, so much pride filled him, I thought he might explode. He straightened his back and offered his arm to her. 'Shall we, my lady?'

Selena gratefully took his arm, and the two of them started off towards the bridge, leaving me behind. I stared at nothing in particular for a moment longer, thinking that I should perhaps just pick her up into my arms and run. Surely this initiation was not that important, after all. Conor could represent us. I'd authorise it!

Then I turned, and my eyes met Ithorion's frosty gaze. He looked down from this side of the Bridge of Honour, by all accounts appearing mightily unhappy with me. Remembering that he could read my thoughts was more than sufficient to stifle the fire in me and cool my head once more. I quieted my mind and hurried after the others. I knew we had an assignment to go on today, but how I was going to concentrate on any of it with Selena around, especially looking like that, I had no idea! I would have to keep my distance from her as much as I was able to. Surely, I should be able to do that for ten days? I just needed to keep reminding myself why we were there and what would happen if we failed. I needed to get a grip on myself if I was going to make this work!

Ithorion gestured for me to walk past him, which I did, and stopped in the middle of the bridge behind Conor and Selena.

'On one knee!' ordered Quede, who stood facing them. She tilted her head to look at me in a way that made me think she expected me to go to the front. I kneeled where I stood instead, making her raise an eyebrow. The way I saw it, I was the tora of this circle, no matter where I stood. And I would always prefer a position where I could keep an eye on the other two and knew them to be safe, to flattering myself with meaningless privileges.

'Kristian Del Rosso, Selena Soto and Conor Drew,' Quede said, her clear, strong voice like a sword cutting through the excited murmur that reached us from our small audience. 'As you already know, the Order of the Dragon exists to defend the known worlds from external and internal threats against freedom and peace. To save, preserve and build, to heal, educate and inspire. To invest our strengths and gains in resources to make civilisations prosper. Guided and aided by our divine Gods, we stand to serve all lifeforms across the universe. Upon becoming initiates, I ask you now: do you sincerely swear that you will defend the Order to the utmost of your power against all harm, conspiracies and ill attempts?'

'I do,' we responded as one.

'That you will uphold its values, abide by its principles and keep its existence secret?'

'I do.'

'That you will bear faithful, true allegiance to our most divine Deity, Meroth, the Dragon, and to his descendants, the lesser Gods, to the Order of the Dragon, to your Dicto and to your Supreme Leader?'

'I do.'

'That you will respect your Dicto and follow their instructions to the best of your abilities?'

'I do.'

'And you, Ithorion Altaronos. Do you sincerely swear that you will be a true mentor to the three initiates in front of you; that you will guide them on their path with all your wisdom, might and heart?'

'I do.' Ithorion's deep voice boomed behind me.

Quede stepped closer and put her palm on the top of Selena's head. 'Selena Soto. I, Supreme Leader Quede Ocana Idashi, with the power granted to me by the Gods, accept and acknowledge you as an initiate of the Order of the Dragon. *We are the fire that keeps away the dark.*'

She then turned and did the same thing with Conor. Finally, she came to me, put her hand on my head and said, 'Kristian del Rosso. A tora's service is always the hardest. And in your case, given who you are and who you are in charge of, perhaps expectations are even higher than usual. But I have faith in you, that you will carry out your duty and make us proud. That you will show me that my trust in you wasn't misplaced. I, Supreme Leader Quede Ocana Idashi, with the power granted to me by the Gods, accept and acknowledge you as an initiate of the Order of the Dragon. May we soon call you all Champions.'

With that, she walked back to her initial position, lifted her arms high and said, 'Our beloved, divine and mighty Gods, who favour us with your strength and wisdom, so that in turn we may help those in need: I respectfully ask you to bless the joining of these three initiates so that they may share our task in protecting ...' Quede abruptly fell silent, her eyes widened, something only she knew or realised causing her a sudden shock which soon turned into amazement. I tensed, suddenly unsure whether this development was a good sign or a bad one, wishing very much in that moment that I could sense her mind, too.

I turned and looked up at Ithorion, who was staring at her, too, but unlike me, his eyes glinted with understanding. Ever so slowly, he tilted his head, his cold gaze meeting mine, and I was stunned to see that on his stony face, in the corners of his stern, thin lips, there was the shadow of a smile.

I felt it then. A force like a stormy wind swept through me, and from a distance, I heard the call of a creature that reminded me of a bird of prey, only much louder. A resounding thunder rumbled across the sky, where clouds now raced with impossible speed. Between them, large, dark shadows appeared, piercing through that swirling curtain, descending on the city of Pantheon as the rising sun glinted on their scales. Dragons. Real dragons. I couldn't count how many. Most stayed far above, several circled close by, and there were countless in between. Green, blue, black, red, golden, their reptilian bodies long, their wings enormous.

A deep sense of wonder gripped me and grew in me, until I realised it had nothing to do with the legendary flying creatures. I felt the presence of a powerful being surround me, move through me and touch my soul. Awe filled me, shading into joy, rushing out of me and bouncing back at me from Selena and Conor. Then, like a mirror broken into three parts, a range of emotions raced through us. Delight and vitality radiated from Conor, fondness and devotion from Selena, all shifting and turning into a fast-whirling wave of other feelings: gratitude, kindness, grace, understanding, affection, gentleness, power, happiness, clarity, greatness, glory, excellence, courage, until I could no longer differentiate between their minds and mine. The strength of our combined experience hit me with a force that had me shaking like a leaf in a storm. I reached my hands down, my fingertips pressing against the stone in an attempt to steady myself. And just when I thought I could bear no more, there seemed to be an explosion turning up both volume and quality to the next level, until my whole being buzzed with it and with so much love, a deluge of tears ran down my face from my tightly shut eyes.

A cold splinter of fear penetrated through my heart. I forced my eyelids open to see Selena rise into the air. But before I could jump up, a heavy weight settled on my shoulders, pushing me down. A soft, icy touch on my forehead, like a kiss, from which serenity washed through me and anchored me to the bridge. I could sense Selena calming, too, as her ascent stopped high above us, surrounded by circling dragons. She opened her arms, and I watched her slowly turn around and around, as if this God wanted to take a proper look at her from all angles. Sunlight dimmed, then dusk bled into night, painting the deep blue sky above the clouds full of stars. A moment of pause, then darkness broke and waned, our world filling once again with daylight. A moment of pause, then the light slowly died again, as night and day chased each other around us like two butterflies. A small part of me wanted to turn and check what was happening to the sun behind me, but I couldn't take my eyes off Selena. Her long, red hair flew in the wind as she kept on turning and shone with a golden glow like a star.

Sunshine brightened our day again, staying this time, and I heard the dragons call out as they made a final circle above the city and flew off. Selena stayed where she was, motionless now, but she looked up, and as I followed her gaze, I could see pink flower petals falling from the sky. They looked like the blossoms of that magnolia tree we had stood under yesterday. First, just a handful, here and there, then like guarded rain growing into a storm, the air was suddenly thick with them, laying a soft, scented carpet all around us.

Through that heavy swirl, I watched as Selena was slowly lowered to us, and sensing no more resistance, I stood. Conor also got up, and the three of us wordlessly hugged each other in the middle of the bridge. My heart filled with relief, mixing with their joy, and I could hear loud cheering from below. I raised my head to see that the streets around us were filled with members of the Order, although I could hardly see their faces through the magnolia petal shower. I smiled and waved in the direction where I remembered Ramin standing, then put my arm back around the others and held them tight.

Chapter 22

Conor

Pantheon, Styx, BD19S2 11-78Δ

As magnificent as the city of Pantheon was, to tell the truth, I couldn't wait to be out of there. Despite the ceremony, it just didn't seem like I belonged there. I wondered if Kris somehow knew how I felt, too, because when Ithorion prompted Quede to arrange a more permanent accommodation for us, he politely turned it down.

'That won't be necessary, thank you. This is not where our home will be,' he informed them, making them gawk, which he promptly ignored and looked at me instead. 'It will be on Drelos.'

Ithorion said that it was fine by him, and Quede agreed that it was a perhaps unusual, but not an unprecedented choice. And as for my part, I appreciated his gesture. A lot. But deep down, I couldn't dismiss the nagging suspicion that no matter how thoughtful it sounded, in the end, it was still a trap.

Would we really own a house somewhere and sit at home all day in between running all over creation for this lot? The whole idea sounded absurd. I cared about him. I truly did! And having to say goodbye would break my heart. But this wasn't me. He must have known that!

He was now back in our room, sorting out his stuff because he wasn't allowed to take his advanced technology into my world. He even had to leave his needle tube behind, which had me smirking when I heard.

I turned and watched Selena, walking up to Ithorion with determined steps. He seemed to know what was on her mind because by the time she reached him, he had his dagger in his hand, offering it to her.

For me it took a moment to work it out what this was about. Of course, sleeping again in that room last night had healed her arm. Our fierce little Scarlet Witch wanted to show the boss that she wasn't too delicate to have herself cut again and practice her presumed skills.

I was going to object, that the witch we were taking to heal the king should not have any visible wounds, but it looked like she had already worked that out. Instead of grazing her arm, she tugged her skirt down a little on the side and cut her hip. I winced with her.

Ithorion nodded his approval and produced a white handkerchief, which I thought was an uncharacteristically caring move from him.

Those damned healing rooms! When I noticed the first morning that all my old scars had disappeared, I was shocked. How would anyone believe now that I'd seen any action when my skin was as smooth as a baby's bottom? Surely, they'd removed a part of me. There was history there! Women especially liked tracing their fingers around my scars and making me tell them how I'd got them. All gone now.

Selena and Ithorion were still talking—I imagined discussing something about her arrangements on Earth. I couldn't decipher a word of it, but it sounded like they might be a while. At least in Elesean, the adopted language of the Order, I already understood some words and could speak a few phrases. This so-called "English" was still pretty much all gibberish to me.

I checked the street again, but there was still no sign of Kris. Knowing what our tora was like, I would have expected him to be finished with things by now. To be jumping up and down in front of the skygate, telling us to go. A minute later, I decided that Selena was probably safe enough with Ithorion and went to look for him myself.

I found him sitting on the bed of our sleeping room, holding the hilt of that fucking sabre that belonged to Laro. He was so deep in thought, he didn't even notice me come in. I wanted to hit that thing out of his hands and kick it far away, but his miserable face had me reconsider.

I sat down next to him and put an arm around his shoulders. 'I don't have any brothers, but from what I've heard, they are extremely overrated,' I said.

'I just wish I could have known him,' he said without looking up. 'When we were younger. Maybe he wouldn't have turned out the way he is now.'

I squeezed his shoulder and tried to think of something wise to say. But I couldn't. The sheer thought of his half-brother made me sick to my stomach with rage.

'Well, he's certainly nothing like you,' I managed finally, not that it added much to the conversation.

'Do you have no family at all?' He looked at me.

I shook my head. 'My father was an adventurer like me. He met my mother in a whorehouse. I was an accident. Or so my mother claimed. She made some deal there so that they would allow her to keep me. But a few years later, she still sent me off to the monastery, and I never heard from her again.'

'You grew up in a whorehouse?' His face was shocked, as if not sure he had heard me right. Here he was again, worrying about me, when if what Quede claimed was true, he had been handed a much worse deal.

'Just for a few years,' I said. 'I was still very young when I was re-located to the Shield of Heaven Monastery.'

'I'm so sorry.' He put his arm around me, mimicking me. It would have been strange to sit like that with anyone else, man or woman. But with him, I somehow didn't mind. Was this what Ithorion meant when he said "closer than friends, closer than family"? It certainly calmed me. I just wished he would put that bloody sword hilt down.

'It was fine,' I said. 'In the monastery, I had a clean bed every night and plenty of decent food every day. I learned a lot there. Not that I appreciated it at the time. But it was the best place to learn how to fight.'

'You're certainly pretty good, from what I've seen,' he acknowledged, his praise lifting my spirit.

'Which reminds me,' I said. 'In the monastery, all the monks lived in celibacy. You don't think that members of the Order practice similar restrictions, do you?'

'No. I asked Terek yesterday.'

'*You* asked?' I laughed. I never thought that would be one of his earliest concerns.

'What?' He shrugged. 'It's something we should be aware of. Especially knowing your temperament.' He grinned.

'I'm just surprised then that we haven't seen any children around,' I pointed out.

'Oh, that. He also mentioned that Champions very rarely have children.' His face darkened, as if, for some reason, he wasn't entirely happy with that fact.

'Sounds reasonable to me. I wouldn't want any, either.'

'It didn't sound like it was a choice. Just something that usually "failed" to happen to them. Although surely there must be other ways to have children if it didn't happen naturally,' he mused, then laughed at my horrified face.

All this weird stuff within the soul circles, within the Order … I wondered if this was the root of how I felt about Selena, too. Or more like how I didn't feel about her. No matter how gorgeous she was, I just couldn't think of being with her that way. Not that I hadn't tried. But somehow, it just felt wrong. As if I would make her dirty. I adored her more than I have adored anyone else. Way more! Even just her smile filled me with joy. Only while other women made me hard and lustful, Selena made me soft and cuddly.

'So how do people in Coroden go about it anyway, hmm?' Kris asked, and I needed a moment to remind myself what we'd been talking about. 'How does Conor Drew not have any children?' he prompted with a smile.

'There's a herb for it,' I informed him. 'Redthorn leaf. Women drink a tea made of it if they don't want to conceive a child. The men can drink it, too, before bedding a woman, or chew some of the leaves, although they are very bitter.'

'Sounds like another thing you no longer need to worry about if you become Champion,' he offered with an encouraging smile. 'Although there have to be exceptions. The Supreme Leader's daughter is a case in point.'

'Oh yes.' I smiled wistfully. 'The lovely Aiki.'

'Just be careful,' he warned in his teasing voice.

'You're not worried about her now, too, are you?' I grinned back.

'Not in the slightest,' he reassured me. 'I'm worried about you! Aiki is a smart one. She'll break your heart before you get even near her skirt.'

'I'm tempted to try,' I said. 'I could really use a challenge!'

'And, of course, Quede would kill you afterwards.'

I thought back to Aiki. 'It would probably be worth it.'

'Obviously, were you to somehow succeed and find yourself in bed with her, I might just need to send you to sleep again before anything happened. Strictly for security reasons, you understand.' He grinned, but before I could retort, he raised his head and hissed, 'Selena!'

We jumped to our feet like two guilty boys just as she opened the door.

'Is everything alright?' She looked us up and down, her eyes pausing on the sword hilt in Kris's hand. He dropped it then as if it had stung him.

'Yes, all fine. We were just leaving.' He gave her an innocent smile as he passed her in the doorway and started down the stairs.

'I haven't interrupted anything, have I?' she asked.

'No,' I said, smiling at her affectionately for fixing so efficiently what I couldn't. 'In fact, it was perfect timing.'

'Is that …?' Her eyes lingered on that piece of junk on the floor.

'Come on.' I opened the door wider and pulled her out with me. 'Coroden is waiting!'

When Terek told us that they were packing our carriage on the other side for us, for a moment, I thought that perhaps I had heard him wrong. A carriage? They'd got us a whole carriage? But then, when I saw how much stuff Selena had, it suddenly made sense. She claimed most of it was clothes. I had to admit, I'd never really considered before just how many dresses a woman needed. My interest in the subject usually only extended to removing them.

Speaking of which, a few members of the Order lingered near the Pantheon's skygate as we approached it. One of them was Aiki. I peeled off from the others and went to say my farewells.

'On assignment so soon?' She smiled at me.

'Well, you know,' I said. 'Important initiates such as us can't just put their feet up and chill here when the Order is in desperate need.' She faked a sorrowful expression at that, curling those delicious, full lips in a way that made me step closer and add, 'As much as I'd love to.'

'You think that you might sort it all out soon and be back?' Her eyes flashed with that little mischief I so loved, and I was ready to promise her anything.

'Maybe,' I teased, enjoying the way her smile turned into mock disapproval. 'Definitely,' I murmured and watched the sun come out again. It was a smile that teleported me far away from here, into a bed where she was already half-naked and sighing under me with lust and pleasure. She might work for Gods, but I would show her what real heaven felt like!

Her eyes shifted from mine, the coyness disappearing, as she word-lessly exchanged a look with someone else, an understanding passing between them. I turned uneasily, but it was only Kris behind me, treating me to that innocent smile of his.

'Ready?' he asked.

'Um … yes, sure,' I said, suddenly uncertain whether that look between them was about something more than just him fetching me, or if I was only imagining things.

'Good luck!' Aiki said, the playfulness back in her eyes as they met mine. 'I look forward to hearing all about how it went.'

I took one last look at her, drinking her in like a man about to leave for the desert, then turned and followed Kris to the swirling gate. Selena stood in front of it, fidgeting anxiously.

'Not afraid of teleporting, are we?' I wrapped her in a hug. 'Surely not the Supreme Key of the Dragon who opens doors into other worlds!' I looked down at her embarrassed face.

'It's pretty ridiculous, isn't it?' she complained. 'But I'm a nervous flyer, too. Anyway. What is it like?'

'It's not too bad.' I shrugged, half-wondering what she meant by being a "flyer". 'But I honestly preferred when you brought us. It was nicer. You don't remember, do you?'

She shook her head.

'Well, best just get on with it.' I took her hand in mine and looked up at Kris. He tapped a combination of symbols on the side, and the gate lit up with a blue light. Then he took Selena's other hand, winked at her, which made her smile, and led us back into my world.

The Coroden Gate was well hidden in the belly of the Ceteres mountain range that cut across the kingdom. Hans waited for us with two torches in the large cave we entered on the other side. He handed one of them to me, and I took up the last position in our little line behind Kris.

Only a few weeks ago, I had been on my own as usual in the Holt Catacombs, holding a torch like this one. Then, under the ruins of Borond Castle with Kris. And now, there were four of us. If I carried on like this, I'd be marching with a whole army soon!

Still, it wasn't bad. Hans led us with practised steps, the black cloak on his broad shoulders shining like silk in the torchlight. I kind of liked their uniforms. They looked very practical, yet carried a hint of that majestic elegance that seemed at the heart of all design in the Pantheon. I wouldn't have minded having a set of something similar myself.

My eyes moved over to Selena behind him, and my heart soared with joy. She was the best thing I could have brought back with me! More precious than any gems. She looked simply stunning in her tantalising dress and with that long, red hair. I'd be the envy of the whole kingdom with her by my side. I adored her with all her cute insecurities. She was a little star. The Supreme Key of the Dragon, whose potential and impending power clearly even Quede feared. Yet, Selena didn't see herself that way. Sometimes it seemed to me as if she was hiding behind a mask. As if too afraid to come out and shine.

But she did shine for me. I saw it every time she smiled at me. It was in the warm affection in her eyes. In that profound connection between us that felt as obvious and solid as the ground I walked on. In the way her happiness always mirrored mine. She knew it, too. We belonged together, whatever the Order of the Dragon believed. She was my key. And there would be hell to pay if anyone tried to take her away from me again!

Which brought me to the last member of our party, who walked between us. This strange guy, who not so long ago I had tried to get rid of. And now? I said to him that I had no brothers, yet he sure felt like one. Unlike his real brother, I could never hurt him, though. If anything, it was the opposite. How had this happened? How did we come to this?

'People you meet are like seeds,' Aiki said when she asked me about our friendship in the middle of the street yesterday. 'Sooner or later, most of them are blown away from your life, and you forget all about them. But a few will stay and grow roots while you're not looking. Before you know it, they take hold in you so deeply, you can no longer remove them without tearing off a part of you. And sometimes you will find that it is a part you cannot live without.'

I still wasn't sure if that was true. I could definitely leave him behind if he carried on insisting on this Champion business! I just didn't want to do it. Maybe there was still a way to convince him that there could be another life for us. I knew he was attached to Selena just as much as I was. Maybe

I'd take them to Manessa once we'd finished this job and show them what it could be like. I'd take them to see the Great Fortress of the Selvik, the Enchanted Gardens of Antiria, the Sacred Baths of the Fire Island! They were both so into books, I'd take them to the Merdillion High Library in Andastos. Then a visit to the famous Herend Market. We could buy Selena a hundred dresses there!

I was sure there was a way to get ourselves free from the Order. There was always something that someone needed more. Everyone had a price. And so what if we couldn't have any gifts because of it? I'd been perfectly fine without any all my life. We would have each other and the freedom to do what we liked. That mattered more.

That little plan cheered me up as we stepped into the sunshine outside. Spring was blossoming into summer in Coroden, and the forest around us buzzed with life. Selena slowed considerably behind Hans, following him now on a narrow path, taking in the world around her as if it was even more fascinating than the one we had just left behind.

'You don't get out of that London much, do you?' I called after her in Wedan, my mother tongue.

'Is that so obvious?' She turned and grinned at me, making me laugh. 'What's so funny?' she asked, lifting her skirt as we crossed a small stream.

'Your accent,' I said.

'You didn't find it that funny when you needed me to translate between you and those girls at the party,' she pointed out.

'That's because I didn't want them to think I was laughing at them!'

She spun around, and I ducked behind Kris, using him as a shield. 'Don't hurt me, Miss Soto! Please don't hurt me again! I'll be a good boy, I promise!'

Kris turned his head to look at me. 'She has the same accent as me.'

'I know,' I said and released his shoulders. 'You both sound a little foreign. But it fits her type of character perfectly, so it's all good.'

'My type of character? And what's Kris's type?' she asked.

He was suddenly too busy smiling at her at that, so I answered the question. 'He already introduced himself in Beren as Kristian del Rosso, a scholar from the far away Alba, so we both can only play ourselves.'

'So, you both get to be who you really are while I have to pretend to be a powerful sorceress?'

'Sums it up.' I nodded. 'Just take it as a rehearsal session for a potential *key* role to come!'

She stopped and waited for Kris to pass her by, which he reluctantly did.

'So clever!' she stabbed an accusatory finger into my chest as I stopped and grinned at her. I took her hand and kissed it.

'Don't worry. You'll be great!' I said.

'Is my accent really ridiculous?' she demanded with a concerned face.

'No, it isn't,' I admitted. 'I was just teasing you. You sound like Kris. You know …' I tried to find the right word. 'Well-educated.'

That seemed to reassure her. I offered her my arm as the path ahead of us widened, and she took it. 'It's the month of the Red Blessing here,' I informed her.

'What do you mean?' She frowned.

'Just what I said. This month is called Red Blessing,'

'You're teasing me again.'

'I'm not!' I laughed.

'Why is it called Red Blessing then?'

'Because there are many types of red fruits that are in season this month.'

She nodded like that made sense. 'I hope I get to try some.'

'You'll love them.'

As I said that, my own eyes widened, impressed. The path crossed a paved road and on that road stood our carriage with four beautiful horses. Practical, with a hint of majestic elegance. Made of dark wood, polished to a shine, and not a scratch on it anywhere. Unlike most coaches I'd seen, this had shafts that could pivot, allowing the four large wheels to turn. Wheels with circular iron bands fitted around them. On its doors, the emblem of the Scarlet Witches was painted in magnificent detail, although I doubted that the witches had ever seen, let alone owned, anything like this. No, this was clearly made by the Order, possibly even overnight.

'Is it a good one?' Selena asked from next to me.

'It's so good, people will be staring with an open mouth. And that's before they even see you!' I added.

I opened the door for her. From under the body of the carriage, a step slid out, allowing her to climb up easily. I laughed in wonder. Inside were soft leather seats, and with all our stuff on the roof, plenty of space to stretch your legs.

'Are you going to be alright in here?' I grinned at her.

'Are you coming already?' Kris called down from the driver's seat, where he was looking at a large map with Ramin and another man I didn't know. Boy, I couldn't wait!

I shooed the others away and took my seat next to him.

'You can put that map down. I know where we are,' I told him and reached for the reins.

'There's no way we can make it to Caledon by tonight.' He lowered the map into his lap, annoyed. 'Not even with four horses!'

'No,' I agreed. 'We need two days, and even that would be a record. We'll be stopping for the night here.' I pointed a finger at the map.

'Abor? Do you know this place? What is it like?'

'It's a wealthy market town built on the River Abora, and closely administered by the royal household. A good place to find a clean room and a proper dinner for our delicate sorceress.'

'Will this cover it?' He turned a black leather pouch full of coins towards me.

I peered into it and whistled. 'Should be enough for a year!' I laughed and flicked the reins.

The carriage swept along the Farand Road like a dream. I drove the horses hard, enjoying the speed. Whatever suspension we had, I hardly felt a bounce. Kris sat deep in his thoughts next to me, neither worried nor impressed by our pace.

'Are you hungry yet?' I asked him after a while.

'No. Why?'

I'm just thinking about when and where to stop for a rest,' I said. 'I have a few places in mind.'

'Let me ask Selena.'

I watched him turn around, grip the side rail and push himself back to the window of the carriage. When the distance proved too long, he let go of the footrest and stretched further back only holding on to the rail and keeping the rest of his body in the air, more or less horizontal. I didn't know what exactly they did at this university of his, but there was clearly a lot more involved than just reading books!

By the time he climbed back, I would have guessed they'd discussed Selena's every dietary wish for the day, down to the last slice of cake.

'She's asleep,' he said.

'Hmmm. In that case, Era's Kitchen it is.'

'An old girlfriend of yours?'

'You could say that!' I laughed. 'Except that she's old enough to be my grandmother. But she's a very warm-hearted lady with a good sense of humour. She has a well-known tavern in a small village called Isher further down this road. At this speed, we'll be there in less than two hours.'

'Won't the horses need to rest before then or slow down?'

'I'm not sure,' I admitted. 'I don't know what kind of horses these are. I slowed them to a gentle trot earlier, but they soon picked up speed again on their own account. It's as if they just loved running.'

'Interesting, but works for us.' He laughed.

'You don't think they were built like Storn?' I asked him.

He shook his head. 'Storn doesn't eat or defecate. These horses do.'

'Well, we'll give them a good rest in Isher with plenty of food and fresh water,' I said.

'Sounds good.'

'Have you travelled in a carriage like this before?' I asked.

He shook his head. 'Have you?'

'Only once. Although that was a considerably bumpier journey, and not only because the suspension wasn't this good.' He grimaced and turned away upon realising what I was talking about, making me laugh. 'There are often long hours between stops, and there isn't much else to do when you need to spend that time in a small, confined space with a woman. Especially on a nice summer's day like this. With the curtains down and comfortable seats like these, there are lots of ways to enjoy a ride.'

He groaned and buried his forehead into his palm. 'Thanks for that, Conor!'

I laughed again and patted his shoulder. 'It's been a long time, I know. Don't worry. We'll sort out something once we conclude our business in Caledon.'

'Thanks, but I'm fine,' he grumbled.

'Well, don't say "no" until you've seen the places I'm going to take you!'

He sighed and raised his head, studying the countryside around us. 'Two more hours?'

'What do you usually drive back in your world when you're not with Storn?' I asked. 'The kind of things we saw in London on the roads?'

'No, we don't really have those. Not where I lived, anyway. We mostly use vehicles that fly.'

'That fly? What? Like a bird?' I thought of the boat we both travelled in but didn't want to upset him with the memory.

'Better!' He grinned, his eyes glinting with excitement.

'You'll take me to this university and teach me?' The carriage I'd so admired before seemed suddenly simple and childish. His smile faded. 'What?'

'Just this strange feeling,' he said. 'I don't think I want to go back there. But don't worry,' he added. 'I'll still teach you. Just probably somewhere else.'

'Great!' I grinned and handed him the reins, making sure that he held both correctly in his left hand. 'Here, I'll show you how to drive in the meantime.'

Two hours later, we stopped the carriage at the tavern. It was a popular resting place for those travelling the Farand Road. What had once been nothing more than a simple house with a handful of tables and seats in its yard had now taken over the land of its former neighbours. In their place was a vegetable garden where fruit bushes bordered neat rows of potatoes, onions and carrots, and beyond that, a large stable block. All this had sprung up to service the demand caused by the aroma from one woman's cooking pot.

I had hardly opened the carriage door for Selena when a stable boy hurried our way to help with unharnessing the horses. Kristian opened the black purse next to me.

'Do we have any coppers in there?' I asked him.

He shook his head.

'Then give him the smallest silver you can find.'

A moment later, the boy arrived, and I watched, stunned, as the coin exchanged hands. The thrilled excitement on his young face was priceless.

I leaned close to Kris and whispered, 'That was our smallest coin?'

'Yes,' he said.

Great. I leaned down to look at the stable boy with a serious expression. 'Listen. This is the first time we've brought these horses here. You make sure they enjoy their stay.'

Based on the profound reassurances that followed, I wouldn't have been surprised to hear that they were even treated to the owner's famous apple pie! The boy was soon joined by one of his older brothers, and by the looks of it, they knew what they were doing.

I made Kris and Selena sit down in the garden, where the number of tables around the fruit trees and flower baskets extended to about twenty now, and where we were still close to the carriage and the elegant wooden chests on its top.

I looked towards the door to the house and saw Era watching us from there. She threw me a look, and I followed her in. Inside, I only saw empty tables, all the customers clearly enjoying the lovely weather in the shade the trees provided outside. The smells from the kitchen had my mouth watering.

Era sent her granddaughter out to our table with drinks and nibbles, and once it was only the two of us, she turned to me.

'I'm glad to see you, Conor. I was starting to get a little worried about you,' she said, wiping her hands on a cloth.

'Come on, Era, it's me!' I laughed and watched her wrinkled face relax into a smile. 'You know I will always come back. I love your cooking!'

'Very nice lady you have there. Even for you, Conor.' She nodded, impressed.

My chest swelled, and I almost blurted out what was on my mind. Luckily, I remembered myself just in time. 'She is one of the Scarlet Witches. We're taking her to cure the king.'

'You have come all the way from the Isle of Yres?'

'I have!' I picked up a fried chicken leg from a nearby plate, unable to resist the temptation any longer.

'Do you know there's an astonishing price on your head in Coroden? A thousand golden ducats! They're charging you with treason.'

Laro's face appeared in my mind, and the meat suddenly turned bitter in my mouth. Rage boiled in my veins, and I thought to myself that if the Dragon really wanted me to become his Champion, he'd surely give me an opportunity to kill that worm!

'All false accusations,' I said. 'We'll lift the curse soon, and my name will be cleared.'

'I never doubted you for a second. But there are plenty who would, for that kind of money. You travel like a rich lord with a beautiful woman and only one man to help you defend it all. I hope he knows how to use a sword!'

'He's not bad.' I smiled. 'He's actually a really good friend and still new to Coroden. My impression is that the food is rubbish where he's from. I was rather hoping you'd show him what proper cooking looks like.'

'Leave that with me.' She flipped her hand dismissively. 'We'll give him a lunch he'll never forget!'

I walked out to the garden, pausing in the doorway to look around. There was a mixed crowd outside. A noblewoman with two female companions, three groups of soldiers, a merchant family, two groups of men in expensive clothing and without apparent weapons, a bard, two priests, and a bunch of weather-beaten thugs, whose look I didn't like.

There was one thing they all shared in common. They were all watching the two in the middle, who stood out like two roses in a clover field. One of them an exquisite beauty of a woman in a flirtatious dress, the sunshine playing magic with her long, red hair. The other, a tall, blond guy, lean, toned and wiry. He was good-looking, but it wasn't just that that had the three women at the nearest table excitedly whispering about him, or that the warm weather made him open the top of his shirt and tuck his sleeves up to his shoulders. It was more than that. He had a quiet confidence about him. A perceptive intelligence in his eyes. Like he knew something the rest of us didn't. The smile on his face as he looked at the woman seemed to say he could see right into her and what he'd found there was all he cared about.

I chewed my lips and looked over at our carriage. Our swords were secured to the top. I had an urge to go and get them, but I had a feeling that those thugs might take it as an invitation to cause us trouble. Would anyone recognise me? All the men seemed content enjoying their meals and feasting their eyes on Selena as an additional treat. Should I at least say something to them? Warn them? I watched their happy faces and reminded myself that this would be the first time the three of us shared a meal. I wanted us to come here to have a good time. I wasn't about to spoil it.

I loosened my shoulders and confidently took the empty seat next to the Scarlet Witch. She shot me one of those affectionate smiles she only kept for me, and all was well with the world.

It was the best few hours I'd had in a long time. A gentle breeze blew, just enough to take the edge of the midday sun, and for the first time, it seemed all three of us were able to just relax. We improvised playful conversations in Wedan, so Selena could practise her role, and once we got bored of that and of not being able to speak our minds, we switched to Elesean. The food kept on coming from the kitchen, starting with Era's famous chicken soup, followed by buttered boiled potatoes, cherry sauce and freshly fried duck legs with crispy skin, which were so delicious I burned my tongue rather than wait for them to cool. There was apple pie, walnut cake with rum and strawberry compote, and some excellent chilled white wine from the cellar.

We ate with dedication, complimenting the cook at each round, our joy and satisfaction infectious. Not a single guest approached us or frowned upon seeing my face. If anything, everyone was friendly, smiling or nodding our way amicably, as if we had woven a spell over the place. Even the thugs had disappeared—I didn't notice when.

'Maybe some sweet cherry wine to finish it off?' I asked with an innocent face.

Kris narrowed his eyes at me.

'I meant for the Lady Selena!' I grinned at him. I knew he'd pick up on it. That wasn't an evening he'd entirely forgiven me for.

'Oh, no, thank you, I'm so full,' she said. 'I wish I could have a coffee.'

'A what?' I asked, mystified.

'Do you remember that tea we had in Castle Beren?' Kris asked.

'Edernut leaf tree?' I looked at Era, who stood behind him waiting. She nodded.

'It's not exactly what you have in mind, but it has a nutty flavour and quite a bit of caffeine in it,' he told Selena.

'Add a little honey, too,' I suggested. This might have been the first meal the three of us had shared, but I'd already been to a feast with her.

Kris pursed his lips, looking at Selena. 'And perhaps some milk,' he said.

'Milk?' Era pulled a face.

I gestured to her to just do it.

'So, depending on how the horses take it after this rest, I expect we should reach Abor in about four hours.' I spotted the stable boy and waved at him to get the carriage ready.

'Can we walk around a bit?' Selena asked. 'I can't sit for another four hours without moving a little first.'

'There isn't much to see here, but sure, we can have a look around the garden. See the horses in the stable. Abor has a pretty waterfront, though. We can go for a walk there at sunset.'

'You know, this isn't half-bad!' Era appeared with a cup and put the drink down in front of Selena. 'I made some for us to try, too. What do you think?' She looked at her granddaughter, Clara, who followed her out, holding a similar cup. Clara was only a few years younger than me, but it never crossed my mind to consider anything more than a passing glance between us. I wouldn't have risked my place at one of their tables for anything!

'I like it.' Clara nodded her approval.

Selena reached for her cup, but I stopped her and added a touch of rum. 'Now try it.'

I leaned back in my chair, waiting for the verdict.

'Oh, this is too good,' she announced after a few sips, making me share a satisfied smile with Kris.

I sorted our bill afterwards while the two of them went for a walk. I knew Era wouldn't accept the number of coins I wanted to give her, so I left it with Clara instead. Then I went to check on our carriage and that the horses were properly harnessed. I marvelled again at our ride. I had seen carriages with brakes in the past. They called it a spoon brake and operated it with a lever, pressing a big block of wood against the wheel. Ours had callipers around the wheels, which I could control with a foot pedal. I'd never seen anything like it.

Once Kris and Selena reappeared, we said our goodbyes and were soon back on the Farand Road. For the first hour, all was as it was supposed to be. We passed another village and had a long stretch of the road ahead, surrounded by nothing but green meadows and pastures spotted with sheep and cows, the rolling fields crowned by the occasional farmhouse.

I noticed them from quite some distance away. On the right, an abandoned building, partially overgrown with vines. Around it were ten men, jumping into their saddles upon seeing us. Kris watched them, too. 'Not good,' he said. He handed me the reins and turned to get our swords from the roof. 'Do you have the keys to any of these chests?'

'Selena has them. I think there might be only two. In the black chest, there are some daggers,' I added.

He got Selena to pass him the keys through the window, warning her that we expected some trouble ahead, and in less than a minute, he had the daggers out and the black purse locked up in their place.

I waited until we got near the bandits before showing them what our unusually fit horses and modern carriage were capable of. The speed surprised them. Hell, it surprised me! But as single riders, they still had the advantage over us and soon caught up.

The next moment, a bolt from a crossbow sailed past my ear, shortly followed by a knife. The carriage was surrounded by the ten riders, jeering and calling out to us. I recognised the thugs from the tavern among their number.

As I ducked and dodged whatever missiles came my way, I watched Kris take out the four closest men with the throwing daggers. He wasted precious time ensuring the wounds would incapacitate rather than kill. He was soon out of daggers, though, and for a moment, I wondered why he was still standing next to me. Then I realised that however agile he was, apart from Storn, he'd never ridden a horse. We would have to work on that, I thought, as I handed him the reins. I raced across the carriage roof as fast as I could and threw myself at crossbow-guy.

I got lucky, as always. My sudden arrival surprised him so much that even if he'd had time to reload, he didn't have time to aim. I got unlucky, too, as my arrival knocked him off his horse completely. I really could have used that crossbow! I twisted around in the saddle to sit properly and encouraged the horse towards his nearest friend. When in close range, I pulled my legs under myself into a crouch, then sprang at my next victim. His knife went flying, and a few well-aimed punches had him tumbling from the saddle.

A young robber next to me had been struggling to pull his sword from his scabbard while maintaining his speed, but now that it was finally out, he started poking it ineffectually in my direction. I rolled my eyes, then pulled up my legs again and, while balancing on the left, I stretched out and kicked up at his wrist with the right, the impact sending the sword flying away. I didn't bother trying to catch it.

'Idiot,' I hissed at him. 'Why do you think I left mine on the carriage? It's near useless in a close-range fight like this!'

A movement caught my eye, and I looked up to see two of the more adventurous bandits on top of the carriage, making Kris abandon the reins and engage in a sword fight. But it was seeing the carriage door open on the other side, and someone climbing in, that stopped my heart. The kid came close to me and tried to grab me, presumably to push me off, although why he didn't attempt to hit me instead, I couldn't imagine. As it was, class was over. I got rid of him with a powerful kick to the ribs and launched myself back at the carriage door. Inside, Selena stood hunched with her back against the door, brandishing a dagger at the burly scar-faced guy closing on her and laughing.

'Selena, sit down!' I shouted at her as I tore the door open. I grabbed the railing that kept our luggage on the roof and propelled myself into the carriage feet-first. My heels hit the man in the chest, helping him out the same way he entered. I threw myself after him and climbed onto the roof on the other side to relieve Kris of one of his attackers. I didn't understand how he hadn't fought them off yet, until I noticed blood on his right arm and realised, he was using his left. Together, we made short work of the remaining opposition.

'Have you done this before?' he asked once we got rid of them, and I slowed the horses.

'I have,' I admitted with a rueful smile. 'Only back then, I was playing for the other team.'

'Do I want to know?' He sighed, wincing as he cleaned his arm with a cloth and some of that herb spirit Terek had packed for us.

'It's not what you think. I'll tell you later.' I stopped the horses and jumped off to check on Selena.

It was shortly before sunset that we made it to Abor. We'd only just entered the town when a small army stopped us.

'Conor Drew, I'm Captain Trevor Oldbriar, in charge of the City Guard of Abor. In the name of the king, I hereby arrest you for treason,' the one in the middle of the front line announced without preamble. He didn't look much older than me, only twice as smug on his chestnut Gelferland stallion.

'We are on an important mission, escorting the Lady Selena to the king himself,' I said in an even tone. 'She's here on behalf of the Scarlet Witches, who have finally agreed to lift the curse and cure the king.'

'A Scarlet Witch, you say?' He chuckled, as if claiming a unicorn was in the carriage would have sounded a likelier tale.

I got down and went to open the carriage door, hoping that Selena's appearance would be convincing enough. The captain also dismounted, along with some of his soldiers, and they surrounded me, sneering as if expecting a good joke. The door wasn't even half-way open when I felt it pushed from the inside and a woman I didn't recognise exited the carriage.

Her face was a picture of upper-class fury, sparks flying from her eyes, her hands in fists by her sides in a way that would make any rational man take a step back.

'Captain Oldbriar, is it?' she snapped at him. 'Just what the hell do you think you are doing?' She marched right up to him, getting a Scarlet Witch medallion out from her neckline on the way and shoving it into his surprised face. 'After four hundred years, my coven finally consents to this ridiculous, incessant begging from the Coroden court,' she raged, stamping her right foot, 'and I'm obliged to journey across the Nineteen Kingdoms, sitting in this box for weeks, bruising my backside on your tragically kept roads, attacked by bandits! My driver got injured.' She pointed at Kris. 'While my escort, had to fight off a dozen of those scum because Corodien soldiers are too busy loitering about instead of keeping the area safe! Delay him just by one more minute, Captain, and I'll turn around, go all the way back home, and you can tell your king not to annoy us with his pleading for another four hundred years!'

I pushed the back of my hand into my mouth and bit on a finger as I watched Captain Oldbriar's ears turn very red.

'Pardon the intrusion, my lady,' he bowed to her. 'Robert,' he turned to one of his men. 'You and ten of your soldiers are to accompany this carriage to the White Dove Inn and make sure that Lady Selena gets their best room for the night. You will station there and ensure that her stay remains undisturbed. In the morning, you will be given ten more men to escort the lady and her companions to the Royal Palace in Caledon with a personal note from me to the knight-commander.'

Selena pursed her lips, nodded at him, then turned on her heel, making me jump to open the carriage door for her. Once I closed it behind her and climbed back up next to Kris, I gave a sigh of relief. Surely this wasn't the same woman I had comforted after the attack just a few hours ago? How fast her heart still beat as I pulled her close to me. And now? Sure as hell, I never wanted to be on the receiving end of that!

'Why was she even nervous about this last night?' I muttered to Kris.

He opened his arms with an amused smile on his face. I picked up the reins, and we followed the soldiers to the inn.

The next evening, we arrived at the Royal Palace to a reception fit for a princess. Servants rushed up and down around us, sorting out the horses and carrying our belongings. Selena was greeted by no less than the knight-commander himself, as well as the steward and a line of well-dressed domestic staff. We were then politely escorted to a set of guest rooms, with hot bathwater prepared in case we wanted to wash ourselves before joining the king at the dinner table. The luxury of the palace took my breath away. Gold and silver on everything, the rooms full of fine works of art, soft linen covers on the beds. I could get used to this, I thought, as I sipped a well-balanced red from a beautifully crafted glass while soaking in the wooden tub.

The king welcomed us warmly, as if we were the only piece of good news he had received in weeks. Selena explained to him that she needed a few days to assess the current state of the curse and pick out the best method to break it—a task at which our scholar companion would help her.

The king apologised for not having much free time available to answer all her questions due to frequent strategic and military meetings regarding the situation with the Harags, but he showed us to the library where their family history was kept in excessive detail going back five centuries, describing, among other things, not just the circumstances of the curse, but every single method tried to lift it in their thick volumes. His wife died in childbirth a few years ago, leaving behind a little girl, but he assured us that the Lady Selena would be properly looked after by her court ladies and the royal household.

After dinner, we had our own little meeting in Kris's room, where we decided who would do what. He was to go through the library books and share any important details he found regarding the curse with Selena. Selena was to spend as much time with the king as she could, making sure she didn't venture too far from Kris and lose her grip on our language. Conveniently, the library was very close to the throne room, but even if Selena had to go further away, Kris could always pick up a book and follow her to the next location. As for me, I was to use my own magic and enchant the king's closest advisor's, Lord Dranos's daughter, Lady Aurelia, who had already been eyeing me up at the dinner table. According to Kris, this way we would have access to three types of information, which he seemed to consider important: official, through him and the written records; unofficial, through me and the advisor's daughter; and personal, through Selena's conversations with the king.

The first few days went fast and easy. Everyone seemed keen to help us with whatever we needed. Even Aurelia, who was distressed by some family drama, had fallen for my charms quicker than I expected, and while still guarded when it came to discussing matters regarding her family and the king, she gradually loosened up as we spent night after night together. She warned me to keep our nights of passion secret from her father, but all that sneaking around just added further excitement to our evenings.

I was really impressed by how well Selena had settled in, too, convincing everyone she was exactly who we claimed her to be. Even now, as she sat between Kris and me in the dining hall, she was precious. She was sweet, she looked gorgeous in a beautiful red dress that left her arms and shoulders bare and wore a scent that was discreet but enticing. More than a few men watched her as we dined, and some of those sitting closest did everything they could to charm her. She pretended to enjoy their mostly feeble attempts. She giggled at their jokes. She thanked them warmly for their compliments. She made up intriguing tales when they asked her about her coven and politely inquired about their ways of life in return. She even teased one or two. Needless to say, they all loved it.

The only man who had grown more distant from her these last few days was Kris. To be fair to him, he did spend most of his days reading. You almost never saw him without a book anymore. Nonetheless, even I started noticing at meals and at our catch-up meetings how he was always serious and never smiled at her anymore. I knew he was taking this job very seriously, and so I wasn't going to say anything, but at that night's dinner, he was taking his aloofness to a whole new level and even avoided looking at her. When Selena asked him to pass her something from the table, he did so with the briefest of glances her way. Otherwise, he was even less chatty than usual, and I had to wonder if that, too, had something to do with Selena sitting between us.

I watched Selena grow a little more disheartened by his behaviour day after day, pushing herself to excel even more in response, keen to prove herself and impress him. I knew the feeling. In some ways, I had been the same when we had met. Instantly had this urge to try and look good in front of him. Ordering everyone the most expensive beer in the tavern just to get a table. Showing off with my fighting skills whenever I had a chance. If I was entirely honest, even that anger that burned in me follow-ing my release from the prison had more to do with shame that he had to meet me under such stupid circumstances than it did with the duke keep-ing my medallion. Any other time would have been fine. Any at all! No. He had to arrive exactly then and save me.

I wondered what it was about Kris that made you feel like you should be a better version of yourself. Maybe it was just as Ithorion had said and, as a tora, he inspired us. I didn't know for sure. But the way Selena glowed with joy at even his slightest approval made me think that her feelings towards him had perhaps started growing in an entirely new direction. And if that was the case, I actually didn't mind. If anything, I was relieved that it was Kris for her. Selena falling for anyone else carried the risk of her being swept away from my life again, and I didn't want that. Besides, Kris was a great guy. Nobody I knew came even close to him in my estimation. If only he would stop acting like an idiot! I saw the way he had looked at her before we arrived here, and I knew he wasn't indifferent. Yet here we were. At a long table full of men who could hardly keep their eyes off Selena, while Kris pretended she didn't exist.

'I'm sure you must hear this all the time, Lady Selena, but painting such an exquisite beauty as yourself is every artist's dream,' Duke Albury was now telling her, taking advantage of his prime position sitting opposite us and making her laugh politely. Albury was one of the wealthiest aristocrats in the country with an arrogance to match. As one of the kingdom's most eligible bachelors, he had, of course, been invited to the Beren wedding, too, although I had paid little attention to him at the time. He was tall, well-muscled and handsome. His face had a hard, dangerous quality to it when he was serious. As far as the ladies were concerned, it seemed to make him all the more attractive when he smiled. That, and his dark curly hair about which I had heard excited whispers on more than one occasion.

'I dabble a little in the art myself and would love an opportunity to paint you, my lady.' He leaned closer to Selena with an admiring smile.

From the corner of my eye, I caught Kris move a little strangely at that, but by the time I properly looked at him, nothing indicated that anything had happened at all. I carefully pushed my chair back a bit and leaned back to have a better view of him. He seemed focused on his dinner, but there was a tense set to his shoulders, as if he was paying careful attention to the conversation taking place beside him.

'I'm afraid I'm a little too busy to sit for you, Duke Albury,' Selena responded politely. 'Maybe another time.'

'Perhaps a gentle walk, then?' the duke pushed on. 'Have you seen the palace grounds yet? I would be more than happy to show you around in the evenings if you're occupied during the day. How about the lily pond? Have you seen it yet?'

'No, I don't think I have,' she admitted.

'Oh, you must come! It's simply stunning at sunset.'

'Is it really?' Selena hesitated, some intrigue in her voice now.

'Absolutely.' Albury smiled, sensing that he had her. 'There's a little green bridge across it that looks lovely at dusk. And the whole pond is surrounded by beautiful magnolia trees.'

Kris lowered his cutlery and finally looked at Selena at that.

'I love magnolia trees!' Selena beamed at Albury without noticing, clearly excited now.

'My lady,' Kris spoke quietly to her. 'We have a lot of work in the morning. I'm not sure that tiring yourself out tonight might be such a good idea.'

'A little walk before bed is known to be beneficial for sleep!' Albury narrowed his eyes at Kris.

'No, no, Kristian is quite right,' Selena agreed hurriedly. 'There are a lot of records we need to go through in the upcoming days. Perhaps once the curse is broken.' She tried to appease the duke with a smile.

The duke nodded unhappily, then they all went back to eating again— Selena a little awkwardly, Kris more relaxed, Albury looking like he was ready to kill him.

'Maybe you'd come and see my estate, Lady Selena, once the curse is broken,' he said again in a little while.

'Your estate? Whereabouts is it?' Selena asked conversationally.

'It's out to the west. I actually have a lily pond, too. And an orchard. Do you like apples?'

'I do.' Selena smiled again.

'It's a big estate.' The duke smiled back. 'I'm sure you'd love it.'

'I'm sure I would,' Selena responded warmly, making Kris clench his jaw in the background.

'And the food,' the duke continued, watching Selena more eagerly, 'is fantastic! I mean, don't get me wrong. The food is obviously excellent here, too. But I have some of the best cooks in the country. One of them is from Orean. He makes the most delicious game stews you've ever tasted. He's also very good with cakes,' he added with a conspiratorial smile.

'Is he really? Sounds very accomplished,' Selena agreed.

'We could have dinner right next to the lake. Surrounded by dozens of candles in the dark. What do you say, Lady Selena?'

I watched Kris go very still, staring at his plate as we both waited for Selena to say no.

'That sounds so lovely!' She sounded more than a little enchanted. 'I'll definitely consider it.'

'Wonderful!' The duke smiled triumphantly, glancing across at Kris, who chose that moment to look up at him. The duke's smile twisted into an ugly smirk.

Kris returned to eating his dinner once more and ignoring what went on around him, although when Lady Elisa, who sat on his other side, dropped her hairclip in between them, he instantly reached for it for her. Lady Elisa, a niece of one of the earls and still new to court, clearly had yet to master the subtlety required to make the act look accidental, but even so, succeeded in her overall goal. Kris didn't just help her fasten the decorative clip back into her lush auburn hair, but even leaned closer to her with a smile to exchange a few quiet words.

I watched Selena tentatively reach into her own hair with a little frown, adjusting a similar hair ornament, hesitating.

I leaned forward, gesturing widely. 'Drop it, drop it!' I mouthed with a grin. She dropped her hand instead and laughed.

'He'd never notice it,' she muttered to me under her breath.

'What would I never notice?' Kris turned and looked at us.

I was about to make a joke, but his eyes were on Selena now, watching her so intently, I thought it was best to leave them to it. She remained silent and I leaned forward a little more to see her face, resting my chin on my hand, elbow on the table.

'What would I never notice?' he repeated in a softer voice, a smile tugging at his lips.

'If …' Selena hesitated like a misbehaving schoolgirl caught by the teacher. 'If …'

'Yes?' His smile widened in encouragement.

'If I stole some of your food while you weren't looking,' she managed finally.

'Are you that hungry tonight, my lady?' He tilted his head theatrically to look at Selena's near-full plate and then continued with an amused look on his face. 'Or perhaps you think mine tastes better than yours?'

'Well, I'll never know unless I try.' She beamed at his rare playfulness.

'Let's see, shall we?' He started cutting small pieces of chicken, potato, and vegetables, carefully arranging them on his fork with an unhurried calm, as if it was just the two of them and not half the table watching him curiously at the royal court, a clearly annoyed Duke Albury included.

Kris lifted the fork up to Selena, his left hand hovering underneath, and waited. For a long moment they just gazed at each other, Kris with a passion I'd never seen on his face before, Selena utterly mesmerised by him. Then she opened her mouth, and he slowly guided the fork in, his eyes deep in hers as he did so.

Nobody moved as we all watched Selena chew with a smile. I imagined quite a few men around us had their blood circulation suddenly re-distributed, leaving only a few after-images in their minds. As for Kris, I had a pretty good idea where his mind was at.

'So? Do you like mine more, my lady?' he asked in a soft voice, gently tucking a lock of her hair behind her ear.

Selena nodded. Kris exchanged their plates with a smile and started eating again.

I could sense Duke Albury's fury from across the table, but at least he remained silent. Selena turned and looked at me wide-eyed. I grinned at her in response, slowly shaking my head at the pair of them as I moved to finish my own food.

The conversation gradually re-started around our half of the table, too, a little laughter mixing here and there into the general noise of cutlery clinking, dishes clattering, servants walking around offering more wine and collecting empty tableware. Only the three of us remained silent, and of course Albury, who looked positively murderous.

'I'm too full for cake tonight!' Selena announced as dessert was about to be served and the musicians started playing from the gallery.

'What? No cake? Are you well, my lady?' I teased her.

'No, I think I'm a little tired,' she said. 'Kristian, would you mind walking me to my room, please?'

'Of course, my lady.' He swallowed. 'Conor, would you mind accompanying us, please?' he added suddenly. 'There's something I'd like to talk to you about afterwards.'

I stood, puzzled, but did as he asked. We wordlessly made our way up the stairs and through corridors to our allocated rooms. Judging by

Selena's expression, she was, like me, wondering what was going on. Kris seemed distant and didn't even glance at us until we reached Selena's door.

'I'm sorry if I got a little carried away with the improvised roleplaying in there,' he eventually said with a nervous laugh, making me stare at him in disbelief. 'I was only trying to discourage the duke from pestering you.' He frowned at Selena. 'I just really don't think it's a good time for you to get involved with other people right now. I hope you agree? Of course, you're allowed to, if that's what you really want, and you can absolutely go and see the duke once …'

'No.' Selena shook her head at him. 'I don't want to get involved with the duke.'

'No?' Kris shook his head, too, as if he needed to be sure they were really saying the same thing. 'Well, just know that of course you're absolutely allowed to. And please forgive me for getting carried away like that in the dining hall. It was, of course, wildly inappropriate. I didn't mean anything by it. Just wanted to protect you and save us from unnecessary distractions until we complete the assignment.'

'Of course.' Selena nodded, her face frozen into a polite smile. 'No problem at all.'

'Well, good then—and thank you. See you in the morning. Good night.' He tried to smile reassuringly but was failing by a mile.

'Good night, Selena.' I shot her a genuine one and would have hugged her, too, had I not been so desperate to grab Kris and shake some sense into him. I followed him along the corridor instead, towards his room.

'Stop looking at me like that,' he muttered as he opened the door.

'Roleplaying?' I laughed as I closed it behind me. 'Roleplaying? Really?' If anything, it looked like the opposite to me. He was finally showing how he really felt.

'I'm sorry! I'm sorry!' he pleaded as he walked up and down, raking his hair. 'I know I messed up. I shouldn't have done that. I lost my head. It won't happen again, I promise!'

'It was fine by me,' I informed him calmly, making him look at me surprised.

'It was?'

'Of course it was. I mean, maybe I would have suggested you try flowers or jewellery first, but it's not like what you did in there didn't work.' I chuckled. 'But maybe it's not too late to add a few romantic touches. And if that's how you really feel about her, you should go back to her right now!'

'No. I can't do that.' He sat down on the bed, burying his head in his hands.

'Why not?' I sat down next to him.

'Because we're here on an important assignment, on behalf of the Order of the Dragon!' He lifted two old volumes into the air from the bedside table. 'This is what I need to focus on right now, not on romancing Selena! Besides, we're supposed to work together. What if whatever this is between us just fizzles out quickly, leaving an awkwardness? How would we still work as a team?'

'Does it feel like something that might fizzle out quickly?'

'Not to me.' He sighed.

'Is this why you've been avoiding her?' I smiled now I finally understood what was going on. 'You'll have to stop doing that.'

'I know.'

'And it clearly doesn't help if you bottle it all up.'

'Clearly.'

'Albury will be back, too. He won't give up chasing Selena that easily. Especially if she keeps on spending her nights alone. Besides, he hates you now with a passion!'

'I will have to find a way not to get into a fight with him over Selena.' He sighed. 'He's a powerful nobleman. We don't need more complications on top of everything else.'

'Oh, no. You should absolutely fight him.'

'Why?' He looked up at me, puzzled.

'Because women love it when you fight for them!' I grinned.

'Okay, Conor, thank you. You can go now.'

'No, really!' I insisted, even as he pushed me off the bed. 'And if you injure yourself during the fight, she'll be all over you, trying to tend to your wounds and make you feel better …'

He stood and started shepherding me out of the room. 'This is not helping.'

'Selena hasn't even seen you fight yet. She couldn't have seen you on the top of the carriage when we were attacked. All she knew was that you got injured. Maybe she thinks you're a wuss who can't even fight!'

'Don't you need to be somewhere else?' He pushed me towards the door and opened it for me. 'There won't be a fight.'

'I bet she thinks you're rubbish!' I laughed as he forced me out into the corridor.

'She saw me fight Laro in the library.'

'Oh, come on! That was hardly anything. You lowered your sword then he sent you to the floor in no time.'

'Out!'

'Wuss!' I pushed my head in once more, grinning as he tried to close the door on me.

'Thank you. We're done here,' he announced as he finally got rid of me.

I turned, smiling, and walked away. Faint strains of a ballad still reached me from the dining hall, but dinner was more or less over, and I had a nightshift to do. I left the building by the kitchen's door and hurried down the dark garden path.

I always made sure with whatever job I took that I also had some fun along the way. Why wouldn't you? Kris seemed too stiff to have fun most of the time, let alone mix it with work. One of us would have to change our ways if we were planning on doing this long-term, and it was definitely not going to be me! It might take him some time, but he'd get there. Selena was clearly a good influence on him already. I laughed as I recalled his embarrassed face, admitting that he had lost his head. Who would have thought? Between us, Selena and I would sort him out in no time, I was sure.

I opened the door of that little shed near the rose gardens that had been recently pointed out to me. Inside, a woman sat on the middle of the empty workbench, her long, dark brown hair only partially covering her delicate naked body.

'I'm sorry for the delay. I hope you haven't been waiting long.' I stroked her lovely face.

'Stop wasting my time, thief!' Aurelia pulled me closer, and only a little laugh escaped me before she shut me up with her lips.

Chapter 23

Selena

Caledon, Drelos,
7th The Month of Red Blessing 1575

I finished putting on the make-up the way Saya had taught me. I placed all the powders, brushes and little vials carefully back into their box and glanced in the mirror. The woman on the other side looked nothing like me. She seemed almost like a dress too daring for me to wear.

When I first saw myself like this, I was thrilled and terrified in equal measures. But I also knew immediately the only way I could pull it off. This hair was so like Rhia's. Except, maybe even she would be a little jealous of this colouring. It was like one of those impressionist paintings. When you looked very close, you could see lots of different shades, which when you stepped further away all merged into a vibrant wonder of fire.

I still remembered how much my scalp hurt and itched when Saya put that strange-coloured, smelly paste on it. I wanted to touch it, but she pushed my hands away, and said something that sounded like women needed to suffer sometimes in the name of beauty. The way I watched incredulously as my hair started growing was apparently so funny, she was in a fit of laughter. I tried to ask her afterwards if it came off when I washed it, mimicking the movement, but she shook her head and spoke dismissively.

I pulled at a long curl, marvelling at it, and my thoughts went back to Rhia. I couldn't have done this without her. Without being such close friends with her all these years. All I had to do to complete the Scarlet Witch look was to act like her. To walk with her confidence, to talk in her self-assured way. To address people in her charismatic manner that made them listen and do what she said. It worked like a charm, and it wasn't without its gratifying, joyous moments. But it was also exhausting sometimes. Like wearing a heavy coat I longed to take off.

I sighed and went to make sure I had locked the chests. They were packed with clothes, shoes, necklaces, rings, hairbrushes and ornaments, white towels, creams, scented soaps—you name it! I wondered who in Terek's team prepared all this for me. I doubted very much that it was him.

I was supposed to go over to Kris's room when I was ready, and he would walk me to find the king. What I was going to talk to His Majesty about today, I had no idea. I'd run out of topics after just a few days.

I went out and closed the door behind me, my hand hesitating on the door handle. Had I blown out the candle? Surely, I'd blown out the candle last night? No way it would still be alight in either case. The unreasonable urge to go back in and check grew, making me groan in frustration. *Not this again!*

I opened the door and went back in. The candle stood innocently in the middle of the table, definitely no longer burning. I touched the black wick, emphasising for my brain what it didn't seem able to remember alone. I pushed everything a little further away from the candle on the table, as if I expected it to light on its own account once I left. Then I went back to the chests to check again that they were locked.

I knew what had happened last night wasn't particularly helping my mental state. I re-opened the first chest, but my thoughts were on Kris. I played back our conversations in my mind, trying to read between the lines. I'd been holding my breath ever since we met, not daring to hope, not daring to rush into things, in case I'd misunderstood the situation and made a fool out of myself again. And yet here we were. *He*'d made a fool of me last night.

But why? I didn't get it. I thought back to the way he held me that day in the Pantheon. The way he moved to protect me on the train. The way he looked at me last night as he tucked my hair back. Surely, he was different to all the other guys in my life before. Or was he? Did he maybe have someone else? Was that where he disappeared to that night when he left us alone with Conor? But wouldn't he have mentioned that when he told me about the plan to settle down in Coroden? Or was this some kind of religious thing? Or a cultural one from his planet? Or was it just simply that he didn't like me that way? But the way he looked at me sometimes...

The last chest was a little looser than the first two. I unlocked it, lifted the lid, closed it, then locked it again. I tried to lift the lid. It was locked. I put the key back in and unlocked it. Lifted the lid. Closed the lid. Locked it. Tried to lift the locked lid. I couldn't. I pulled the key out, fighting an urge to put it back in.

I had no idea how I was supposed to lift the king's curse when I couldn't even lift my own! I stared at the red chest in front of me. Kris had shown me so many excerpts already about methods others had used to break the spell. Inventive and interesting, sometimes complex procedures I could never have come up with myself, let alone do them! Surely, I should have attended some kind of course before coming here. Something where I could have learned at least the basics. *Focus on what you know,* Ithorion said sagely. He clearly had no idea how little that was! I put the key back into the lock and opened the lid again. It was easy for him to talk like that. It wasn't like it was him on probation. I closed the lid and locked the chest. Some Scarlet Witch I was! They were lucky if I could brew a pot of tea.

But, of course, Kris had lived with his uncle, who probably made sure he learned everything he might possibly need as a Champion of the Order. Conor had been brought up in a monastery among martial monks, trained to serve the Gods from an early age. It was only me who had to be hidden away, clueless that someday my life might be about more than fulfilling purchase orders behind a desk. Why did women always have to be at a disadvantage? Joining the game late when the men were brought up with a head start.

When I asked Ithorion after the initiation, he said that I was too important to draw attention to. That I had to be old enough to cope with my gifts. That there was some organisation trying to undermine the Order from which they wanted to keep me hidden while I didn't possess my gifts. At the same time, they wanted to give me a chance to enjoy and experience a carefree life with friends and family, from which there was apparently also a lot to learn! I wouldn't have exactly called it carefree.

I sighed and pushed myself up. I went out and closed the door behind me. Had I locked the red chest the last time? Or did I just mean to do it? I couldn't say for sure. I pushed my forehead against the door and groaned.

'Are you alright?' Conor asked next to me, making me jump.

He looked up and down the corridor checking it was empty, then led me back into the room. We sat on the bed, and he pulled me into a hug, closing his arms around me. For a minute, we sat there, nothing but my frequent swallowing breaking the silence.

Then he lifted his head from mine. 'What's wrong? Talk to me.'

'I have no idea what I'm doing,' I confessed.

'What are you talking about?' He raised his eyebrows. 'You've been brilliant!'

'All I'm doing is pretending to be someone I'm not. I wish I wasn't this useless. The days are flying by, and we're none the wiser about how to break this curse or how to stop the Harag army from attacking the kingdom.'

'We're working on it. It's going to happen.'

'But how?'

'Well, for one thing, we have Kris with us. Given the speed he's been going through those books, he'll soon know more about the history of the kingdom than anyone else. He'll come up with a plan for how to negotiate peace with the Harags, I have no doubt about that. You know what he's like. I bet he never failed a test in his life!'

'And the curse?'

'We also happen to have the Supreme Key of the Dragon with us.' He smiled.

'Who can't do any spells or break them. And it's not like the Dragon actually talks to me.'

'Just relax and stop worrying so much. When we got into trouble just a few days ago, you teleported us to a completely different world, purely on instinct! You have the solution in you, Selena, I'm sure of it. Have a little faith and stop tormenting yourself. Take a few deep breaths, give yourself some credit for getting us this far, and just carry on as you've been doing. Keep talking to the king. Keep studying those records with Kris. At some point, somewhere, something will click into place. You'll see!'

'I just wish there was something more specific for me to do. That I could actually see the route to the solution and my part in it.'

'Selena, if it was that easy, the curse would have been broken by now. Sometimes, life is like sailing towards land that you can't yet see. Instead of burying your head in your hands and fretting over uncertainties, you need to stand tall and open your eyes. Check the wind! Check the map and the compass! Steer that ship to the best of your knowledge, then enjoy the journey. Chances are, you will reach the shore. And if you don't, you did all that you could and had a good time while you were at it. There's nothing more in life that any of us can do.'

I relaxed at that, resting my head against his shoulder.

'Feeling better?' he stroked my back.

'Yes, thanks.'

'Good. Any other worries this wise, strong, perceptive, famously good-looking, legendary thief can help you with?' He grinned.

I laughed, hesitating.

'Anything, at all?' He watched me knowingly, waiting for me to confess.

I sighed. Without my friends, I had nobody else to talk to. And wasn't he my best friend now? Always watching over me, making sure that I had everything I needed, hugging me whenever I was anxious, even saving me when we were attacked … he was like a brother, but more than that. A guardian angel. Well, guardian thief, apparently.

'Did you think Kris was a little strange last night?' I ventured.

'That's a very polite way of saying that he was an ass.' He laughed. 'But for what it's worth, he sorely regrets it now, and I'm sure that none of it was intentional. No. I think Kris is just incredibly disciplined, you know? It's like he has his own rulebook and keeps himself to it at all costs. But you—' He grinned, poking me playfully. '—have been confusing him! You've been crisscrossing lines for him and drawing little hearts on the pages! And he doesn't know how to handle it. Just give him some time to adjust.'

'Okay.' I smiled. 'I will.'

'He's lucky to have you. We both are.' He rested his forehead against mine, smiling. 'Let's go and get him, shall we? I'm sure he's itching to hurry back to the library and get his hands on the next book.'

After Conor coached my confidence back into place, things started to go much better. Kris was much nicer than he'd been the past few days, clearly eager to make amends for last night, smiling all the while as we went through the excerpts he had prepared for me to read in the library. Later

I met Jon, Aurelia's younger brother, who came to court to visit his family. He was a lot friendlier than their older brother, Aron.

I knew from Conor that Jon lived in Hort, where the family had lands, including a big vineyard. Apparently, there was some big family argument going on, where Aron and their father, Lord Dranos were on one side, and Aurelia and Jon on the other, so Aurelia was especially pleased about Jon's arrival.

According to Kris, the Dranos family went way back, serving the kings of the kingdom as advisors even before the current king's ancestor, Renold II, took the throne from the Bors, the previous royal dynasty. Renold II was allegedly some nasty piece of work, which Kris said was apparent even through the carefully worded accounts of the family historians. A terrible ruler, who wasn't just ruthless, but a narcissist, too. He wasted fortunes on extravagant celebrations and parties, headed into pointless confrontations and wars until the population of the kingdom almost halved within a decade. His son, Renold III, was a slight improvement, but Kris still considered him hardly more than a spoiled brat.

The current king, Sirion, seemed rather nice and friendly to me in comparison. Almost modest. Although how well he ruled, I had no idea. Wasn't this situation with the Harags partly his fault? Didn't he say something that offended the ambassadors? But then again, I knew there were always people out there, looking for any excuse to be offended. They could always find something if they really wanted to, no matter the intentions in the background.

It was strange to think that King Sirion was only a few years older than me. He looked much older, way into his thirties already. I guessed taking over the ruling of a country at eighteen, knowing you had ten years to live before you went blind, could do that to anyone.

In the afternoon, when the king had his strategic military meetings with his advisors, I left him to it. Thankfully, I wasn't allowed to attend. They might have been the kind of thing Kris would have enjoyed—how many and what type of soldiers were stationed where, where they should be instead, what parts of castles needed to be mended, and so on—but I would have found them terribly boring.

Luckily, it was also the time of the day when a group of knights practised outside, and I had grown accustomed to watching them from an upstairs window. There was a part of the training when they worked in pairs. One would hold up a shield while the other hit it with a sword from various angles. It was such a perfect opportunity to practise what Ithorion had shown me back in the Pantheon. Not that I had any success in stopping their blades, but it wasn't for the lack of trying!

When the household staff first noticed what I was doing, they became ridiculously attentive. Every ten minutes, someone showed up, trying to bring me a chair, or some water to drink, or a glass of wine, snacks, or perhaps a cup of tea! By now, I knew all these words in Wedan, even without Kris around, as we repeated them every day. Together with "thank you" and "no, thank you". And "good day"!

When news of my watching reached the knights, they started looking up towards my window and had to be told to pay attention to their training. I was afraid I might have to abandon my own practice on them, but the knight-commander sent word through Conor that my presence was welcome as it apparently improved the soldiers' posture and enthusiasm.

In the end, I didn't know if it was Conor's reassuring words that morning or my own unwavering eagerness, but that afternoon, for the first time, I managed to block one of the soldiers' strikes. He looked confused, especially when I did it a second time. He kept on massaging his arm, as if that would solve the situation, making me laugh. I stopped for the day, not wanting to raise suspicion. I was supposedly a witch, after all!

Later, we had our daily catch-up in Kris's room, which we'd moved to late afternoons since Conor usually spent his evenings with Aurelia. Then we had dinner in the dining hall with the king and his guests. This time Aurelia and Jon sat opposite us; Duke Albury thankfully nowhere in sight.

Unlike on the previous nights, Kris was unusually talkative, discussing everything from politics to wine-making with the Dranos siblings, frequently pulling me and Conor into the conversation with questions, too. He was also very attentive to me, with an adoring warmth in his eyes which made me wonder whether it was a continuation of his "roleplaying" from last night. But then, when he walked me to my room after dinner, all by himself this time, it was still there.

'Good night, Selena. Sleep well!' he said to me with such a sweet smile, I couldn't stop thinking about him afterwards as I soaked myself in a hot bath. Little did he know that sleeping well wasn't exactly one of my strengths, especially since we'd left the Pantheon and arrived at the palace. I tossed and turned for hours every night, sleep only finally claiming me around dawn.

Tonight was no different. I sighed, adjusted the pillow under my head and turned to my other side. Wearing a set of night-time underwear that had definitely not been made primarily for sleeping probably didn't help. These Scarlet Witches must have been some sort of cross between regular witches and courtesans because they certainly knew what might draw a lover's attention! Not that they weren't comfortable, and they were nice to have. I'd never owned anything so beautiful and sensual at the same time. But did they really all have to be like this? Short, erotic nightdresses, all lacy, intricately split or see-through, some with more romantic touches and all with matching seductive knickers. Just what did the Order assume I would be spending my nights doing? Sleeping with the king? I imagined our curmudgeonly dicto saying to Terek, 'Give Selena the steamiest lingerie you can find!' and giggled. Maybe I was letting them down by spending my nights alone. But the only man I would have enjoyed sharing my bed with had no intention of sleeping with me. If anything, based on last night, he would have probably considered it wildly inappropriate!

Tonight, I had left a few candles burning in their holders, coming to the conclusion that extinguishing them made no difference to my sleeping abilities, but once they were out, I had no way of re-lighting them unless I tiptoed out to the corridor and lit a taper from one of the lanterns there.

At some point, when I was finally half-asleep, I heard a noise as if someone had tried to open the locked door. My first thought was that it had been maybe Kris or Conor, but then there was a knock, and someone said, 'Lady Selena?' in a voice that didn't sound like either of them. Even as I hurriedly put on my kimono-style dressing gown, I fretted that something might have happened to them. Why else would anyone want to talk to me in the middle of the night? Was it possible that the curse had manifested early or that the king suddenly felt unwell?

'Yes?' I said as I opened the door and looked out.

It was Duke Albury outside, his face serious. 'Lady Selena!'

'What is it?' I demanded. 'Is it the king?'

'No, my lady.'

'Then what?' I stepped out into the corridor and looked left and right, half-expecting to see some turmoil, but of course, it was all deserted at this hour. 'Has something happened?'

'No, my lady.' He smiled and now that I stood closer to him, I realised how strongly his breath smelled of alcohol. Not even wine. Some sort of liquor. 'I just needed to see you.'

I didn't like that smile. He looked menacing in the dim light.

'In the middle of the night, Duke Albury? What can be so important?' My words were loud and clear, but even as I said them, I started backing towards my room again, only for him to follow me like a dark shadow.

'You!' he said, his face serious again. 'For all the Gods, you!'

'Me?'

'You, my lady, are important to me. Too important! I can't stop thinking about you.'

I was inside again, my hand on the door as I faced him. 'I'm sorry, but I'm sure this can wait until the morning,' I announced and started closing it. He leaned against it, stepping forward to stop me.

'No, it really can't. You see, Lady Selena, women never say "no" to me. And once they say "yes", they don't start flirting with other men right in front of me.'

'How dare you? I never said yes to you!' I was angry now. Not only was he harassing me at night, but he was actually trying to make out it was my fault!

He took another step in, making me retreat further. 'You might have not said "yes", but you meant it!' He leaned closer. 'I saw it in your eyes. You wanted me—the way you want me now!'

'Never!' I informed him, still trying to close the door. He forced it further open, smirking at my pathetic efforts.

'Who is it, my darling?' Kris's sleepy voice made us both pause. It came from behind me. How was he behind me? Did he climb through the window? He must have, I thought, puzzled, as I turned and looked. He was walking towards me, smiling, wearing nothing but a pair of grey boxers. I watched him, stunned, my eyes taking in his toned body, as he called out, 'Ah, Duke Albury!' in a friendly manner, as if the duke were an old acquaintance who popped in to say hello. Then he was there, wrapping me in his arms and kissing my head as he said, 'Why don't you go back to bed, angel? I'll talk to the duke. I'm sure he's just lost or something.'

The duke recovered quicker than me, but even so, all he managed to say at this unexpected development was an angry, 'You!'

Kris was still looking at me, however, ignoring the threat altogether, his face close to mine as he said again, 'Bed, darling? Yes?' He smiled at me sweetly, stroking my lower back, patiently waiting for my response as if my reaction mattered way more than the duke's.

Kris was clearly trying to signal to the duke that I was already taken, hoping that he might leave us alone, but the duke seemed too arrogant to take the hint. At the same time, all I could think was that Kris was playing the same game with me that he had before. Did he really think he could just take my breath away, make me gaze at him all doe-eyed, turn me on, then leave me for a fool by announcing later that he had faked it? No! No way! If this was the part where we just did what we liked and denied everything later, I wanted in! I'd show him roleplaying!

'Are you coming soon, too?' I pressed myself against him, stroking his face.

'Of course,' he breathed, surprised, watching me intently, his mouth slightly open.

I looked deep into his eyes, leaned closer and kissed his lower lip, gently pulling at it with my teeth before slowly letting it go. He watched me, dazed, hardening against me. We both smiled then, despite the duke fuming nearby.

'Don't keep me waiting for long.' I stepped back but put the end of my dressing gown belt into his hand, closing his fingers around the silk. Then I continued stepping back, letting the motion untie it. He watched me, spellbound, as I opened the gown further and let it fall to the floor before climbing onto the bed.

'I'm talking to you, scholar!' The duke slammed his fist into the door next to Kris, his fury making me flinch. Kris stood there staring at me with my belt still in his hand as if he hadn't even noticed.

'I said I was talking to you!' The duke bellowed and threw himself on Kris. Kris stepped out of his way, deflecting the move with so little effort it made the duke look like he was just fooling around.

'Duke Albury, I'm sure this is just a misunderstanding,' he said as he moved away once more, tying my belt around his hand.

'Oh, it definitely is.' The duke circled him. 'So, let me make this clear for you: you are in my way!'

'Lady Selena is not available, I'm afraid.' Kris spread his hands in a placatory gesture, but the flowery silk tied around his right hand was a statement on its own, declaring loud and clear what he left unsaid.

'And who do you think you are to make such a decision for her?' The duke sneered at him.

'I'm her ...' Kris hesitated, glancing at me. 'Her Champion.'

'You're what?' The duke laughed. 'Why don't you go back to your books? You're overstating yourself.'

'I'll go back to my books, if you go back to your own room and leave the lady alone,' Kris offered.

'How dare you, you little nobody? And it's "Your grace" to you!' He threw a punch at Kris's head, but Kris diverted his attack again, grabbing his shirt and stepping close to bring their faces only inches apart.

'I'm asking you one last time, Your Grace,' he warned him coldly. 'Leave!'

'You still don't understand, do you?' The duke chuckled dismissively. 'It doesn't matter what you do; I'm still going to have her. Do you know why? Because you're nothing but a foreigner with no power here, whereas I am the Duke of Albury, and she is a little bitch in heat, begging to be fucked.'

Kris moved so fast at that, all I saw was the blood running down from the duke's broken nose.

The duke touched his face, staring at the blood on his fingers in disbelief. 'You little ...' He launched himself at Kris again, only to be rocked back by another punch.

'Apologise to the lady, and we'll forget that anything happened.'

'You want to lecture *me* about manners? *You*?' The duke seethed. 'You have no idea what you've done. I'll see you rot in prison for this for the rest of your life!'

'Apologise!' Kris repeated, unmoved. He hit the duke a third time, who staggered back half-shocked, half-furious, and pulled a dagger from his belt.

'I'm going to kill you!' he roared as he stabbed at Kris's naked torso.

I heard voices come from the corridor, accompanied by clanking noises as two soldiers appeared in the open doorway, staring wide-eyed, making me hurriedly wrap the bed linen around myself.

'Get the knight-commander,' one said to the other, possibly viewing the situation, where a bloody-faced Duke of Albury threatened a half-naked man in the Scarlet Witch's room with a knife, to be above his paygrade.

An ugly smile spread across the duke's face. 'You're going to get what you deserve, scholar! You are a man of no consequence who'll rot in prison for assaulting a duke. But don't worry. Lady Selena will be in good hands.'

I stood from the bed, pulling the white bedlinen after me like a long cape. 'Nothing is going to happen to him while I'm here, you understand? Nothing!' I stomped towards the duke indignantly. Albury turned my way, surprised, still holding his dagger, prompting the remaining palace guard to rush in to protect me, while Kris forced the weapon out of his hand, locking his arm behind his back.

Several soldiers marched into the room a few moments later, followed by a grim-faced knight-commander. Duke Albury looked at him gleefully, only for the smile to freeze on his face when the king followed the knight-commander in, looking furious.

'My Lord King!' The duke bowed deeply as Kris released him and went down on one knee himself. 'I was merely protecting Lady Selena from this madman who attacked us! He clearly has no—'

The duke's voice faltered at King Sirion's raised hand. I'd never seen the king this angry before. His eyes travelled from the duke's bloodied face to Kris kneeling behind him, undressed, solemn, and without the slightest injury on him, then to the dagger on the floor, not far from my dressing gown, and finally to me awkwardly curtsying in my improvised outfit.

'My lady, are you well?' The king hurried to me. With two fingers beneath my chin, he tilted my face towards him, looking closely. 'You're not hurt?'

'No, Your Majesty, I'm unharmed,' I said, clutching the bedlinen closer to myself, embarrassed. I wanted to tell him more and argue what the duke had said, but King Sirion turned after a quick nod and started talking to the duke instead.

'Duke Albury. You understand that our current political situation is such that instead of sleeping, I'm concerned enough to be discussing military matters with the knight-commander at this hour?'

The duke nodded, looking a little nervous.

'Can you imagine, then, how news of a fight in Lady Selena's bedroom added to my distress? Duke Albury, Lady Selena isn't just my guest here, enjoying my full protection. She is right now the most important person to me in the whole palace! In the whole palace, you understand that? Her well-being, her every wish, anything she needs at all, is my concern.'

'Yes, Your Majesty,' the duke muttered sheepishly.

'Excellent. Then we're finished here, Duke Albury.'

King Sirion waited until the duke had left, then turned to Kris and gestured to him to get up.

'Thank you, my friend,' he said to Kris. 'Duke Albury will be leaving court in the morning, and my men will make sure nothing like this happens again. But I feel better knowing that you'll be guarding the lady, too.'

'Of course, Your Majesty.' Kris bowed his head.

'My lady.' The king nodded at me with a smile. Finally, he turned and walked out of the room. The soldiers followed him out, except for the one who had hurried to my defence earlier.

'My lady, if you leave that with me, I'll make sure the blood is cleaned out of it by the morning.' He gestured at the silk tie around Kris's hand.

I smiled at him. 'Thank you …?'

'Jerric, my lady.'

'Thank you, Jerric.'

'Sorry.' Kris grinned as he unrolled it and handed it to Jerric. The soldier collected the duke's dagger from the floor, wished us goodnight, then disappeared after the others, closing the door behind him.

'Well,' Kris said as he picked up my dressing gown from the floor and offered it to me. 'I think I'd best go and put on a shirt now, too. And get some clothes for the morning. I can sleep on the carpet.'

'Don't be silly. Of course, you won't sleep on the carpet!' I waved the idea away. 'This bed is huge!'

'If you're sure about that, I'd be happy to join you. Thank you. Only to sleep, of course,' he added with a serious face.

'Absolutely! Only to sleep,' I agreed hurriedly. But I couldn't help myself and continued, 'I'm sorry if I got a little carried away with the roleplaying before.'

'Don't!' He laughed. 'I completely deserved that. Besides, it's not like I can pretend I didn't enjoy it.'

I smiled back. His body certainly hadn't been able to lie. I'd felt how much he wanted me.

'Right, I'll be back soon,' he said finally, before he disappeared, too.

I stayed where I was for a moment longer. A sweet excitement swirled in me, like a soft breeze gathering strength, spiralling into a hurricane. 'He said only to sleep. Only to sleep!' I tried to tell myself, even as I let the bedsheet fall and jumped on the bed. I leaped into the air, silently screaming my joy to the world, bouncing up and down, making a handful of feathers fly around me. Then I quickly re-adjusted my underwear, put on the thin dressing gown to avoid looking too naughty following his "only sleeping" directive, made the bed and lay down under the covers, waiting for him as if nothing had happened.

He came back fully dressed, carrying a bundle of clothing that he deposited on the chair on his way to the bed.

'Still awake?' He glanced at me with a smile as he took his shoes off.

'Um, yes. About that … I might as well mention now that it takes me ages to fall asleep, so being awake at this hour for me is not that unusual.'

'Well, that's not very good.' He frowned. 'But I might be able to help you with that.'

'Really? How?'

'Magic.' He grinned.

'You have magic?' I laughed, sure that he was joking.

'Why can't I have my own magic?' He hesitated as he sat on the bed, looking uncertain about taking off his linen trousers, too.

'Oh, just get comfortable!' I told him. 'No need to be shy. I've seen everything already. Well, almost everything,' I added with a grin.

'You did get a good look, didn't you?' He grinned back as he got out of his trousers and climbed into bed, lying down facing me.

'I was concerned about your safety, so obviously, I had to watch.'

'Obviously. By the way, any time you want to save me again wrapped in a bedsheet, please do. That alone was worth my whole evening!'

I laughed again, trying to imagine how I must have looked. 'Thanks for coming over. It was lucky for me that we woke you,' I said finally.

'I was awake, too,' he admitted. 'I can fall asleep quickly, but I've been having bad dreams that wake me during the night. Then I end up thinking about things I shouldn't.'

'What things?' I shifted a little closer to him with a smile.

'So eager to know my wayward thoughts!' He grinned instead of sharing them.

'Fine.' I rolled my eyes. 'Tell me about the bad dreams, then. Have you had them for long? What are they about?'

'No, it's a recent thing.' He sighed heavily. 'They're early childhood memories, I think.'

'From that time Ithorion and Quede talked about?' I bit my lip.

'Yes,' he admitted, looking uncomfortable.

'I'm so sorry,' I said, a wave of compassion rushing through me. 'Is there anything I can do to help?'

'Like what?' He smiled again.

'Um …' Like what, indeed. 'Well, we Scarlet Witches have a number of very effective rituals to keep away bad dreams,' I informed him.

'I'm sure you do.' He grinned. 'I've seen the ceremonial outfit already!' He pulled an impressed face and whistled, making me laugh.

'It's nice, isn't it?' I smirked a little self-consciously.

'Very nice,' he agreed with a smile. 'You look very good in it,' he added more softly, making my body tingle and tighten in all sorts of places in response.

'Right. Shall I try and help you fall asleep, then?' He pushed himself upright.

'How are you going to do that, exactly?' Was this really a thing?

'You'll see,' he said, climbing out of bed.

'Where are you going?'

'To blow the candles out.'

'You can only do it in the dark?'

'I'm blowing out the candles because we're going to sleep.'

'I don't know! You're making me a little nervous now!' I giggled as he climbed back next to me in the dark.

He let out an exasperated sigh. 'Turn around.'

'Why?' I laughed.

'Safety reasons.'

I did as I was told, grinning, my heart beating fast.

'Come here, you.' He wrapped me in his arms from behind and pulled me close. Needless to say, that did nothing to calm my excitement. If anything, I felt more awake now than before.

He pushed himself up and leaned close to me. I waited, not even daring to breathe.

'This is for the nerves,' he said, then gently kissed my hair like that time we stood under the magnolia tree. Not once, but again and again and again. Each kiss like a hot drop of sunshine, melting me.

'Mmmm … this is definitely helping.' I sighed.

'I hoped it might,' he murmured in my ear.

'So, how many times have you done this thing before?' I asked as he settled again behind me, holding me tight.

'Only once. With Conor,' he said.

'Like this?' I giggled.

'Of course not like this!' He laughed.

'So, he didn't get the kisses, either?'

'No. Those are only for you,' he confirmed in his soft voice.

'Poor Conor.'

'Yes. I'm sure he's been agonising over it ever since!'

His hand found mine, making me feel like he was leading me somewhere. 'Just give me a little time, then hopefully you'll soon feel it, okay?'

'Okay.' All my nervousness was gone now. I was in a soft cloud of heaven filled with love. I listened to his breathing, feeling it on my neck. It gradually slowed and deepened, until I thought he'd fallen asleep. A few minutes later, a strange sense of sleepiness pulled at me out of the blue, and I let it take me. The next moment, I was out like the candlelight.

I woke as Kris was getting out of bed in the morning. I watched him get dressed, waiting for him to turn his attention back to me.

'Good sleep?' he asked.

'Mmmmmm.' I stayed where I was but smiled up at him like a bride on her honeymoon—not that anything had happened. 'How about you? Did you have any bad dreams?'

'None,' he informed me with a smile as he leaned down to me and kissed my forehead. 'Same thing again tonight? Just much earlier, obviously?'

'I think we'll have to. I would hate to disappoint the king.'

'Of course, my lady,' he mused. 'I'm going to let you get dressed. Come over to my room when you're ready.'

I stayed there for another minute, stretching luxuriously, then jumped out of bed and dressed quickly. Let's just get on with what needed to be done today, I thought. The faster the day went, the sooner it would be evening again.

As I approached the door, I turned to look around once more. My eyes lingered on the chests for a moment. 'Silly!' Conor had grinned when I quietly confessed the thing to him over lunch yesterday. 'I'm the most famous thief in the Nineteen Kingdoms,' he whispered in my ear. 'Nobody would dare to steal from you, anyway.' I smiled at the memory and exited the room without a second look.

Duke Beren had come to court last night, the man who had accused Conor of stealing that old crown and offered a large reward for capturing him. Kris and I were invited to meet him and the king after breakfast.

'We're sharing the money, right?' I said to Kris in Elesean on the way. 'How about seventy-thirty?'

'Seventy sounds about right.' He nodded. 'But it comes to me for finding him first and paying the duke to let him go free.'

'Is that how the two of you met? You bought him?' I laughed. 'Was he expensive?'

'Very. He cost me a high-tech invisibility cloak, which let alone the expense is now costing me more since I have to get it back from the duke. Ithorion wants us to retrieve it and even if we can persuade the duke to sell it back to us, the price will be a fortune! Not to mention, he was hoping for political advancement from removing the curse through that crown, which is now lost to him. Even if we break the spell, he gets nothing out of it. We need to be careful with him. He's no fool. He won't leave here empty-handed.'

'Well, he's certainly not taking Conor!' I made a fist.

'Look at the tigress!' He grinned at me.

'What did he do, anyway?'

'Conor? As I later found out, he was at a wedding where he slept with the duke's daughter.'

'He is Conor!' I laughed. 'And why is that such a big crime?'

'She was the bride.'

'Oh. He slept with the bride on her wedding night? How did he even…?'

'As you said,' Kris mused, 'he is Conor!'

'Even so. He's our Conor. The duke's not getting him!'

'No,' he agreed. 'But just be careful.' He slipped his hand around my waist and kissed my head mid-step. I didn't know what gifts the Dragon was to empower me with, but he had nothing on this. Nothing! I felt like I could take on the world!

I sat down opposite the king and the duke, and with Kris on my side, I nailed that meeting. Nobody in the castle even mentioned the crown to me. Everyone considered me the real deal! Even my name was similar to Lady Selia, the curse bringer. As far as everyone was concerned, I was the absolute authority on the subject.

I told the duke that Conor had nothing to do with the disappearance of the crown. It was a powerful warlock taking revenge on him for some-thing Conor had done in the past. And that the only reason Conor hadn't got it back yet was that he came to negotiate with my coven instead and brought me here. But the crown didn't matter now anyway, because while I understood how he might have come to that conclusion, it wouldn't have helped. However, I reassured them that I already had three possible meth-ods in mind that would successfully break the curse. I was only making sure now to pick the one which would cause the least amount of incon-venience or pain to the king.

Then, remembering that we needed that cloak from him later, I smiled at the duke sweetly and added that it would please me very much if he stayed at court until the king's birthday and celebrated with us.

I only realised once we'd almost finished the discussion that I com-pletely forgot to copy Rhia's mannerisms. Yet somehow, I felt more confident than ever. By the end of the meeting, the king looked happy, the duke defeated, and Kris proud. Conor was under my protection. Shielded by my lies. I had bought us time again, but I knew the bill was on the way and getting heftier by the day. And our pockets were still empty.

After my morning success, the afternoon took a bad turn. When I couldn't find the king after lunch, one of the knights told me he'd ridden out.

'He does this sometimes,' he admitted. 'Just disappears on a whim. Too fast for anyone to join him, and when we try, he tells us he wants to be alone. The knight-commander isn't very happy about it. Even Lord Dranos is against it. Perhaps you, Lady Selena, could go with him next time. Perhaps your company he wouldn't mind.'

I told him I would see what I could do, knowing that it was nothing. I couldn't ride or speak Wedan much when alone. Still, I mentioned it to Kris as I joined him in the library, and he nodded thoughtfully like he was already thinking of a solution. Then he made me sit down and read all the sections he'd marked off for me to read. It was a lot.

In the meantime, Conor arrived, and the two of them pulled chairs into the furthest corner so they wouldn't disturb me as they caught up with each other. I watched them sometimes, their heads together, teasing each other, their laughter unguarded. When we had company or an audience, they acted like the other men in Coroden, keeping their distance, the occasional pat on the back perhaps the most they would display as a sign of their affection. I thought back to my world, where formalities were more relaxed, but still probably everyone would think them a gay couple. Of course, if they were two women, nobody would take any notice. I wondered if, on Alba, where Kristian lived, society had reached a point yet where this was commonplace.

I was pleased to see them happy, but I couldn't understand how they could be so relaxed. Every time I read through another page of curse-breaking attempts, I despaired. Surely there was nothing left they hadn't already tried? Not to mention that I had no way of knowing whether certain rituals were even done correctly, nor could I replicate them. Conor said something somewhere would click if I carried on, but nothing seemed to volunteer itself so far. The only thing that I noticed was that none of the attempts made before the kings' twenty-eighth birthdays worked, but some that were made afterwards worked temporarily. Occasionally, a healer or a powerful sorceress would come along, and whatever they did made some improvement, but then the kings would lose their eyesight completely again, as if the curse had been stronger and kept on winning the fights.

Due to dinner being later than usual, I got to spend another hour getting miserable in the library, when all I wanted was for the day to finally end. At least the food was delicious, once the king and his thirty-something guests finally gathered in the hall. We also had the sweet wine again that Jon brought with him from their estate. The Golden Kabar. Apparently, it was the king's favourite, and I could see why. I didn't think those barrels in the cellar would last long.

Conor warned us that the Duke of Beren secretly had Kris's invisibility cloak with him in the palace, and we should be careful to always use Elesean when talking among ourselves in case he was spying on us, too. He said he could easily sneak back into his room and lift it, but he was likely to be the duke's first suspect once he realised it was gone. Kris said he didn't want to rock that boat, and the duke was more likely to use it to attend the king's meetings rather than to follow us around, but he agreed that it was best to stay cautious.

I asked him if this high-tech cloak didn't need charging sometimes, to which he said that it did, and while its battery fibres should last quite a while, it all depended on how much it was used. I imagined the duke revealed while spying on one of those meetings and couldn't really feel sorry for him.

When the wooden tub was taken out of my room later, I sat down at the dressing table and started to brush out my hair. Soon there was a knock on the door, and Kris came in.

I watched in the mirror as he undressed, just like last night, leaving a short-sleeved shirt on and his underwear. I was on my feet as soon as he was in bed.

'Shall I blow out the candles?' I smiled at him.

'I think so. It's late,' he said in a voice that made me decide to leave my kimono on again as I approached the bed. It wasn't completely dark. Torches burned on the palace walls outside, allowing a touch of light.

'Is everything alright?' I asked as I settled down, facing him.

'Yes, why?' He raised an eyebrow.

'I don't know. You just seem a little tense.'

'Braving a Scarlet Witch's lair every night is no small feat.' He pulled a face.

'Was it that terrible last night?' I shifted a little closer, longing to be in his arms again.

'No.' He sighed. 'It was the best night I've had in ages.'

'But?' I almost asked, stopping myself just in time, suddenly worried what the answer might be. 'I told you, we Scarlet Witches are good at warding off bad dreams,' I said instead.

'You did,' he agreed with a little smile.

I shuffled a little closer again, watching him. He grinned. 'Turn around,' he said softly.

To my shame, I didn't even argue. If those were the rules, those were the rules. I just needed those little kisses again and his arm around me like an addict. 'I think I should have at least as many of these as I did yesterday,' I informed him as he started kissing my head. 'That is, if you want me to keep away those bad dreams again.'

'Is that so? How many did I give you last night?' he murmured into my hair as he carried on.

I thought about that for a second. It was probably around ten or twelve. 'Twenty-five,' I said confidently.

'And where am I at? Are you counting?'

'Two.'

'Two?' He chuckled but carried on kissing me. 'I think you might need a little math tutoring, you know.'

'Do you know anyone good who could do it?'

'Maybe.' He kissed me one more time. 'Ready to sleep now?'

I really didn't want to sleep yet. It was too nice being in his arms. 'I just have one question,' I said, desperately trying to think of one.

'Go on.'

'How come you can make me and Conor fall asleep? Is it because you're our tora? The same way you can sense it when we're near, too?'

'I think it's more like a gift. Or part of one. It's something I believe my uncle can do, too, so I don't think it's a tora skill, no.'

'Oh, okay.' Damn, that was quick.

'I have a question, too, if there's nothing else crucial?' he said, and I could tell he was smiling.

'Yes?'

'Do you mind if I take off this shirt? It's quite a bit colder on Alba, and I'm still not used to this warm climate here.' He was shifting around behind me already as he said it, but he pulled me back into his arms afterwards, so that was more than fine with me.

'Good night,' he whispered in my ear, and for a minute, I wondered if I should try and resist falling asleep. I wanted to enjoy being snuggled up with him, not just wake up again alone in the bed. If I was honest, I wanted a lot more than that, but it seemed like I was alone in feeling that way. He did say last night that he was only in bed with me to sleep. In the end, though, I gave in and fell asleep shortly after him.

In the morning, I woke to find myself without my dressing gown and with my face on Kris's chest. I remembered, suddenly, what had happened. After all that late night feasting, it had been me this time who had nightmares and woke in the early hours, sweaty and my heart still pounding fast from the dread.

'Selena, Selena,' he had mumbled my name, but as I turned towards him and looked in the dim light, I could tell he wasn't properly awake. What's more, I felt that strong pull of sleepiness again that was almost impossible to resist. All I could do was quickly get out of the kimono, so I wouldn't feel so hot as I lowered myself back to sleep.

Now I was on top of him, my arms around him, and his around me, his palms on my lower back under the night dress. My right leg was between his, our naked thighs pressing against each other. For one glorious moment, it was wonderful. The next, I knew that he'd woken too, similarly assessing the situation. and that this was not going to go down well.

He pushed me off him, not roughly but decisively, and started dressing as if the house was on fire. I stayed where I was, feeling discarded, unloved and hurt.

'I'm not going with you this morning,' I said without turning to look at him. 'You can go alone. I'll find the king later.' I knew this was childish, but I was too upset to care. Why did he have to be like this? Surely, I wasn't that hideous!

He hesitated at the door, then went out without a word and left me there. I turned and buried my face into his pillow, quietly whimpering to myself.

I hated everyone! We had three days left and nothing to show for it! I hated him for being so cold. I hated myself for being so useless. I hated this stupid curse! I hated Ithorion for not giving me more help. I even hated the Dragon for not providing any guidance. I didn't even care anymore! I was going to stay in bed all day. They could all do whatever they wanted without me.

It was so nice and warm where he had slept. I could still smell his scent on the pillow. I closed my eyes and imagined myself in his arms. My body relaxed, and my mind went blank. I could hear my heart beating, and further down, a little above my navel, a warm sensation swirled in me.

I had practised the healing exercise that Ithorion talked about. Mostly in the carriage on the way here and then in the evenings. I usually felt nothing or just a tiny bit of warmth. But now, it was much stronger. I shifted my focus and tried to move it with my thoughts. It wasn't easy. But it wasn't going anywhere, and neither was I.

I stayed in bed all morning, breathing slowly and deeply, working on growing it, turning it, making it flow towards my hip until half of my body felt hot. In the end, I pushed down the bedcover and checked the cut on my hip. It seemed like before. Or was it a little smaller? I should have looked before I started, marked it off with a pen!

I got out of bed and dressed quickly. I had no idea if this would work or not. There had been so many healers for centuries who tried and failed to cure the royal heirs. Why should I be different? Not to mention, my power wasn't even working properly yet. But I was so frustrated, so fed up with doing nothing, that I was ready to try anything.

I found the king in the throne room. There were several other men around, Conor among them. I couldn't see Kris anywhere, but I knew he couldn't be far because I understood every word I heard around me. I walked up to the king and told him that I had decided on the treatment I was going to use and that we would have to do it every day from now until his birthday. He swallowed excitedly and asked if I wanted to start right then and there, but I told him it was probably best if we did this privately in his bedchamber, perhaps after lunch. Conor stared at me with a raised eyebrow, but I shot an I-know-what-I'm-doing look his way and confidently walked to the hall where lunch was usually served. I was starving!

After a momentary pause, everyone followed me, and the table was soon filled with steaming dishes.

Kris appeared, too, and sat down next to me, at which point I stood and walked out of the hall, only to come back a few minutes later and sit somewhere else. I saw him and Conor talking among themselves, the latter giving him some hard looks, but I ignored them. After lunch, they were apparently going to meet someone who they both knew and had just arrived. It sounded like they wanted me to go with them, but I paid them no attention. I told them to go about their business and that I had more important things to do. Then I looked at the king, nodded and followed him out of the hall.

As we approached his bedroom, the king smiled and said something, but I moved my index finger to my mouth to silence him. I gestured that I needed to concentrate, and he seemed to accept that. Once inside, he started to undress, checking if that was what I had in mind, but I stopped him after his boots were off and made him lie down on his bed in his clothes. I walked around and sat, positioning ourselves so that his head would be in my lap. Then I put my right hand on his forehead and tried to concentrate.

For the longest time, nothing happened. I bit my lip and tried to swallow my frustration. I was determined to make this work. I tried to remember how I'd felt this morning. What it was that helped me. I thought of Kris. His scent on the pillow. How it felt to have his arms around me. The longing I felt for him. And suddenly, the feeling was there again, like warm sunshine under my skin.

I focused on it, making it swirl and grow until it was all around me. An invisible bubble of power, born out of love, its loss, and most of all, the desire to restore it. To mend. To heal. To wash away all that was wrong.

Once I finished and lifted my hand off the king's head, he got up and excitedly started talking to me, his dark eyes full of joy. I just nodded along, smiling, feeling a little tired. He said something again, gesturing for me to stay, and I lay down on his bed to rest.

When I finally left the room, he was nowhere to be found. I stopped at an open window in the corridor, looking out at the garden, wondering what to do with myself now. Some of my misery returned to me, souring my mood again. My mind replayed how Kris had pushed me away that morning, and I tightened my jaw. Wasn't he just playing with me, using me like Jake had?

That was where he found me, slowly coming close, but I turned away and pretended to be more interested in the garden. He took my hand into his, but even then, I didn't look at him.

'Come on,' he said softly, 'I'd like to introduce you to someone.'

'I don't care,' I said and didn't move.

'Selena, please.'

When I stayed unmoved, he did something Conor would have done. He raised my hand to his mouth and kissed it. I turned then, torn between wanting to snatch my hand back and throw myself into his arms. Our eyes met, and the way he looked at me stole all my objections.

I nodded, and he led me out of the palace. I wasn't paying close attention to which way we went or who was around. All I was acutely aware of was how tightly he held my hand in his. As if he feared I might run away at any moment. I could feel people's eyes on us as we walked, the fierce Scarlet Witch smitten under the spell of the quiet scholar.

We crossed the garden, turned towards a line of buildings, and went into the stable. I wondered if he had found a riding instructor for me. There was only one young guy in there, busy with a brush and bucket, but we passed him by without a word. Then a little further in, he stopped me in front of a stunning black horse.

'Selena, this is Storn,' he said and patted his neck.

'Is this your horse?' I asked awe-struck, the name familiar.

'I prefer to think of him as a friend.'

The stable boy sniggered at that, which seemed to annoy both Kris and the horse.

I wanted to reach up and stroke Storn's head to comfort him, my hand hesitating mid-air.

'Here,' Kris said, 'let me show you how he likes it.'

Storn, sensing what we wanted, bowed his head for us to reach him more easily. Kris stood right behind me, our arms touching, our hands brushing each other as I tried to mimic his movements. I could have spent all day like that. Then he slowly lowered his arms around me, placed his hand on my waist, and gently stroked my side as if I were another horse that needed calming. He leaned closer and kissed my hair. The horse, in turn, widened his eyes, tilted his head and studied me, as if I had been some strange bug or a rather unusual flower.

'You surprised him.' I smiled.

'I did, didn't I?' he murmured into my hair and kissed me again and again, making my knees go weak. I closed my eyes, wanting very much to turn and have him kiss my mouth for once, but this was a spell I was too afraid to break.

'Gone?' he asked after a while.

I didn't understand what he meant and opened my eyes. The first thing I saw was Storn watching me with a completely stunned expression now, that was so comical I laughed. He didn't seem to like that! I quickly reached up, stroking him as I was taught.

'You are so beautiful,' I told him and watched him half-close his eyes as I scratched his head behind his ear. 'So, so beautiful.'

Once I lowered my arm again, he nodded towards Kris, but he left his arms around me, holding me tight. I half-turned to look at him. 'He's the most beautiful horse I've ever seen.'

He returned my smile with one of his own. 'He's not real,' he said.

'What do you mean he's not real?' I laughed. 'He's right here!'

'What he means is that I only look like a horse,' Storn said with some melancholy in his voice, and I would have jumped had Kris not held me so tight.

It came to me then why the name was so familiar. "It's like Storn," Conor had said on the night we met when he was looking at the spider.

'James built him,' Kris said, his hand returning to stroke me again.

'But he looks so real. His eyes …' I looked at the horse next to Storn, then back. 'His eyes look just like the eyes of the other horses.' Soft, fragile-looking and so alive. 'His hide.' Warm, underneath something soft like flesh, not hard like metal. 'Even his mouth and tongue and teeth.'

'It's practically impossible to tell if you don't know,' Kris agreed. 'This is why you can go out for a ride with him. He will look after you. He even speaks English, I already checked. Only, of course, if there are no other people around,' he added, making me realise what the earlier 'Gone?' was about. He wasn't talking to me. He was talking to the horse!

'Storn, can you please print a set of earbuds for Selena? Transparent where you can, and match the rest to her skin tone.'

There was a quiet burring noise, and a minute later, I watched, astonished, as Kris removed two small earphones from the horse's mouth.

'Don't worry, it's not saliva,' he laughed as he wiped them off on his shirt. Then he turned me to face him, tucked my hair behind my ears and carefully placed the earbuds into them. 'Don't lose them.' He kissed my forehead. 'Ithorion would have a heart attack!'

'We definitely don't want that,' I laughed and moved my hair back to cover my ears.

'Ready?' he asked.

'Not quite,' I admitted, and he opened his arms, knowing full well what I wanted.

We stood there a little longer, lost in each other's arms as he stroked me and kissed my head again. Not wanting to push my luck, I let him go. He showed me how to climb up into the saddle and how to sit properly, adjusted my long skirt around the horse's back, then led Storn out of the stable into the Corodien summer.

The world looked like a different place from horseback. I held on tight, so weak from happiness, I thought I might slide right off if I relaxed just for a moment. Two knights stood outside, abruptly stopping their conversations as we passed them, and stared at us in wonder. Then, remembering their manners, they bowed and greeted me, and I nodded at them graciously. Kris pulled the horse's head down in the meantime and whispered something into his ear. Then he looked up at me, a touch of longing in his eyes that quickened my heart again.

'I hope you have a pleasant ride, Lady Selena,' he said. He patted the horse's neck and let him go. Storn set off at a gentle pace, carrying me out of the palace grounds and into the town.

Shreds of conversations reached me through the earphones, in English and in the voices of their owners, as we passed through the streets, but I soon stopped paying attention to them. The city of Caledon might have tried to impress me with all its glory on that fine, sunny afternoon, but all

I saw was him. His smile. The way he kissed my forehead. That look in his eyes.

'He intoxicated you,' Storn pointed out, talking to me for the first time and not through the earbuds, which woke me from my daydreams to find that we stood on a road somewhere, the city well behind us.

'He did,' I admitted as I looked around.

'How?'

How indeed. Just by being him? 'I'm not sure.' Then after a pause, I asked, 'Have you not seen him like this before? You know, with another woman?'

'He knows that human mating habits and reproduction are topics I like to avoid if we can. But he's certainly never introduced another woman to me before, if that's what you mean,' he said, the answer filling me with a foolish joy. 'This makes you happy,' he observed.

'You can tell, huh?' I laughed.

'I can,' he said. 'I'm monitoring all your system functions. Sorry, it's part of the safety protocol he selected for you.'

A breeze blew a small leaf into his mane, and I picked it out, stroking his head. 'Sounds like I should be pretty safe,' I mused.

'Well, it's the highest level. Anyhow, which way would you like to go?'

I looked around once more. There was a crossing not far from us. On the left, a narrow road, empty and leading towards Tittere, according to a sign. Ahead of us, a cart was coming our way, pulled by two oxen. This was the road on which we travelled to Caledon from Abor. On the right, a big forest in the distance. I looked at the leaf in my hand. I kept waiting for the Dragon to guide me somehow. Wasn't I supposed to interpret his signs? Could they be something as simple as that? But then again, what did I expect? That they would appear written in the sky? Surely, they would have to blend in around me somehow. Maybe he had been sending me signs all this time, and I wasn't paying attention. Or more accurately, all my attention was elsewhere.

'Let's go into the forest,' I said.

I heard noises from behind and saw soldiers riding towards us, catching up.

'Are you ready to try a faster speed yet?' Storn asked.

'Um …' I panicked suddenly. 'How fast?'

'Don't worry,' Storn said confidently. 'You are safe with me. Just lean forward a little. That's it!'

He took off, turning onto the forest road at speed, and accelerated until my skirt flew behind us, leaving my legs bare. I made a mental note not to repeat this when I rode with the king. I enjoyed it, though. There was a thrill to it that, instead of scaring me as I expected it would, flooded me with happiness. A strange intimacy between rider and horse. A trust. A shared experience of sailing through the world and leaving it behind.

He slowed to a walking pace once we reached the forest, and we took a less travelled path at the first opportunity.

'Have you known Kris for long?' I asked him.

'All my life. The Professor built me when Kris was eight years old. They already lived in the University of St Mark at the time.'

Imagining him as a child made me smile. 'What was he like back then?'

'Very different. Troublesome. Loquacious. Always running around, exploring everything, injuring himself often. He is a lot more agreeable now. All that education went a long way.'

'Wasn't he a little young to be schooled at a university?'

'He was always more advanced than his peers, but he didn't attend classes for the first few years. The Professor taught him. And in any case, in Alba's schools, students from a certain age mostly self-study. There is a huge volume of material available for them to choose from. Recordings, simulations, AI tutors, interactive textbooks, tests. In fact, there are relatively few living teachers at St Mark's.'

'It must have been a very different life from the one I had, not to mention Conor. I can't even imagine.'

'I can show you recordings of him from the time if you'd like,' he offered pleasantly, making me laugh.

'I'd love to see those. But probably later.' I knew I had to change the subject soon, before Storn informed Kris that all I wanted to talk about during the whole journey was him. Had he found out that we spent the time watching childhood footage of him, he probably would have stopped me from going out for a ride again, or even worse, diminished my kiss allocation in the evenings!

'So, how did you find us?' I asked instead. 'How did you know we were in the palace?'

'I met Kris and Conor at a prearranged time and place outside of Caledon. We came all the way from Borond with Conor's horse, Athos.'

'Prearranged? How?' I frowned.

'I was actually going to ask you about that,' Storn said with some hesitation, then stopped, as if approaching a delicate matter he wasn't sure we should be discussing. I leaned closer to him, ready to supply whatever information I might have in return for his intel on the man I was in love with. 'Kris contacted me seven days ago, using what he said was another droid made by the Professor.'

'Seven days ago? But then we were still … oh.' So that's where he went when Conor and I spent the evening without him at the feast! Suddenly, I felt very foolish for having assumed anything else.

'I always thought I was the only droid the Professor built. He never told me otherwise.'

'Maybe it was a new invention,' I offered and stroked his head. 'Maybe Professor Montgomery hasn't had the opportunity to mention it yet. He was on my planet at the time. He could have made it there.'

'What was it like? This spider droid?'

'What do you mean? It just looks like a spider.'

'Do you know any of its specifications? Its components? Capabilities?'

'No, I never asked, sorry,' I admitted. 'But it was definitely clever.'

'Clever?'

'Oh, yes.' I nodded. 'Even Kris was impressed.'

A pause. Then, 'Really?' Something in his voice I failed to notice before, but it clearly hit me now. What was it? Insecurity? Jealousy, even?

'Obviously, nothing like you,' I backtracked quickly. 'When I say clever, I just mean, you know, clever for a spider.'

'Nothing like me?'

'Of course not.' I put my arms around his neck and rested my head against him. 'You are magnificent!'

'I have some extremely unique capabilities.'

'I'm sure you do,' I said, which didn't stop him from launching into detailed technical descriptions that meant nothing to me.

After a while he seemed to sense my disinterest because he suddenly exclaimed: 'Oh! I tell you what. I'm detecting a small group of two horses and two humans about three hundred meters north from here. If we go just a little closer, we can spy on them.'

'Are they coming towards us?' I asked.

'No, they are stationary.'

I bit my lip and wondered if I should tell him what two stationary humans might be up to alone in the middle of the forest on a fine afternoon like this, but he was already on the move, eager to show me what he could do.

Soon, he stopped and projected a life-size holographic image in front of us. Just as I thought, there was a half-naked man and woman in each other's arms but looking somewhat distraught.

'Oh,' Storn said and stopped the footage.

'Wait!' I hissed at him. 'Back, back, back, back, back, back! That was the king!'

The image reappeared, showing the two people in conversation, a sadness between them.

'Can we hear what they're saying, please, Storn? Can you record it?'

Their voices started playing in my ear in English, and I listened intently.

'No, Isabell, listen to me!' the king was saying, his face agitated. 'You can't tell him about us. He'll hurt you or worse.'

'But this might be the only way.' The dark-haired woman cupped the king's face in her hands. 'And once the curse is broken, we can finally be together.'

'We don't know for sure if the curse will be broken.' The king reached for his shirt and pulled it on. 'What if it isn't? None of the healers have succeeded before. I might well be blind in three days with no way of seeing or knowing that you are safe. Even if I found out that he's done something to you, there will be precious little I can do to help. Please, Isabell, I must know that you'll be safe! You've been the only thing that's kept me going these last few months.'

'Then let's talk to him tonight,' she pleaded.

'And what do you think he'd say?' he snapped. 'How do you think he'd regard a man who in three days' time won't be able to cross the room without tripping over the furniture? No, my love,' he added, more softly. 'There's nothing we can do. I want you to go back and be safe. And with time, even if the curse persists or if I die, I want you to find happiness again. With another man who can give you all that you deserve.'

'Never!' Isabell said fiercely and kissed the king. 'I love you.'

'Promise me,' the king insisted. 'Promise me, that you won't tell him. In turn, I promise you that I'll talk to him if the curse is broken.'

'But what if it's too late by then?'

'It won't be.'

'But I've seen—'

'Hush,' he said and kissed her. 'You haven't seen everything.'

They kissed for a little longer before finally saying goodbye to each other.

'Let's go before he sees us,' I said to Storn, and we raced back to the palace.

Once back inside, I went to find the men with a matchbox-sized thing in my pocket that Storn reassured me Kris would know how to use. The three of us gathered in his room, locked the door, closed the window shutters and settled down on the bed. For a strange moment, it almost felt as if we were about to have a cosy movie night in, and I wished very much that would be the case, instead of standing defenceless as a malicious curse and an impending war came crashing down on us.

We watched the footage quietly, in the original Wedan this time. The picture was so clear in the dark room that, if not for the trees and the forest floor, we could have thought them really in front of us. Seeing their sorrowful faces again, my own heart filled with sadness, too, and I vowed to spend the remainder of the day in the library, re-reading all those excerpts in case I had overlooked something.

'It would be good to know who this woman is.' Kris looked at Conor.

'On it.' Conor jumped up and, without another word, dashed out of the room.

Kris stood and opened the shutters, watching him march through the garden from the window. He rapped the back of his fingers on the nearby table and gazed ahead for a while, his eyes lost in the distance, as if looking at an incomplete puzzle only he could see and was wondering where this new piece should be going.

Chapter 24

Conor

Caledon, Drelos,
9th The Month of Red Blessing 1575

As far as jobs went, I had to admit that this hadn't been too bad so far. Living in the Royal Palace, filling my belly at the king's table every day, chatting to people … I bet this was just a probation period thing to lure me in, though, and Ithorion would drop us into some rathole next if we properly joined the Order! But for now, the only thing I could even call an inconvenience was bedding the same woman every night, which after four nights in a row was an unheard record for me! I had a reputation to protect, after all. On the plus side, she was surprisingly creative. So much so that even I learned a few new things from her!

But apart from that, there was nothing really, besides getting a little bored. Yet even that I couldn't fully claim. Not with those two continuously expanding my horizons, with their mind-blowing artifacts they called technology and their magic they called supernatural powers.

Ithorion said what magic was simply depended on your definition. It seemed to me that it was different for all three of us. Selena, our powerful sorceress, was clearly enchanted by the smallest things sometimes. In turn, Kris, who made fun of me once for believing in such things, now spent most of his time studying ways to break a curse and didn't even blink when I switched to Elesean in our conversation, using the knowledge in his head. You'd think any man would surely feel a little uncomfortable about that. Someone reaching into their mind and taking from what they spent years learning. But if anything, he seemed pleased. In fact, I was learning a lot from him every day, often without even realising it. He had a natural talent for explaining things in a logical way that was easy to understand, driven by a genuine desire to see others grow. But most of all, me.

I entered the stable and went to find my saddle. Once I had it, I walked over to where Athos and Storn stood side by side. I turned to Athos first and patted him.

'What's up, buddy? Enjoying the royal fare, I hope?'

Then I moved over to Storn and put the saddle on his back—a move that proved unpopular with both horses.

'Trust me, I'd rather go with Athos, too,' I muttered to Storn, not wanting to be overheard. 'But I need you to show me where you saw the king.'

Considering that we were supposedly here on behalf of a secret order, we really had an aptitude for drawing attention to ourselves, I thought as I crossed Caledon on Storn. Perhaps something we could work on later. As it was now, he ignored me completely and trotted through the streets with a snobbish dignity that somehow made him look even more impressive. A little more of this and surely the king would want to keep him.

I made him take a longer route to avoid being seen from the road, and by the time we reached the rendezvous spot, I knew we didn't have long before sunset. I dismounted and looked around.

'See?' I showed the hoof prints to him. 'They clearly met up somewhere else and came together here from that direction.' I pointed eastwards. 'Then one left towards south, to Caledon, and the other went north. We follow her north!'

I got back into the saddle and clicked my tongue.

'You know that you don't need to do that for me.' He looked up at me annoyed.

'Force of habit.' I shrugged. 'Come on then, let's go!' I clicked my tongue again and grinned. He rolled his eyes but moved on.

In truth, as much as I enjoyed winding him up, it was a temporary distraction. A diversion from something I didn't want to think about. But there it was on my mind again. Of course, she had to go north. In the footage she spoke with a northern accent. I knew what accent it was exactly, I was just hoping I was somehow wrong.

We spent the last few hours of daylight tracking her. The forest darkened gradually, wrapping us in a night blanket of premonition. A breeze made the trees whisper a tale of sorrow, their leaves falling quietly, whirling as if trying to escape the inevitable. A whiff of smoke in the air. A faint smell of brimstone. A cold dawn was reaching for me whichever way I turned, its hard fingers snapping dry twigs about me in anticipation.

'I'm detecting about a hundred people ahead of us with horses and temporary accommodation,' Storn informed me.

'Take me as close as you can without us being noticed,' I said quietly.

'You don't want to meet her people?'

'Not if I can help it.' I patted his neck. 'They are the enemy.' I knew from the knight-commander that negotiations had been slow, and Harag troops were already bothering the villages along the border. Never an official attack. Just savage bullies too impatient for spoils and blood, eager to find men who might say no to their plunder or prove too protective of their daughters. After our luxurious stay in the palace, it was sobering to find some of them already this close to the heart of the kingdom. It was unlikely they would welcome me with open arms and grant me a private audience in a tent with one of their women. A woman who, if found out, could possibly be charged not just with infidelity but with treason, too. Seemed like we already had something in common.

Storn stopped in a while. From his eyes, a vision took shape in front of us. A map of tents. Then, as if we were a hawk falling on its prey, the picture closed in on the camp and raced in between them. It split into three parts. One showing the area from the side, like a wolf circling it. The second darting around the tents. The third displaying it all from above, a small red dot indicating the viewpoint of the second. In the right top corners of all three, a set of records, numbers changing fast as the pictures moved.

I kept my eyes on the second footage, looking for her.

'Stop there!' She sat around a fire with a group of men, cleaning a shield. I wondered if she was the wife of one of them. Her long, black hair the king had so lovingly fondled not long ago, was now tamed into a single braid, her face hard, her lips pressed into a thin line of defiance. Her skirt was gone, too, I noticed, replaced by a pair of black trousers, like the ones the men around her wore. I studied the other two angles briefly, then dismounted.

'Good job!' I patted Storn's neck again, then checked that all my knives were in place. My sword was back in the palace, but it would have only hindered me anyway. The knives would do. 'Wait here.'

'Where are you going?' he asked.

'Where do you think?' I turned.

'That is an irrational idea I strongly advise against. Perhaps you're not thinking clearly.'

'I need to talk to her,' I said. 'I need to find out who she is.'

'Can't it wait until she rides out to meet the king again or they are all asleep?'

'These are Harag soldiers. They will never all be asleep!'

'But there's an eighty percent chance that you will be seen and potentially hurt,' he argued.

'Eighty percent?' I laughed. 'How did you even calculate that? Wait. Don't tell me. It's insulting as it is.'

'But—'

'But what? You don't even like me. Does it really matter?'

He considered that for a moment, his big eyes studying me in the moonlight. 'Your loss would cause me a temporary software malfunction.'

'Touching!' I shook my head and turned to go.

'Wait!'

'What?' I snapped.

He bowed his head, looking up at me with big puppy eyes. 'Just come back to me. Promise that you'll come back.'

'Awww.' I scratched his head behind his ear, the way I'd seen Kris do a dozen times. 'Come on, little horsey. We don't have time for this. I have a lady to meet. And, as you'll see, in such cases even an army can't stop me.'

I had to slow considerably in order to move through the trees quietly. But I preferred stealth to speed right now. I knew I didn't have to go far.

Soon enough, I heard two men walking towards me, their approach underlined by their conversation and by the torches they held.

I had two options. I could easily avoid them and press on towards the camp. Or I could kill them and change into their uniform. A hundred soldiers would know each other well enough to recognise me as an outsider if they saw my face. But it would still help a great deal in disguising myself, not to mention that the light armour they wore could also be useful if it came to a fight. Which I really hoped it wouldn't.

I didn't like killing. I knew men who enjoyed it. But not me. I considered it a necessary evil that sometimes just had to be done. The same way a farmer would kill a chicken, a pig or a cow they had previously cared for. For months or for years, they would look after them, feed them, clean up after them; not a few would even talk to them, pet them. But when it came to it, the knife had to do its work. Otherwise it would be the farmer and their family who starved and died. At times, it was the same with people. It was either them now or you later.

I knew this to be true. I certainly had been through enough to realise it. Yet no matter how educated my dear friend, Kris, was, this was still a lesson that had so far escaped him. He'd had a chance to end Laro in the library. Yet, Kris chose to lower his sword. Brother or not, couldn't he see what a malicious, sick bastard he was? Laro would keep coming after us until one day he succeeded. Or died trying. Why delay it and hope that our luck held up?

I saw Laro so clearly in front of me now, framed by the soldiers' torchlight in the distance. It made me think back to the Day of Revelations in the Shield of Heaven Monastery all those years ago. When I somehow punched fire into the shield in front of me. Surely, the Dragon would give me back that fire magic if he wanted me to become his Champion? I would treat Laro to such a warm welcome when he came to visit next! How unfair it was that he had all those powers, advanced weapons, and I had nothing. A supposed initiate of the Order of the Dragon! If only I could use fire like that again. He would be no match.

I sighed and dispelled my daydreaming. It was time to focus on the task at hand.

I knew Kris would prefer it if I incapacitated these soldiers rather than killing them. Him and that silly horse both, who I was sure was watching me like a hawk even now. But Harag soldiers were a tough breed. Chances were, I couldn't knock out both quietly, and even if I somehow succeeded, who could tell for sure when they might get up again and come after me?

I jumped, catching the lowest branch of a big oak tree, and climbed up. I watched the two swaying torches come closer, considering my options as I crouched. I would try to incapacitate them for Kris if I had the chance. But surely, he'd prefer me alive and them dead, rather than the other way around!

'Just go ahead. I'll catch up soon,' I heard one say to the other in the Haragi tongue, and he stopped nearby. 'After all that beer, I need a piss.'

The other said something I didn't understand and went on, passing under me with quick steps, carrying a bow. I couldn't see a way to avoid bloodshed. In this dark I couldn't make sure I wouldn't step on a twig or something, and alert either or both of them. Or confronted one so quietly, the other wouldn't hear it this close. At the end of the day, these guys would be killing my countrymen and raping their wives in a few days without a second thought unless we stopped them somehow!

I had four knives on me. I selected a throwing knife. The nearby soldier was holding his cock with one hand, the torch still in the other. I aimed carefully, his neck an easy target with the flame near it. I pursed my lips, hearing myself explain it to Kris in the morning. Oh, for fuck's sake!

I quietly jumped down from the tree and snuck up behind the man. That must have been a lot of beer, indeed! I was almost there when something snapped under my foot. He turned slowly, as if unsure, while my body instinctively coiled into a fighting position, ready to punch.

'Deliver it from your heel!' I still heard Brother Peter's voice in my ear, crystal clear, as if it had been only yesterday and not a decade ago.

'Oy!' The Harag soldier objected to my presence, just a moment before my fist connected with his face and sent him to sleep.

'You're dead, you fucking bastard!' It was my turn to turn around, surprised, only to be presented with the second soldier pulling an arrow back in his bow, his torch thrust into the ground. The throwing knife flew out of my left hand without thinking. I was never too good with my left hand. But it looked like I was still lucky! The man gave out a short, muffled sound as my blade embedded itself in his neck. I sent a second knife after the first with my right hand this time, just to be on the safe side. He fell on his knees and collapsed.

'Oh, well.'

I put out the torches, collected my knifes and changed quickly. Then I dragged the dead guard and the unconscious one a little further away from the path and proceeded towards the camp. The trees around me thinned, then the forest stopped suddenly like the tree-god had just hit the brakes hard. I could see more fires now, as well as outlines of the nearest tents. I approached quietly, waiting for the right moment behind the last wide oak.

'Calling it a day already?' I heard a voice call out.

'I thought I might as well try to get some rest before they arrive,' someone muttered nearby. 'Even if they don't need us to help, a thousand men setting up tents and chopping down more trees isn't likely to aid my sleep tonight.'

'There might be some truth in that,' said the first voice, and the noise of footsteps was soon followed by flaps of heavy fabric.

The fact that among a thousand soldiers, I would have a much better chance of keeping my cover provided little consolation. The clock was ticking, faster and in more ways than I liked.

I stepped out from behind the tree and confidently made my way through the camp. I avoided the fires, and whenever someone came my way, I crouched, pretending to examine my boots, or turned off the path to check on a guy line. Finally, the group she sat with came into sight. They were busy eating some stew and so I could come fairly close before either of them looked my way. She stood suddenly, and I stepped behind a banner, the ominous Harag flag hiding my face.

Isabell put her bowl down and started towards me, moving quietly but purposefully. She stopped at the banner and looked behind it, but I was no longer there. She turned around slowly, her eyes carefully studying her surroundings. In turn, I studied her, her fierceness appealing.

After a few minutes, she gave up looking for me and went into one of the few large tents nearby. Candles burned inside, providing a vague, dark outline of tables, a bed, boxes and other furniture. She was alone in there, right in the middle, and on her knees. I waited for a clear moment again, then flew in after her to answer her prayers.

I entered the tent without the smallest noise. Isabell kneeled with her back to me, her head bowed slightly. I didn't want to frighten her or be rough, but I knew I had to act quickly to stop her from calling out before I had a chance to explain myself. I stepped closer silently, all of me gearing up to arrest her move with one arm and silence her with the other. In the last moment, she turned like a snake, two curved, wicked knives flashing in her hands.

'Wait, wait!' I hissed, suddenly busy blocking her competent strikes.

'Who are you? What do you want?' she hissed back without slowing her attacks in the slightest. We knocked over and broke some pots from one of the tables, causing a racket. I could hear voices outside, coming closer. Shit!

'King Sirion!' I grunted as her heel found its way to my stomach, grateful her kick wasn't any lower than that.

'Are you here on behalf of King Sirion?' she whispered wide-eyed, dropping her blades and grabbing the front of my shirt, yanking me closer.

'Yes!' I leaned closer than she intended, very aware now of the approaching steps not far behind me.

She pulled her head away with a stern look.

'They can't see my face! They'll know!' I explained in a whisper urgently. 'And … mess …' I mumbled, my lips suddenly too busy under hers.

'Is everything alright, Lady Isabell?' a voice behind me asked.

She continued kissing me instead of answering, moaning with pleasure. She took a slow step backwards, pulling me with her, and sat on top of the table, making space on it with a wave of her hand, casually smashing more stuff.

The soldier turned without another word and left the tent.

'Who are you?' She pushed me off a moment later.

'My name is Conor Drew. I'm the one who escorted the Scarlet Witch to the Royal Palace to break the curse.'

'I've heard of you. How is the king? Do you think the Scarlet Witch can really break the curse?'

I thought of Selena. The determination in her eyes as she studied those texts with Kris. The way she had slowly twirled above us in the Pantheon, turning day into night and night into day, circled by dragons, held by a God. She was my Supreme Key. Of course, she would unlock the curse!

'I haven't the slightest doubt. If anyone, she can and she will,' I reassured Isabell.

'Is that why you're here? Did the king agree to talk to my father?'

I opened my mouth, still trying to work out which question to ask first. Someone approaching the tent with quick steps made her close the gap between us and start kissing me again, even more passionately than before. I wrapped my arms around her, my mind swirling with what I was putting together just now.

'Lady Isabell?' a deep voice said behind me.

Isabell pulled away and looked at the man over my shoulder. 'What is it, Resh?' she snapped at him. 'Can't you see I'm busy?'

'Please forgive me, my lady, but the meeting has started.'

'You can stand in for me and brief me afterwards.'

'And what if the Khagan arrives in the meantime?'

'Then you can tell my father that I shall be with him in a moment!'

Her eyes followed him out of the tent, then returned to me. 'We'll have to speak to him,' she said quietly, her voice suddenly shaky, an unsettling worry replacing her fierceness.

'We?' In the eyes of the infamously cruel Harag warlord I was little more than fresh meat to feed to his dogs. All alone in the middle of the enemy camp, after killing one of their men in the forest, I was a dead man walking. And that was before even mentioning that our king was fucking his daughter! Besides, I had a terrible track record when it came to women's fathers. I was practically the worst man for the job!

'Please.' Isabell squeezed my hand, her eyes suddenly filling with tears. And there it was. The perfect death-trap. I could make my escape now. I knew with every fibre in me that I should. Then stand as a coward in front of Kris, Selena and the whole Order for abandoning a terrified woman in her hour of need. Or should I convince her to keep quiet and sacrifice what might be our only chance to speak with the warlord and convince him to stop this madness? But honestly, what were my chances when even the king's ambassadors had failed at the task? I knew what Kris would do in my place. Negotiate peace. I wished he was here now. He would be so much better at this than me! I wondered what chances his horse calculated for me now. Forget about getting out of this unhurt, but just alive? Then I decided it was best not to know.

'Fine,' I said and smiled weakly as Isabell threw her arms around me. No executioner ever had finer features.

Her dark hair reminded me of Aiki, who had often entered my thoughts these past days. I wondered if she could watch me sometimes. Wasn't she a Test Master apprentice or something? How did Test Masters spy on people, anyway? Well, if she did, I bloody well hoped she would pick this moment! The possibility filled me with some comfort. And even a little excitement.

We settled on Isabell's bed, sitting side by side, waiting for her father to arrive with his army, like two convicts waiting for their final call. Soon we were chatting with a confidence in each other you only gain by facing a certain end together.

'So, how did you meet the king, anyway?' I asked. 'What were you doing in Coroden?'

'I was secretly investigating the strengths and weaknesses of the castles for my father. The Royal Palace was, of course, one of the most important.'

'What? You came here to spy on King Sirion and you fell in love with him? Surely, you are the worst spy ever!' I laughed.

She tightened her jaw at that, but the king's name also brought a smile to her face. 'He thought I was a foreign merchant's daughter, at first. We met at the market. He was riding through with some of his men when I caught his eye. I tried to hide, but he was quicker. He came to talk to me and ended up buying me a necklace as a present. He paid for it even when it was offered to him for free. It was all very romantic.

'The next few times he caught me within the palace walls he didn't even ask what I was doing there. He was just happy to see me. He might have assumed that I sneaked in, hoping to have a glimpse of him. In the end, he took me around the palace himself, showing me absolutely everything.' She laughed.

'So, what happened? What stopped you visiting him, or staying with him in the palace?'

'Lord Dranos.'

'What?'

'Yes.' She nodded. 'He's hoping the king might marry his daughter.'

'Aurelia? But she's not of royal birth!'

'Even so. He thinks he might be able to convince the king once the curse takes effect. He made it clear to me that he didn't want to see me anywhere near Sirion again. In the end, I was worried he might start investigating who I really was, and I didn't enter the palace again.'

'Have you told the king?'

'About Lord Dranos? No. Dranos is like a father to him. Sirion trusts him more than anyone else. And at the time I still had my own secret to reveal.'

I scratched my chin. So, this was why Aurelia was still not married. Her father had other plans for her. Was this at the root of that big family argument? I thought of how resourceful she was. How adventurous. Just like me, she wasn't made for a life of sitting at home. 'It would be a forced marriage,' I said. 'I don't think Aurelia wants to marry Sirion or become queen.' Not that it mattered what she wanted in the eyes of her father.

There were voices outside, and I knew that our time was up. I'd never in my life felt more reluctant to leave the side of a woman and get up from the bed. 'Come on, Conor,' I told myself. 'Just this once. Next time you're in bed with a beautiful woman, you can stay where you are. Whatever happens,' I promised. 'Not even lift a muscle. Just now. Come on!'

I pushed myself up and Isabell joined me a heartbeat later.

'What is this?' Kohl, the Great Khan of the Harags entered the tent, followed by several of his men. He was at least a head taller than me, twice as wide, and heaped with muscle. His scalp shaved bald, a brow ridge to rival Ithorion's, under which a pair of bloodthirsty eyes pierced into me like two blades, ready to cut out my heart.

'Great Khagan of the Harag.' I bowed.

'A Southerner?' he roared and four of his soldiers jumped on me. He grabbed Isabell's hair right behind her head and pulled it hard enough to make her whimper in pain.

'What is a bloody Southerner doing in your tent?' he bellowed into her face, forcing her to look up into his.

'Father, he's here on behalf of the Coroden court. King Sirion sent him!'

The soldiers around me paused for a second and looked at their ruler.

'What are you waiting for?' he snapped at them. 'Stop once more and you'll be next!'

They stripped the clothes off me, setting my knives out on the floor in a line, one tying my ankles together, and another my wrists behind me with a rope. Then, they shoved me to my knees, and the next thing I knew, my face split open under the spiky rings of the khan as he sent me to the floor with one powerful punch. My whole head buzzed with pain as I pushed myself back up, preparing for the next that I knew was coming. Without delay, I was down again, the world spinning as I struggled to get back on my knees, bloodying Isabell's carpet all around me. I felt her concerned eyes on me from behind her father.

'This was for my soldier, Ambassador,' the Khagan said, picking up one of my knives from the floor and coming around to face me again. He drew the sharp blade across my neck, watching me. 'What's your name?'

'Conor Drew,' I said.

'Like the thief?' The Khagan raised his eyebrows at me.

'The very same, great Khagan.' I bowed my head.

'Conor Drew!' He gestured to his soldiers, like I was someone dropped among them from the legends, and who upon second glance, naked and bloody, wasn't actually that impressive at all. 'You look more like a thief now. I imagine the women won't find you that pretty anymore!' The soldiers politely laughed around me.

'So, what does King Sirion want now?' he asked, carving more red lines into my neck and chest like an artist's sketch.

I swallowed and closed my eyes for a moment. 'Your daughter Isabell's hand in marriage.'

'What?' The khagan paused, then burst out laughing. 'That's a good one, little thief! This is going to be more fun than I thought!' I watched him detach and uncoil a long whip from his belt, with little hook-shaped iron stars worked into its many tails. 'Jokes aside, what does he really want?' He struck me, and I bit into my lip hard to stop myself from crying out. 'Faster!'

'As I said, great Khagan, he wishes to make your daughter his queen.' I stifled a yelp as the whip bit into my flesh again, the iron stars holding on to some of it.

'Why would I allow that?' He hit me again, harder.

'Because I love him!' Isabell cried out behind him, making him stop and turn.

'What?'

'We love each other, King Sirion and I!'

The Khagan raised the handle of the whip towards his daughter. 'Out!' he shouted at his soldiers. 'Out! All of you!' He grabbed Isabell's hair again and shoved her down next to me. He was already raising the whip as she fell.

'No! Father, no!' Isabell yelled and held her arms out before her body. 'I'm pregnant!'

'What did you say?'

'I'm pregnant!' she sobbed.

He moved to strike her even so.

'Don't hurt her!' I yelled at him, causing him to shift and start pummelling me instead with his fists in his fury.

'No!' Isabell pleaded. 'Please, Father, stop!' She tried to shield me from him, only to be shoved away again, but to her credit, she kept coming back.

'Sirion will be blind soon! You are my only daughter. I'm not marrying you to a blind man!' The Khagan raged, breathing hard.

'Conor brought a Scarlet Witch to Caledon. She's going to break the curse.'

'A Scarlet Witch?'

'Just give him a chance at least to speak. Father, I'm begging you. Please!'

'What?' He grabbed my neck with one massive hand. 'What could the king possibly offer me for her?'

'The Kenesi Goldmine,' I croaked. It was the first thing that came to mind from what Kris explained to me.

'What else?' He shook me.

'Belar Forest.'

'I have plenty of forests. Why would I need another?'

'It has several hot springs with healing properties.'

'What else?' The whip bit into me again.

I closed my eyes and saw Kris's face in front of me, telling me all the territories and natural resources he thought the Harags would have an interest in. I tried to recite them all. He had a shorter list for a best-case and a longer one for a worst-case scenario. I felt we had passed the realm of best-case scenarios already.

'I can take all this for myself. Why should I agree to anything?' the khagan demanded once I had finished.

'Your daughter is a strong woman,' I said. 'Strong and clever. Our king is madly in love with her. He'll do whatever might please her. By letting her share his throne, you'll practically have influence over the whole kingdom without wasting a single coin on war. And why not allow her to be happy? One's achievements on the battlefield don't guarantee contentment in life. Her joy would bring pleasure not just to you, great Khagan, but to all of us!'

He released me and turned to Isabell. 'Is this really what you want?'

'More than anything, Father.' She took his hand into hers and kissed it. 'Please!'

'Only if the curse is broken.' He looked at me. 'If the king goes blind on his birthday, we attack the next day.'

He called in his men to cut my ropes and give me back my clothes. Soon, I was roughly escorted out of the camp and thrown onto my front on the forest floor. I tried to push myself upright, the pain excruciating.

I was usually luckier than this. On those rare occasions a more serious injury or illness had struck me down, I usually hid away from the rest of the world in one of my favourite inns. But strangely enough, and for the first time ever, it wasn't solitude that I wished for just then.

As I stumbled and whimpered with each step in the dark, my mind was on Selena. How gently and carefully she had cleaned the cuts on my arms the night we met. And on Kris, too. With that bloody needle of his! I grinned, even if it hurt my face. Much colder by temperament, but even more efficient. When I thought of being with them, I felt a strange sense of safety that was new to me. Perhaps this was what other people did when they were in pain. Perhaps it was normal to long for those who cared about you. I'd just never had anyone like them before.

I wondered how the two of them were getting on tonight. Kris had asked me over lunch to let him sort out the disagreement between them and that it was apparently nothing to worry about. He also said that he was sure Selena was only trying out some new treatment in the king's bedchamber that she thought might work. But even if that wasn't the case and they'd gone beyond that, she was a grown woman, and it was her decision to make. Not ours.

It was a good speech and I'm sure he would have convinced anyone else of his disinterest. But I saw right through him. In the end, I told him again that I didn't care what he did or didn't do with Selena at nights, I just wanted to see some improvement by the next day!

A dark shape crossed my path, stirring me from my thoughts. Storn's big eyes studied me with concern.

'Despite how it looks, it was a successful trip,' I stated.

'Fortunately, I always have some emergency first aid supplies with me,' Storn informed me and licked my face.

'Hey, stop it! What are you doing?' I scolded him as he did it again. I tried to wipe off my face on the sleeve of my shirt.

'No! You stop rubbing those wounds with your dirty clothes! This will sterilise them and dull the pain.' He licked my face again and I could feel it starting to go a little numb already. If I had learned one thing by now, it was that no matter how strange some of Kris's things were, they always worked. I sighed and let him get on with it.

'Take off your shirt.'

'Seriously?'

'Yes.'

'You're not recording this, are you?'

'Of course not, what a strange thought.'

'Good.'

'Turn around.'

'Up there on the left.'

'I can see it.'

'And on the right.'

'Almost done.'

'Great. I'm exhausted.'

'I know. Don't worry. You'll be in bed by sunrise.'

'Best words ever.'

'Now climb up! Let's go home.'

'Aaaaah.' It took me a while, but I was eventually in the saddle again.

'What? No clicking with your tongue?' he asked.

'Too tired.'

'Oh, come on. Just a little click!'

'No.'

'Come on, Conor! Just a little one!'

'No.'

'Ha-ha!'

Chapter 25

Kristian

Caledon, Drelos,
9ᵗʰ The Month of Red Blessing 1575

She lay in front of me with her eyes closed. I gently kissed her head again, enjoying the wave of her happiness that washed through me, as if she was an ocean on whose shore I stood, inviting me to go deeper. And I wanted nothing more.

I knew I should have called it a day, but I couldn't.

'So, how did it go with the king today?' I did my best to sound causal. Nothing to show that this had been something very much in the back of my mind all day.

'Good, I think,' she said quietly and stopped there.

'What did you do?' I prompted, stroking her gently while all of me tensed.

'I sat on his bed and made him put his head on my lap.'

'On your lap?' The words were out before I could stop them, an incredulous jealousy clashing with my rational thinking and threatening to take over. 'And?' I added, more softly this time.

She remained silent, but I could see a smile tugging at the corner of her lips in the dim light. What was this? A little revenge attempt still for this morning? Just unbelievable!

I moved closer and slowly kissed her ear. Her lips parted slightly, making me smile. 'What did you do with the king?' I whispered, keeping close.

Her lips curled into a slow smile, but she still refused to volunteer more.

I started kissing her ear again, my lips and tongue teasing her, my teeth biting gently, bringing myself dangerously close to a point where I knew I wouldn't be able to stop. 'What?' I whispered into her ear again.

To which she finally admitted that they had both been fully dressed, the king lying on his back with her hand on his forehead, and the only reason she positioned them this way was that it was close both to her tummy, where she felt the healing power originate from, and her hip, on which she had previously practiced. I silently sighed with relief and kissed her ear once more.

'Do you think it might work?' I stroked her.

'I'm honestly not sure,' she admitted. 'I don't think I'm doing anything majorly different to what other healers have done in the past. I might achieve some healing now, but I don't know if it will actually stop the curse. And if I continue once the king goes blind, the spell might persist like it did before.'

'Carry on with it, regardless,' I suggested. 'It can't hurt. Do you want me to stay nearby while you're doing it tomorrow?'

'Yes.'

'Okay.' I kissed her head softly. 'Good night.'

'Already?' she objected.

'Yes,' I murmured into her ear.

'Can't we just …?'

'No.'

I pulled her close to me and closed my eyes. I slowed my breathing and made myself fall asleep. Then I reached for her. It was so easy. I didn't even have to look for her, like I did with Conor back in the caves. She was just there. So close. After the first time, I didn't even need to see her anymore. Just think of it. And she was asleep, in a shared dream which I quietly exited as soon as she appeared, leaving her to the privacy of her mind.

I knew she would have preferred to spend time together each night before we went to sleep. I would have, too. But even just a few minutes with her in bed stretched my self-restraint to its maximum now.

Something woke me early. She was deep asleep in my arms, but the sun outside was already climbing out of the horizon, painting warm colours across the sky. I sensed Conor pass by in front of our door, heading towards his room. I carefully peeled myself away from Selena, fighting the urge to place a kiss on her forehead that might wake her. I dressed quickly and went after Conor.

I knocked on his door, opening it slightly. 'It's me,' I called.

'Come on in,' he said in a tired voice.

I entered the room and stopped short at the sight that greeted me. 'What happened?' I closed the door behind me.

'I negotiated peace.'

'With your face?' I went closer, a dull pain hitting me.

'Among other things.'

He lay on his side. I moved to lift up his shirt. He let me. His injuries shocked me as my eyes travelled across his torso and back. They looked much worse than the pain indicated. They were, just like his face, also covered in some slimy stuff. I carefully scooped up a little from his skin with a finger. 'What's this?'

'Storn.'

'Oh.' I grinned upon realising what must have happened. Then, despite myself, I burst out laughing.

'Shut up!' He struggled not to laugh with me, then lost the fight. 'Stop it, Kris! It hurts my face.'

'I'm sorry.' I sat down next to him, trying to control myself as I hurt with him.

'Promise you won't tell anyone. Not even Selena!'

'I won't,' I said. 'And don't worry. He used to do this to me all the time. I always injured myself somehow—when I was around eight or nine,' I added quickly upon seeing his expression. 'Storn used to hate babysitting me. But this will help.' I checked his forehead to make sure he had no fever, but his skin didn't feel warm to my touch.

He turned his head to look up at me and winced with pain. I felt it between my neck and shoulder. 'What's wrong?' It was one of the few places on his body I couldn't see any wounds or discolouring.

'Just the muscle. I think I was holding my neck in an awkward position on the way back.'

'Let me see.' My fingers found the knots in his shoulder and I started loosening them, literally feeling my way through the tight tissue. 'Now tell me what happened.'

'I followed Isabell into a Harag camp. She's the khagan's daughter!'

'Just our luck.' I shook my head in disbelief.

'It actually turned out to our benefit. But bloody hell! You have a gift, my friend!' he exclaimed as I eased another painful cramp in his neck.

'Perhaps.' I smiled, still unwilling to confess that I did, just not quite the way he thought. 'Then what happened?'

And he told me the whole story.

'This Khagan sounds like sadistic brute,' I said once he finished his tale. 'You should have never ended up in his clutches. We're lucky to have you back at all. Especially after you killed one of his soldiers. I'm amazed that he let you go!'

'I think he was more pissed off with those two soldiers for not stopping me. Two against one Southerner,' he said.

'What's his daughter like?'

'A good kisser!' He grinned, lacing his answer with pain. I squeezed his shoulder, making it worse. 'Ouch!'

'Behave yourself, Conor. She might well be your queen soon. Our queen,' I corrected myself.

'*Our* queen, eh?' Another smile curled his lips.

'That's still the plan, isn't it? That we settle down in Coroden somewhere?'

'I will have to check the regulations with the scribes. Those folks on Alba are a pesky lot! They think that after helping to save our kingdom they can just move here with their vast knowledge on everything, their show-offy fighting skills and their weird pets. The cheeky bastards!'

'You should get some sleep.' I grinned. 'You're so tired you no longer know what you're saying.'

'Isabell is great. You'll like her. She'll make a fine queen.'

'Good. Well done for stopping the war, Champion!' I patted his shoulder carefully and stood to go. 'We'll celebrate once the curse is broken and you're feeling better.'

'How is Selena?' he asked suddenly.

'She's fine.' I smiled.

'Happy-fine?'

'Yes. Her healing powers have started to emerge. That's what she was practising on the king.'

'That's great to hear! Don't tell her how I look,' he added after a pause. 'Let her spend her magic on the king this afternoon. We really need to break that curse somehow.'

'Of course. Is there anything I can get you before I go?'

'A glass of that Kabar would be nice.'

'There's some next door. Selena likes it even more than you do! I'll get you some.'

'Did you know that it's based on a recipe that's hundreds of years old?'

'Impressive! Now get some rest. I'll be back in a minute.'

I quietly entered Selena's room and poured some wine into a glass for Conor, its rich, complex aroma reaching my nostrils. After my first night in this room, wine had started appearing on the table every evening. The maids apparently brought it in now along with the scented candles and massage oils when they prepared Selena's bath. It almost seemed as if they were disappointed not to find any signs of passionate lovemaking in the mornings and did what they could to aid the process. Like Selena wasn't enough temptation already and needed additional tools in her weaponry!

I tiptoed out of her room and returned to Conor's. He was already fast asleep. I left the wine on the table and made my way to the library.

I sat at a table and opened the last remaining volume of the royal family history records. On our first day here, I started with the oldest book, then half-way through the sequence I grew impatient and jumped to the current one. Once I finished that, I started working my way back from the most recent to where I left off. Most of it was tedious, but with time I learned to look forward to the sections after the kings' twenty-eighth birthdays. Those were the years in which each king had made some of their best political and economic decisions. As if going blind somehow gave them a strange, tactical insight into governing the country.

Of course, after Conor's heroic venture last night, all that remained to do now was to break the curse. So, all I had to look for were the various attempts in that regard. In some ways, I still hoped Selena's emerging heal-ing powers would do the trick, but her own uncertainty when I asked about it wasn't a promising sign. In comparison, when she told us about the way she had temporarily paralyzed one of the knights from the win-dow, she was bursting with excitement. But who knew? Maybe she just needed some more time and practice. Not that we had much more time. Today and tomorrow were all that remained.

It was way too early for her to rise, but I knew that sooner or later, I should go back to her room. I didn't want her to wake alone and get upset again. She was so sensitive! One tiny sign of my feelings for her and she glowed with joy, enticing me. But one little step in the opposite direction and she went crazy! Finding a middle path each evening was like balancing on a knife's edge. Not to mention the way her desire always woke mine. Like spark to fuel.

It was hard enough to get her out of my head each morning as it was and try to concentrate on our task. Had I spent the nights exploring, kissing and pleasuring every single bit of her as I wanted to, no mental training in the world would have stopped my mind from replaying those scenes all day instead of engaging with the dreary historical journals of the Coroden Kingdom. We had two days to break the curse, and if that wasn't done, I could clearly see Ithorion's face after one of those tell-me-all confession sessions, pointing out in no uncertain terms that perhaps I had failed at our task because I was too busy fucking the Dragon's Supreme Key! How the Dragon himself would assess the situation, I wasn't sure, but I very much doubted that it would be a good step in his books, either. Besides, I wanted to make James proud, too. Not disappoint him. I needed to focus and find a way. Yet, here I was, thinking about Selena again. You had to wonder which one was the real test. I bet the solution to the curse was something really simple, I just wasn't seeing it yet.

I could sense her before she even stepped through the door, and I knew I was in trouble. I stood and had my arms around her as soon as she entered the library.

'I woke early today. I was going to come back,' I murmured into her hair. 'You never get up this early!'

'Maybe I don't sleep so well anymore when you're not there,' she complained but snuggled against me. She wore one of those dresses again that drove me crazy, but she would have turned me on in a space suit. I sighed into her hair and wondered how to step away without causing offence before I lost my mind completely.

'I'm going to need your help with the king today,' I said.

'Are you? Why?' she murmured, staying exactly as she was.

'We'll have to explain to him somehow how Conor found out about his affair with the Harag ruler's daughter and negotiated peace with them last night.'

'What?' She stepped back and looked at me. Mentioning that Conor got injured in the process would have been my last resort, but I was glad I didn't have to go that far.

'Why don't we sit down? I'll tell you all about it.'

She took a chair at the long table while I walked to the serving trolley in the corner.

'Would you like some water?' I asked.

'No, thanks.'

I lifted the jug, wishing I could just pour its contents over my head.

'So how shall we play this?' I asked once I'd sat down opposite her and briefly told her what took place last night, playing down Conor's injuries as he had asked me to. 'We can't really say that you rode out yesterday and happened to spot them in the middle of a huge forest. We could say that Conor secretly followed him because the knight-commander was concerned, but I'm sure he wouldn't like that, either. Any suggestions?'

It took her less than a minute. 'We could say that I had a vision. About this woman in the north of the forest who was in danger and so precious to the king that any harm to her would jeopardise the breaking of the curse.'

I leaned forward with a mischievous smile. 'Could work. Do you think you could sell it to him?'

She mirrored me, eager to impress. 'Watch me!'

Good. This was exactly how we needed her. Happy and confident, like she was with Duke Beren the other day. 'Let's go and see if he's up yet.'

We presented the case to the king over breakfast. He seemed to buy Selena's tale of the vision, then listened to me wide-eyed as I listed all that Conor had promised the Khagan for his daughter's hand. There came a point when I thought he might get upset with our interference, pushing me to inform him that Isabell was pregnant. I watched him recalculate the value of those territories in his mind rather quickly at that. Besides, this was a long-term investment, buying peace for possibly centuries if all went well, as well as the alliance of a much larger and more powerful country. I hoped he could see that, too.

When I then reassured him that Isabell was well, and Conor shielded her from the Khagan's wrath, he wanted to see Conor straight away and thank him in person. I managed to persuade him to let him sleep for now, but he promised to visit him later along with his personal physician to attend to his wounds.

We went to have our own breakfast with Selena afterwards, then visited Storn in the stable. I sent her out with him for a ride after I quietly warned Storn about keeping Conor's injuries to himself. I wanted to make some progress with that last book, just in case I found anything in there. At noon we re-joined the king for lunch, then the two of them headed to his bedchamber again, with me following not far behind.

To distract myself from any irrational jealousy, I thought of Conor instead as I waited. Would he appreciate those healing rooms now in the Pantheon more? Would he want to come back with us, so his face healed properly?

Persuading him to stay in the Order as a Champion reminded me of those documentaries from primitive planets, where capturing a large, powerful beast took multiple attempts with various harpoons and nets. He knew the three of us could stay together that way. He was promised money! Powers! I'd said we would settle down in his home country because he didn't like the majestic city so much. Even Aiki had cast her own spell on him, and although I secretly relished her efforts, that was a risky game to play. She seemed to have her own reasons, I just hoped she knew what she was getting into.

The door opened, and I saw the king leave his room. After a minute or two, I went and looked for our girl. The two guards outside stopped me briefly, but after a brief explanation, let me through.

She lay on the king's bed, her tiredness creeping into my body as I entered. She pushed herself upright when she saw me and smiled, but I could tell how much effort it took her.

'It went much better than yesterday,' she told me excitedly. 'The king had an old scar on his ankle, and even that disappeared. And watch this.' She untied her dress on the side and pulled the material away so I could see her hip. There was only a faint line where she had apparently cut herself in the Pantheon. I kneeled beside her and kissed it, making her shiver.

'Come on.' I tied her dress back. 'I'll take you home.' I lifted her into my arms and carried her out of the room.

It was strange to feel tired but have my muscles work as if it had nothing to do with them. Because it didn't. It was only my brain confusing the two. In the end, we reached her door, and I put her down on her feet. She looked at me, and I knew what she was going to say before she asked.

'Won't you come in?'

There it was again, like a test I had to pass daily. Only instead of getting easier, it only grew more difficult. Say "no" and she would be sad again. Say "yes" and it was impossible to tell what she might do once we were inside.

'Best not.' I kissed her forehead softly. 'There's something I should go and check,' I said, inviting her to ask what, so I could say "I'll tell you later", and go.

She remained silent instead, making me linger. And just when I thought she had accepted my decision: 'How about just for five minutes?'

I wanted to say "no". But my heart already said "yes". Let's be honest, I wanted to go in. I wanted to go in and not come out for days. Weeks, even!

'Only five minutes, and you promise me you won't be upset when I leave. Deal?'

'Yes.' She smiled.

'Promise me!'

'I promise.'

We went in. She lay down on the bed facing away from me, waiting, and I followed her like iron drawn to a magnet. I held her and kissed her head like I always did, making her smile. Then, despite knowing better, I slowly slid down and kissed her neck, moving on to her shoulder where her dress left it bare and kissed that, too. I pressed my forehead against her back. My desire fused with hers, and I tried to resist them both like a dry leaf might resist an inferno. I knew that to succeed, I had to sacrifice what I wanted now for what I wanted eventually, but it was so hard. The only thing that kept me from devouring her was wanting to be a man who deserved her. Not someone who failed at his task. We only had tomorrow now to make this a success, and I needed to make sure we did, not spend the day in bed!

I pushed myself up and held her a few minutes longer with my head against hers.

'A glass of Golden Kabar before I go?' I murmured into her ear.

'Yes, please.' She smiled.

I got up and poured the drink for her. She sat up on the bed, and I joined her, watching her sip the sweet wine.

'Did it feel any different today? Apart from the strength of the healing increasing?'

She shook her head, as I thought she might. I raked my hand through my hair. I knew I was missing something. But what?

'The annoying thing is,' she said, 'that I feel like I could eventually heal the king if he was blind right now. But I'm worried that if I did this after his birthday, I wouldn't succeed. The curse would just, you know, strike and strike again until it won the fight.'

Which was more or less what she had told me before, only phrased differently.

I stared at her. 'What did you say?'

She repeated it, but I no longer heard her. The whole picture clicked into place in my head, my mind busy turning it around and around to look at it from every angle. Could this be true?

'What is it?' she asked.

'Just something occurred to me that I should check.' I took the empty glass from her hand. 'Get some rest.' I leaned down to her and kissed her forehead.

I closed her door behind me and forced myself to walk along the corridor in a causal manner. I wanted to run. I wanted my invisibility cloak on my back. But I knew neither was an option. My mind raced along all the relevant pieces I had collected from Conor, Selena and the books since we arrived. Of course! This had to be it!

I headed towards the west end of the building, where Conor usually disappeared in the evenings. I passed various people on the way. Maids, workmen, knights, kitchen staff—all looking at me curiously. In their eyes, Conor had almost a kind of celebrity status, I noticed, while Selena was the incarnation of the powerful witch their ancestors had wronged in the past and now was their only chance to make things right. How I fitted into the picture they couldn't fathom. The strange man who just read all day, but somehow still managed to find a way into the Scarlet Witch's bed at nights. Not that he took advantage of his good fortune. The fool!

I turned a corner and found the place I was looking for. A quieter part of the palace, but still too busy for my liking. The corridor was narrower, the tapestries less fancy but still grand and glorious in the afternoon sunshine that poured in through the large windows on the right. On the left, a few closed doors, among them the dark green one Conor had described to me. This was the one he had to avoid at all costs when sneaking around with Aurelia. It was the one I had to go through.

A grey-haired man carrying an awl and a chisel approached from the opposite direction, and I passed by the door, pretending to head towards the exit to the garden at the end of the corridor. Once he was out of sight, I stopped and turned, eyeing the door nervously. Conor would be so much better at this! What should I do? Wait? Go and knock? I didn't want to speak with anyone in there or be seen entering. As I mulled over my options, the door suddenly opened. I watched Lord Dranos come out, close it behind him and hurry down the corridor without even looking my way. I waited until a knight passed me by, and once he went outside, I darted for the door, hoping no one else was inside.

I entered a large study and quickly closed the door behind me. I had no idea how much time I had or what exactly I was looking for, but so far, I had been lucky for once! He could have locked the door.

There were a couple of bookcases around me, a set of other shelves, a large, elegant desk, a few chests in the corner and several chairs around a smaller, round table. From the study, another room opened, which looked like a bedroom from where I stood. A set of large windows were open, long, green curtains half-drawn across them. Outside, someone walked past, whistling to themself. I went and closed the curtains completely. A low growl behind me made me pause.

A wolf-like hound came slowly out of the bedroom, baring its sharp teeth at me. I had zero experience with dogs, but the way it shifted its weight to its front legs told me that it was preparing to lunge.

'Easy! Easy!' I panicked and hurriedly searched my pockets for anything useful. The beast took a few more steps forward, wrinkling its muzzle and snarling. My fingers caught on something smooth, and I pulled out Storn's projector. The dog's eyes followed my hand with interest.

'What's this? Shall I show you? Yes?'

The dog barked furiously, then growled again.

I cast the footage between us, lowering the volume as the king started speaking. The dog tilted its head, seemingly impressed by my magic trick, then started wagging its tail and barked at the king a few times.

'Who's that? King Sirion? Do you know him?' The dog kept shifting its eyes between me and the king, but it looked more relaxed now. It panted with its tongue poking out and lowered itself onto the carpet, its front paws stretched out. I stopped the recording, at which point the hound lifted its head, closed its mouth, and sternly looked at me.

'Alright, alright! Here!' I restarted the footage, then looked around. On one of the higher shelves, there was a plate with some kind of biscuits on it. I carefully took a few slow steps towards it. The dog stood but made no attempt to stop me. By the time I reached for the biscuits, it was at my feet, sitting straight, looking at me excitedly, its tail pounding against my legs.

'Is this yours? It's nice, is it? Want some more?' I put away the projector while the dog was distracted with the biscuits, then went to the desk.

I started shifting through the contents of a wooden tray full of letters and other documents, freezing every time I heard someone approach along the corridor. Would I even hear Lord Dranos coming back, or would he surprise me? I'd be tempted to lock the door, had I seen a key in it. It made complete sense now why Conor was a thief, the little adrenaline-junkie.

There was a locked drawer in the desk. I shook the handle gently. I could have forced it open, but I didn't want to raise suspicion.

The sound of female laughter made me pause.

'I think it might be just so her magic doesn't weaken for when she needs it with the king,' one voice said as they passed in front of the door. 'Maybe he would tire her out too much after just sitting in the library all day.'

Exactly! I thought. You go, tell them, girl! I left the desk and went to check the chests in the corner. The first one was open. I started unpacking it quickly, rummaging through Lord Dranos's personal items.

Suddenly, there was a knock. I turned and saw the dog stand again, looking at me. Then it turned and ran to the door with such menacing growling and barking that even my heart started hammering again. I understood now why Lord Dranos didn't bother locking his door. I doubted many who lived or worked in the palace ever entered his quarters uninvited.

'Are you looking for Lord Dranos?' the same female voice asked outside.

'Yes,' a man said.

'I just saw him talking to Jon at the falconry.'

I reached for another biscuit for the dog as the voices quieted. It came and took it from my hand this time, licking my fingers.

'You really love these, don't you?'

It agreed with a short, high-pitched whine, then closed its mouth and looked up at the plate with fake agitation. I passed him one more, then put everything back into the chest and tried to open the other one. It was locked. I eyed the lock wearily, screaming Conor's name in my head in frustration. The dog came to supervise my attempts, sniffing at the chest.

'Do you know where the key is?' I asked causally.

It closed its mouth, tilted its head and looked at me thoughtfully. I patted its head the same way I did Storn's, then got up and went to search through the bedroom. I found a key rather cleverly hidden in the inside of a wardrobe after I practically took the whole thing apart. I went back to the chest and opened it.

Inside, almost on the very top, was a book that looked older and plainer than the ones on the shelf. I untied its leather bindings and carefully opened it. On the first page was a recipe. On the second, another that looked even more interesting. In the rest, chronological recordings going back centuries. I didn't think the book was actually that old. It was probably just a copy. But even so, it was impressive. I could have digitalised the whole thing with my lenses within a few minutes. Now, I had to spend those minutes memorising the first two pages.

I understood why Ithorion disapproved so strongly of us carrying modern objects with us. He wanted us to exercise and improve our bodies and brains instead of relying on technology that could be taken away from us. And in theory, I supported his way of thinking completely. But just then, as an approaching storm of angry voices hit me from the corridor, I wished it all to hell.

I shoved the book back into its place, then looked around. There was absolutely nowhere to hide. I could hear Lord Dranos's voice among the others and a woman's I recognised as Aurelia's. Through the window, I thought, and rushed to open the curtains. I closed them immediately with the same move. Outside on the garden path, the king stood talking with the knight-commander. No, no, no, no, no, no! The door was opening now, and I jumped next to the window, pulling the long curtain over me.

I was sure they must have seen the fabric move, but the four people entering were talking over each other in a heated conversation and paid little attention to the surroundings they knew so well.

'Lower your voices and get in there. Felix, down!' Lord Dranos ordered his three offspring and their dog around. 'Aurelia, close the windows!'

I swallowed and watched Aurelia enter my line of vision as she closed the glassed panels. Had she looked to her left, she would have spotted me standing there, pressed against the wall, but her eyes were on the king. Then she turned right, following the others to the bedroom. 'Listen to Jon, Father. This is madness!'

They closed the bedroom door behind them and talked more quietly, but I could still hear snatches of their argument.

'… in this situation because that fool Kenter was leading the negotiations,' Lord Dranos was saying now. 'Once the war breaks out, proving them to be unsuccessful, and Sirion loses his eyesight, I can persuade him to let Aron take over. We'll convince the Harags they have a better option …'

I thought of making my escape now. I had what I came for. I could even pick up the book on my way out as evidence. Alert the king and stop this all now! He would never lose his sight, could marry Isabell, and we would be free to leave. Easy! I thought of Jon and Aurelia. All the friendly conversations we'd had over dinner. They were both so bright. They had inherited their father's resourcefulness and tactical skills that clearly ran in the family, but unlike their father, who was ambitious, and their older brother, Aron, who was arrogant and selfish, their hearts were in the right place. Jon had two young boys and a wife waiting for him at home. Would he be executed along with his siblings and his father as a consequence of my actions?

Maybe there was another way. But then I needed Lord Dranos to stick to the plan he was forcing on Aurelia and Jon even now, with Aron backing him up. Knowing exactly what he was up to was the only way to play this right.

Which meant staying where I was and waiting for a chance, no matter how risky or how foolish I felt. The missing biscuits could have been just down to a maid who did the cleaning or one of his children coming in earlier, but he was bound to notice the missing key. I had to put it back at the earliest opportunity, after adjusting the book's bindings and locking the chest.

'I hate you!' Aurelia shouted as she burst out of the bedroom sobbing and ran out of the study, leaving the door open. I heard the dog scurry after her.

'Aurelia, come back, immediately!' her father called out, then started off after her, too. Aron chuckled and made his exit, too. Jon was the last one to leave, his steps slow, like a defeated man walking to meet his end.

I rushed to the chest, adjusted the book, and locked it in record time, then darted into the bedroom and put the key back. Jon hadn't even bothered closing the door behind him, so I just slipped out as soon as the corridor was clear.

I made my way to the library to see if the king had a book on herbs. Once I found it, I picked it up and headed off to take Storn out for a ride myself.

I returned at sunset, my head full of plans. But with darkness spreading its wings above me, my heart also filled with a longing for Selena. Would she have had her bath yet? Was she waiting for me in bed? I knew I had to speak to her, and Conor, too, before pulling her into my arms under the blanket tonight, but maybe I could just hold her again for five minutes first.

I found them in Conor's bed. Him without a shirt, feeling guilty and calmly holding her in a way I couldn't. Not without losing my head, anyway. She snuggled against Conor, exhausted.

'What's going on?' I asked, but one more look at Conor and I knew. His face wasn't completely healed, but it was vastly better than this morning. Only a little swelling and a light purple line indicated that anything had happened there. His torso, where it wasn't covered by Selena, looked even better.

'She insisted,' he said defensively, stroking her in his arms.

She rolled over and turned to face me, worry now in her eyes over what I thought of the situation, but too tired to get up. I walked to the bed, expecting Conor to sit up at least, but he seemed to have decided not to even lift a muscle. I couldn't help but wonder where his head had been during all this big healing treatment!

I sat down on the edge of the bed, then leaned down to Selena and kissed the wrinkles away on her forehead. 'You should be more careful not to overdo these things,' I scolded her gently.

I glanced over at Conor as I straightened up, but he was smiling at me, content. They both were now.

I guessed it was time for me to talk. I was pretty sure this wasn't how other toras briefed their circles before their last day on a job. I imagined Clive Walker sitting around a table with his team, going through every little detail with them multiple times. Whereas we looked like I had come in to tell them a bedtime story.

But did it really matter? Selena's exhaustion was pulling at me with the gravitational force of a black hole. I kicked off my shoes and squeezed onto the bed next to them.

'So, the reason why nobody was able to break the curse before is that there is no curse,' I informed them. That stirred them enough to remind Conor how to lift his head from the pillow, and even Selena sat up, both looking at me, confused. I put my hands under my head and stretched, taking my time to find a comfortable position.

'What are you saying?' Conor prompted me when he couldn't take my games anymore.

'It's the Dranos family who's been poisoning the kings all this time.'

'But why?' Selena asked.

'I imagine the first time it happened, four hundred years ago, they did it because they found Renold II too awful to bear. He wasn't just a terrible ruler, he was also a cruel psychopath who enjoyed tormenting others. He used to organise orgies. According to the records, the Dranos family had a young daughter at the time, and this is just speculation, but anything could have happened.

'They shifted the blame onto the Scarlet Witch, who was the King's mistress at the time, and it's difficult to tell now whether that was intentional or accidental, but the fact remains that she was executed for their crimes. With time, they gained Renold's trust, and convinced him to take a number of steps which all turned out very beneficial for the kingdom. They slowly started building it back from the ruin the king's first seven years on the throne had left it.

'The king's firstborn was a spoiled brat, but he still inherited the throne on his eighteenth birthday, as everyone, apart from the Dranos family, agreed that it's better to have a king who can see, even if he was young and inexperienced. After ten years of wasting the gold from the treasury on meaningless wars, however, the curse struck again, and the Dranos family once again gained influence over the leading of the country. Then they just kept it up. They've been technically governing the country for centuries from the background.'

'How do they do it?' Conor asked. 'They use the wine, don't they?'

'Yes.' I nodded. 'It has such a sweet, complex aroma that it hides the poison relatively well. I found the recipe in Lord Dranos's study, and I've already collected and verified the ingredients with Storn. Some of it was easy to find and buy on the market, some of it more difficult, but nothing is impossible when you have the kind of coin we do. The rest we just picked up in the forest. The combination of toxins from a certain fungus and a poisonous plant can attack the eye, cause inflammation and seriously damage the optic nerve. The rest is there to help to mix them easier and dull the taste.'

'So, every time someone healed the king, they just used the poison again?' Selena looked aghast.

'Exactly as you said this afternoon.' I smiled. 'The curse just struck again! Until the healers gave up or the poison eventually did so much damage, nobody could do anything about it anymore.'

'And how about all those sorcerers, witches and wizards? Couldn't they tell there was no curse?'

'I imagine, as Conor told me once before, those who can actually wield magic are incredibly rare on Drelos. Most were probably just trying their luck, hoping for the reward.'

'And those few who could wield magic?' she insisted.

'I don't know,' I admitted. 'Could you not tell there was no curse, oh Supreme Key of the Dragon?' I grinned at her. 'Maybe you can ask Ithorion about it when you're next feeling brave.'

'How do you want to handle this?' Conor asked, his eyes thoughtful.

'Surely we tell the king?' Selena argued.

'We might not,' I admitted.

'What? Why?'

'Various reasons. Lord Dranos has been the king's closest advisor all his life, while he only met us last week. Which doesn't mean we couldn't eventually prove our case, but it could get ugly. Lord Dranos is a cunning man. He could try to twist this around or blame others. And even if we succeed, a well-loved and respected family would be executed based on the word of a thief and two foreigners, which would leave a bitter taste for many. News travels very differently here to your world or mine. People are far less educated. Even if the king believed us, others in the country might not—which doesn't bode well for us if we want a home here. Not to mention, Aurelia and Jon are against it. It's their father blackmailing them to accept his decision. Which wouldn't save their lives if the family secret was found out. Plus, that would also mean no more Dranos Golden Kabar for you and Conor anymore! Ever! Imagine!'

'You're not suggesting that we let them get away with this?' She frowned at me.

'Oh, no.' I smiled. 'See, the real shame in all this is that they are such excellent tacticians! They *should* be involved in the running of the country. But not like this. It's going to be on our terms.'

'But how can we ensure they keep to anything we might agree with them once we've left?' Conor pointed out. 'It's not like we're going to stay here to supervise them.'

'This is why I thought we should involve Duke Beren. That way, we can get the cloak back from him, too. Two birds with one stone!' And I told them my plan.

'I like it.' Conor grinned at me.

'I thought you might.'

'And all I have to do is pretend again?' Selena complained.

'Come on, Sel, it's an important part of the job. It will be much safer to make it look like you broke the curse. It's what everyone expects to happen anyway. This way, Conor gets a full pardon from the crown, and we'll be welcomed here at any time.'

'I just feel so useless. I wish I could do stuff!'

'But you've been doing stuff …' I trailed off when Conor shot me a warning look from behind her. I couldn't understand why she didn't see the value in what she'd been doing. We wouldn't even be here if not for her! Never would have found out about Isabell, either. 'What stuff would you like to do?' I asked instead.

'I don't know,' she grumbled. 'Real stuff!'

I wrapped her in my arms. 'Come on, you're just tired.' I made her lie down on the bed.

'Real stuff like you and Conor can do,' she muttered. 'Will you teach me?'

I had no idea what this was all about. 'Of course, I'll teach you,' I murmured and kissed her hair the way I did in the evenings. It didn't make her happy like it normally did. 'Conor will teach you, too,' I added and looked at him. 'Conor?'

'Of course, I will,' he confirmed.

'All the stuff!' she insisted in a quiet grumble now.

'Yes. Conor will teach you all the stuff,' I repeated, kissing her hair again and again. It seemed to calm her. 'I will teach you all the stuff, too.'

'Good.' She sighed and closed her eyes.

I looked at Conor, puzzled, but he just shook his head. I had a feeling that whatever the problem was, it wasn't just about her skills or capabilities. No, this went deeper than that. I stroked her arm thoughtfully, wondering what I could do to help.

I talked quietly for a long time after that with Conor in the dark, our murmurs sending Selena between us asleep. In the end, I was tempted to close my eyes, too. But I gathered the Scarlet Witch into my arms and carried her next door instead. There was no need to confuse the staff even more.

Chapter 26

Selena

Caledon, Drelos,
11th The Month of Red Blessing 1575

Sourcing Specialist, Scarlet Witch, Supreme Key of the Dragon … everyone seemed to know what those meant and who I was more than me! I'd started to get fed up with putting on the make-up every morning and getting into character. It wasn't even pretending to be a Scarlet Witch that made me unhappy if I was being honest. It was the uncanny feeling that I'd been pretending all my life.

I wanted to be myself again. But when I tried, there was nothing there. Or I just couldn't see it. Couldn't find it. I just was. Empty and lost.

On top of everything, I lay now on the bed alone and terrified. After breakfast, where I told the king that today was the third and final cleansing ritual which would complete the breaking of the curse and that he was only allowed to drink water all day until sunset, as Kris advised me to do, I excused myself and said I needed to rest first. I did feel tired.

I lay down in my room and stared at the open window. I listened to the sounds from outside and eventually closed my eyes. I think I was awake, but I saw images in my mind and heard voices as if in a dream, until something snapped, and my eyes flew open. My heart was beating fast, my head felt heavy and dread, like a dark, hungry beast that knew me too well had crawled up inside me. I tried to shake it off, but I couldn't. Inside my head, it kept me paralysed, holding me between life and death, pushing me down a path I didn't want to follow.

I sat up and got out of bed. I walked around a little, staring into the mirror, then at the garden through the window, hugging myself and shaking. I felt dizzy and tired, and all I wanted to do was to go back to bed again. I knew I shouldn't. I had to distract myself somehow. But I didn't want to leave the room like this, and eventually, I found myself crawling back into bed.

It had been some time since I was this unwell. Kris's presence kept the panic attacks away at night, and before I met him, reading Dr.

Montgomery's book had helped a lot. I wished I had it with me now. I tried to think back to what he told me. His reassuring tone of voice. It wasn't even what he said, but how he said it. Making me understand and believe, that this was just a phase. Something that would pass. Not the end.

My mind relaxed a little at that, and I clung to the memory of his face and smile like a shipwreck casualty might hold on to a wooden board out on the stormy sea.

Kris said that he wasn't just his uncle, but also part of our soul circle. Which explained why he looked so familiar at the counselling session and how we bonded so quickly. James. I wondered where he was now. I knew Kris and Ithorion were trying to find him. I hoped he was alright and we would see him again soon.

There was a knock on the door. I pushed myself upright and went to see who wanted what now. My terror was tamed, but its residue still pulsed in me like an icy fog, making me cold and weak.

I opened the door. It was Kris outside, unwilling to come in.

'Ready for lunch?' he asked.

'Is that the time already?' It seemed impossible. Lunch, then I had to do healing on the king, powerful enough to convince him he was free of the curse. I felt it was too much effort to just stand there and keep my eyes on Kris.

He nodded with a small frown. I tried to smile. 'I'll come around soon. I just need a few more minutes.' I closed the door and went back to bed. If he didn't want to come in, he should stay outside. I had stuff to deal with. I collapsed on the bed and buried my face into the pillow.

I heard the door open and close. He sat on the bed and stroked my back. 'What's wrong?'

I didn't know what to say. Me? That I was just like this? Broken? Not strong enough to keep it together on the last day? I had only ever described my struggles to his uncle and even that was hard. I didn't want to talk to Kris about it. I was too afraid what he might think of me afterwards. How he might feel about me then. I didn't want to lose what we had.

'My head,' I said in the end. It was true enough.

He combed my hair aside with his fingers and started massaging the back of my head, his hand slowly moving down to my neck.

'So tense,' he said, as if it was all my fault.

'I'm sorry,' I mumbled into the pillow.

'It's only because we've been cooped up here all this time with hardly any exercise. It will all change after tomorrow.' I didn't respond to that. We could have exercised plenty! At nights. But I wasn't exactly sure why we weren't. I was too afraid to find out the reason, so I just kept quiet, letting him talk about all the training he had in mind for us in the upcoming months, as if that should please me.

When I gave no sign of enthusiasm, he took his hand away and kissed me instead. Once. Twice. Three times. His lips burning a path along the curve of my neck, relaxing a set of muscles in the area instantly, tightening others lower down.

'Better now?' he murmured in my ear and I could tell he was smiling. Then, without waiting for an answer, his fingers were back, playing a symphony along my spine.

I wanted to turn and kiss him, but I chickened out again. My mind was on those kisses, though. Surely, he didn't just do it to loosen my neck. He could be remarkably practical sometimes, but surely not that practical? Could he?

There was another knock on the door.

'What are you doing? The king is waiting!' Conor walked in. 'He hasn't started eating without you, so everybody's just sitting there, waiting with him.'

'How are you feeling now?' Kris made me sit up.

'Just a bit weak.'

'Some food will help. Come on.'

I re-adjusted my make-up and hair in the mirror, then went with them.

A general delight spread across the table in the dining hall once Conor reappeared with the two of us, everyone smiling, exchanging looks and whispering comments behind their hands. I wanted to apologise, but I knew that I mustn't. I was a powerful witch once again, who could fool around with her lover and make kings wait if she wanted to, before getting a quick bite and breaking four-hundred-year-old curses nobody else could.

I smiled at the king, though, then took my place with my head held high. I put some food on my plate, but I couldn't eat, so I sat straight for a while, forcing my back muscles to do the work, despite wanting to just collapse over the table. I kept my face blank, but inside, my mind was churning. Why did it have to go all wrong at the last minute? Wasn't this typical? What would I do if the panic attack returned while treating the king, or if I was still too weak to start? Last night I was unhappy with the smallness of my role, and here I was today, unable to do even that. I bet Kris was disappointed in me now. They probably both were.

Suddenly I was back in that counselling room, sitting behind the desk. Outside it was gloomy, raindrops pattered on the windows. Inside, I was facing James, his light blue eyes never leaving mine as he went through those unhelpful thinking patterns with me.

'How about assuming we know what someone else is thinking or predicting what's going to happen?' he asked.

'Jumping to conclusions.' I said at the time.

'And blowing things out of proportion?'

'Catastrophising. Viewing situations as worse than they are.'

'How about focusing on the negative part of a situation and forgetting the positive parts?'

'Mental filter.'

'Mental filter. What are the positive parts of our current situation?'

I stared in front of me. The positive parts. What were the positive parts? I looked to my right. Kris turned his head and looked at me, too. Calm, serious, focused. Ever since we'd met, all I'd done was try to impress him. And the same urge was there even now. But maybe it was time that I tried to impress myself for once.

I turned back to my food and started eating. He was right. I needed some energy in me from somewhere. He shifted closer and put his arm around my lower back. I carried on slicing, chewing, swallowing, as if nothing had happened. He stroked me and pulled his hand back. There was enough determination in my eyes to show him that I needed to swim without a lifebelt now.

I finished my food and looked around. The king was no longer eating, either, but chatting with the others around him. My eyes caught on Lord Dranos among them. I noticed that only Aron was at lunch with him. Aurelia and Jon were missing.

'How are you feeling? Do you need some more time?' Conor asked quietly. I looked at him and saw something more than concern in his eyes.

Guilt. He had wanted me to rest yesterday and not waste my magic, as he put it, on him. I convinced him to let me. I told him it was out of the question. I was still furious at the Harag warlord for what he'd done to him. And now Conor blamed himself for my weakness. That gave me the final push I needed.

'No.' I smiled, then leaned close to him. 'Go, do your thing. I'll do mine. We'll celebrate tomorrow,' I whispered.

He smiled back and nodded.

I stood and the king stood with me. I went to him, and he offered me his arm.

We walked up to his bedroom and closed the door. The window shutters were also pulled to keep away the afternoon sun, casting shadows across the room. I sat down on his bed as usual and took a deep breath. I knew that if I thought of how I'd felt that morning in my room, it was likely to start again. Still, a part of me reached for it, as you might scratch a scab, making it bleed again.

In the meantime, the king took off his boots and, just like on the last occasion, undressed down to his waist. Conor did the same thing half-way through our session last night. Apparently, whatever I did, it generated a lot of heat.

My hands felt cold now and shaky. The king looked at me as he climbed up onto the bed. I knew it was certainty he needed to see in me, not despair. The curse will be broken, I thought, regardless of what I do here today. The king can have Isabell in his arms tomorrow! That made me happy, and I smiled.

'Please lie down, your majesty,' I said briskly, but I kept my hands on the bed by my sides, wishing I could sit on them for a while. He settled down, and I watched his bearded face relax as he closed his eyes. I wondered if he was thinking of Isabell, too.

My own thoughts flew to Kris, his features blurry in my foggy mind. But I still remembered how his kisses felt on my neck. The longing to turn and have my lips on his. How I missed him even now! And just like that, the swirling was there. See? Nothing to worry about, I told myself. It works like magic!

I found the escape I needed in the work. It focused me in ways that left no room for anything else. I could make the energy flow through me as if it was a warm river and pour it into the king, looking for anything to mend, anything wrong to wash away. It was calming, but at the same time, it also filled me with a happiness unlike anything else. A glow almost. Which gave me an idea. If I could somehow shine, that would help convince the king that I'd done it. That this was different from what other healers might have done in the past. I knew I had glowed back in the Pantheon, when I was up in the air. If I could just do that again somehow.

'Don't overdo it.' I heard Kris's voice in my head. I knew he was nearby, waiting. Would he carry me back to my room again? I was sure he would, and that made me smile. I closed my eyes and thought back to the initiation ceremony.

What happened on that bridge still filled me with awe. That powerful sensation of connecting. Bonding. The ceremony wasn't just about joining an order. It was also joining him. Meroth. The Dragon. I felt him in my heart at the time. In my mind. In places and ways I had no words for. No understanding of. A spark of that memory pulsed in me still.

I remembered how he lifted me. How he turned me around. A clarity flashing through me. A drop of perfect awareness, echoing between me and the stars. It quieted into a glow, as if I were a piece of iron lifted from the forge. I thought of that glow now. How it throbbed in me, making my skin tingle, my eyes light up, allowing me to look beyond the world as I knew it.

I held that spark in my mind and blew on it. Making it clearer, brighter, until its light spread through me. It lit up the room and I felt the king sit up. I opened my eyes. He was sitting opposite me now, his expression full of wonder. He saw more than just a woman in front of him, and in turn, I saw more than a man. A contour of his past, present and future. A potential in him.

I placed my right hand back onto his forehead and combined my healing energy with the glow, letting it flow through him.

'Your curse is broken, Sirion,' I said. 'May you now fulfil your destiny and become the best king this kingdom has ever had.'

The light intensified for a moment, then rapidly diminished. The king took my hand and kissed it. 'Thank you, my lady.'

A darkness descended now, and I needed all the energy I had left in me and more to smile and say, 'I need to rest now.'

'Selena! Sel!' I heard Kris's voice in my ear. I opened my eyes. I was back in my own bed, the fading light outside turning the room dark.

I sat up fast, crashing into him. 'I didn't miss it, did I?'

'No, the dinner is just about to start,' he reassured me. 'But you can stay here and rest, we have a plan B. I just knew you'd be upset with me if I didn't wake you.'

'No, no! I'm coming! Help me with the candles.'

He made some light while I brushed my hair quickly and picked out my most daring dress from the wardrobe.

'I'll be outside.' He smiled and let me get on.

We joined Conor at the long table in the great hall. He smiled up at me appreciatively. All around us, finely dressed ladies and men were settling down. The usual group of court musicians set up their instruments in the corner and started to play.

'Oh, not this again,' I muttered under my breath. Opposite to me, Baroness Greta heard me and shot me a look of agreement.

'You ladies don't like music?' Conor recoiled in mock horror.

'Certainly not this mouse whining!' The Baroness rolled her eyes, sharing a flirtatious smile with Conor. I was getting used to it. Ever since the feast in the Pantheon, or even at Rhia's party before that and then almost every day since when Aurelia wasn't around, or occasionally even when she was, something like this would happen. Conor radiated a natural charm, a charisma most women found irresistible. And he wasn't shy to take advantage of it, either! Kris told me Conor was one of those men who didn't get attached to women. I could see what that meant. Which wasn't to say that I didn't find it sometimes a little awkward sitting beside him. When I showed the slightest sign of it, he would laugh and start paying attention to me as if nobody else mattered, and I knew he would hug me if I wasn't there as a Scarlet Witch. Then he would go back to flirting with the other women.

We went through the courses, and I made sure I hardly touched my red wine, opting for water instead. Finally, they began serving dessert, and sweet wine started appearing in front us. Thankfully, the musicians also decided to take a break and stopped torturing us. The Dranos family had been ominously absent from dinner, save for Aron, who sat not far from us, but now Lord Dranos came into the hall, holding two glasses in his hand.

'Our best vintage!' He offered one to the king and started chatting with him. Kris stood up beside me and wandered over to them. Conor turned and grinned at me, his face like a child's at Christmas. I tried to not to stare, even if I knew what was happening. Instead, I sat motionless, waiting for my turn. A few minutes later, an invisible hand squeezed my right shoulder. I knew this meant two things.

One was that Lord Dranos had unknowingly poured a harmless substance into the King's wine that Kris had made, and Conor secretly swapped for his poison that afternoon. The real poison was now added to Lord Dranos's wine instead by an invisible Duke Beren. The other, since the squeeze was at my right shoulder and not the left, was that Aron had opted not to have Kabar this evening and was sticking to his red instead. I took Kris's untouched glass and filled it with the sweet wine along with mine. I waited, and soon enough, I could see the top part of a vial appear over the brim and a small amount of liquid fall into Kris's glass. It was such a quick, barely noticeable action, you really had to look close to see it, and even then it was hard to believe.

'Are you deserting me?' Conor asked as I stood, pretending offence. 'Just so you know, I shall be keeping my eye on you!' He shot me his flirtatious smile.

'Maybe next time you'll make more effort to impress me, my dear.' I raised my eyebrows, making him gasp in indignation. I walked over to Aron, smiling at him.

'Lady Selena!' He stood, surprised, but seemingly pleased. I guessed he was merry at the sight of the king finishing his drink.

'I thought you might share a drink with me to the king's health.' I offered him Kris's glass.

'Ah, that's very thoughtful, but I don't really feel like sweet wine tonight,' he said flatly, his dark eyes watching me carefully.

'Oh, but I insist!' I sweetened my smile and looked deep into his eyes. 'I love this wine so much, and I shall be leaving the day after tomorrow. I'd love to have a glass with the man producing it before I go.'

'Well, that would be more my brother, Jon, but I guess I can stand in his place.' He smiled and took my glass from me, instead of the one I was holding out for him. He raised it. 'To the king's health!'

I raised mine, the smile frozen on my face. 'Why don't we sit down?' I pulled Lord Dranos's chair out next to his, playing for time. He took his own chair, smiling, then looked at me.

'Your Majesty, my dear lords and ladies!' I heard Conor's voice from the middle of the hall, loud and clear. 'I must beg your forgiveness in advance if this is a little rusty. It's been a long time since I last held a guitar in my hand. And to be fair, even then I was drunk!' he admitted to the crowd, raising a laugh. Aron held on to his glass but turned to watch, eager to see Conor make a fool of himself. Conor did mention before that he had lived in a monastery where they sang and played instruments on occasion, but he never elaborated, and I had quite forgotten about it. As it was now, he confidently plucked the strings and took everyone by surprise with his voice, commanding all eyes on him like a star. He must have also worked on his repertoire in subsequent years because this was definitely not a song for monks! He sang to the baroness, which just made all the other women in the room yet more keen on him.

Even I was so mesmerised by his performance that Duke Beren had to squeeze my shoulder, prompting me to subtly move my glass to the side. I could feel it being removed from my hand and replaced with another. I glanced over at Aron's glass and I thought I saw the wine sway in it a little. I hoped that meant that the duke succeeded on both accounts.

I had asked Kris whether we could trust the duke. What if he reported all of us to the king, in the hopes of getting an even higher reward? But Kris reassured me that the duke was smart enough to want us as his allies rather than his enemies. I really hoped that was true, or things would get even more interesting in the morning.

Aron drank his wine, annoyed, but not before making sure I had finished mine. Not wanting to seem suspicious, I talked to him for a while even as the king stood, ready to call it a night. In truth, I could hardly wait to leave. Aron's whole personality repelled me as if I had been trying to make friends with a snake. I didn't understand how Lord Dranos's children could be so different from one another.

'Not much Golden Kabar going around tonight, Lord Dranos!' I heard the king remark. 'Are we running out already?'

'Fear not, my lord king, there should be six more barrels arriving on the morrow for your birthday,' Lord Dranos said. 'And just to ease any qualms you might have during the night, I also personally delivered a bottle to your bedchamber on my way here.'

'Good man!' The king smiled then turned to leave.

I glanced over at Conor. He was sitting next to the Baroness on the opposite side of the table. His lips formed a thin line as our eyes met and I could tell this was not part of the plan.

Two hands appeared on my arms, stroking them, and I looked up to see Kris standing behind my chair. His eyes were on Conor.

'There's a bottle in Selena's room. Go!' he called out to him in Elesean in a friendly manner, as if exchanging pleasantries.

'Leave it on the windowsill.' Conor winked at me, then changing back to Wedan, 'Enjoy your night!'

'My lady?' Kris looked down at me. 'Ready to retire for the night?' I stood without a second thought. 'I'm sorry for stealing her,' Kris said to Aron in an apologetic tone, but even the deaf would have been able to tell he wasn't sorry at all. He put his arm around me and leaned close to kiss my hair. 'Slowly,' he whispered in my ear.

My heart was in my throat and all I wanted to do was run after the king. Instead, I smiled contentedly and let Kris make a show of us ambling towards the opposite exit.

Once we were outside, he took my hand in his and we rushed through the corridor and up the stairs.

'I'll distract him if you get the bottle,' I offered as we reached the second floor and finally spotted the king.

'Other way around,' he said. 'The guards will be more likely to let you in.'

'My lord king!' he called out once we caught up with him. 'I hope you don't mind, but I wanted to ask something.'

I passed them with an apologetic smile and hurried on. A few more turns and I was at his bedchamber, the guards outside looking at me, puzzled.

'The king is on his way, he just stopped to talk with someone.' I saw one of them hesitate, so I added, 'You don't want to displease him by not letting me make myself ready for him, do you?'

The guard bowed his head at that and let me pass.

I entered the room and went straight to the bedside table. On it were a clean glass and the ominous bottle of Golden Kabar. I picked it up, holding it away from me, as if just the smell alone might cause harm. To the windowsill, Conor had said. I went to the window, opened it wide and looked out. The moon shone at me from the middle of the sky, surrounded by a multitude of stars, as if all watching to see what happened next. I wanted to know, too. I looked down, my eyes travelling across the palace wall in the dark. Did Conor mean to climb up here? How?

I could still hear loud voices from the great hall and saw the light spilling out of its large windows onto the dark grass. I watched two knights walk past through the grounds, holding torches. I saw other movements, too, a solitary figure here and there going about their business.

I moved the bottle from the middle of the window to the side, then turned towards the door, wondering if it would be Conor or the king who appeared first and what I would do if it was the latter. Both of them seemed to take forever. Kris was clearly doing his best to give us sufficient time, but I knew he couldn't delay the king forever. Conor must have been similarly held up somewhere, or perhaps had to wait for the right moment. I eyed the bottle nervously. I could just pour its contents out below but then what would I say to the king? That I drank it all? Maybe I should just throw it out and be done with it.

'Lady Selena!' I heard the king's surprised voice behind me, and I knew that my time was up.

'Your Majesty.' I smiled and went to him. 'I hope you don't mind my company.'

'Not at all.' He smiled back, clearly wondering if I was there for the reason, he thought I might be. I was doing my best wondering, too, what other reasons I could possibly have to be in his bedroom alone at night, after the curse was broken, wearing a dress that begged to be taken off me.

'I'd like to make sure that you sleep well tonight,' I said softly, digging myself into an even bigger hole.

He reached up and gently stroked my hair. I reached up, too, and started to unbutton his shirt, wondering what Kris would make of the situation. Would it matter to him? It wasn't like he wanted to do anything of this sort at night! I saw his face clearly in front of me now, twisting my heart, and I knew I couldn't do it. Of course, I couldn't! I loved him. But what now, then? I wondered, and he gave me the idea.

'Lie on your front, Your Majesty.' I smiled as I took the shirt off him.

'On my front this time?' the king asked, intrigued, but he did as I asked.

I kicked off my shoes, climbed onto the bed and started massaging his back, remembering Kris's fingers on me that morning. I felt the king relax under my touch, stretching out and enjoying it.

I saw something from the corner of my eye, and I watched Conor replace the bottles in the window. In turn, he watched me with a face that made me think he might just pick me up and take me, too.

'Go! Go!' I mouthed at him. If the king decided to turn his head, he would notice him instantly.

He shook his head, frowning at me, then jumped into the room without making a sound, and took a few steps towards me. I was so stunned by how quietly he moved that for a while I let him. Then I started gesturing to make him understand that I was trying to make the king fall asleep and had no intention to do anything more. That seemed to relax him, but he still settled down in the room, waiting, making me roll my eyes.

Luckily, the king seemed content with being only massaged, and remembering the look in his eyes when he was with Isabell, I thought I knew why. He was utterly in love with her. Still, it took a long time, but he did fall asleep eventually, and I stood, straightening my dress. By the time I turned and looked at Conor again, he was no longer there.

I told the guards outside to make sure nobody else disturbed the king that night, no matter the reason. I said he needed to rest peacefully for the curse to be completely gone. Then I went to find Kris.

'Nothing happened,' I told him this time straight away. 'I just massaged him until he fell asleep.'

He smiled at me, looking surprisingly unconcerned, but he still pulled me into his arms.

'I'm not going to lie, I had an overwhelming urge to just take out those guards and break down the door on you in the first ten minutes,' he confessed. 'But then I could tell that Conor had joined you and I had to wonder what the two of you were up to with the king for so long.' He chuckled. 'Did he help or was he just taking notes?'

Of course! I kept forgetting that Kris could sense it when either of us were near him. I thought Conor stayed in the room because he felt protective of me. But maybe it was more than that.

'What does it feel like? Sensing that I'm near?' I asked.

He considered that for a moment. 'Like the sun coming out from behind the clouds.'

I grinned up at him, but he just kissed my head, as usual. 'Come on, it's late. Off to bed with you, sorceress.'

In the morning, I woke for a serenade that was nothing like Conor's. It was as if the whole palace were clapping, shouting, singing, making loud noises with whatever they could find.

We jumped out of bed, dressed quickly, and not a moment later, there was a loud knock on the door. I hurried to open it. The king caught me in his arms and lifted me up in the air with a laugh, causing the crowd surrounding him to cheer even louder. Conor was grinning at me from behind him.

'Happy birthday, Your Majesty!' I managed with a smile once he put me down and kissed my hand.

'My lady, I will be forever grateful! Who's coming with me for a ride?' he shouted and turned with a mischievous smile. 'Knight-Commander?' There was an uproar at that as all the soldiers wanted to ride with their king. He made his way down the corridor, his knights in his wake.

People bowed to me happily as they left, shaking the two men's hands on my either side.

With time, everyone disappeared, leaving only the four of us standing there. Conor, Duke Beren, Kris and me. We looked at one another, and with a nod from Kris, we made our way down to Lord Dranos's quarters through the empty corridors.

Kris knocked on the green door, and without waiting for an answer, opened it. There was an angry barking which quieted as soon as he entered. I watched him reach up to a high shelf and put a plate of biscuits down in front of the dog. We followed him into another room, where Lord Dranos sat in bed with Aurelia standing beside him, holding his hand and looking pale.

The men pulled in chairs around the bed, and we sat down.

'What is this?' Lord Dranos asked, staring in our direction without seeing us.

'Two medium-sized Derella roots, three Greenclaw mushrooms, one tablespoon ground sweetnut … shall I continue, Lord Dranos?' Kris asked, his face hard, his voice sharp and frosty like icicles.

'You, scholar?' Lord Dranos grimaced. 'I should have known. It's always the quiet ones you need to watch!'

'A bit late now, I'm afraid,' Kris responded in a sarcastic tone.

'And I'm guessing, since it's you and not the knight-commander, this is going to cost me quite a bit more than just my eyesight?' Lord Dranos asked.

'But less than your life and your children's lives.'

'And your terms?'

'You inform the king that you've fallen unwell, and he shouldn't visit you for a while. Once a week has passed, you tell him that you've been suffering from worsening eyesight for some time now, you just didn't want to worry him. Unfortunately, the feverish sickness that took you to bed on this occasion finished the job and left you blind. You quietly send your son, Aron, away immediately to one of your more remote estates and replace him with Jon at court.'

'And?'

'Duke Beren?' Kris prompted.

'Ten thousand golden ducats. Your estates in Redwood, Koron and Silverside. And Aron's place for me in the king's privy council,' Duke Beren listed.

'Is that all?' Lord Dranos pursed his lips unhappily.

'You will send your very best wishes to the king upon hearing of his wedding plans to Isabell Khatun, the Harag Khagan's daughter,' Conor added, 'and Aurelia will be free to marry whoever she wishes.'

I watched the dog come into the room and put his head in Kris's lap, looking up at him. Kris stroked his head then caught my eye, shooting me a quick smile. 'You will carry on advising the king to the best of your knowledge and skills,' he continued, his face stern once again, 'with the help of Jon and Aurelia.'

'Not that I will have the same skills blind!' Lord Dranos complained bitterly.

'Duke Beren will send us regular reports,' Kris said at that. 'If we find, in a year or two, that you have earned it, we might return with Lady Selena and see if we can do anything about regaining your eyesight. But you will have to work hard for that. In the meantime—' He stood. '—enjoy your rest!'

We followed Kris out of the room. As I turned for a last look, I spotted Conor giving Aurelia a wink.

Two hours later, I was outside, watching Conor passionately kissing yet another woman. This one was called Olivia, apparently, and she was presented to me as the one who had been imprisoned with them by Duke Beren.

'Took you two long enough,' she complained, looking nothing like someone who had spent even a minute in prison. Her green eyes watched me like a cat's when Conor introduced us, something in her look telling me she knew that I was no Scarlet Witch. Even Kris greeted her rather sweetly, making me dislike her even more. He was now inside the palace, talking with Jon, while I'd spent an hour with the king's falconer, who showed me all their hawks, owls and falcons. The king wanted to gift me one of them along with an already overgenerous reward I didn't truly feel I deserved. I didn't want a bird, either, but Kris persuaded me to pick one and not to offend the king.

On my way back to the palace, I caught sight of Conor, although he was clearly too busy to notice me. I stood uncertainly, knowing I was being unfair to him. He deserved to have fun now. I was only grumpy because I was jealous of the kind of attention he was paying to other women. The kind I could only dream of.

He lifted his head then, as if sensing my unhappiness. He said something to Olivia and came over to me, as I knew he would. He wrapped me in his arms and rested his head against mine.

'What's wrong? Why so sullen? Are you tired? Have you not slept much?'

'I slept plenty, thank you,' I grumbled.

'You did?' He looked at me in surprise, then his face hardened. 'He … Kris … didn't hurt you, did he? He isn't rough with you, is he? Does he spend enough time …?'

'Oh, no, no, no. Nothing of that sort!' I reassured him quickly. 'In fact, I'm not even sure he's really into me like that.'

'Who? Kris?' Conor laughed.

'Yes.'

'You mean Kris? Our Kris? Just making sure that we're talking about the same person here!'

'Yes!' I repeated, more annoyed.

'Selena, he's obsessed with you.'

'Not like that,' I insisted. 'Every night he makes me lie down facing away from him. He kisses my head, puts his arm around me and within minutes he just falls asleep. And then he helps me fall asleep, too!'

'I can't believe he's being such a good boy.' Conor chuckled and shook his head.

'Do you really think he's interested?'

'Oh, he's definitely interested, trust me!'

I was completely lost now. 'Then what am I doing wrong?'

'You're not doing anything wrong. Just go and tell him that he can have some fun now!'

'Are you really sure?'

'I'm really sure.' He laughed.

'Don't tell him we spoke about this.'

'I definitely won't.' He confirmed. 'Feeling better? Can I go back to Olivia now?'

'Yes, thanks.' I squeezed him and let him go.

'He's yours,' he said. 'Go, take him!'

I turned after him and saw Kris standing further down, watching us. I meekly went to him as Conor walked away with Olivia, giving us space.

'What was that about?' Kris asked, but he was smiling.

'Just about us not having enough fun,' I said.

'Typical of Conor!' he laughed. 'On the way here, he was telling me what brothels he'd take me to once we'd finished here.'

I looked at him like I heard him wrong. 'No!'

'No?' He had his teasing smile on.

'No!' I repeated more loudly, cross now. Was he enjoying this?

'Right. Right.' He laughed and pulled me into his arms. 'I shall tell him it's most definitely a no!' he clarified, kissing my head. 'So, where would you like to go?'

'Where would I like to go? What do you mean?' I grumbled.

'Maybe we could go and see that pond with the magnolia trees around it now. Would you like to sit there for a bit?' He stroked me, talking in his soft voice now like in the evenings. 'Or we could go and have a look around Caledon. Maybe you'd have lunch with me somewhere outside of the palace for once. Or perhaps you'd like us to just go back to your room. How about a warm bath, then giving some attention to those massage oils that have been sitting there all week unloved?' he murmured into my ear. 'Or do you have any other plans for the day, Miss Soto?'

I lifted my face to him, drunk from his words. He looked down at me with a lust in his eyes that had my heart doing all sorts of things. He gently kissed my forehead, then tilted his head, his face stroking mine. My eyes closed, my lips waiting for his to arrive.

'Oh, Kristian,' I heard the king's voice from nearby, making us pause.

'Give it some thought?' Kris squeezed me a little before reluctantly letting me go. 'I shall be with you in a second.'

'I'm sorry, my lady,' the king apologised before steering him away from me. 'Kristian made some very good suggestions last night, one of which I'd like him to explain further to our chief architect and his engineers.' He indicated a small group of men and a woman behind him. 'I swear, this won't take long.'

I watched them encircle him as the king left, eager with their questions. Kris's face was relaxed as he explained the answers to them, his hands joining the lecture from time to time as he drew his ideas into the air for them. A tinge of pride pushed its way into my heart through the happiness that was boiling in me, electrifying to a point where I couldn't just stand there any longer. I had to walk around.

I strolled over to a fountain, restless, looking at it but not seeing it as I circled its stone base. My eyes moved back to the group, and as if he'd felt it, he shot me a quick smile, igniting a promise that sizzled between us like fireworks.

I turned and went further, not caring where to as long as it wasn't too far. I just had to move. I wanted to jump, to run, to fly! A pink cloud descended over me, love blinding me faster than any poison, all of me lost in him.

I thought I heard Conor's voice coming from somewhere, and without thinking, I followed it.

A large outbuilding stood in front of me, its entrance leading into a pool of darkness from the dazzling sunshine. 'No, no, no, no, no!' Conor was saying to someone, and I wandered in to see what that was about. It was some sort of barn, but without any animals, I observed as my eyes got used to the change in light. Just hay everywhere, in great stacks that reached up to the ceiling and completely covered the ground. Conor lay on his front further in without his shirt on, Olivia sitting astride his back naked, massaging him.

'Yes, there!' he said happily as I turned to leave, red with embarrassment.

One more step, then I paused and turned back, certain that I saw that wrong! One of Olivia's hands was high up in the air, and in it a long knife with a green blade. The muscles in her toned arm flexed as she moved to strike. My heart jumped, flushing with dread, and I instinctively blocked her arm, screaming Conor's name at the top of my lungs. I saw him lift his head, looking at me and starting to turn, but then something flashed past my vision, and my back hit the wall with a thump. Pain like I'd never known exploded in my chest, blurring the face in front of me.

'Missed me? I bet my brother was less fun!'

His dark eyes held mine, but I tore my gaze away and looked dazed at the black handle sticking out of me. It was above my right breast. Did that mean that I might still live? I wondered. I could hear shouting outside and I knew Kris was on his way.

'He'll be too late,' Laro promised and moved closer to me, somehow trapping me with more than just his body. The air shimmered as time plunged into an infinite hole, slowing the world around us to a crawl. He unhurriedly pulled the knife out of me, the size of the blade making me feel sick. Had that really been all inside of me? He smiled and pushed it into me again, more to the middle this time.

'Good-bye, Selena,' he said in a soft voice that wasn't unlike Kris's, pulling the knife out and kissing me on the lips.

All my life, I was terrified of dying. But just then, as my body started shaking and the world went dark around me, it wasn't fear that I felt. It was frustration. I was angry at never having kissed the man I loved, furious at being robbed of a life I could have spent with him! Let down by the world that I knew would continue without me just the same. But most of all, I was disappointed with myself. This was all my fault! Other people seemed to find life so easy. They just got on with it, achieving so much that was somehow always beyond me. I'd never got anywhere. Even now, when I'd been given a unique chance to do something great, to make something out of myself, I'd failed. And in that moment, it occurred to me, that maybe it never really mattered that I didn't know who I was. All that mattered was who I wanted to be.

Darkness closed around me, stealing my thoughts. A velvety black, like the ocean, rocking me. Nothing melted over everything, and everything melted into nothing. No centre, no edges, no directions. Yet a spark flared up somewhere and pulsed like a heartbeat. A breeze now, turning it into a fire, fierce like a storm, bright like a star. It burned, spreading across me, a pain screaming through my body, turning into fury. Fury bled into strength, strength into determination, determination into life, a force light-ing up the world around me as I found my way back into that kiss.

My lips moved under his, startling him, but I held him now. Not just his arm—all of him! My healing energy swirled around my navel, flowing up into my chest, mending all that was broken, washing away all that was wrong. I willed it higher, my tongue tingling as it moved across my mouth and into his. My eyes shone with a light that worried him and he tried to break free again, but I was stronger.

He thought of the blade in his hand, an ability in him changing its structure, moving it towards me. I saw it in him for the broken, corrupted gift it was, and I washed it away, curing him of it for good. Horror in his eyes now, as if he no longer enjoyed our shared intimacy. I was just getting started.

I looked closer until I found his skill to change shape, and just like before, I melted it into nothing. He jerked, trying to get away, using all the might of his inhuman speed, but I was there again, touching it with my mind where he did, taking it away from him.

Time jumped back to normal with a jolt. Laro was shoved off me with an unstoppable force as my legs shook and I slid down a little along the wall. I saw Conor watching me, shocked, holding Olivia in front of him with her arms twisted back.

I looked to my left to see Laro seemingly unconscious on the ground, then Kris was there with me, pulling me up, his hands shaking so badly as he tried to expose the wound, I thought I might need to help. His mouth opened, but no words came out as his fingers caressed the faint white lines he found on my skin under the blood stains.

'I'm fine.' I smiled at him. 'It's all healed, I promise,'

He pulled me to him then, holding me so tight I thought he would break me. But even then, I didn't complain.

Chapter 27

Kristian

Caledon, Drelos,
12ᵗʰ The Month of Red Blessing 1575

H er heartbeat against mine. Nothing else existed. Selena's filled
with relief and love now, as if it was my body she wanted to
pump life back into, not hers. Mine strong and frantic, as if
showing how it should be done.

My brain a bruised frozen thing somewhere on the outskirts, in its
depths, a battle of two halves. On one side the old champion, rational
thinking, protesting that none of this was possible. How could she be alright? I needed to take her back to the Pantheon immediately! In the
opposite corner a new challenger. Divine, confident, and—surprisingly—
winning the fight: faith. Selena was the Supreme Key of the Dragon, glowing with golden light only a moment ago. Just because I didn't understand
how a God's power worked in her, that didn't mean it was impossible.

There was some movement around us now, shapes drifting in. Conor's
voice reached me, talking to them. Then he was there, his need to hold
her crushing against me in waves, and I reluctantly pulled back, allowing
him closer, the only person I was willing to share her with in that moment.

I watched as the guards thoroughly searched Olivia and Laro, giving
the former her clothes once they'd emptied the pockets. They collected all
their weapons, and carried them both out in handcuffs, Olivia on her own
legs, Laro still unconscious.

'Laro no longer has any powers,' I heard Selena say. 'I erased the three
skills that he had.'

Conor twitched as he heard Laro's name, a decision forming in him,
and he gently handed Selena back to me. He turned away to follow the
others, leaving me torn between wanting to stay with her and needing to
go after him.

'Are you sure about erasing Laro's powers?' I asked her.

'Yes.' She nodded confidently. 'They felt wrong, broken, so I was able
to cure him of them using my healing energy.'

As you kissed? I wanted to ask, struggling to push away an unreasonable jealousy. My eyes lingered on her lips, a need in me to show her how she could be kissed. How she should be kissed.

'I think it's my turn now with this healing energy of yours, Miss Soto,' I suggested and watched her smile disappear.

'I don't think I can do it with you.' Some sort of regret in her now, confusing me further.

'Why not?' Did she not want me anymore?

'Because,' she said after a little hesitation, 'it only starts when I think about how much I miss you.'

'Really?' The number of times my imagination had conjured up the king's head resting in her lap, torturing me, and all the while she was thinking of me?

'Yes,' she said. 'How I miss your arms around me. And your little …'

'Well, that's a shame,' I announced, happier than I'd ever been. 'And what else?' I murmured, tilting my head to close the gap between us.

'And how much I want to …' She trailed off, her lips suddenly too busy learning from mine what else to miss next time.

We kissed, and within minutes, our passion burned so hot that all of me yearned to get her out of that dress and make love to her right then and there. But she deserved better. And I needed to go.

I lifted my head reluctantly, holding her tight against me. 'I can't leave Conor and Laro alone together, no matter the circumstances,' I sighed.

'Of course,' she said unhappily, but knowing what I meant. 'Let's go.'

'Thank you, my love.' I kissed her hair, soaking with joy as my words melted her in my arms. 'Are you not too tired to come with me?'

'No, actually. If anything, it's the opposite for some reason.'

I looked at her, remembering how Conor had been much the same once we crawled out of that coffin miraculously alive. 'Come on, then.'

Back in Renold II's day, the imposing dungeons under the far end of the palace would have been filled to the brim, torture being one of the psychotic tyrant's favourite pastimes. But these days, apparently, only a few prisoners were kept down there. Depending on their crimes, criminals either purchased their way out or were executed shortly after trial.

The entrance was strangely deserted, with the gate left slightly ajar, so we hurried down into the murky darkness without waiting for permission.

'Why, Olivia? Just tell me why!' Conor's voice. Not shouting, but close.

'Who wouldn't betray you for the right price?' Laro snapped back. 'Or do you really think that you're so important to anyone? Even my brother takes you for a fool!' A laugh. The dull thump of a fast punch, crunching bone.

'Any last words, you snake?'

I took the last five stairs in one jump and ran. I could see them now through the metal bars of the cell. Olivia and Laro were chained to the stone wall a few metres apart, Conor inside with them, holding a sword against Laro. No guards anywhere in sight. I wondered if he had bribed them.

'Conor, wait!' I yelled, rushing in after him.

'Why?' Even his question sounded like a threat. Inside him, red hot fury mingled with hate, dangerously close to exploding. 'Do you want to do it?' He pinned me with his eyes, holding me in place, too.

In that moment, I knew that whatever I did next, something would break between us. The question was only how far the damage went. I had a feeling Laro was waiting to find out the exact same thing. Waiting and probably enjoying the show.

'We're not going to kill him,' I said calmly.

'Is this because he's your brother? It is, isn't it?' Conor fumed, his anger tinged with pain now.

'No,' I said slowly. 'It's not.'

'You don't care what he does to us? What he did to me? What he did to Selena?'

'Of course, I care.' I was doing my best now not to get infected by his temper. I wanted to put my hand on his shoulder, but he looked like he might chop it off.

'Then why?' he shouted at me. 'Tell me why!'

'Because we're not like him, Conor! We don't want to be like him. We want him to be punished and we want answers from him. We'll take him to the Order tomorrow. They'll know what to do with him. Think about it! Ithorion can make him tell us everything he knows.'

'No, that's what you want,' he retorted. 'I don't want answers! I don't want to look good in front of the Order! I just want him to end. I don't want him in a different prison cell, never knowing if he might escape and come after us again. He will never give up. Just look at him!'

I followed his gaze. Laro smirked at me with blood streaming down from his broken nose. Behind me, a second source of resentment started to boil, a steely determination that made me turn and remind myself that Selena stood there, wordlessly watching us.

'He no longer has any powers.' I turned back to Conor. 'He won't be able to escape the Order's prison.'

'You don't know that! You don't know what will happen. He could cut our throats one night easily without any powers.' He lowered the sword finally and stepped so close our faces were but an inch apart. 'Look, I know you're not a killer. But let me do it!'

'That's where you're wrong.' Laro chuckled. 'He is a killer. More savage than you've ever known.'

'Shut up, nobody asked you!' Conor roared at him. Then he turned back to me. 'Please!'

'Conor, no,' I said softly, watching his eyes fill with angry tears. 'I know how you feel, but this is not the right thing to do.'

'Do you? Do you really have any idea how I feel?'

'Trust me, I do.' I felt the hurt tormenting him because, in his mind, despite all that had happened, I was still choosing my half-brother over him. And it was silently killing me inside. I put my arm over his shoulder. 'We're in this together.'

'We are clearly not!' he snapped, breaking away from me. 'I don't want to join that stupid order, anyway! So, you can't tell me what to do!' He raised the sword again and turned towards Laro with intent.

'Conor!' My voice a cold rumble now, like an approaching blizzard. A warning to convey that, by killing Laro, he would end more than just him.

Conor hesitated, hating me. But not hating me enough to entirely give up on me. The blade shook in his hand until he threw it away. Then he turned on his heel and left without another word.

'Interesting,' Laro remarked, finally snapping the last thread keeping me together.

I hurled him against the wall, shoving the back of his head against it.

'Don't think you'll get away with this!' My hand was on his neck now, throbbing with a desire to break it.

He remained calm, infuriating me further with his lopsided smile. 'He'll never stay with you in the Order now. Even you must know that! But it will be all the easier for me to kill him when he's alone again.' His smile widened as he watched me boil with rage. 'You don't really think they can keep me locked up for long, do you? Or do you think them so almighty? They can't even find our uncle! I hope you're not too worried about him. The world is a dangerous place; anything can happen.'

'Have you hurt him?' I roared, tightening my grip on him. 'What happened to him?'

'Nothing yet, as far as I know. Trust me, I'm a lot more interested in Selena now. And if I can't kill her, I might as well find a way to fuck her finally before you disturb us again! Did she tell you how turned on she was that night in the library? How she enjoyed me hardening against her or where my hands had been? How she had her tongue in my mouth today in the barn, begging for it? Did she?'

A dark cloud descended on my mind, reaching for what lay beyond a locked door. The dark energies that leaked out from there were only a taste of what James had buried in me. A weak shadow of what was to come. Someone put their hand on mine, trying to pull me away. I kept my eyes on Laro as the lock turned in my head, wanting to have what was hidden there. All of it. Nothing else was good enough to hurt him with.

A kiss above my collarbone now. One on my neck, then another, making me pause. Selena's hand on the back of my head, pulling me closer. I looked down at her. She was talking to me, but I couldn't hear her words. A terrible anger pulsed in me, looking for a way out. I let Laro go and swept her up into my arms, taking her further away. Her lips found mine, like a key locking that dark door in my mind. And opening another.

I carried Selena along the corridor, turning into a long-deserted cell. A human skull and some bones on the floor, nothing else in the empty cubicle. I put her down, pressing her against the cold wall as we kissed, eagerly, deeply, my hands busy unlacing her dress. The material slid down her body, and I followed it with my lips, losing myself in those breasts that had tantalised me for so long. She rested a hand on my head, stroking me, her eyes closing as I made my way further down, lingering in places that I felt gave her the most pleasure. Her black lace underwear was already wet with lust by the time I reached it, turning me on even more. I kissed her through it until it was soaked. I tugged it aside, my tongue making her moan, teasing her ever closer to her climax. Finally, I stood, reached back and pulled off my shirt in one move, her hands on my belt, freeing me. I lifted her a little, opening her legs and wrapping them around my waist, pushing myself into her. Her mouth was back on mine, hungry, and I wouldn't have stopped kissing her had the world collapsed around us. I rocked her faster and faster, her thighs tightening around me as I buried myself in her again, and I could feel a slow orgasm spread up through her legs, igniting mine on the way.

'I love you,' I breathed into her ear, stealing her chance to reply with a kiss. I could tell the answer anyway.

I held her like that a little longer, unwilling to let her go, then gently released her. I sat down on my shirt and pulled her into my lap.

'This is really not how I planned to do this.' I smiled at her, stroking her in my arms.

'Planned?' She smiled back. 'Weren't you just going to make me fall asleep as soon as we were in bed again then?'

'Definitely not. The only reason you might fall asleep tonight will be exhaustion, I'm afraid,' I murmured.

'I love you, too.' She sighed happily, snuggling against me.

The rattle of metal keys echoed across the walls, making us look up.

'As romantic as this place is, we probably shouldn't overstay our welcome.' I reached for her dress and handed it to her. I lifted the skull next. It looked like something the crows had picked clean outside decades ago and had been subsequently brought in to unnerve criminals. 'Want a souvenir, too?'

'Unless it's Laro's, no, thanks!'

'Touché!' I laughed.

I watched her examine the dried blood stains on her dress. 'So, is it back to your room now?' I asked.

'I should think so,' she said. 'I definitely need a bath and another set of clothes. It's been a busy morning!'

'You go ahead. I'll join you in a bit.'

'Are you not coming with me? What do you want to do?'

'Don't worry. I won't be long. I just want to double-check that the guards didn't miss anything when they searched Laro. Make sure he has no modern equipment on him they didn't know to look for. And I should also collect Conor's sword,' I added after a pause. The thought of him sobered me, but it was Selena whose heart filled with sadness. A longing grew in her to comfort him, the way he always did the same for her.

'Do you want to spend some time with him?' I offered, reluctantly suppressing my own desire to be with her. I knew she could do what I couldn't: ease the pain I had caused him.

She looked at me, surprised.

'It's okay.' I pulled her back into my arms. 'Just come and find me afterwards.'

'I will,' she promised, her lips suddenly back on mine, kissing me passionately.

'Are you mine?' I murmured, kissing back.

'I'm yours, my love.' She had her hand in my hair, stroking my head. 'Just make sure you rest plenty this afternoon. I might tire you out tonight!'

I smirked. It was the best challenge I'd heard in a while. 'I certainly look forward to seeing you try.'

I had to get the guards to re-open Laro's cell for me, asking for a few more minutes with the prisoners. I waited until we were alone, then had a good look at him. He seemed to have forgotten how to smile, whereas nothing he said anymore could have washed the grin off my face.

'This is not over,' he warned me through gritted teeth as I forced his head down and checked the top of his spine for implants. He didn't have any.

I knew the guards did a thorough body search and went through his clothing. I watched them do it. I checked his eyes, ears, nose and even shoved the hilt of Conor's sword into his mouth, feeling around his teeth and gums. I pursed my lips as we eyed each other, he defiant, me still on cloud nine, armed in Selena's love and feeling unstoppable. The memory of her hands on me gave me an idea, and I raked through Laro's thick, jet-black hair, my fingers locating something solid in there, clinging to him. I fastened my hand around it and tore it off him.

'Oh, I'm sorry! Did that hurt?' I asked once he finished yelling, examining the small, crab-like droid in my hand.

I did the same searches on Olivia, but the way she let me do it told me she had nothing left to hide, and sure enough, she was clean.

'Feel free to stay up late. I'm not planning on rising early!' I informed them before taking a final look around and having their cells locked once more.

As I headed out into the corridor, a new inmate was carried into the dungeons. A skinny guy covered in dirt, regretfully keeping his eyes down as they passed me by. I might have recognised him under all that black soot and grime had I taken the time and effort to go after them. But by then, my head was filled with Selena again. Her naked body pressed against mine, the feel of her nipples between my lips, and all that I was going to do with her that night. And so, I didn't even look twice.

I went over to the stables and pretended to groom Storn until everyone disappeared for lunch.

'Conor rode out with Selena on Athos! Why didn't they take me, too? I wanted to go with them,' Storn complained. 'He completely ignored me, no matter what I did!'

'It's my fault.' I patted his neck. 'Don't worry. He'll come around. In the meantime, I have some important tasks for you.'

'Important tasks? Really? You're not just saying that to make me feel better?'

'Oh no, they are absolutely crucial. Here.' I opened my left palm enough to show him the droid. 'We have to find out everything about this little guy here. But you need to be extremely careful with him, Storn. Expect the worse.'

He took the small thing out of my hand with his teeth, holding it trapped there as he examined it. 'It has a customised, layered protection shield. Nine levels, each designed to be more difficult to get through than the one before. The first layer released an array of viruses, three of which I've never come across before.'

'As I said, be extra careful! If you're not sure about anything, just pause and wait for me.'

'Is this the owner?' he asked, projecting an image of Laro in front of us.

'Yes. Which brings me to the second thing I'm going to ask of you. Can you see the entrance to the dungeons from here?'

'No, it's too far.'

'In that case, I'd like you to sneak out after sunset and, avoiding all humans, move closer to monitor it. If Laro gets out of there somehow, I want you to alert me straightaway. Is there a way we can keep an eye on him down there?' I wished very much Storn could see through stone walls, but I knew he couldn't.

'I can give you a microcamera you could take down. The live feed will be poor, but we can watch it back in proper resolution later.'

'Give me one I can stick to the wall on the corridor outside his cell. If I try to set it up any closer and he sees me, he'll just get the guards somehow to take it off once I'm gone.' Had things gone differently, I could have asked Conor or Selena later to distract Laro while I positioned the camera at him, but all things considered, I didn't want either of them near him again today. Alternatively, I could have used the invisibility cloak, had the batteries not run out after last night's events. Due to their special fibre structure, I couldn't even charge it through Storn. Just typical! Anyway, surely one on the corridor would do. He no longer had powers. I'd checked his handcuffs, chains, his door. The place was guarded by armed men. If he got out of his cell somehow, Storn would know and would alert me. Even if I arrived once he was outside of the dungeons, the horse could keep an eye on him and lead me to him.

I picked up the transceiver and the camera Storn printed for me. I pocketed the first and set up the second after telling the guards I was doing a survey for the king on the state of the facilities. Once everything was in place, I wandered through the palace aimlessly. The others were clearly not in a hurry to get back, and after a while, I started to feel their absence like never before. In the end, I found myself on the outer walls, my eyes on the road leading up to the gates, my thoughts further afield.

Maybe Conor was right, and it was too dangerous to keep Laro alive. But I couldn't trust a word my half-brother had said, and I wanted to know all of it now. The truth. About our family, about how he knew of the Order, why he was really after me and why now. What he knew of James's whereabouts. Everything!

But, of course, I had other reasons for not wanting him dead, too. Conor thought it was because Laro was my half-brother. And there was some truth in that. I did wish deep down that Laro had been different. If he had just come and talked to me at the start. Maybe we could have understood each other. Maybe I could have helped him. Maybe we could have got to know each other better. But not after all he'd done. Slaughtering my students. Beating Conor half-dead and repeatedly threatening to kill him. Stabbing Selena in the chest.

My breathing quickened just at the thought. Had it not been for the Dragon, she would be dead now. I never thought I would believe in Gods, let alone love them. Now part of me felt like crawling to him on my knees and kissing his feet for giving her back to me.

So, why did I still insist on not killing Laro, apart from the answers I sought? It was because of something I knew now, just didn't want to face it. Harsh truths, James called them once. The really painful ones we avoid. And he was right. I did everything I could to deny it. But the truth was that, at our cores, Laro and I were the same.

For the longest time, I wondered why James had nagged me to leave the university when he knew about my condition. Didn't he worry that a little blood would eventually turn me into a monster? But of course, it wasn't the blood. I'd seen blood before at the university and felt nothing. I'd even tasted it a few times at martial arts practice. No. It was since Laro turned up in my life that the mental veil James covered my past with frayed, and the contents started to leak. Certainly, blood had triggered me since the massacre. But it was something in him, in his eyes, in his voice, in his words, that I recognised. His demon that now woke mine.

I remembered now how that dream ended, too. The nightmare in the storm that was a locked memory. The really disturbing part wasn't the brutality with which I'd killed that man and then the little girl. It was how much I'd enjoyed it. An echo of that pleasure lived in me still. Wasn't that why I convinced Selena to accept the king's gift and choose a hawk? Because I wanted one? Because I couldn't wait to hunt with it? Excited at the thought of a merciless kill masked as a native pastime?

Of course, I hated myself for it and fought it whenever I could. This was why those bandits managed to cut my arm open on the top of the carriage as I'd wrestled with my instinct to just run my sword through them. As a lover might hold back from pushing themselves into their woman hilt-deep. And this was why I didn't want to kill Laro now, either. It wasn't affection, as Conor thought. It was the fear of replacing him. As long as Laro lived, I knew on which side of the line I stood. Once he was dead, either by my hand or by Conor's, who was but an extension of me in this act, I wasn't sure what would happen. But whatever followed, I knew it would destroy what was left of me. The person I was when I laughed with Conor. When I kissed Selena. When I wanted to serve in the Order and fulfil a higher purpose in life. When I swore an oath to the Dragon.

Quede was right to be wary of me. Not who I was now, but the potential of who I could become. With time in the Order, Selena and Conor would grow more powerful, and in turn, their bond to me would grow stronger. Even if I was not granted gifts of my own, apart from those that already supported me in being their tora, my power would grow through them. Even now, Conor wanted to kill for us, and the only thing stopping him wasn't the Order; it was me. And Selena, who like a red phoenix, came back even from death and had already manifested multiple gifts, some unique to her. She was clearly destined for great things. Terek had said that each circle took after their tora. It was their tora's personality that would influence and form each circle's qualities and character. The harsh truth was that they deserved a better person than me. That staying with them meant that I needed to fight who I was for the rest of my life. And that it was Selena, again, who saved us from our worst enemy. Not even of Laro this time. But myself.

I had to examine that mental protection James had created in me. Study it and fix it. Which meant facing all that I wanted to look away from. I knew it would take a while. It would take strength to repeatedly make time for it and not to just give in when I faced my deepest desires. Could I really do it alone and without James's help?

Something bright caught my eye, and I finally saw them coming my way. Conor on Athos, Selena on a white mare, both riding at a leisurely pace, talking and laughing. My heart filled with something warm at the sight of them. Surely, I could do it for them? Surely, it was a price worth paying.

The sun was already low in the sky as I hurried down to meet them. They stopped at the sight of me, both getting down from the saddle. I went and reached up to help Selena, even though she seemed to be managing fine. I had to touch her and feel her close to me, even if just for a minute.

'Had fun?' I asked. She was bursting with excitement. I just hoped that some of it was due to seeing me again.

'So much. Everyone cheered us wherever we went and wanted to give us presents. We had to stop at every single tavern and have a drink with the locals. I obviously couldn't, even after we had lunch. I had to start saying no after three, but Conor kept it up!'

'I'm not surprised!' I grinned, my eyes looking for him, but he had his back towards us, fidgeting with his saddlebag, sulking again.

'And he bought this horse for me—isn't she beautiful?' She stroked the animal with the fondness of a proud owner. 'He said, we should send the carriage along with most of my dresses and shoes to the Scarlet Witches, to appease them for pretending to be one of them and acting on their behalf. I only get to keep one or two.' She pulled a devastated face, eyeing me like I might overrule the clearly shocking decision.

'Conor is right,' I said firmly. 'In fact, I think it's a great idea. We can always buy you more clothes later.'

Her eyes darkened further, unhappy lines creasing her forehead. 'Even my underwear?' she silently mouthed at me.

'No!' I mouthed back, trying to look mortified, but the nature of her distress ruined it with a smile. 'Hide them in my bag.'

'We got a few things for you, too,' she announced, happy again.

'You did?' I asked, surprised.

'Well, mainly Conor did.' She looked at him pointedly.

'Really?'

'Just a few things for the road. Nothing to get excited about,' he stated without turning or looking at me.

I walked to stand by his side, patting Athos but looking at him until he could no longer ignore me. 'So, is it Manessa we're going to first?'

'Is it?' He gave me an annoyed look, suggesting we both knew it wasn't.

'Oh, we're not staying long in the Pantheon,' I said quickly. 'We're just going to drop off those two, have a chat with Ithorion, and then come straight back, I promise. We must see this town you love so much! Not to mention all those other sights: The Great Fortress of the Selvik, the Enchanted Gardens of Antiria, the Sacred Baths of the Fire Island,' I quoted to show I had been paying attention the other night. 'Where do we start?'

'They are all quite far away. It would take weeks, some even months, to visit. Are you sure you wouldn't prefer to spend all that time with your new friends instead?'

'I'm sure.' I put my arm around his shoulders, half-expecting him to shake it off. 'Ithorion said we'll have long breaks between assignments. I don't see why we couldn't fit in one each time.'

He pursed his lips at that, as if not entirely happy with the concept. 'Let's go to Manessa first, and then we'll see. Maybe we'll find a place there you'll like.'

'I was actually thinking we might build one,' I admitted.

'Build one?' He laughed.

'Why not? It's the best way to make sure it's exactly what we want. I have a few ideas already …'

He laughed again and shook his head at me. 'Building a house. Right. What's next? Keeping chickens? Digging up the backyard? Stop tearing up my reputation piece by piece, will you?'

'Why don't we start with that bottle of Golden Kabar in Selena's room?' I squeezed his shoulder. 'Then we'll go to the king's birthday feast. Aurelia was already looking for you earlier. How about just enjoying our last night here and having a lie-in in the morning? You don't need to worry about her father anymore.'

'A lie-in? You?' He grinned like I just presented him with some funny paradox. For a moment he stared at me, reading my thoughts clearer than Ithorion ever could, then we both turned and looked at Selena behind us. She smiled back at us innocently.

'Fine,' he announced at last, patting my back. 'Let's go. That Golden Kabar does need drinking!'

And so, we spent the next hour in our blessed threesome once again on Selena's bed. Conor with his back against the raised pillows, talking about their afternoon in town and what we might see on the way to Manessa, holding a glass of wine in one hand, stroking Selena's hair with the other. Selena leaned against Conor, watching me from under his arm with the unashamed joy of a woman who felt wanted and knew I would spend the night worshipping her. Her feet in my lap, my fingers busy massaging them, not quite able to keep my hands off her, but not trusting myself not to start kissing her, were she any closer.

I hardly touched my glass, my unspoken excuse being my tastes and being otherwise engaged, but the truth was, I didn't want to drink much in case there was an emergency with Laro during the night. Last time I checked, Storn was still only on the third level of his firewall system, which didn't help with knowing for sure that he had no backup plans. I just hoped that, if he did have anything up in his sleeve, it would wait till the morning.

There was a knock on the door to let us know dinner was soon to be served, and I pushed myself up from the bed, wishing we could skip it. But of course, we couldn't. Not this one.

Whether I liked it or not, with Selena on my right and Conor on my left, I was in the centre of all attention as soon as we entered the great hall. Guests mingled here before food was served next door, with a new group of musicians playing lively songs in the corner.

'Is that Isabell?' Selena eyed a magnificently dressed woman standing next to the king with some envy. 'I wish I had something like that to wear, too.'

'That's a Khatun's traditional robe. You're here as a Scarlet Witch,' Conor pointed out, even as his eyes travelled over to the huge man standing on Isabell's other side. 'And that's the khagan.'

A strong dislike bubbled up in both of them instantly, just as the king noticed us and gestured for us to come closer.

'Be nice,' I warned them quietly. 'This is not a boat we want to rock before the wedding.'

'Do you mean I can't even stick my tongue out at him?' Selena teased me, clearly fearless after all that sweet wine.

'I'll deal with your tongue later,' I murmured into her ear. 'For now, just smile, my beautiful.'

The knight-commander stood with the royal trio, who now also turned our way and bowed to Selena with clear admiration. 'My lady!'

We went through the formal introductions and curtsies, while the king looked on us with something that seemed close to pride on his face. Isabell Khatun greeted us warmly, and the khagan frowned at Conor's spotless face. My lot acted innocently enough, not counting the flirty smile Conor pulled upon kissing Isabell's hand. Fortunately, it was only me keeping a close eye on him in that moment.

'My falconer tells me Lady Selena unknowingly picked one of the Imperial Hawks out of all my birds this morning,' the king remarked with a smile.

'Only the best for our lady!' Conor laughed.

'They are the most vicious, too,' the khagan added.

'Only if not trained or kept well,' the king assured me before we moved on so that a group of aristocrats holding presents behind us could be introduced.

'Really? The most vicious?' I mock-scolded Selena as I pulled out a chair for her at one of the long tables in the dining hall.

'He didn't look vicious,' she objected as she sat down. 'And none of those birds liked me. He was at least interested.'

'I bet he was!' I kissed her neck before taking the seat next to her.

'I'm being persuaded to sing more songs after dinner.' Conor caught up with us, taking the seat on Selena's other side.

'After dinner? Can't it be during dinner?' I muttered.

He abandoned his chair and came over to lean against the table next to me. 'We're not in a hurry to go anywhere, are we?' An amused smile curled his lips.

'That obvious, huh?' I unfolded my linen napkin.

'You know, I was thinking I might do some of those nice, long ballads,' he mused, watching me. 'A few of them go on for about thirty verses!'

I groaned, fiddling with my cutlery.

'You'll have to learn some of these songs, anyway,' he stated.

'I do?'

'Of course, you do, if you really want to settle down here. These are the songs we'll be singing with folks in taverns in the evenings after our fair share of Doreni High Ale. You learn the songs I teach you on the way to Manessa, and I'll keep it to three short, straightforward ones tonight. Deal?'

'Fine,' I conceded grudgingly.

'Can you play any instruments?'

'No,' I admitted.

'What? Don't they teach you these things at that university of yours?' He raised his eyebrows at me.

'They just never seemed that useful.' I shrugged.

'We don't learn music because it's useful,' he lectured me with a frown. 'We learn music because it makes us better people! Better fighters! Better lovers! We sing because it's fun and makes us happy!'

'Aha, I'm sure it does.' I treated him to a wry smile.

'You'll learn all the songs I teach you *and* an instrument,' he decided.

'What? No! I'll learn the songs, no instruments.' I pushed back.

'You'll learn the songs and an instrument, and in return, I keep it short tonight and make excuses on your behalf when the dance starts after dinner.'

'Dance?' I tried to play for time, frantically looking for a way out.

'Songs and an instrument!' He observed his fingernails. 'Or …' His mischievous smile promised nothing good.

'Fine! Fine!' I gave in. 'Guitar will do, I suppose.'

'Guitar it is!' He patted my back, satisfied. 'I'll be on your case until you start enjoying life like normal people do.'

'See the things I have to do for you?' I turned to Selena once Conor let me be, only to find her watching me with a knowing smile. 'You're not in on this, are you?'

She leaned close to whisper in my ear, placing her hand on my thigh in the process and stealing all my objections. 'Maybe I am.'

'Then maybe we should see if I can play any tunes on you tonight,' I murmured, caressing her back.

It was a long dinner that I thought would never end. I had my arm around Selena's waist for most of it, struggling not let my hand wander. There were additional tables laid out as Harag guests mixed with the

Coroden nobility, and even from the latter we had at least twice the usual number turn up to celebrate the king's birthday and the breaking of the curse. The Dranos siblings sat framing us, less shocked now than they were in the morning and more cautious when talking to us, but by the time we reached the last course, Jon was once again relaxed enough for a few jokes, and I caught glimpses of Aurelia sharing smiles with Conor. I wondered whether he would end up in her bed again tonight. If any of his songs were like the one from last night, he'd have a line of women queuing for him soon enough!

After dessert was served, the king made a speech in which he thanked all his guests for their good wishes and gifts. He said he received the two best presents of his life from Lady Selena and the Great Khagan, though. One was breaking the curse, and the other, his beautiful bride, Isabell Khatun, whom he would marry next month. A huge cheer followed the announcements, during which Conor disappeared from our table and took his place with a guitar at the front, bowing to the king and Isabell as he started to play.

His first song seemed a well-known, cheerful tune, and he had half of the room singing with him soon enough. The second was a ballad of bloody battles and glorious victories, some of which he sang in another language I guessed to be Harag, causing much appreciation among the foreign guests. The third was about a pretty girl and love, which had most of the women craning their necks and trying to catch his eye. He ignored them all and was grinning at me instead, as if the two of us shared a private joke. In truth, I knew he was laughing at me, knowing I was on the edge of my seat.

On the edge of reason, more like! We used the loud applause he received as cover for our early disappearance as I took Selena's hand and stole her out of the hall. As soon as we were out in the empty corridor, I was all over her. She laughed with joy, wriggled out of my arms and ran to her room, making me chase her. I pressed her against her door as we kissed, my hand blindly searching for the handle, eager to be inside. She found it for me, half-opening the door as she stepped in and stopped, her hand on my mouth gently pushing me away.

'Are you sure you want to come in?'

I kissed her palm, reaching for her hand with mine. 'I'm sure.'

'But look! My bath is still here with steaming hot water. Don't you want to wait until I'm safely in my dressing gown, as usual?'

I took her forefinger into my mouth, biting it gently as I looked into her eyes, slowly shaking my head with a smile. I breathed into her palm once more, turned her arm, kissing the inside of her wrist, and from there made my way up, closer and closer, until her lips were back on mine. I pushed her into the room, closing the door behind us, unlacing her dress even as I turned the key in the lock.

I didn't think I'd slept, because even after Selena drifted off at dawn, I didn't seem able to entirely stop kissing her. But I must have slept because I was dreaming when I woke. Even in my dream, I made love to her, on a warm beach somewhere, so it was quite a shock when a red flashing light broke through my eyelids, accompanied by Storn's voice.

I flew to the table, muting the transceiver to let Selena sleep on as I jumped into my trousers, shoes, then picked up my shirt and ran.

'I'm on my way!' I told him as I put on my shirt mid-sprint down the stairs. 'Talk to me!'

'I think he's gone,' he stated, almost making me lose my footing on the last step.

'What do you mean he's gone?' I demanded. 'How?'

I reached the dungeons in about ten minutes. A group of guards outside were talking among themselves, their faces shocked.

'It's bad,' one informed me as I arrived, but let me go through.

I passed a dead soldier in the corridor who looked half-frozen, a few of his comrades around him, looking grave. But that wasn't what the man at the entrance had referred to when he said "bad". Outside of Laro's cell was a smaller crowd, which meant I didn't see immediately what they were gaping at—only that two of them were vomiting a little further away. I pushed my way in to assess the situation for myself. I had to close my eyes and grip the bars, pressing my forehead against them as a vicious madness exploded in me.

Inside, a blond man lay on the floor who looked like the one they brought in yesterday, except I knew it wasn't him, and not just for the lack of dirt on him. A third of him was missing, as in cut through vertically by an uneven blade. What remained of his organs, intestines and brain were dipped into the pool of blood around him. There was a tall, narrow shadow near him on the wall, which seemed to be bleeding, too. Olivia still had her hands chained to the wall, ending in her shoulders, neck and head that now all flopped down with nothing to support them. Apart from a piece of her upper body, that was nowhere to be seen, the rest of her was on the ground, blood still oozing from her torso where she had been horizontally sliced apart.

From the camera footage, a message found by Storn in the droid, and from what the guards told me, I gradually put together the full story. Laro wasn't alone here on Drelos. He was with his guy Lerkin in Caledon, while Lerkin's twin brother, Seth, waited for them somewhere closer to the Coroden Skygate.

Laro messaged Seth yesterday to come and get him, while I was otherwise engaged with Selena in another part of the prison. There must have been a soul circle connection between them, and by using that, Seth opened the Coroden Skygate to Laro's cell that morning, just like Conor had opened the North Sentry Gate in Borond to Selena's location a few weeks ago. But as Terek pointed out in the Pantheon, we were lucky to be teleported into the middle of a library, which was large enough to contain the skygate. With a small cell like Laro's, the story would have been very different. Part of the gate must have materialised inside the wall and the rest cut through Olivia. Just as there was a non-negotiable pull as soon as you entered or even touched the skygates, there was also a rigid push upon exit. Which must have meant that the bleeding shadow on the wall was the missing part of Seth, stuck between the stones.

Lerkin quickly broke his and Laro's chains with his freezing powers, just as he broke the locks on their cells and, presumably, they were then still able to use the gate to journey back. Whether they remained on Drelos, though, or left the planet entirely, only someone from the Order would be able to tell me. I expected that, since discovering the security breach upon his return, Ithorion had now made sure that the gates were more tightly monitored.

I wondered if Laro's original plan was to simply break out of the dungeons with Lerkin during the night and have Seth meet them somewhere in the open. But I specifically asked the knight-commander yesterday to heavily guard the exit, and once news of Laro's attack on Selena spread among the soldiers, many of them volunteered for night duty. Nobody thought it wasn't enough to triple the guard on the main gate, though. Not even me. In consequence, my half-brother chose this dangerous and ultimately bloody escape, rather than face the army stationed outside the dungeons. Not without his powers, anyway. I had a feeling he really wanted to avoid a meeting with Ithorion. Not that I was looking forward to seeing him after this!

I slammed the wall in frustration. The hell I was going to get for this from Conor! Still, there was nothing to do now. When the knight-commander questioned me, I told him that the case looked to me like a sorcery-aided escape gone bad, but that I had no reason to believe the culprit would return. Especially since he knew we were leaving this afternoon.

Laro's droid turned out not to contain anything interesting apart from a lovely personal message to me that made me want to chase after him to the end of the world if I had to and comply with Conor's wishes. As it was, I left it with Storn to hold on to for the time being.

It took me some time before I felt calm enough to return to Selena's room. Going back to bed was the last thing I wanted to do, but I knew she would be upset if she woke alone while I sat brooding somewhere else. I couldn't do that to her. Not after our night together.

I entered her room quietly, stopped by her bed, and for a while I watched her sleep. I undressed, as if by leaving my clothes behind I could also shed my troubles. I snuggled against her warm body under the soft linen cover and buried my face in her hair. She moved without waking, turning towards me, as if she knew even in her sleep that this was now part of who we were, and she could wrap herself around me. It made me wonder how I'd managed to deny myself this wonder for so long. I put my arms around her, gently stroking her back, until I selfishly woke her. She was smiling before she opened her eyes.

My lips were back on hers, even as I turned her onto her back, pushing myself even closer, kissing her deeply. I caressed her enticing body, wanting it all, wanting to pleasure all of her, make her mine. To love her until she wanted to belong to me, too, the way she owned me already. The way she had bewitched me right from the start, making me long for her from half a galaxy away.

I slowly lifted my head and looked at her, smiling as her joy spread through me. I stroked her nose with mine.

'I will have to kiss you everywhere, Miss Soto,' I murmured. 'It would be best if you just let me.'

'Everywhere?' She widened her eyes in mock shock. 'Really?'

'Absolutely,' I insisted. 'It's really not my fault that every part of you is so delicious.'

She closed her eyes and smiled, letting me get on with it. I smiled, too, eager to explore her. Last night was intense as our passion ignited. Now I wanted to take my time. To enjoy her scent, her taste, how her breathing quickened as I gently licked and sucked her nipples. To slowly pull that red thong from her with my teeth and to tease her little trigger with my tongue. To hold her tight as she lost control and climaxed under my lips.

I immersed myself so much in her, her sensations washing through me, that I had to look down to confirm what my body was telling me, yet I couldn't believe.

'You came, too?' She smiled at me, amused, as she sat up and checked what I was staring at.

'Looks like it.' I smiled back at her sheepishly. I crawled up and gathered her into my arms.

'I thought I could feel your hands on me,' she said, stroking my face.

'They were on you,' I admitted. 'You're just too sexy.'

'But …' she insisted with a little frown.

'Your butt especially,' I murmured and quieted her with my lips. I loved kissing her and she enjoyed it too much to interrupt with more questions for a while. When I finally let her go, I knew it was time to confess at least one thing to her. I went with the more important one. My special 'gift' could wait.

'I need to tell you something,' I started as I caressed her in my arms.

She looked up at me. 'What's wrong?'

I told her everything that happened that morning then, the circumstances of Laro's escape, expecting her to be worried or angry or upset, but she was none of those things. She stroked my arm as she listened, admitting in the end a relief that it was nothing to do with us. That I still loved her and that she could love me back.

'I can handle Laro any time!' She kneeled to kiss me. 'As long as I have you.'

'Then he'll never have a chance.' I pulled her into my lap.

I wished we could have stayed there all day. But when we did eventually emerge a few hours later, we were fully packed, relaxed and happy. I knew I had to face Conor next and he wouldn't be as forgiving. But I felt stronger now and certain that we would get through this.

He was fuming, just as I expected, but we did still manage to sort out a few last-minute things together. Duke Beren knew someone we could trust to take the carriage all the way to the Scarlet Witches for a good fee, along with many of Selena's belongings, some gold, and a letter from Conor. He went to check on the horses with Selena while I walked over to the falconry to fetch the hawk. He was handed to me in a cage, along with a thick leather glove, jesses and tethering equipment. I thanked the old falconer, who told me to ask for some meat from the kitchen to take with us for the bird.

'Seriously? You have more stuff than Selena!' I chided our new pet once it was only the two of us. He watched me curiously, as if trying to decide what to make of me. 'You don't really want to travel in this, do you?' He tilted his head, considering his options. 'Don't worry, we'll figure something out.'

We were invited to have lunch with the king before leaving, then we finally rode out and took the road back towards the Coroden Skygate. We stopped every few hours to rest, partly due to the heat, partly considering that Selena was still new to horse riding. In the end, I got her to sit with me, so she could relax, and I could enjoy her arms around me.

For the hawk, I got Storn to print a pair of lightweight socks, containing a microcamera and an Olso-trap, which worked like an invisible string, pulling the bird back towards the horse when it flew off too far. He hated it at first and tried to chip them off with his beak, so we had to reinforce them with metal fibres. He did enjoy the meat scraps we treated him to, though, and the freedom after the falconry. Once we'd watched it dive after a pigeon from above, Selena named him Bolt.

At sunset, we stopped near a stream that cut across a flower-spotted green meadow and lay the blankets they'd bought in Caledon the day before. They were made of decent quality fabric, thick and soft, but it was still a far cry from the comfortable beds of the Royal Palace. Concerned that Selena might find the ground too cold during the night, we agreed to place them all on top of each other and sleep like we had in the Pantheon. Conor hardly spoke to me all day, so it was good to see him put aside his frustration with me, at least for the evening.

Just as we were arranging the bedding, Ithorion appeared out of nowhere like that last time weeks ago. He didn't even wait for wine offerings this time. After a quick greeting, he turned to me expectantly, and I knew what was coming.

'So, Kristian. Start from the day you left the Pantheon and tell me all!' he prompted me, making it sound like he had just announced my death sentence. From the corner of my eye, I could see Conor pulling Selena up from the blankets to lead her away, and in that moment, I loved him for it. I knew this was going to be a long one, and I managed to squeeze in a walk request quickly and grab a waterskin, even as I started to fill him in on a painfully detailed account of our first day.

By the time I made it back to the others, hours later and guided by the fire Conor had lit, I felt like a complete failure. Who was I kidding I could do this? A Champion of the Order? Not to mention a tora? I wanted the earth to open and swallow me whole!

'How was it?' Conor asked as I dropped to my knees on the blanket, slumped down on my front, and groaned. 'That bad, huh?'

'Worse. We apparently relied on technology far too much, and our solution wasn't exactly the best. Not that he told me what he would have preferred! But he was positively furious with me for letting Laro slip through our fingers. It sounds like he was just as eager to question him as I was, if not more. He said Laro and Lerkin took the gate to a planet called Eris, and we are not to pursue. They apparently sent others after them. But he did give us more money, so I guess we're still on the payroll.' I threw Conor the purse.

'Not bad!' he observed, checking the contents. 'And what does he want us to do for it?'

'Just spend time together, for now,' he said, 'rest, train—that's it.'

'Works for me!' He laughed.

'Great!' I buried my face into the blanket. It was nothing compared to the hell he gave me for losing my head in Laro's cell. "Brutal" seemed a charitable word to describe it.

Selena shuffled closer to me, stroking my head. It took me a few minutes to stop feeling sorry for myself and register her discomfort.

'You're still cold?' I managed to make it sound like a question in the last moment.

'Just a little bit.' She shrugged. 'It's nothing.'

'Wait.' I got up and started to fold up my end of the blankets towards the middle. Conor stood, too, pulling Selena along with him, and soon we had six layers in a much narrower pile. She hesitated around it, feeling guilty.

'Come on. You know what to do!' I grinned at her.

She looked lost for a second, then realised what I was talking about and laughed. She lay down in the middle, facing away from me. I positioned myself as close to the edge as I was able and pulled her to me.

'Cosy!' Conor chortled as he took his place, his laughter infectious.

'I'm sorry!' Selena giggled, their noses barely inches apart.

'For what?' I objected. 'I'm sure Conor won't mind if I accidentally poke his eye out during the night!'

'As long as your finger doesn't get stuck in my nose, I'll be fine,' he confirmed.

'Well, I don't know. Do you normally keep your mouth closed when you sleep?'

'Normally. But I'll make an exception for you.'

The flapping of wings cut across my response as something flew dangerously close to my head, alighting nearby.

'Bloody hell! Don't you keep him in its cage at night?' Conor bristled.

'I don't understand. How is he not scared of the fire?' I wondered.

'Who cares, Kris, have you seen his talons? If he comes any closer, I swear, I will break his neck, royal gift or not! Should have asked for a puppy instead. Do you hear me, Bolt?'

'What is he doing, walking around us like that?' Selena chipped in. 'Like a field marshal!'

'Marking his territory.'

'More like his breakfast!'

'He can't be hungry.' She laughed. 'We've given him plenty of meat today.'

'Well, if he's even a bit like Conor, anything is possible.' I sighed and got up. Storn left the other two horses and came to me. 'Thanks,' I said to him, rummaging for the bird's food. I put on the glove and whistled to him.

'That was quick,' Conor observed as the hawk alighted on my arm.

'Was that a hint of envy in your voice? Let me know if you want some as well.'

'Why? Do you think you can support my weight, too?'

'Before or after dinner?'

The banter went on long after I finished feeding the hawk and asked Storn to keep him away from us during the night, our frequent laughter ringing out across the quiet meadow. It was followed by a peaceful morning and glorious days as we slowly journeyed south towards Manessa.

We spent most nights in inns after that, and occasionally in the houses of people who Conor knew. We played card games with the locals in the evenings, listening to their stories, and of course, celebrated that the royal curse was finally broken. Conor started to teach us his songs and how to play the guitar. In turn, I introduced morning training sessions before the days turned too hot. To start with, I mixed core strength exercises with unarmed martial arts practice. They were met with less resistance than I expected, despite our late nights. In fact, Conor announced that this was the only thing he actually missed from the monastery, and even Selena took to it with so much dedication that I constantly had to keep an eye on her to make sure she didn't overdo it or injure herself.

She cut her hair much shorter after the first few days, making us gasp with indignation that we were not consulted before such a drastic decision. She wore less alluring clothes these days, but the warm weather meant that still a lot of her was on show, so I had no complaints. Especially since I had all of her to myself every night now, falling in love with her even more.

We agreed not to display our feelings for each other outside the bedroom to avoid making Conor feel awkward around us. Not that they stopped their big hugs in front of me. Whenever it happened, every part of me tensed, waiting for the inevitable punch of jealousy to hit me in the stomach, but it never came. There was never any sexual tension between them. I knew how Selena felt when she was in my arms. The longing wrapping her when I just looked or smiled at her sometimes. I also knew whenever Conor desired a woman. It certainly happened often enough.

No. I could tell it was none of that when they shared a moment, even as I pretended to look the other way, but was shamelessly all over them like some octopus with invisible tentacles. They were just two people who had perhaps grown up without a supportive kind of love, and now that they'd found it in each other, they couldn't get enough of it. Given that I couldn't get enough of her in other ways, I really had no right to complain.

Storn took a keen interest in Bolt. 'Your pet has a pet!' Conor pointed out one day when he got tired of Storn's never-ending reports on the bird's activities. Athos, on the other hand, seemed to develop a very different kind of interest in Selena's mare, Angel, that made me raise an eyebrow. Conor, of course, just laughed and proudly patted the horse. All in all, though, we were all happy as we reached the foot of the Ceteres mountain range and started our way upwards. Because Conor's favourite town had to be on the top! To be fair to him, this section of it looked more like a range of hills, far lower and less steep than where the Coroden Skygate lay hidden. Much of it was also covered by forest, which meant a welcome break from the sun after the lowlands.

Manessa perched on the hill ridge about seven hundred meters above the sea. The view along the great sweep of ragged coastline to the south stole our breath away. The charm of the town itself lay in the narrow winding of its cobblestone paths and in the picture-perfect, stone-built houses they threaded. And amid all that rock and stone waited a riot of flowering green, hanging above doorways, creeping up any vertical surface and trailing from every ledge. Every now and then, a temple, a pleasant fountain with benches around it, gardens declaring ownership of any even vaguely flat area or tumbling down the slope. In the centre, a lively marketplace, taverns huddled in tight corners, apparently offering some of the best food and finest wine in all of Coroden.

Attractive shops crowded several streets. To distinguish one establishment from another among the anonymity of all that stonework, alternately thrown in black shadow and dazzling sunlight, signs hung, beautifully painted and artfully crafted, to draw the eye and declare the business carried out beneath them. When the evening came, lanterns on the walls were lit, casting the alleyways in rainbow hues as flames danced behind stained glass of every colour.

The place boasted no fewer than five inns. Conor led us to his favourite, called the East Wind. Its white terrace of flagged stone hung above a stark drop, beyond which green treetops fringed a view to the rocky shore and the azure sparkle of the ocean. Several tables scattered the area, nudging up against a cast iron railing.

This was where we sat the first evening, the setting sun turning the sky into a magnificent landscape of striking colours which would have had any painter's hand shaking with fervent inspiration. Even if I had not wanted to please Conor by settling down in a place he liked, one look at Selena's face in the candlelight would have confirmed that we had arrived. This was it.

But more than the beautiful exteriors, Manessa's real treasure was its people. Friendly, caring, proud of their town but in a humble sort of way, as if trying to live up to expectations to match its loveliness. They all seemed to know Conor, including the family who owned the East Wind, and they must have liked him, too, because we were given rooms with breath-taking views, and the best table was reserved for us on the terrace every evening.

The first few days went by in a bliss of charming walks, grand lunches, shopping, and getting to know the locals. When news reached the town that the woman with us was responsible for breaking the king's curse, they became even more taken with us. Once they learned that we were thinking of moving to the area, they were beside themselves with excitement. I couldn't tell if it was a Scarlet Witch leaving her coven and finding a home here, or Conor finally settling down that they found more incredible, but they all looked at me as if I was some magician to make it all happen. And I guess, in a way, they were right.

Every evening now we had a small crowd around us on the terrace once we'd finished dinner, waiting to hear Conor's stories. He told them heavily edited but nonetheless colourful accounts of recent months, some of them from the time before I met him. This was inevitably followed by music, singing, more wine and me looking for an opportunity to take Selena to bed. But it was always worth the wait. She was enchanted with the town, her joy irresistible. She also gradually grew more relaxed and confident than I had ever seen her before, making me the happiest man alive every night. If this was Conor's idea of living, I thought I could get used to it.

He thought we could make some sort of deal with the Order to let us be, and given my science knowledge, I could perhaps open my own business as a glassmaker, which was one of highest-paid crafts due to the skills and technical understanding required, although he still would have preferred us to do work that required travelling as he thought even Manessa could become boring after a while.

'Or if you're really a glutton for punishment, become a teacher at the local school.' He grinned, certain that that would make me opt for travelling in no time.

In the end, I promised him I would consider his suggestions.

'What would *you* like?' I asked Selena one night, stroking her hair. The sun had lightened it considerably on the way here, and she had washed it with some herb she bought in the market until it was back to blonde again. It gleamed like gold between my fingers in the candlelight.

'I don't really mind, either way.' She snuggled closer sleepily. 'I'm sure there's something I could do for the Dragon here, too. Healing people seems like an obvious choice.'

It certainly sounded like an easier life. A safer one, too, where at the end of each day, I could be at home in bed with her. I closed my arms around her, smiling as I fell asleep.

Our happiness didn't last long. The next evening, Ithorion appeared on the terrace, his stern face like a merciless wake-up call ending a dream. My first reaction when I caught sight of him was to smile, offering him a seat at our table. I was so transformed by the last few days, I saw no reason why he wouldn't share a few laughs and some good wine with us. He gestured to me to follow him, and we ended up back in our room, taking two chairs at the window. For a while, he just looked at me silently, not even bothering with his pipe, which was unusual.

By then, I didn't know what to think of his presence here, but I could tell it wasn't good news. Had they decided against letting us join, I wondered? Had we broken some rule? Had my nature, my condition, my past meant that I couldn't become a Champion and certainly not a tora for those two? Was this the part where I needed to negotiate some deal for us? My hands turned cold in the warm room, my stomach in a knot as I waited to find out what he had come to tell me.

'It's your Uncle James,' he said finally.

'What happened to him? Is he alright?' I demanded, even as a heavy weight settled in me, a sense of what was coming pulling me down.

'He was killed last night, his body sent to the Pantheon through the skygate from a planet in the Corloba system.'

'Killed?' I felt dizzy for a moment. 'You mean he's dead?' Like it could have meant anything else. But surely, it had to.

'Yes, he's dead,' Ithorion confirmed. 'I'm sorry.'

'But when Selena was stabbed, she came back. Couldn't the Dragon bring him back, too?'

'Champions die just like other people, Kristian. What happened to Selena was an exception, due to the circumstances at the time, due to who she is and what she's capable of. The rest of us are not that lucky.'

The thought of what happened that day brought back memories of someone else. 'Who killed him?' I asked through gritted teeth.

'We don't know.'

'Didn't you say that planet Eris was also in the Corloba system?' Surely, the answer was obvious.

'I did. But that doesn't prove anything.'

It did to me.

'You told me not to start investigating where he was!' I turned on him, my voice growing louder with each word. 'You told me to leave it with you! That I should not pursue Laro, even after what happened in Caledon!'

'You forget what almost happened in that cell in the dungeons,' he warned. 'You were not ready to pursue Laro. Nor are you now.'

'Who cares what would have happened?' I shouted. 'He's dead now!'

'I do. And I know James would have, too.' His frosty eyes pierced into mine, holding me as if waiting for more. But I knew he was right. Of course, James would have cared. That broke my heart even more, and my hot anger turned into cold sorrow, the way thunder was followed by rain. Ithorion had just left me then.

'The funeral is in two days. I will open a gate where the road leading to Manessa forks to Lelke. Be there with the others tomorrow at midnight,' he said on his way out.

I stayed where I was, numb with pain and guilt. Conor was right. We should have killed Laro while we had the chance. What had I done? I wished I could go back to that moment and choose differently. I thought I was doing the right thing. That it wasn't my business to decide whether someone should die just because I could make it happen. Because what would that make me? It seemed to me now that it was very much my business, after all. That I had to make it so!

I told the others briefly what had happened and that I needed a walk alone. I went out and only returned in the morning. I kept my distance even then, unable to face their sympathy.

I stood with them at the funeral though, as if nothing between us were out of place. Yet I had to force myself to hold Selena's hand in mine and stand close to Conor. James's body lay in front of us in an open casket as Quede made a speech, followed by many others. I was offered the chance, too, but I had to refuse.

Before the ceremony, I was left alone with him in a small room. He looked like he was merely asleep in that coffin, but of course, he was icy cold. I lowered my forehead onto his chest and sobbed like a child. Grateful for everything he'd done for me, I could now never thank him for or return. Feeling like a failure but promising to do better in the future. Missing his wisdom, missing a future that he should have been a part of, where I could have made him proud. Where he could have spent more time with Selena and Conor, and they could have got to know him better, too. And hating myself for allowing this to happen. That I wasn't strong enough, wasn't clever enough, wasn't concerned enough to save him. I was the reason why he left the Order, and this was how I'd repaid him.

I was all but drained now, standing there, listening to the others. Drained of words, drained of tears, drained of life. A ghost of past mistakes that led to this.

A golden light burned his body to ashes under a glass lid before the coffin was lowered into the ground in the Pantheon's cemetery. A long line formed of those who wanted to say something to me, and I stayed to listen to their words, not that I really heard or remembered them after. I waited until it was all over, then went to the skygate without a word, Conor and Selena following me like shadows. I didn't bother with the buttons this time. I visualised the exact location Ithorion used as I remembered it. The wooden sign on the side of the road. The trees around it. The smell of the forest. The sound of the birds. Mixing it with my request to be there. The gate lit up with a powerful blue light in response.

'Come on,' I said, grabbing Conor's arm and Selena's hand, my mind firmly on the destination. Two steps forward, and the familiar pull of the skygate swallowed us, spitting us out at the forest crossing.

We walked back to Manessa, then all the way to the inn, where I disappeared into our room. Selena came in after me, tried to hold me, but I pushed her away and asked her to leave me alone. At night, we lay apart, not that she didn't try to comfort me. I just couldn't take it. I felt too rotten for her love. Undeserving. I wanted to be alone with my pain. Numb in my madness. Blind in my darkness.

I couldn't eat. I couldn't sleep. During the days, I disappeared from the town into the forest with the hawk, who'd spent most of his time in his cage since we arrived, and now appreciated the attention. But the nights became so unbearable with Selena, that in the end, I had to beg Conor to take her away somewhere for a few weeks. Even then, she didn't want to leave me there. So, to break her spirit, I called her selfish, insensitive and clingy, even if she was none of those things, but when she heard me say it, she believed it to be true. I shouted at her until she cried, and when I thought I couldn't possibly sink any lower, I still hurt her until she finally left the room and told Conor that they could go.

'Take Storn for her,' I said to him when he came in to say goodbye. 'I need her to be safe.'

That he would obviously keep her safe was written on his face, but he knew better than to argue with me then, and just nodded.

I carried on spending the days with the hawk or brooding in my room, and when even the innkeeper's concern for me became too much, I packed a few things, rode out on Selena's horse and stayed the nights in the surrounding hills.

I took the equipment off the bird's feet. It was useless without Storn around. But Bolt acknowledged my leadership now anyway and always flew back to me, regardless of whether a treat was offered or not. More than that, it seemed to me as if we were forming a bond. Not just as owner and pet. Something more elemental than that. An understanding when either of us noticed a possible prey and I sent him after it. A sharing of excitement when he closed down on it. A flicker of satisfaction when he caught it. Even when it was a rabbit, and I had no way of seeing it happen, I felt it. And I liked it.

Every time I took that pleasure and examined it closely, disgusted with myself even as I looked for its roots and tasted the yearning I felt for it. I wanted to rip it out of myself, and I tried to. But I couldn't. It went too deep. The only way that remained for me to beat it was to become stronger than the longing. To master it. Not to turn away from it, scared when it came over me. But to be able to say yes or no.

I sent the hawk after quails, my mind sharp on his, like a sixth sense. And when the prey came within reach, our shared eagerness to sink his claws into it amplifying, I stopped him by shoving him away in the air. I let him get a little closer each time, making it more difficult to resist the urge, but I carried on doing it until I finally let him catch the bird.

Ithorion visited me on my second week in the wilderness. Unlike the others, he had no kind words to offer, but I found his coldness oddly soothing. He told me that our Attainment Ceremony, in which we became Champions of the Order, would take place two weeks from now. I was surprised to hear that it had come so quickly, despite his criticisms of our curse-breaking assignment, but I didn't object. I needed something to focus on. And perhaps he knew that, too.

I wanted to learn what exactly had happened to James and how. And I wanted to hunt down Laro. But I knew that I could do neither without the Order. I had to play by their rules, to be a part of them. To learn more about how they operated. To be accepted and trusted by them. And I knew that would take time. But I had time. There was no rush now. Ithorion told me that corrupted gifts like Laro's didn't just grow overnight. He wouldn't be back until he was stronger again. Especially with us becoming Champions. He would be the underdog now. Whereas I would make sure that I excelled in everything.

I stayed a few more days, then went back to the East Wind. I washed, put on clean clothes and waited for the others to arrive. They came the next afternoon. Conor entered my room, leaving Selena behind until he made sure I was safe enough to come back to. When he decided that I looked close to normal and I told him I would have dinner with them on the terrace, he hugged me.

'If you carry on like this, you'll look like Selena soon.' He ruffled my hair. 'Why don't we cut it tomorrow?'

'Why not?' I nodded.

He smiled approvingly and let go of me.

Something flickered in my chest. A ray of sunshine finding its way into my darkness through a crack between closed shutters. I looked up to see her walk in like a frightened deer. Not scared of me, but scared of my rejection. I opened my arms to her, and she came to me, her eyes full of tears by the time she reached me. I hadn't cried since the funeral, but I cried then, holding her close. She wiped her face and tried to kiss me, but I stopped her.

'No, please!' I stroked her face. 'Not yet.'

She nodded that she accepted that, even if she didn't understand it, and buried her face in my shirt instead. I kissed her hair like I used to, again and again, until I felt her calm in my arms. 'Just give me some time,' I murmured. Maybe I would hate myself a little less with every coming day. Maybe a time would come when I could allow myself to be happy again.

I held her until the sun started setting through our windows beyond the vast, blue ocean.

'Hungry?' I asked her. I could tell that she was, but she shook her head, unwilling to let go of me. 'How about I hold your hand, and we go together? Yes?'

I led her out to our table, where Conor was waiting for us. I ate with them, talked with them, even had some wine and forced a weak smile on my face every now and then. Once the food was all gone, I told Selena I was going to go to bed and that she would have more fun if she stayed. She said she would have a bath in Conor's room and come in after. I paused at that, but then nodded and took my leave.

She followed me into the room not long after. She wished me goodnight but made no attempt to come close. She lay down instead, facing away from me, leaving it up to me whether I would pull her to me. The first night I didn't. The second night I did. The third night I kissed her. It was a quick, awkward thing. Joy, like a stranger, lurked around me, unable to make it past my defences. I slumped down behind her, defeated, wondering if I would ever be able to love her again. The fourth night she snuggled against me. I let her. The fifth night she did the same, and I even put my arms around her this time. The sixth night I kissed her again, my lips lingering on hers, as if trying to remember what to do. She showed me, the way I showed her that first time. Deeply, passionately, as if the love of your life had been taken from you and you've just got them back. As if you wanted to make sure that no matter what, they would remember that kiss forever. On the seventh night I made love to her.

The last three days before the ceremony went even faster. I was out and about now with them, walking the winding streets, visiting the shops, having fancy lunches. That was when I noticed that as I was getting stronger once again, Conor seemed to be fading away. He grew quiet, fidgety. He looked away when I was watching him, avoiding my eyes. And the most telling sign of all, he went to bed alone at nights.

I knew exactly what this was about. His own demon he couldn't get the better of: commitment. I was still hoping against all hopes that he would somehow come around.

The last morning, Selena was out when he came into the room, and I knew what he was going to say before he even opened his mouth. I stood at the window, looking out at the sparkling water, waiting to hear it.

'I'm not coming to the ceremony with you tomorrow,' he said. 'I was asked to do a job for the Duchess of Arundel. It's a very important one. I couldn't refuse! And it's not like the two of you really need me anyway. I don't even have any powers!'

I gripped the windowsill in my anger, wanting to grip him instead and shake him. 'If that's what you think,' I said coldly instead.

'I'm going to the market to buy a few things for my trip. I'll leave in the morning,' he added. 'See you at dinner!'

'Enjoy your shopping,' I managed, not even looking at him. I listened to his steps quieting as he walked off, leaving the door open.

I buried my forehead into my palm, my elbow on the windowsill, my eyes lost in the distance. I heard the door close behind me as Selena walked into the room and wrapped her arms around me.

'I really hoped he would stay,' I said bitterly, my arms on hers.

'He was always hesitant about joining the Order. You know that.'

'Yes, but maybe he would have been more keen had I not been like this lately.' I opened my arms in frustration. 'If we had more fun.'

'You had your reasons,' she stated. 'And so does he. But you need to stop blaming yourself for everything.'

'What am I supposed to do then?' I turned to face her.

'Come to bed with me,' she said simply and kissed me. 'I want to spoil you.'

I slipped my hand behind her head and kissed back. 'If you say so.'

I let her lead me back to bed, pushing me down onto it, and I watched her slowly undress in front of me.

'Is that a smile?' she mused as she climbed on top of me naked.

'Maybe.'

She leaned down to kiss me. 'Expect more to come.'

I was ready for more. More of everything. And she gave it to me. All of her. All her love. And whatever your definition, it was magic.

In the afternoon, we rode out on Storn, and I showed her the place I imagined our house could be. It was outside of the town, as I felt it should be with all our strange connections and activities, but not too far. It was part of the woodland that had a stream, but due to the steep hillside, we could still have stunning views down to the shore from the upstairs windows. The king had said to pick any location in the country we liked, and it would be ours. I thought with some adjustments and making a road to lead to it, this would do very nicely.

I sat down with my back against a tree, put the wooden board with the large parchments stretched out across it on my lap, took the charcoal into my hand and started to draw the plans of the building. I wanted to create a modern house that looked like an old one. Something that would make our lives easy, safe and comfortable here, but seemingly fitted right into this world in case any locals came to visit or even stayed in a downstairs guestroom. Something that would have made even James proud.

'Any special requests?' I asked Selena when she stopped walking around and came back with Storn.

'Will we have running water?' she asked. 'Can we have proper bathrooms and a shower?'

'Of course we'll have running water, my love! You'll have the most amazing shower ever!' I promised her. 'Tell me something more special.'

'Um … not sure. How about some secret doors?'

'Secret doors?' I looked up with a puzzled smile.

'They always look so cool in the movies,' she protested.

'Fine. We can have secret doors,' I agreed. 'Anything else?'

'How about …?' She leaned down to whisper into my ear so that Storn wouldn't hear, but I knew he could anyway.

'I like the sound of that!' I grinned at her, loving where this was going.

'And we'll have a washing machine, too, right?' she demanded suddenly, making me laugh—both with the suggestion and by how her thoughts followed a certain line that started in the shower.

'Sel, I said a modern house. Of course, we won't have a washing machine.' I laughed again.

'Oh, so when you said modern house, you didn't mean modern by the standards of my primitive world, did you?' She patted my head.

'Not in terms of washing machines, no. But don't worry. We'll have something way better. You'll see.' I pulled her down to me and kissed her. 'Anything else?'

'At work, there's this Japanese-style dojo where they organised classes for us. I attended a few yoga and tai-chi sessions there and always found it really nice with its little gardens and water features and tea corner. It has some big mirrors, which would help me a lot when you're correcting my stances or showing me how to strike.'

'Sounds good.' I stroked her. 'You'll just have to tell me more about Japanese style. Anything else?'

'No, I'm sure I can just leave the rest with you, my love.' She kissed my head and stood.

'We'll need a large enough stable to house other horses when you have guests,' Storn pointed out, starting to detail his requirements. I stopped listening within a minute. I wasn't sure if it was just my imagination because I wished it to be true, or if it was real, but I stayed where I was, not even daring to look behind me, and waited. It always surprised me how quietly he could walk when he wanted to. My tora sense was all I could rely on when it came to him.

'Can we have a bar, too?' he asked, placing his hand on my shoulder, peeking at my drawing.

'A bar counter?' I looked up at him.

'Yes,' he nodded. 'I always wanted to have one of those. To fill it up with drinks I liked. To organise it all in a way I thought was best.'

'Sure,' I said.

'And a cellar, obviously,' he continued. 'Ithorion is our boss now. We can't give him some horsepiss again like we did that first time, when he comes around. No offence, Storn!'

'Obviously.' I smiled at him.

'And where are we going to practice our fighting? Not on this slope?'

'Oh, no. We're going to have a terraced garden with lots of flat surfaces. And a big room inside, too.'

'Good. I seem to remember you wanted to learn that sword flourish pattern back in Borond. We need somewhere to do that.'

'I seem to remember you said you would teach me everything you knew if I helped you find the Key,' I reminded him with a grin.

'That would take a veeery long time.' He grinned back.

'Why, are you in a hurry to be somewhere?'

'Not anymore,' he admitted.

'What happened to the Duchess of Arundel?'

'I couldn't abandon your music education. Not now, when you're finally showing some appreciation of the subject.'

'Completely understandable.' I nodded. 'Anything you'd like in return?'

'That all the training aside, we'll always have some fun between jobs.'

'I can promise you that,' I said. 'In fact, I already have a suggestion for you.'

He crouched down next to me, as if he might have heard me wrong or was witnessing a miracle. Based on his expression, it could have been either. 'A suggestion for fun from you? Tell me! I'm all ears!'

'Well, Selena wants to go back to Earth for a bit to arrange some things there. How about we go and pick her up once she's ready?'

'And … we'll go to a party like the one where we collected her the first time?' he ventured, unclear where I was going with this.

'We could do that.' I nodded. 'But I was going to say that we could spend a few weeks visiting those islands you both liked so much on the footage in the train station. Based on what Ithorion told me, we should have plenty of time to fit it in before we're called away again.'

'You don't mean the footage with all those half-naked women drinking and dancing, by any chance, do you?' He grinned.

'I do. We could go out partying every night. And we could try some other things, too. Hire a few vehicles and fool around with them, see if we can find one that flies. Go out to the sea on a boat, swim around, do some fishing. Play silly games, sing. I'll even do a treasure hunt for you. What do you say? Sound fun enough?'

'Not bad for a first suggestion!' He laughed.

'Only if it's something Selena would like to do, too, of course.' I looked up at her.

Conor rose slowly from my side, looking at her with big, pleading eyes and his best smile in place.

'Only if you teach me that sword pattern thing, too.' She crossed her arms.

'I'll teach it to you right now! Why don't we go a little further up and let Kris get on with his drawings?'

'And, of course, we'll continue with our morning training after tomorrow,' I called after them. 'Even on holiday!'

There was something odd that I had been ignoring in my excitement at having him back. I reached up to my shoulder where his hand had been earlier. Even my linen shirt felt warm there, almost as if it had been pressed against hot metal. I hoped he wasn't going down with some bug. I turned and looked after them, but he seemed perfectly fine.

I dismissed the notion and crossed a line over in my plan, making space for Conor's bar downstairs. Under the charcoal, a blue line ran over mine, spreading out to cover everything I put on the parchment so far and rose into the air. I looked up at Storn.

'Don't worry.' He shook his mane, 'We won't mention this to Ithorion. We'll say you drew it all into the dirt with a stick.'

I laughed, even as I flicked the crossed-over line into the recycle bin with my little finger. I rested my arms on the invisible energy board he'd created and drew on.

'I'm adding some menus for materials, measurements, colours and systems into the right top corner,' he informed me, making the work surface multi-dimensional. I picked up a small twig, sharpened its end with my knife and continued the work. Conor wanted a cellar, and of course, we would have one, but I had more ambitious plans for the belly of the hill under the house. And we'd have one of those comfortable libraries looking out to the garden like Duke Beren's, thank you! A meeting room for any Order gatherings. Soundproofing, obviously. And should we have solar energy? Wind? Gravitational? A mix?

As I sat there—Conor and Selena's voices reaching me amid the birdsong and the distant rumble of the sea, the sun stroking my face through the tree branches above, Storn recording my ideas for our place—I realised something. For the first time in my life, I felt at home.

Epilogue

Ithorion

'So? What do you want?' I lit my pipe with the match and leaned back in the chair. 'Do I need to forge the Skygate reports for you again? Or are you staying put on Drelos?'

'You're my eyes in the Pantheon now, Ithorion.' He sipped his coffee. 'Tell me what's going on.'

'Nothing out of the ordinary. Everyone's on their best behaviour since I arrived.'

'I bet.'

'My initiates became Champions, of course. Needless to say, you were very much on Kristian's mind during the whole ceremony.'

A smile at that. Not an ounce of remorse.

'I really wasn't sure he would make it.' I fidgeted with the pipe. 'Not after the funeral. He was a broken man.'

'You're getting sentimental in your old age!' He shook his head in mock disappointment.

'You didn't see the state he was in. When I told him …' I couldn't stay in the room. Even for me, it was too painful to watch. 'And for weeks afterwards …'

'But he came through in the end.'

'Oh, he was more keen to become a Champion than ever! And that's despite Conor practically convincing him not to.'

'Two birds with one stone.' He smiled.

'You thought this would happen? No,' I corrected myself. 'You knew this would happen.'

Another of his bloody smiles. 'Maybe.'

'Everyone thinks me uncaring, and maybe rightly so, but I swear you can be such a cold-hearted bastard sometimes!'

'I learned from the best.' He laughed.

'Oh, I think it runs in the family,' I deflected his flattery.

'But no.' His face grew solemn once again. 'This really wasn't what I wanted at all. But given the circumstances, this was what was needed. Besides, he's safer in the Order. You know that.'

I sighed, but he was right, of course. 'Do tell me your secret investigation is going well, at least. I'd hate to think that all this theatre was for nothing!'

'I'll have to lay low for a little longer before I can really get into the midst of it, but my job is already easier with nobody looking for me. In addition, Laro thinks he killed me and will now stay put, satisfied. Kris thinks Laro killed me and is now determined to progress within the Order. Their father thinks I'm dead and will not be so guarded in his plans anymore. With all eyes on young Kris, I will be able to quietly get on with things in the background without any notice.'

'Sounds like a big, happy family!'

'I know. But we can't be all as lucky as you are! How are they, anyway?'

'Fine, thanks. Esmeralda thought that going back to the Order might be good for me. Then I told her that my team was settling down in Manessa instead of the Pantheon. First, she just laughed and said she hadn't agreed to me bringing work home. But now she wants to meet them. Especially given that Kristian is your nephew.'

'Have you told them that you will be practically neighbours?'

'Dragon's breath, no! And I want to keep it that way as long as I can.'

'I've seen his house plans. Even you must admit, some of his ideas are brilliant.'

'No half-measures there, that's for sure.' I sighed. 'I'll get Terek over there with his team to help. Otherwise, they will never be ready.'

'They're lucky to have you as their Dicto.'

'Not that they see it that way. Kris especially will never forgive me for letting you die.'

'Just give them time.'

'Anyway.' I stood, ready to call it a dream, then paused, as if I'd just remembered something.' 'Oh, and about Storn …'

'Yes?'

Was that a flash of concern in his eyes? I knew I could still take him by surprise, despite all his mind-cloaking skills.

'Quede doesn't like the idea of the horse staying with them …'

'Oh, please don't take Storn away! He's my only way to see Kris now,' he admitted what I suspected already.

'But I managed to convince her to let him stay,' I finished the sentence.

'Thanks for helping.'

'No problem.' So, there it was. He did miss his nephew, after all. But the harsh truth was … 'I guess he's my boy now.'

No confident smiles this time.

'Best not get too sentimental.' I patted his shoulder. 'I shall keep you posted on his achievements. Sometimes.' I walked to the border of our mutual dream, and before finally disappearing, I still turned and added, 'Welcome back to the Order, James!'

Acknowledgements

I worked on this book on and off for almost five years. Often it was time that I didn't have (a full-time job, studying, blogging and beta-reading keeping me busy). Sometimes it was the lack of energy (fibromyalgia making my life more challenging with fatigue, muscle pain and brain-fog on a regular basis). Other times it was simply self-confidence that I lacked to carry on. As a non-native speaker, I convinced myself that I'd never be able to master English to a level I'd expect from an author. Then the pandemic hit, and I was made redundant. Working only part-time allowed me to finally focus on the story properly. In only four months, I wrote the remaining sixty percent of the book, finishing it on 19 January 2021.

During these years, I was lucky to have some very supportive people around me, and I'd like to thank everyone who helped me on this journey.

First and foremost, I must thank Mark Lawrence for his unrelenting faith in me and for his stern but kind critiques. I've been Mark's beta-reader for his last fourteen books now, reading chapters and providing feedback on them as he wrote, and it was both educational and rewarding to switch roles for this story. Mark has always encouraged me to write, pushing me on when I wavered, at times going so far as not giving me his next chapter to read until I finished and sent over mine first. Even now, as I'm writing this, he has just messaged me to let me know that he won't send me the ending of his latest trilogy before I complete work on my copy edits. As it turns out, these measures can be fairly motivational when your beta-reading partner happens to be your favourite author.

Another author friend who was incredibly helpful and tolerant with my slow progress was Matthew (T.O.) Munro. Where Mark provided broad structural feedback and expert advice on my attempts at clever or beautiful lines—something for which we share a passion—Matthew went into great detail with every scene, providing perceptive, valuable commentary and often humorous insights that made editing a lot more fun than it normally would be. I'm incredibly grateful to him for the time and energy he put into supporting me in the writing of this book.

The first person to read the finished manuscript in full was Goodreads reviewer Queen Melanie Parker. Melanie's enthusiasm and wonderful counsel were both heart-warming and reassuring. At the same time, she didn't shy away from pointing out possibly problematic parts where my characters might have gone a step too far.

Mia Caringal was also an early reader of the book, providing much valued constructive criticism as well as encouragement, both of which were highly appreciated.

I would also like to thank those who read some of my early chapters and cheered me on: Joseph Lopez, David Menashy, Rita Sloan, Kareem Mahfouz, G. R. Matthews, Robin Carter, Adriano de l'Orange and Peter Hutchinson—thanks so much!

Finally, I'll be forever grateful to Karrah E and Shawn T. King for their hard work in making this book look amazing: Karrah, by wonderfully bringing the characters to life and Shawn, by crafting an incredible cover design around the artwork.

With gratitude,

Mitriel Faywood

London, United Kingdom
19th August 2022

Lightning Source UK Ltd.
Milton Keynes UK
UKHW030326281022
411213UK00004B/59/J